RUBY'S REDEMPTION

EDWINA KIERNAN

Visit the author's website for updates:
EdwinaKiernan.com

ENDORSEMENTS

Ruby's Redemption is a gripping tale of redemption from the sins that separate one woman from God. The love story is told with the spirit of grace beautifully woven throughout and is one that is hard to put down. I highly recommend it.

- **Jennie Goutet**, author of the *Clavering Chronicles*

Edwina Kiernan delivers the first of her Gems of Grace series with a strong start in *Ruby's Redemption* and one that is likely to hook readers who enjoy Christian fiction in historical settings. The narrative and descriptions are good without dumping information into the plot, a credit to the author who has the skill and courage to elect for a slower unpeeling of backstory. In the context of a solid love story in this specific genre, Kiernan does not shy away from plot elements that rarely come into play. Religion is deeply woven within this but is still allowed to blanket all aspects. Many contemporary Christian authors temper religion to appeal to a broader readership, but Kiernan holds unapologetically tight, and as a result, so did I to the story.

- **Readers' Favorite** 5-Star Review

CONTENTS

A NOTE ON SPELLINGS

PLEASE NOTE:
This novel is set in Regency England, therefore, the spelling used is UK (British) English.

This means, you'll see words like
- "realise" instead of "realize",
- "colour" instead of "color", and
- "travelling" instead of "traveling".

This is intentional, and I hope you find that it gives an authentic flavour to the story.

For Jesus,
the Author of my redemption

Above all, keep fervent in your love for one another, because love covers a multitude of sins.

— 1 *PETER* 4:8

CHAPTER 1

AN UNEXPECTED MEETING

IT WOULD NOT BE long until the arrival of Ruby's next customer.

She quietly drifted through the preparation routine she had developed over the years, yet reluctance slowed her movements, her muscles weighed down by some invisible oppression.

Vacantly, she glanced in the mirror.

She tried to inhale deeply despite the bricks on her chest that stifled each breath.

Her hands went automatically to the decanter of whisky on her dressing table, and she raised the crystal bottle to her lips, welcoming the familiar feeling as the liquid ran down her throat, warming her shivering frame.

As she took another generous swig, a knock sounded at the door.

Drawing in a deep, slow breath, she forced herself into a more confident posture, stuffing all her true emotions down into the last surviving piece of her spirit.

With a tremulous hand, she twisted the doorknob and pulled the door inward in a graceful arc.

"Do come in, sir," she breathed, trying to sound convincing in her invitation, though to her ears, her voice sounded flat and drained.

"Thank you," came a kind voice, as the man walked in.

Ruby was stunned. No one had ever thanked her. For anything.

"Would you like to sit down?" she offered, still somewhat rattled by his manners. Or rather, the fact that he had any manners at all.

"Yes, thank you."

There were those words again. She didn't quite know how to respond.

As the man sat down, she looked at his face, surprised to notice a complete lack of lust in his eyes. He seemed almost *gentle*.

He looked at her, his brow slightly furrowed. The expression in his kind eyes made her cheeks burn. What was he thinking?

For the first time, she felt painfully aware that what she saw in the mirror every morning was what the gentleman before her was now seeing. Her pale cheeks, highlighted by the dark circles so deeply ingrained below her eyes. Her dull, lank hair. All of it was on unveiled display.

She cleared her throat, remembering her duties. With a flourish of her hand, she unfastened her plain grey peignoir. Letting it fall to the ground behind her, she walked toward him in her undergarments - a long chemise and loosely-fitted stays.

The man jumped up in alarm, moving away from her, swirling to a stop behind the chair upon which he had sat.

His dark eyes were wide, diverting their gaze from her face to the floor and back again in rapid succession.

"I beg your pardon," he said. "I was under the impression that I was to meet a Dr. Tewby here . . . regarding a patient of his."

He paused, clearly overwhelmed by the unexpected reality in which he found himself.

"I suspected that you might have been a patient yourself," he continued, rather flustered. "Perhaps even the one in question, and that was why you were present. I did not . . . That is, I do not . . . "

She sank to the floor, fumbling to grasp her peignoir with trembling fingers. As she pulled it back over her bare shoulders and tightly around her, she kept her gaze low.

Hadn't she suspected him of being a gentleman? She silently scolded herself for ignoring her suspicions, even though she had long been instructed to ignore decorum and act with impropriety.

Then she registered what he had said. Forcing herself to meet his gaze, she frowned in confusion.

"Forgive me, sir. Who is Dr. Tewby?"

The gentleman frowned, too. "He is not here?"

She raised her eyebrows before frowning again. "Sir, there is no doctor on *these* premises."

Realisation dawned in his eyes. "Oh!"

She felt a sudden rush of shame. "Please, sir, forgive me. I thought you were my next customer," she said, her voice as low as her gaze.

His eyes closed in reluctant acknowledgement. "I must confess, I wondered as much when the gentleman downstairs asked for remuneration, but I had hoped . . ."

He sighed, but it was not the type of sigh she had been

expecting. There was no air of judgment. Instead, it seemed almost mournful.

Despite her shame, she could not help but look up at him again.

Here stood a man who seemed to embody everything of humanity's goodness. And here she was, the embodiment of all that belonged in humanity's gutter. She was disgusted by herself even more than usual, now that this stranger's purity so distinctly contrasted her own depravity.

He strolled back around to the front of the chair and lowered himself into it with another sigh. This one sounded like a sigh of resignation.

Ruby could translate sighs with startling accuracy - a skill garnered by years of creating them herself.

He sat for a moment, his head resting in his hands, his face hidden from her view.

The next few minutes that passed felt torturous to Ruby. She was completely disarmed by this gentle stranger. She didn't know what to say - she barely knew what to think.

There was a curiousness about it all. An odd, lingering atmosphere, as though time had stopped. As though their different worlds had collided, and they'd landed in some strange new place, where the air was quiet and calm.

Peaceful.

That was it, she realised, with utter astonishment. For a moment - a brief glimpse of a moment - the bustling and clamour had all grown silent, and peace governed the room.

The man lowered his hands from his face and looked up at her.

"Forgive me," he began. "This has all been a most awful misunderstanding. You see, I am not too familiar with this part of town, and I asked a gentleman for directions, but I was not entirely sure that I had heard him accurately. I am even less certain seeing as how the twists and turns he instructed led me here. I must have taken a wrong turn," he said, shaking his head gently. "I am deeply sorry for the intrusion. I should have known . . . I did think it an unlikely meeting place, but . . ." His voice trailed off in another sigh.

Ruby could scarcely believe what she was hearing. Had he really just apologised to her?

The unfamiliar bewilderment she felt grew stronger. Never had she encountered anyone like this man.

Nor did she expect that she ever would again.

She swallowed hard. "Please, sir, it is certainly not your place to apologise. It is I who should be sorry for . . . my impropriety."

His eyes softened, though they had been tender from the start. "You were . . . You were merely doing your job."

She did not know how to read his expression. There was noticeable discomfort, and an element of uneasiness, without doubt, but no judgment in either his words or deeds. Mostly, he seemed genuinely sorrowful.

He looked her in the eye again. She couldn't remember the last time a man had looked at her eyes. She stared back at him, perplexed, yet oddly brave enough to hold his gaze.

It was most peculiar to her that a gentleman, who was undoubtedly of fine breeding and professional standing, should look at her at all, never mind look at her with such a blend of care and kindness.

"What is your name?" he asked, a hesitance in his voice.

With her eyebrows raised slightly, she answered in a barely audible voice, "Ruby."

He exhaled sharply and nodded to himself. She noticed a flicker of something else in his eyes - something she couldn't quite read.

He gave a small smile. "Ruby. That is a beautiful name."

She stared at him for a moment then lowered her gaze to the floor.

She didn't tell him that she always thought it ironic that her name was Ruby. A ruby was something precious. Something valuable and beautiful.

No one had ever described her with any of those words. She didn't deserve such a name.

"And you are Doctor . . .?"

It was his turn to look surprised. "Oh no, I am not a doctor!" he exclaimed.

She frowned. "Forgive me. Only, I thought that you were hoping to meet another doctor here to discuss your patient?"

She could not believe how freely she was conversing with this gentle stranger despite the shame knotted deep in her heart.

"Regarding *his* patient, yes. But I, myself, am not a doctor. Forgive me - I am Mr. Henry Stratton, parson of a little church about fourteen miles or so from here. I was informed that Dr. Tewby's patient was eager to speak with me, seeking prayer for their health, and to discuss some ecclesiastical matters."

Ruby's eyes were wider than they had ever been.

A clergyman! In her chamber! Her heart thumped. She had disrobed in front of a clergyman.

A clergyman who had visited her by mistake.

"Oh! I am sorry! Oh, I am so sorry!" she half-spoke, half-gasped.

"No, please. I beg you, do not apologise." He gave her a sympathetic look. "You were not to know. It is all an unfortunate mishap."

HENRY GAZED into Ruby's eyes. The vacant expression that had struck him upon his arrival was still there, yet had been eclipsed by sheer horror at the offence she must have felt that she had caused.

It was remarkable, he thought. He had encountered various prostitutes on his visits to the city. They had all accosted him as he travelled through the streets. He had always tried to show kindness to them without encouraging their desires for either flesh or money. But this young woman sitting opposite him did not seem to fit their type.

She seemed quite lost in her surroundings, yet painfully resigned to them. Her eyes showed no hint of greed or lust.

Rather, they seemed filled with an infinite sadness, and a dullness that he imagined had been caused by years of spiritual destruction.

She looked as though her very soul had been chipped away, piece by piece. It grieved him on a level deeper than intellect, deeper than expression.

He longed to ask her what had brought her to this horrid place for, now, as he looked around him, he could see the signs of her trade in the dingy light.

Dare he ask? He had already been so bold as to converse alone with her.

In fact, he had already been so bold as to enter this place, suspecting as he had that it might be a place of unseemly activity.

She looked at him, almost questioningly.

It occurred to him that perhaps there wasn't anyone she could truly converse with. To remain and converse further would surely go against decorum and decency, especially considering his own profession.

But, at that moment, he realised his own profession was worthless if he could walk away from her without another word, without allowing her the opportunity to speak with him and without, perhaps, even uncovering an opportunity to help her.

That being resolved in his mind, he still had no idea what to say next.

"So." He cleared his throat. "Miss Ruby."

He stood up, and began searching the inner pocket of his jacket for something. After a moment, he pulled out a few coins and held them just in front of him.

"Well, then. I already gave some money to the gentleman downstairs, but you were expecting a customer. And therefore, you would have received a gratuity. So . . . Although I am not . . . I am not . . . here to . . . I am not here for an appointment with you - please, allow me to ensure that you will not suffer any loss due to my witless error."

He extended his arm, offering the coins to Ruby.

"Oh, sir. Oh, no, I cannot accept that! Not from you!"

"Please, miss, I do not wish to create any difficulties for you, nor induce any suspicions from the person who runs this . . . establishment."

Ruby's expression altered instantly.

A cold shiver swept through Henry at the depth of terror he saw in Ruby's eyes.

It was almost as though he could hear her soul screaming.

RUBY FROZE.

For the first time in her life, she had managed to completely forget *him*.

He would certainly be outraged if she failed to provide him with any of the extra money expected from any of the customers. Even though this gentleman was no customer at all.

Her thoughts drifted to the last time Millforte had accused her of withholding money from him. The last thing she wanted was to be beaten and left for dead outside again. The candle delivery that arrived that morning had been covered with a faint dusting of snow.

Henry remained with his arm extended, the coins held firm between his thumb and fingers.

Reluctantly, she accepted the money.

"Thank you, Mr. Stratton." She frowned. "How shall I ever repay you?"

Henry gave a little smile and sat down again. He motioned for Ruby to sit opposite him, which she did, slowly.

"Perhaps we might sit and converse for a while. What do you say?"

Disbelief washed through her, and she heard herself give an abrupt kind of laugh. Speechless, she could only nod in response.

He smiled again, deeper this time, a sincere gladness shining in his eyes. His friendliness encouraged her to voice her true thoughts without much further hesitation.

"Why did you not rush away when you realised where you were? I imagine this is not the type of place you would usually visit."

He chuckled softly.

"No, you are correct - I can safely say that I have never been anywhere like this before. At least, not to my knowledge . . . which today has proved somewhat lacking."

A genuine smile rose up from deep within her, warming her chest as it travelled to her face. It was a welcome change from the forced, empty smiles she offered when amusement was expected of her.

Henry seemed to hesitate a moment.

"Truthfully, there was something about you. Something different. Genuine. And, I wanted to stay so that I might speak with you and tell you that if there is anything that I might be able to do for you, to help you in any way, I will do so. You have my word. I will gladly do so."

Ruby blinked a few times, taking in his words. She folded her hands in her lap and looked down at them.

Never had a man treated her with respect or compassion. Why was this gentleman doing so?

She had learned at a young age that nothing was free. If only her mother had known it, too. How different Ruby's life might have been if her vile uncle had not been appointed as her guardian.

Sorrow pierced her. Consumption had taken her parents, and with them, the hope that she would ever belong or be loved again. The fresh mounds of cemetery earth had barely begun to settle when her uncle had dragged her here, forcing her into depravity, beating her within an inch of her life each time she had tried to leave. How nobly he had whispered soothing promises to Ruby's mother as she lay upon her deathbed, only to break every one of them as soon as he had Ruby's limited inheritance legally within his grasp.

Surely, this man must have an ulterior motive, too. Kindness never came without strings attached.

Then she remembered his profession. She nodded, disappointment settling on her like a cold, wet shawl.

"You are a clergyman, of course - it is your duty to help those less fortunate than yourself. Thank you, for your kindness and—"

"Oh, no! Forgive my impertinence, please - I did not mean that I merely pity you or see you as, as a charity case of some sort. No," he said, shaking his head.

Ruby looked up at him and was quite speechless at the expression on his face.

She could not understand why it was that he seemed to care as much as he did. It seemed only natural that it should be due to his profession. It was preposterous to her that it should be for any other reason.

Yet, his eyes seemed to burn right through her with focus and fervency. Despite her wariness, she was quite in danger of believing him.

She forced herself to look away from his captivating gaze.

Soon, he would walk out the door and she would be alone in this prison once more. She had already begun to think highly of him - she dared not permit herself to become even more attached.

After today, she would never see him again.

It was a bitter and deflating thought.

"Mr. Stratton, I do greatly appreciate . . . "

She paused with a sigh.

A few moments later, she tried again to express her thoughts, this time forcing firm composure into her voice.

"The kindness you have shown is more valuable to me than anything else in my life. I shall never forget it."

As Henry's brow knit with concern, he fixed his eyes on her once again.

"Might I be so bold as to ask, what it was that, that is to say . . . Through what circumstances did you come to choose this particular occupation?"

Her head bowed low as she fought back tears. "I did not choose it. I have never had the opportunity of choosing anything for myself."

Henry frowned. "But then, how did you come to be here?"

CHAPTER 2

A GLIMPSE OF HOPE

RUBY KEPT her gaze fixed on her folded hands and told Henry what she had never told anyone - not even the other girls who lived there, though they had likely endured horrendously painful experiences of their own.

"When I was around fourteen years old, my mother and father both fell ill with consumption. My mother, suspecting correctly that neither of them would recover, sought to make provision for me. The only living relative I had was my uncle, and he was not even a blood relation. He had been married to my mother's sister, and after she died, years before, my mother and uncle had a falling out. On her deathbed, my mother reconciled with him. My uncle promised her that he would look after me, and compelled her to make him my guardian. Which she did, just before she died."

She paused, and drew a ragged breath.

"My uncle had no intention of caring for me. He cares only for himself. And money. So, once he was legally my guardian, and what little I was set to inherit would be rightfully his in due course, he dragged me away from the little village my parents and I used to live in. And brought me here . . ."

Her voice trailed off as she slowly looked around the dismal room.

Glancing up, she was moved by the look in Henry's eyes.

Noticing how deeply his eyebrows were furrowed, she flinched at knowing there was much worse still to tell.

"We journeyed for days. It all seemed endless. I was not permitted to cry, or to ask where I was being taken. If I spoke, or made a sound, or cried, he would beat me. For days after we arrived he did not feed me, and only once gave me a drink. It was a few sips of gin and it distorted everything, owing to my empty stomach. It was horrid," she breathed. "But that was nothing in comparison to what would come after."

Henry was looking at his hands and shaking his head in agonised disbelief.

Silence hung heavily in the air.

When Henry finally spoke, his voice was grave. "And you are still cruelly treated?"

Ruby nodded.

"Have you ever tried to leave?"

She nodded again. "Each time I tried, he would find me. Then he would beat me until I was almost dead. Then drag me back here, where . . ."

Henry looked as though he felt ill. "Surely, by now, you must have been able to save a generous amount of the money you earn? Enough, perhaps, to enable you to secure your own lodgings elsewhere?"

"I have no money of my own, sir. He takes all that I earn. He gives us our wages in food, clothing and - as he puts it - 'a roof over our miserable heads'."

Henry's expression darkened. "And, even now, if you attempted to leave, he would beat you."

She looked away and fixed her gaze on the empty hearth. She swallowed with great effort, then nodded.

"Girls who have tried to leave, to work at more fairly paid establishments, have been beaten almost to death. If the rumours are true, some have not survived."

He sighed with such force that she almost jumped. It was a deep, mournful sigh. She knew its kind well, yet somewhere along the way had ceased making them herself.

"Might there be anything - *anything!* - that I am able to do to assist you in any way?"

Ruby looked at him, grief flooding her heart. "Sir, I do not know what to say. I do not imagine there is any way I might ever be free from him."

Henry paused for a moment, looking as though he were deep in thought.

Suddenly his expression changed.

He met her gaze. "Then, perhaps - you might allow me to provide an answer?"

She frowned in confusion. "I am not sure what you mean."

His eyes were practically twinkling. "Perhaps, there is something I might be able to do . . . to help you out of this place."

It took a moment for his words to register with her.

Her voice was barely above a whisper. "Out? Of here?"

He nodded gently. "There is room at my parsonage. My aunt lives there with me, so I am not proposing anything improper. You would be more than welcome to stay with us for as long as you need. We would be glad to help you. And we have connections we could call upon to help you find a suitable position, in time." He sighed. "I simply wish to do what I can to help you be free from this horror into which you have been taken."

He spoke with such passion, of things that had been so far out of reach for Ruby to even dare imagine. Incredulity overwhelmed her.

Many minutes passed in which neither party spoke a word.

Finally, breaking the silence, Ruby cleared her throat.

"But . . . *Why?*"

Henry looked at her, his features illuminated with the most sincere expression that Ruby had ever seen.

"Because your life is valuable. You do not deserve this cruelty. You are precious to God. He loves you. And He will help you, if you will ask."

An age seemed to pass in which the air weighed heavy with tremulous hope. Could Henry's words be true? Could God ever love her, after all that she had done?

Her heart sank.

No. It could not be true. Someone like her could never be good enough for God to notice them, never mind love them.

Could they?

As Ruby spoke, her voice started to waver. She tried to force everything from her mind and focus only on what she was trying to express.

"There is no way I might leave without being noticed. And if I am noticed, I may be killed, or at least, very close to it." She shrugged. "I would hardly be losing much, though."

Henry's eyes grew wide and he opened his mouth to speak, but Ruby continued before he could say anything.

"I am completely at a loss to tell you how much I appreciate what you propose," she said. "But there is no hope of accepting it."

He looked almost heartbroken. "There must be *something* I can do."

Silence filled the room again.

Henry soon broke it.

"Are there any secret passages?"

Ruby raised her eyebrows.

"If so, they are secret even to me."

"Would . . . If . . . No."

"What is it?"

He looked down, almost ashamed. "I was going to ask if Mr . . . Forgive me, what is the name of the man who . . . who owns this place?"

Ruby spoke with a firm-set jaw. "Mr. Millforte."

"I was going to ask if, well, if Mr. Millforte would consider *selling* you to me."

Her eyebrows shot upward, then crashed back down in a frown.

"Forgive me, I did not mean that to sound as awful as it did. I do not mean that I wish to *own* you or anything as abhorrent as that. I only ask if it might be possible to buy your freedom, under the proviso of buying, well, you."

She was shocked, though she tried to hide it. After thinking for a moment, she looked at him with an expression of defeat.

"I cannot imagine he would sell any of us. I fear he is too attached to the income we provide him. He is much too shrewd to accept one larger payment over a steady stream of smaller takings. And he most certainly would not sell me to *you*. Your profession would reveal your true motive."

He frowned. "Mm . . ." He ran a despairing hand over his face. "Forgive me. I am at a loss. I know what *ought* to be done, but not how."

Ruby felt a tug at her heart that she could not remember ever feeling before. She could not be sure if it was gratitude for Henry's ardent concern, or a burgeoning hope that it might be possible after all to someday escape the bleakness of her present situation.

Perhaps, it was both.

Henry reached into his waistcoat pocket and pulled out his pocket watch. With a start, he was on his feet.

"Oh, I am dreadfully sorry, but I must away. I have another appointment at half past five, and it is almost a quarter to."

Ruby couldn't believe it. For the first time she could remember, time had moved quickly.

Suddenly, the fleeting fancies she had imagined about escaping evaporated, replaced instantaneously with a terrible anticipation that Millforte, or a new customer, might burst through her door at any moment.

She stood, summoning courage enough to address Henry one last time.

"Thank you for your kindness, Mr. Stratton."

She looked into the warmth and safety in his eyes, knowing that when he walked out the door, she would be trapped again in despair and cruelty.

Silently they both stood, observing one another.

His reluctance to leave was apparent. Ruby was vividly aware of the pressure of time yet longed to once again feel liberated from it. She wondered if he might be feeling the same.

Slowly, Henry gathered up the hat he had removed soon after his arrival and walked toward the door. Reaching it, he turned.

Ruby had followed him, each step heavier and more difficult to traverse.

The reality of his departure welled up inside her, heaping more rubble around her heart, forcing a tight grip on her lungs. Unable to speak, she wanted so much to cry.

Henry bowed. Ruby curtseyed in return.

"Forgive me, for the abruptness with which I must take my leave. Please know that I will not forget you, and . . . " He lowered his voice to a whisper, cautiously glancing at the door. "Please know that I will do what I can to help you, however long it may take."

Upon opening the door, Henry glanced up and down the hall. He whispered a farewell, bowed one more time and turned, walking away from her with visible regret.

When he was out of sight, Ruby closed her door and leaned against it. She closed her eyes, not wanting to leave behind the moments of peacefulness his presence had brought.

But her reflections didn't last long. A heavy knock on the door made her start.

Maybe he'd come back. She smoothed her robe out of habit and opened the door.

"Hello, little lady," leered an older man that she had never seen before. She knew who he was, though.

A customer.

She curtseyed, and motioned for him to come in. Once again, her limbs felt as though they were made from lead and the rubble came crashing back around her chest.

He strode in, commanding and overbearing, as though he owned the room and everything in it.

Ruby peered past the door frame, glancing out in desperate hope for one last sight of Henry.

He was gone.

Closing the door and turning to face her customer, all her hopes vanished. She stood staring at him, forgetting her usual routine, her staged and inviting words.

All she could think of was Henry, and those eyes that had burned through her the right way.

The man before her now - his eyes were burning, but with lust, and glassed from an excess of liquor.

She imagined running out of the room, out of the building, not stopping for breath until she ran right out of the city. Surely taking her chances on the street would be better than this. But deep down, she knew it would not be much different. At least here she had a roof over her head, and meals - though meagre - everyday.

The man walked toward her and grabbed her wrist.

"Well, come on, darlin' - I ain't payin' you to stand and look at me!"

She almost wished that Henry had not stumbled upon her that afternoon.

It had only made things worse - to be treated fairly, then go straight back to being a plaything. It felt like she had been given a fragment of a glimpse - however unlikely - of a different life, then shoved back into a reality that was the complete opposite.

The man glanced at Ruby and burped as he walked toward the door.

"Cheers, darlin'," he slurred as he left.

As the door closed, Ruby stared at it in disgust, then curled up on the chair that Henry had sat on only a short time before.

She knew that he ought to be Mr. Stratton to her, but every time she thought of him, her heart called him Henry.

Each time she closed her eyes, his own were all that she could see. It all still seemed like a dream.

Had it really happened?

Had a respectable clergyman really been sitting in her parlour? Had he really vowed to help her, no matter what?

She squeezed her head in her hands. She had to forget about him.

He had said that he would not forget her. That he would come back and help her. But she had to stop believing that.

He seemed much too important to fret over a worthless prostitute.

Absent-mindedly, she got up and poured herself a drink.

Was he truly a real person, who was out there somewhere, living and breathing - maybe even thinking of her?

She sat back down and sipped her drink. Then, she noticed something strange.

Usually, after an encounter with a customer, she would feel mostly empty. This time, a different sensation filled her heart.

Grief.

All she wanted to do was weep.

It was unnerving. She had learned long ago that she ought to keep her tears tightly contained. Nothing good ever came from releasing them.

But her defences were crumbling, and she feared that if she wept now, she would never be able to stop.

Her heart and her mind were at war.

Part of her screamed that she must stop serving her customers - she must wait for Henry to come back and rescue her.

The other part scolded her to stop dreaming, to get back to her reality and forget Henry completely.

Henry's words echoed in her mind.

You are precious to God. He loves you.

How could that ever be true?

Overwhelmed, she finally wept.

A loud knock sounded at the door. Before she had even thought about standing up to answer it, the door swung open and another customer sauntered in, looking as comfortable as could be.

"Stop that snivelling," he scoffed.

He was an uncouth, uncaring man, if ever she had seen one.

Ruby froze. Despite her crushing shame and grief, a new resolution began to fill her.

From this moment onward, she would not entertain customers who did not show her any respect. She detested all the times she had complied without question.

She brought herself slowly to a stand, then turned to face the man. Tears rolled silently down her cheeks. Looking at him more closely, her despair fused into frustration.

Marching toward him, she gritted her teeth.

"How dare you speak to me in such a manner! Get out - I demand that you get out!"

The man raised a smug eyebrow. "I paid for a floozy. So you best do what you are supposed to, missy."

Unaware of her action until it was too late to change it, Ruby swung her arm back then struck him on the cheek.

"Get out!" she hissed.

His impertinence immediately switched to anger, and he grabbed her hair in one hand, dragging her further into the room.

She struggled against him, punching and kicking where she could, only fuelling his rage. After wrestling her to the floor, he clasped his hands around her throat and glared at her with cold, determined eyes.

"Perhaps you did not hear me. I have paid my money, and you are *mine* for the next hour. I suggest you do as you are told from now on."

He gave her neck one last squeeze, then released his grip.

She gasped repeatedly, welcoming each breath with desperate relief.

The man bent down to yank her up from the floor. As soon as he let go, her knees buckled, and she fell to the floor.

"Now," the man growled. "Shall we?"

She looked up at him, determination in her stinging eyes. She coughed, and when she tried to speak, her voice was nothing more than a thin, raspy wheeze.

"No," she whispered.

"I beg your pardon?"

"No," she said again, trying to strengthen her voice as she spoke but failing to do so.

She was weak not only from the outward struggle against him, but the inward struggle dividing her mind and heart.

She could not stop thinking of Henry. She wished desperately that he were still present, that he could be there to keep her safe at all times. Yet, she knew such a hope was impossible.

Even so, her heart burned for more, for freedom from this nightmare.

"Why, you little . . . "

He grabbed her, his words melding into a raging snarl.

Once again, he knocked her to the floor, ignoring her cries of protest and pain.

CHAPTER 3

TRAPPED UNDER RUBBLE

THE NEXT FEW weeks were a blur of dread and deception.

Ruby refused every customer that came to her, often indicating her inability to comply with a mistruth - that it was the time of her monthly course.

Most of the men appeared to be disgusted, and couldn't leave quickly enough. Others saw fit to punish Ruby for the inconvenience of having to find someone else.

One day, Millforte had burst into her room, glowering as usual. Terrified that he had discovered her ruse and that he intended to punish her, Ruby feigned illness, as well as telling Millforte the original mistruth, hoping desperately that at least one of the fabrications would be believed.

That had bought her some time.

But it was running out.

It was now four days since her conversation with Millforte. She doubted how much longer she could maintain her pretence.

The man who was grabbing her face hadn't believed her.

He squeezed his fingers into her cheeks and told her one

last time how dishonest and pathetic she was. She heard him, despite the ringing in her ears that thundered above the sound of his voice, owing to the collision of her head and the edge of the hearth.

Ruby watched him leave, slamming the door behind him.

She lay motionless on the floor, welcoming the coolness of the air that washed over her. Her throat smarted, and her eyes stung with uncried tears.

A fresh wave of sorrow welled up within her and she remained where she was for a long time, eventually releasing the hot, bitter tears she had suppressed for so long.

Eventually, she sat up and wearily turned to look at the clock. It was later than she had expected. Dinner was long gone, by now.

She dragged herself along the floor toward her bed. All strength had abandoned her, and her limbs shook from weakness. She paused, then with all the might she could muster, pulled herself up onto the bed. Gathering her breath, she crawled beneath the worn satin covers. The faint odour of stale beer lingered on one of the pillows.

Ruby lay staring up at the ceiling, wondering what the next few weeks held in store. She could not go on like this forever.

There was only one thing to be done.

She must forget Henry.

He wasn't coming back. Over two weeks had passed. There had been no visit, no letter, no indication that he still intended to help her.

No evidence that he even remembered her.

As she retraced Henry's face in her mind, she curled up and pulled the sheets over her head, weeping profusely.

SHE AWOKE QUITE EARLY the next morning, each of her muscles tense with pain. Heartache gripped her as she swung out of bed, hoping as she did every morning that this would be the day that Henry would return.

He is not coming back. You must forget him, Ruby, you stupid girl.

She silently argued with herself as she dressed, mindful of how little time remained for breakfast. Though she had no desire for the taste of food, her stomach rumbled relentlessly. She couldn't remember the last time she had eaten anything.

There was a knock at the door just as she approached it from within. Cautiously, she swung it open and found herself face to face with a tall, distinguished gentleman.

"Are you Ruby?" he asked, tentatively.

"Yes," she replied.

A spark of hope fluttered in her stomach. Maybe Henry had sent him. Maybe there was still hope.

"Might I come in?"

"Oh, yes. Yes. I am sorry. Do, come in."

She stood aside to allow him to pass. Closing the door quickly yet as silently as she could manage, she walked toward him and adopted a more hushed voice.

"Why is it that you wish to see me, sir?" she eagerly whispered.

The gentleman looked at her blankly. Then, slowly, a bemused smirk crept onto his face.

"Why does one usually wish to see someone like you?"

He reached for her, but she darted out of his way, coming to a stand behind one of the chairs.

Just another customer. Nausea rose in her throat.

"Sir, I must ask you to leave. I apologise for any inconvenience."

"I beg your pardon?"

She repeated her request, and taut silence filled the room for a few anxious moments.

"But I had an agreement with Mr. Millforte . . . "

Ruby's heart raced. "I understand that, sir, and as I say, I am very sorry for any inconvenience."

He exhaled impatiently and gave her a disapproving look. Then, he left.

He was certainly more of a gentleman than the previous customer. She shuddered to remember him.

Glancing at the clock, she sighed. Too late. Breakfast was over.

She stood for a moment, wondering if it might be worth the risk to see if anything remotely edible remained.

Her stomach growled. She was too hungry *not* to try.

As Ruby headed for the door, it was flung open from the outside. Before her stood Millforte himself.

Suddenly, Ruby felt weak from more than just hunger.

"Well, don't you look pretty . . . "

The sarcasm was apparent in his expression as well as his voice. He looked her up and down, an amused sneer curling his lips. Ruby stood silent, her pulse fast, her mind racing.

He stepped toward her, swaggering with proud amusement.

"You could almost pass for a decent human being." He stopped, inches from her, and bent his leering face to hers so that their noses were close to touching. "Almost."

He stepped away, his hands clasped behind his back and his head tilted to one side in mock thoughtfulness.

Even after all these years, she still had trouble fully reading him at times.

This was one of them.

"Tell me," he said, turning back to face her, "who runs this little establishment?"

Ruby swallowed. Her mouth was dry.

"You, sir."

She silently willed Henry to appear in the doorway and protect her from her oppressor. He did not.

"Correct. Me. Not you." Millforte glared at her. "So, tell me - if it is *I* who runs the place and *I* who makes arrangements for my customers - working my hardest to ensure that their needs are met so that they will continue to bring their custom here - then surely it is *I* who should have sole authority as to whether or not a customer is turned away."

He gritted his teeth.

"I have been more than patient. And now, though you are no longer indisposed, you lied to a paying customer and turned him away! What gives a waste of space like you," he breathed, "any right to be *anything* but grateful to me? How dare you turn my customers away, you insolent strumpet!"

With each word, he lunged closer and closer to Ruby until, having screamed the last three in her face, he grabbed her wrist and flung her sideways onto the bed.

He stood over her, his legs holding hers against the bedside, his rough hands pinning her arms so that she lay stretched on her back, looking up at him. She winced in pain, but he did not seem to notice.

Even if he had, he likely would not have cared.

"How *dare* you insult my customers!" he hissed. "I ought to reunite you with your pathetic parents."

Once again, his face was inches from hers, his warm, bitter breath pouring like a waterfall over her face and neck. A cruel glint in his eye grew brighter.

"I think *somebody* needs a reminder of just *what* they are, do you not agree?"

Ruby's will collapsed, knowing from years of despair that there was nothing she could do to dissuade him.

She tried to imagine she was anywhere but where she really was. She closed her eyes, striving to envision a warm, peaceful place. A place where no one was ever cruel.

No matter how hard she tried to close Millforte out of her awareness and reflect instead on the seed of hope that Henry had planted, her resolve was wearing so thin it was breaking apart.

Henry had forgotten her.

All she had was Millforte, this place, this existence.

She ought to accept what Millforte said about her - what he had been saying for the entirety of her time with him.

There was no hope. No future that didn't include all this.

Her mind warred against itself, struggling against his poisonous words, grasping frantically to hold onto Henry's. Maybe God *did* love her.

Something within her crumbled.

How long ago it seemed since Henry had told her of God's love. Now, here was Millforte, mocking and deriding her, leaving her with no doubt that love was something she could never deserve.

This was reality.

And she would not survive long if she refused any more customers.

Henry was wrong.

Millforte was right.

She *was* worthless. She *was* pathetic.

As Ruby voiced her agreement with the labels Millforte shouted at her, she felt something deep inside her chest snap. For a moment, she could hardly breathe.

She knew she had just felt her soul break all over again.

"Know that this is your final warning."

Millforte's voice thundered in her ears.

"If you fail in *any* way to make my customers happy from this point onward, I will make sure that you will never again be able to utter the word 'no' to anyone - ever again."

His voice was seething, his posture threatening.

"Do you understand me?"

Silent tears slid down Ruby's face, and she nodded, every inch of her in agony.

"I said, do you understand me, *whore?*"

"Yes, sir," Ruby replied in a faint, weak voice.

"Speak up!" he shouted.

"Yes, sir," she repeated in a slightly stronger voice.

He eyed her up and down. "Do not deceive me again."

He turned and walked toward the door.

Just before leaving, he faced into the room and shouted, "Be ready for your next customer in half an hour!"

WHEN NO MORE TEARS WOULD COME, AND the ringing in her ears had settled, Ruby used the last dregs of energy she had to crawl off the bed, dragging herself over to the full-length mirror that stood in the corner of the room.

She beheld her appearance with a start.

Red-rimmed, puffy eyes were set in an eerily pale face. Dark hair wisped out in alarming disarray. Her clothing was rumpled and hitched off-centre, her posture stiffened in a weary stoop. Already, bruises were forming beneath her eye and lip.

Ruby resolved once more to lay aside all hope that Henry would ever return. Survival must be her focus now, and for that, she must be obedient to Millforte.

Since there was now no possibility of procuring any

breakfast, she slipped into her indecorous attire, ensuring her stays were as tight as she could manage without any assistance.

Just as she finished fastening her peignoir, a knock sounded at the door. With a deep breath to calm her trembling nerves, she limped to answer it. Her arm muscles seized with pain as she pulled the door open.

She only hoped that her bruises would not be too much of an offence to whomever this next customer may be. The last thing she wanted was any further complaint reaching Millforte's ears.

Lifting her gaze to look at the face of the man on the other side of the threshold, she gasped.

Was she dreaming?

"Ruby," he said, softly, glancing about him.

"Mr. Stratton?"

He entered the room with respect yet vigour. After closing the door, he moved closer to her, smiling as someone would when they had some happy news to share.

Ruby blinked fast, trying to dispel the fluttering dots that cascaded in front of her eyes. Her limbs grew weak and shaky.

The next thing she knew, strong arms were around her, intercepting her at just the right moment to prevent her from falling to the floor.

"Ruby! Are you all right?"

Henry helped her over to the chaise longue in her little parlour, and eased her down onto its tattered cushions.

She lay there shaking her head for a few moments until she could speak.

"I am sorry, Mr. Stratton. I have had rather a difficult morning."

She looked up at him. A moment later, she surmised that

the sudden alteration of his expression indicated that he had just noticed her bruises.

"I see that," he replied, obviously stunned. His voice deepened. "Who did this to you?"

She sat up, embarrassed. "I . . . I must have hit my head when I fell last night."

He frowned, his face etched with confusion. "I see," he declared, sounding most unconvinced.

Ruby silently cautioned herself to focus on the truth. There was no hope. No matter what Henry might say. This time, she would not be swept away by promises that Henry would never be able to keep.

Soon, he would be gone again, and she would return to depravity - the only life she could ever have. Anything else was a fantastical notion. She could not afford to forget the reality of Millforte's threat.

As such, she resolved that the best thing she could do now was to somehow incite Mr. Stratton - as she ought to think of him, if she was to think of him at all - to leave.

"How may I help you, Mr. Stratton?"

Ruby kept her gaze fixed in his direction, yet without looking him in the eye. She dared not risk being swayed by those gentle eyes. Not if she intended to maintain her frosty demeanour toward him with any success.

"Well, I came because I have some rather encouraging news to share with you."

His tone was flat and resigned.

Ruby glanced at him, a sharp pang of heartache piercing her upon noticing how spurned he appeared.

She looked away again, shaking her head gently, warning herself not to forget Millforte's threat.

Her heart pounded as she forced herself to say, "Very well.

Though I ought to make you aware that I am expecting a customer very soon."

She hated herself. How cruel it was for her to speak to him this way.

But she had to avoid angering Millforte any further. The more she dared to grasp at the dreams of freedom that Henry stirred up, the more she endangered her life.

Henry stood silent. After what seemed a long time, Ruby couldn't bear it any more. She looked up at him, her eyebrows slightly raised in question at his silence.

He was looking at her knowingly. As their eyes met, something appeared to confirm what he had been suspecting.

"He knows, then?"

"Who knows? Knows what?"

Ruby could see plainly the same care and consideration that had enraptured her the first time they'd met, despite the time that had passed and the distance her demeanour had wedged between them.

"Millforte. He knows what we spoke of last time, I presume?"

Henry's tone was firm, but not severe. Not accusatory.

Ruby longed to leave this place with him, regardless of the consequences. A split second later, she chided herself not to be so reckless.

"No, Mr. Stratton. He does not know, and he must never know. I am sorry for allowing myself to be carried away during your previous visit. I thank you, again, for your kindness, but this . . . This is where I belong."

As she trailed off, Millforte's words from earlier that morning echoed in her head.

Henry gave her a look that made her soul sigh.

"Ruby, forgive me for speaking with such boldness, but

you and I both know that you could never truly belong in a place like this."

She opened her mouth to protest, but he spoke again before she could utter a word.

"And that is why I have returned - to reassure you that your time in this miserable place has come to an end."

CHAPTER 4

A MATTER OF URGENCY

WEAKNESS WASHED over her as she struggled to suppress the intensity of her emotions.

She must not even dare to believe him. It was impossible.

An attempt to rebut Henry's claims only came forth as a cracked whimper. She pushed herself up, sitting more than reclining.

He knelt before her, their eyes level, though she tried to avoid meeting his gaze.

"Ruby, please, do not shut me out. I have been discussing with my aunt what might be done to set right the injustice that has been forced upon you - for weeks, now. And, I believe we may have finally devised a solution."

As Ruby's eyes slowly moved to meet his, her head spun, dizzy with anticipation. As her gaze locked with his, her defences finally shattered. Her breathing grew rapid.

Sensing her receptiveness, he quickly explained.

"My household servant, Browne, shall come here during the day," he began, taking care to speak in hushed tones, and pausing at the slightest sound.

"He will dress as a gentleman, and there is no doubt that people will assume him to be so."

His speech was animated, though peppered with a sense of awareness that carrying out such a plan would not be without its dangers.

"We shall bedeck him with a large cloak, under which my aunt will carefully fasten a cushion - or something to that effect - to his abdomen, which will cause him to appear rather plump."

He said these last two words with particular annunciation, as if to imply a great significance.

Ruby's eyebrows fluctuated up and down in confusion throughout Henry's discourse.

"The cloak," he carried on, "The cloak truly is key, for, you see, when he arrives and is admitted to your chamber, yourself and the cushion shall switch places!"

It was obvious that he'd employed extra reserve to hush his voice for the last two words, and more obvious still that he would have shouted them with glee, had he been anywhere other than the very place in which the plot he had hatched was to take place.

Ruby stared at him for a moment, the initial thrill she had felt upon hearing the plan fading with each second that passed, her mind raising question after question.

"You mean, I am to wrap myself around someone and . . . hide under his coat?" she asked, incredulously.

"Browne is quite tall. He does not have a large stomach, but if he did, it would not look out of place on his frame. Besides, you are petite enough to make the whole venture truly possible."

"But, what if I lose my grasp and fall out the bottom of his cloak? Or, or, what if I do not form the same shape as the cushion - which I imagine will be the case?"

"He will pay the man downstairs before he comes up to you, so once you have taken the cushion's place - allowing enough time to pass, of course, so as not to attract suspicion from anyone - he will have only to walk along the few corridors, down the staircase and out the front door, nodding farewell to the porter as he passes. My carriage will be waiting further down the street. Even if the shape is somewhat altered, it should not be noticeable - at least, not for very long, for he will be moving away from the place as swiftly as possible."

Ruby thought for a moment. She sighed, defeatedly.

"I cannot help but think that we will not succeed. And if we are caught, we shall all suffer for it."

He lowered his gaze, his enthusiasm seeming to falter for a moment.

"I confess that there is no guarantee, but I am hopeful - more than hopeful - that we may carry out the plot without failing. If I thought there to be a certainty of danger, I would never expose you to it. There is some risk, yes, but I believe it to be risk that we might readily overcome."

Ruby sighed. "Forgive me. I am a little overcome, myself."

She thought for a moment. "When do you propose that all of this might take place?"

"Tomorrow. Browne will leave first thing in the morning in order to arrive here by early evening."

Ruby's heart sank. She would have to endure another full day and night of this place and all that it required her to do. She could not refuse customers again and risk having all her strength beaten out the day before she would need an abundance of it.

"Mr. Stratton," she breathed. "I must warn you. Millforte said that if I refuse any more clients, he will not hesitate to reunite me with my parents."

Henry frowned, then his eyes widened in realisation.

"He means to . . . to *kill* you?"

He studied her face as she nodded.

"And it was he who gave those bruises to you?" he asked.

Ruby nodded again.

Henry sighed, a sigh so forceful that it seemed to indicate a desire to give Millforte bruises of his own. He opened his mouth to speak, then stopped.

He looked at Ruby intently. "Wait a moment - did you say that you *refused* a customer?"

"Yes." She lowered her head, shame flooding her heart. "I lied. I told Millforte that I was ill. And other things. Most of the time it worked. But last evening it did not. Then, the customer reported back to Millforte. And—"

Henry stood up, abruptly. "That settles it. I shall take my leave now and send Browne immediately. You shall not spend another moment here that is not of absolute necessity. It is not safe."

Silently, they beheld one another, absorbing the burgeoning reality of what had merely been an idea not long before.

"What if he catches us?" Ruby's voice wavered.

Henry's face seemed almost expressionless except for the determination that burned in his eyes.

"Even if he does, Browne and I will do whatever we must to ensure that one way or another you shall be free of this place. But, do not fear. God will provide all that we need."

Encouraged by his hopeful conviction, the hope of freedom seized her with a sensation that made her tingle all over.

"Now," he said. "Are there any small items here of value which are yours, that I might remove with me now, unnoticed? The less that Browne has to carry later, the better."

Ruby looked around the room rather blankly, before returning her gaze to him.

"No. I have nothing of my own. Only some clothes, but they are not really mine. Nor would I wish to wear them outside of here."

A creaking floorboard outside her door made them both start.

They resumed speaking in subdued tones.

"Perhaps I ought to bring them anyway. I have no money to buy anything new," Ruby said.

"Do not worry about that. My aunt will see to it that you have everything material that you need."

"Oh, that is so kind." She paused for a moment. "I do hope that I shall not be too much of an inconvenience. To either of you."

He smiled. "Not at all."

She looked up at him, a question in her gaze.

He repeated himself firmly. "Not at *all*."

A few more silent moments passed.

Henry glanced at the clock and jumped to his feet.

"We have no more time to lose. I must away to fetch Browne and the carriage. It will take some time to get home and back again before evening," he whispered.

Earnestness burned in his eyes.

"I am sorry that I cannot prevent what may take place until then." He grimaced. "Be strong until I return. And take heart - the oppression you endure here will soon be over."

Henry squeezed her hand compassionately then left.

Ruby stood staring at the door in disbelief. Had he really come back? Was she really to be free from her prison that very day?

She set about fixing up the room, ensuring that everything was in order, in case Millforte should arrive and accuse her of shirking her duties. For the rest of the day, she must do everything she could to avoid displeasing him and, thereby, foiling Henry's plan.

Not long after Henry had gone, there was a heavy knock on the door. Ruby moved to answer it, stumbling as she did so. Her senses were heightened and her whole body trembled as she thought about what would take place later that day.

Outside the door was a grinning man. He bowed to her in what seemed a mocking manner due to his overly exuberant countenance.

She stepped back, inviting him in. He sashayed into the room and turned to face her as she closed the door.

"Hello," she said, forcing a smile.

She must try her best to do everything right, lest this man complain to Millforte and dash her chance of escape.

"Hello," drawled the man. It seemed he could hardly speak for all his grinning. "Which one are you? Collette, is it?"

A surge of repulsion coursed through Ruby.

Exhaling deeply, she spoke. "Ruby."

Cooperate. She must cooperate. Soon, all this would be behind her.

"Ooh, is there a Sapphire? I do like blue." His grin deepened.

Not only was she repulsed by him, but she began to question his sanity.

"No, sir. There is not."

"All right. I suppose you will do."

When the grinning man had finally gone, Ruby wept.

Never had she endured such a fierce battle deep within,

believing herself too filthy to leave, yet longing for the carriage to arrive.

She struggled to understand the seeming depth of Henry's concern. She had never met a man whose interest in her had nothing to do with his own pleasure.

Yet another knock sounded. A deep sigh shook her as she moved to answer it.

A very finely dressed gentleman stood in the doorway. He seemed somewhat familiar to Ruby, though she could not place him.

He nodded. "Good afternoon."

"Good afternoon, sir," Ruby replied.

Even his walk was fine, she thought, as the man entered the room. Whoever he might be, he was clearly a man of refined breeding and elevated station.

Ruby had long ago learned that though some men might appear refined on the outside, they could be every bit as corrupt as their uncouth counterparts on the inside.

The only thing she was grateful for was that he did not speak to her. She welcomed the silence as she imagined the evening's impending venture.

It *had* to succeed.

The gentleman handed a coin of no small importance to her, tipping his hat. "I have already paid downstairs for the appointment. Please accept this as a gratuity. Good day, miss."

With that, he was gone, leaving Ruby in possession of the weighty coin in her hand.

Dare she keep it? After all, she would hopefully be gone by the time Millforte made his evening rounds to collect all the tips.

She poured herself a drink, then set the coin on the table in her parlour. She stared at it.

Perhaps, she could present the coin as a token of thankfulness to Henry and his aunt at an appropriate time. Surely, it would be rude to stay at the parsonage empty-handed.

She heard a scuffle at the door latch before the door flung open. Polly, one of the other girls, ran toward her in a fluster.

"Ruby! Ruby, she's gone!"

Ruby stood to meet her, clasping Polly's freezing hands in her own.

"Gone? Who is gone? Gone where?"

"Susanna! She made a run for it, and now Millforte and some of his men are chasing her, hunting her down! Oh, Ruby, they will kill her if they find her!" She broke into sobs.

Ruby froze.

"Oh, Polly."

She helped Polly into a chair, pushing away fresh anxiety regarding her own impending escape.

"I know you and Susanna are very close, but do not fret - I am sure she will be all right. Perhaps they will not find her. She is fast. She may well succeed in outrunning them."

"But she is unwell! One of her customers beat her around last night, and she hit him back in self-defence. Millforte found out and he beat her so hard he broke her shoulder! That is why she fled!"

Ruby shuddered. She was still tender from the bruises Millforte had inflicted upon her earlier that morning. She was suddenly grateful that she had not fared much, much worse.

"Even so," she said. "She is strong of spirit. I am sure that she will do well. Indeed, she will be much better off out there than she was in here."

Polly looked up at her, an incredulous expression on her pale, tear-streaked face.

"But, Ruby! We are safe here, at least."

41

"Safe?" Ruby exclaimed.

"Out there, there is every guarantee of men but no guarantee of money or shelter. At least here Millforte feeds and clothes us, and protects us."

Despair tugged Ruby's heart. She had seen Polly's black eye last year, had tended to her wounds the year before that, and watched her walk with a limp in the breakfast room not four months earlier. Polly spoke of protection and gratefulness, but Ruby knew that it had been beaten into her to do so, just like it had to herself and the other girls.

Millforte the kind provider was nothing more than Millforte the insolent bully. Be thankful to him or be beaten until you are. It pained Ruby to hear Polly recite the words they had all been brainwashed to believe.

"Poor Susanna! How could she be so unwise to attempt such a thing? She will surely be killed if she is ever found. And she might starve to death if she is *not* found!"

Polly was overcome by more sobs, and as Ruby held her, she began to doubt the possibility that her own escape would go undetected.

Her desire for freedom had drowned out the warning voice in her mind that knew the folly of such an attempt, and the consequences they would suffer if they did not meet with success.

But now, the warning voice sounded loud and clear, and its message chilled Ruby.

You can never be free from him.

Would she ever really be safe, even if Millforte did not find her at the parsonage?

She believed Henry to be trustworthy, but doubt swarmed in her mind.

What if he grew tired of her? What if he realised she was

worthless after all? Would he summon Millforte to take her back?

Surely not. But, still, the doubt was there, and it was enough to unnerve her.

"Polly, she will be fine. She will. I am sure she knew the risks involved, and would not have tried to leave unless she truly believed she could succeed."

Ruby's words had little consolatory effect on Polly, whose sobbing and wailing only seemed to intensify.

Ruby glanced up. Just after three o'clock. Browne was due to arrive that very evening. She felt sick thinking about it, especially now.

Eventually, Polly's sobs lessened until they ceased altogether. Ruby gave her a drink and tried her best to steer the conversation away from Susanna's escape.

Just as she had managed, after much exertion, to make Polly smile, there was another knock at her door.

Polly jumped up, thanked Ruby as she wiped her puffy eyes. She opened the door to reveal a tall, stocky man with a very large stomach.

Ruby's heart started to race. Had Browne arrived early?

The man leered into the room, blocking Polly's attempted exit.

"So, I am to have two of you, am I?"

Polly curtseyed and looked at Ruby with a brave smile, before leaving hastily.

Ruby sighed. There was at least one more customer to endure before Browne's arrival.

AFTER THE STOCKY man had gone, Ruby sipped a glass of gin to settle her stomach. As freedom neared, a combination of excitement and terror grew more and more unbearable with each passing moment.

She reclined on her chaise, staring up at the cracked and gloomy ceiling. She tried to force herself to calm down, to stop shaking and relax. If only she could soothe herself as she had been able to soothe Polly.

After a while of focusing on the rhythm of her breathing, she drifted off, exhausted by the events and emotions of the day so far.

Drowsy, she drifted out of her slumber to the sound of a knock that she was not sure she had truly heard. She lay still for a moment until the knock was repeated and she knew it was real.

She jumped up so quickly that her vision clouded over. Standing a moment, she regained clear sight, then nervously hastened to the door.

Upon first glance at the man on the other side of it, she groaned inwardly, thinking the stocky customer had returned.

Glancing at the man's face, however, she froze.

It wasn't him.

A pleasant smile shone out from the stranger's face.

"Please, do come in," she offered.

The man bowed quickly and stepped into the room.

Ruby closed the door, feeling sick at the thought that it was Browne, and sick at the thought that it was not.

He took off his hat and edged closer to her.

"Miss Ruby?"

Her heart leaped, though she answered cautiously, aware of how awful it would be to wrongly presume the man to be Browne.

"Yes?"

It was horrid to imagine the plans being discovered before they could even be put into action.

"I believe you are expecting me, miss? Browne, at your service, by way of Mr. Stratton."

He was whispering, and Ruby detected a nervous quiver in his soft, kind voice.

"Oh, yes," she replied.

He was here. It was really happening.

It was really happening.

CHAPTER 5

THE ESCAPE

BROWNE LOOKED AROUND THE ROOM, his expression that of someone expecting to see foes hiding in every corner. Seemingly content, he proceeded to remove his cloak.

Ruby gave a nervous laugh as she saw the cushion fastened around his middle, and wondered how she had ever agreed to such a scheme. It seemed nonsensical now that it was before her.

"Do you have a fireplace, miss?"

"A fireplace? Why, yes - it is just over there." She pointed to it. "Why do you ask?"

"Well, now - it is up to yourself, miss, but Mr. Stratton said we might want to try burning the cushion, only in an attempt to conceal our methods from your Mr. Millfont."

"Millforte," Ruby whispered in correction.

"I beg your pardon, miss. Mr. Millforte. What do you wish?"

"I do not know. The fire is never lit," she said, hesitantly.

"Ah! But, it *would* be out of view if I were to put it under the bed."

Browne untied the cushion and handed it to her. On top of it were breeches and a shirt.

She looked up at Browne, quizzically.

"Do not fret, miss - Mrs. Jones has all sorts of dresses and garments ready for you. But for this evening's activities she felt that these would be more . . . appropriate. Once we are safely back at the parsonage, Mrs. Jones will see to it that you are dressed accordingly."

Ruby tiptoed over to the bed and crouching down, kicked the cushion as far under it as she could.

"There. That should go unnoticed until he turns the place upside down," she said, more to herself than to Browne.

They sat in her parlour, a heavy silence filling the room as they both anticipated what the next few hours would bring.

"How long have you worked for Mr. Stratton?" Ruby asked timidly.

She hoped silently that she was not being too bold in speaking so directly to him. After all, she had been decidedly more bold with Henry - and him a clergyman. He had just been so easy to talk to.

"Oh, quite a while, miss," replied Browne, jolting Ruby's thoughts back to the present. "Originally, I was employed by his uncle and aunt - Mr. and Mrs. Jones. Mr. Jones was the parson before Mr. Stratton, you see, under the patronage of Sir Anthony Harford. And then, since he and Mrs. Jones had no child of their own, Mr. Jones had always indicated his intention for young Mr. Stratton to assume the elder's duties, in due course. So, when Mr. Jones died unexpectedly a number of years ago, Mr. Stratton came to live at the parsonage, and was installed in the church as the new parson, with the full blessing of Sir and Lady Harford to continue under their patronage. He has been as good and faithful a master as his dear departed uncle."

She smiled in return, then paused. "What is his aunt like?"

She was starting to feel nervous at how vastly her world was about to change. As eager as she was to leave this place, it was all she had known for many years. The thought of being surrounded by new people - people who would, at one time, have been her equals, but whom she could now only view as stations above herself, owing to her lifestyle of debauchery - was only now beginning to sink in.

"She is a lovely lady, miss. Very kind and warm. I am sure that you will get along marvellously with one another. She has cared for Mr. Stratton as though he were her own for many years now. To be sure, I hardly think they could be closer if they *were* mother and son! And it is Mrs. Jones who is largely responsible for Mr. Stratton's fine education. She is very pleased with the respectable young man he has turned out to be. Indeed, we all are."

Ruby was not surprised by his statement.

They continued to converse sporadically as they waited for enough time to pass. Ruby kept looking at the door, dreading a customer. Or, worse - Millforte.

Eventually, Browne broke the silence that had settled upon them.

"Perhaps we ought to make ready, miss."

Ruby gulped, her throat dry as dust. "Yes."

Gathering up the breeches and shirt, she walked over to the dressing screen in the corner of the room and disappeared behind it. She inhaled deeply, unsettled by how real - and how dangerous - it was all starting to feel.

She slipped out of her dress and pulled on the breeches and shirt that Henry had sent. Her small frame was engulfed by them. As she walked back into view, Browne nodded to her with a sympathetic smile.

"Are you ready, miss?"

"I think so."

To Ruby, her hushed voice sounded deafening amidst the tense silence.

"No, wait!" She dashed over to her dressing table and picked up the coin that the gentlemanly customer had given to her. She wondered where the safest place for it might be.

"Mr. Browne?" she said, as she walked back toward him.

"Yes, miss?"

"Could I ask you to be so kind as to carry this in one of your pockets for me?"

"Of course, miss," he replied. She handed him the coin and he slipped it into his waistcoat.

"Thank you."

Browne took up the cord with which the cushion had been fastened to his person.

"Mrs. Jones said that it would be best to use this to tie you to myself so that even if you slip a little, you will not slip so much that you fall off. There are a few more in my coat pockets if we need them, provided it will not do you any ill to be thus positioned, miss."

His concern calmed her slightly. She was beginning to dread the complex practicalities of what had earlier seemed a straightforward, simple idea.

"It will do me no ill, I am sure. Thank you."

"Very well."

Despite her profession, Ruby was surprised by the flushes of embarrassment she felt as she and Browne tried to find the best position for her concealment, knowing that she would have to remain in it, unmoving, until they were far enough away from the brothel to avoid being caught.

When she was finally secured to him, her arms and legs wrapped around his trunk and gravity pulling her practically folded body down to his stomach, he put on his cloak and checked his appearance in the mirror.

Ruby heard him whisper something, though she was unable to decipher it through the thick fabric of the cloak.

Again, she heard his muffled voice. Then, silence.

A moment or two later, he parted his cloak and whispered down to her.

"It does not look so very different from before. Nothing that ought to draw attention during a swift departure in the dark." He paused. "Are you comfortable, miss?"

She could not see his face, but she could tell by his tone that she must have looked the very picture of awkwardness to him.

"Yes, thank you."

At least, she was as comfortable as anyone could be when tied around another person, suspended yet restrained at the same time.

Browne drew his cloak shut, closing Ruby back into a warm and strange darkness.

With each breath she took, she could smell the comforting scent of Browne's clean clothes. She urged herself to focus on it each time the perilous sensation of almost falling overtook her, which happened with every step Browne took and every movement he made.

It was an alarming state to be in, with no end of discomfort in body and mind.

A sudden lurch.

They were moving.

Ruby tried to look down to see the floor beneath them, but it hurt her eyes to stretch them, owing to the position of her head.

Browne stopped and whispered to her. This time, somehow, she could hear it.

"For all our sakes, miss - I will do my best for you."

They were moving again, though to Ruby it did not feel as though they were going anywhere. All she could see was blackness, and her almost folded body bounced and swung repeatedly.

She hushed her breathing as much as she could, oftentimes holding it completely.

A sudden jolt. Then another.

After a few more, she realised that Browne was descending the stairs. She longed to sigh with discomfort, but forced herself to control her breathing.

After what seemed an age, they appeared to be on level ground again.

Ruby could only remember being on the ground floor once before. Her room was on the third floor, and breakfast was served on the second. Below that, none of the girls were permitted to go. The only time she had been there was the day that she had arrived.

Only a vague memory remained of oppressive bleak walls and men on guard to ensure that neither customer nor courtesan would cause any trouble. She'd been whisked up to the room in which all the new recruits had been huddled, before being given a brutal first taste of their new life.

Ruby held her breath as she heard Browne say something.

A distant voice responded to him.

This was it. Something was going wrong.

She squeezed her eyes shut, even though she could see only black when they were open.

Silently, she willed Browne to keep walking. Her heart and stomach lurched within her as he stopped and stood still.

The voices continued, and though she concentrated hard to listen to what was being said, she heard none of it.

Her eyes still clamped shut and her mind racing, she

silently pleaded with God that He would help them leave in safety.

Her limbs trembled with exhaustion and terror.

Her throat tightened, and she wrestled with the impulse to cough in order to clear it.

Beads of sweat broke out on her forehead and on the back of her neck.

Why had she dared to believe that escape could be possible? Her mind raced, her thoughts and feelings a tormented tangle.

She longed to move, to fidget, to run away, but she was trapped.

Once again, she instructed herself to be calm. Everything would be all right.

It must be. It had to be.

She managed to stifle a gasp as Browne started walking again.

She could not see the floor, could not see which direction he was heading, but she hoped with every fibre of her being that he was heading for the large, heavy, double doors that she dimly remembered passing through all those years ago.

She heard a muffled laugh, and her heart sank.

They had been found out.

What else could it be but one of Millforte's many henchmen laughing at their futile plan?

There was a muffled sound, almost a creaking, then she felt a slight draught work its way up over her.

An icy draught. Could it be?

Browne's footsteps sounded quieter, and she strained her eyes downward again, desperate to catch a glimpse of the ground.

White. There was something white on the ground.

A shudder of disbelief coursed down her spine.

Snow.

They were outside.

Ill with excitement, yet still tense, she awaited the moment when one of Millforte's men would stop them, having discovered that she was gone.

As she drew a deep breath, she could feel the chill in the air.

A few moments later, she held back a cry of pain as she grew even more compacted by Browne's movements. Then, he seemed to stop, though she was still considerably more compressed than before.

Suddenly, she was jolted and shaken backward and forward.

Browne slowly pulled his cloak open a little bit, and leaned his head down, whispering, "We are in the carriage, miss. We must remain like this a little longer - only until we get out of the city, to be sure that no one might see you. Are you all right, miss?"

She replied that she was, her voice sounding muffled even to her own ears. Relief washed over her, and she smiled with genuine hope.

There was a shaky jolt, and the carriage lurched forward into motion.

The movement startled her. The whole sensation of the carriage was completely new.

Despite her discomfort, the carriage was a little warmer than the frigid air a moment before, and its rocking, combined with the exertions of the day thus far, lulled her into a light slumber.

But not for long.

The carriage came to a sudden halt. Ruby clamoured to move, but to no avail.

They have found us!

Suddenly she was overwhelmed with bright light and cool air. It took a moment for her to realise that Browne was untying her.

Free from the restraints, she fell backward, too weak to stop herself, and landed on the carriage floor with a thud.

"Oh, Miss Ruby! Forgive me," exclaimed Browne, reaching out to help her up onto the seat opposite him. It was just the two of them in the carriage. Part of Ruby had wondered if Henry might have been waiting in it.

"Are you all right, miss?" asked Browne, genuine concern lining his face.

Ruby smiled weakly, dazed from being able to see and hear properly once again.

"Yes, I am fine. Thank you, Mr. Browne." She looked out the window, nothing but darkness all around them. "Where are we?"

"I would say we have travelled about three or four miles, miss. We are clear out of town now, and as a result, I thought it safe enough to discard our disguise."

Safe enough.

Safe?

"Thank you, Mr. Browne. It feels rather odd to be free. Though, very welcome."

Ruby rested her head against the carriage wall and silently marvelled at all that had transpired since her first meeting with Henry. She had no idea what lay ahead from this moment.

She hoped it would never again include Millforte.

At last, she had broken free from his vice-like grip. Or had she?

Surely gaining liberty from him could not be this easy. At some point or another, surely he would find her and make her pay for her audacious endeavour.

Once they were moving again, Ruby could not help but look out the window, though she was unable to see anything. On the other side of the pane was a world entirely new.

Soon, the rocking carriage made her sleepy and, though she tried to keep her eyes open, a weary slumber enveloped her.

She drifted back into consciousness some time later to find that the carriage had stopped. She looked at Browne.

"Have we arrived, Mr. Browne?"

"Not yet, Miss Ruby. I shall speak to the coachman."

She smiled in return as he nodded to her. As he exited the carriage, she looked out her window, noticing a little more detail than she had been able to see before. Dawn was approaching.

She glanced down and realised she was still wearing the shirt and breeches. Panic started to well within her.

Surely she could not face Henry and his aunt like this. Her dresses may not have been very fine, but at least they had been feminine. How dreadful to meet new people in such a costume.

But then, even if she had been wearing the most exquisite gown imaginable, it would not have eased her shame about facing them. They all knew what she was.

The finest gown, jewels - nothing could redeem her.

For a moment she couldn't breathe. What had she been thinking? At least she had been free from judgment at the brothel. Now, she was to be exposed in a very different way. Now, it would be her soul that everyone would scrutinise.

She shuddered and tried to curl up as much as she could on the carriage's narrow seat, which wasn't very much at all. A yearning to go home filled her, yet she didn't have a home. Not really. Tears stung her eyes.

Browne re-entered the carriage, the very epitome of relaxed.

"One of the horses simply needed a little rest, miss. Not much farther to go, now." He smiled.

She tried to say something in acknowledgement but feared she would break down if she did. Browne looked at her intently.

"Miss Ruby? Are you all right?"

There was tightness yet fluttering in her chest. Apprehension overwhelmed her. "Yes, I am fine," she managed to choke out.

Browne, however, did not seem convinced

CHAPTER 6

NEW SURROUNDINGS

"You look rather unwell, miss. Would you care to take some fresh air before we move on?"

Ruby glanced at him. "Oh. Yes, please. Yes, perhaps I should."

After a short pace around the carriage, Ruby felt an improvement. Before following her back into the carriage, Browne informed the coachman that they were ready to continue their journey.

As she heard him say the word ready, Ruby exhaled. She was anything but ready for what lay ahead.

"Are you feeling better, Miss Ruby?"

"Yes, thank you, Mr. Browne."

The rest of the journey passed in tense silence, at least on Ruby's side. Each time she glanced at Browne, he appeared at ease.

Gradually, the carriage twitched to a stop, and its conclusive lurch echoed the one in Ruby's stomach.

They had arrived.

She did not know what she ought to do. She pulled at the

bottom of the breeches, trying unsuccessfully to cover more of her legs with them.

"Here, miss."

Browne draped his cloak around her shoulders.

"Thank you, Mr. Browne."

As he reached for the carriage door, Ruby looked at him, silently communicating her uncertainty.

He smiled, the lines around his eyes deepening. "No need to worry, miss."

He unlatched the door and gently pushed it open. The air that entered was crisp and refreshing.

As he proceeded out, Ruby heard footsteps race toward them, halting close to the carriage.

She moved toward the door, her muscles tightening subconsciously. Instructing herself to be calm, she drew a deep breath then reached out and placed her hand in Browne's, which he had extended to help her alight.

Her legs shook as she slowly climbed out of the carriage. Even when they reached solid ground, she still felt as though they were moving. She teetered about slightly, trying to gain her balance without revealing that she had lost it.

Browne reached out to steady her.

"There, now, miss, I expect you are not quite used to the carriage movement yet. It is sure to be an odd sensation to you."

He turned and, holding her elbow, led her round the side of the carriage. In front of them stood Henry and a lady who looked the right age to be his aunt.

Ruby did not observe the lady for very long. Her eyes swiftly fixed on Henry's, as though compelled by magnetic force.

How wonderful it was to see him again.

His own delight was evident. A welcoming grin

illuminated his face as he rushed forward, his hands extended toward Ruby. His aunt followed at a less hurried pace.

"Ruby!" he exclaimed, clasping her hands in his.

Ruby was speechless. Was it all real?

"How good it is to see you again," he breathed, letting go of her hands. "I am so glad that everything went according to plan."

He glanced to Browne, a quizzical look on his face.

Browne nodded.

"Splendid! Well, Ruby, may I be the first to say - welcome to Shiloh Hall."

Ruby could not shift her gaze from his warm, kind eyes, despite the shame that usually impelled her to look at the ground. Henry did not seem alarmed at all by her appearance. In all her apprehension, she realised she had forgotten just how congenial he truly was.

"Thank you, sir," she replied timidly.

"May I introduce to you my aunt, Mrs. Abigail Jones."

Henry extended a hand toward his aunt as he spoke. With all her might, Ruby forced herself to look at his aunt, then very quickly shifted her gaze to the ground.

Aunt Abigail extended a hand to Ruby, who accepted it with humble surprise.

"Welcome, my dear," she said, squeezing Ruby's hand warmly. "If there is anything that you need, do not hesitate to let me know. We are all so glad that you are able to be here. To be safe."

She trailed off, clearly not wanting to upset Ruby.

"Thank you, so very much. I do not know quite how to thank you." Ruby looked around her. "I truly cannot believe that I am here."

"Would you like a short tour of the grounds?" smiled Henry, noticing her admiration of their surroundings.

Ruby felt weak from all the activities and emotions of the journey, but such was her gratitude to be outside that she didn't want to go back indoors just yet.

It felt so good to breathe the fresh, countryside air, cold as it was.

"That would be lovely, thank you."

BROWNE DID NOT ACCOMPANY THEM, and as Ruby noticed him heading toward the house, some of her certainty seemed to leave with him. His presence held a strong, quiet calm, one she wished she could lean on as she ventured into the grounds with Henry and his aunt.

The three of them wandered around paths laced with more shrubbery than Ruby had ever seen all in one place, coming lastly to the garden behind the parsonage.

The splendour of the garden took Ruby's breath away. It was like a paradise. Had it not been for how chilly the air was, and how weary she felt from the overnight journey, she would have gladly settled herself beneath one of the trees to bask in the beauty and calm that overwhelmed her.

"Let us all go inside and warm up with some tea," Henry smiled.

Ruby returned his smile, despite her unease.

When the three of them were seated inside, a young, bubbly maid named Bessie brought a steaming tray of refreshments into the drawing room.

Ruby observed an easiness in how Henry and his aunt - and indeed, Browne and Bessie, too - all interacted. It was strange, in a lovely sort of way.

Henry and Abigail did not treat Browne or Bessie as most people would have treated their servants. It almost seemed as though they were considered to be part of the family.

A memory of her old life pierced her. It seemed a lifetime ago that she had been at home with her parents. She forced the thought as far away as she could.

As she beheld the smiles and friendly faces all around her, a new thought presented itself. Could they ever one day treat her as family, too?

Ruby's eyes met Henry's and he smiled. "I really am so glad that our scheme was successful."

"Yes. Mr. Browne has my deepest gratitude for his courage. As do you and your kind aunt for devising the whole idea. And, for welcoming me here."

Henry and Abigail smiled simultaneously. Browne and Bessie had left the room moments earlier, and Ruby's uncertainty heightened her sense of unworthiness. She fidgeted with her hands and cast her gaze downwards, feeling overwhelmed to the point of tears.

"Are you all right, my dear?" enquired Abigail, concern in her voice.

Ruby cleared her throat softly. "Yes. Forgive me, I am very tired after all that has passed . . ." She intended to explain further, but, finding herself at a loss for words, she shook her head gently in dismissal.

Abigail's face softened in sympathy. "Indeed - how silly of me! You have journeyed all night. Here, I will show you to your room now. You may rest there for as long as you wish."

Ruby nodded. "Thank you."

Abigail rose to a stand, causing Henry to immediately do the same.

Ruby stood up slowly and glanced at Henry.

"Please, excuse me," Ruby mumbled.

"Rest well," said Henry, softly. "You are safe, now."

The words made Ruby's heart flutter with delight, despite the emotional turbulence she'd endured.

Safe. Was she really safe? She longed to believe it.

"I shall ask Bessie to bring you something to eat, though if you are too tired, please, do not feel that you must eat any of it," Abigail said to Ruby as they ascended the stairs.

Ruby was awed by Abigail's kindness. "Thank you."

Abigail smiled as they continued down the hall. She stopped outside a door at the far end of the upstairs hallway, turned the handle and gracefully swung the door open.

Ruby followed her inside and gasped. The room was beautiful, so light and spacious. The walls were papered with elegant florals in rich, warm hues. As Ruby looked around, taking it all in, she was struck by how opposite it was from her room at the brothel. This room was inviting, not a trace of gloom or decay was to be found.

Abigail walked to the wardrobe and opened it, indicating the contents to Ruby with her hand.

"Do help yourself to whatever you like, or whatever will fit you." She looked Ruby up and down, deep in thought. "I do hope they are not too big for you. Well, even so, they can always be altered."

She closed the wardrobe and walked toward the door to leave. Turning back, she smiled at Ruby.

"I shall have Bessie come up presently and arrange everything you will need in order to freshen up. Is there anything else you would like, my dear?"

Ruby sighed and shook her head. "No, thank you." She sighed. "Truly, I cannot thank you enough for all your kindness."

"We are only too glad to help you, my dear. Rest well."

Ruby nodded and thanked her. After Abigail left, Ruby stepped lightly over to the bed, pushed on it with her hand a few times, then turned around and sat down on it. It was so soft and comfortable - nothing like her bed at the brothel, with its creaking springs and worn, cold bedclothes.

Free from the gazes of the others, she was free to relax, and in so doing, she was all of a sudden overwhelmed with exhaustion. Rousing herself to stand, she tiptoed to the wardrobe and ran her fingers over and under the beautiful array of fabrics hanging inside. Some were more plain, everyday dresses, and some were truly exquisite, with silks and embroidered embellishments.

Bessie arrived not long after with all the accoutrements necessary for a refreshing cleansing. It felt so good to wash away the dust and dirt of the journey and slip into one of the crisp, white nightgowns she had found in the wardrobe.

As she watched Bessie leave with the breeches and shirt, Ruby realised how very glad she was to be distanced from the final physical reminder of where and how the journey had begun. Not that she could fully forget.

A short while later, Bessie returned with a tray of food. Simple as it was, owing to the awkward time of the morning they had arrived, it was like a banquet in comparison to all the stale, putrid meals she had eaten at the brothel.

When she could eat no more, she crawled under the warm, soft eiderdown and curled into a ball, a habit she'd adopted long ago and resorted to whenever she felt vulnerable.

Around her, everything was the epitome of peace, a contrast to the gnawing sensation she felt inside.

Imaginations of Millforte filled her mind. She saw him discovering her absence, vowing that she would pay, summoning his henchmen and kicking his horse without mercy as he rode far and wide, desperate to find her.

Squeezing the covers more tightly against her, she tried to

forget him. Yet, even if she could, it was unlikely he would ever forget her.

The years had taught her one thing above all. In Millforte's eyes, Ruby was his.

And he would never let her be free.

RUBY AWOKE LATER that evening when a faint knock sounded at her door. Still somewhat tangled in slumber, she wearily pushed herself up, then walked slowly to answer the door. She was relieved that it was Abigail, and not Henry, as she stood shivering in her nightgown, despite the glowing embers that remained in the fireplace.

Abigail walked inside, taking care to both move and speak with hushed gentleness.

"I came to inform you that dinner will be served in around twenty minutes, and to ask if you are feeling well enough to join us," she said with a hopeful smile.

Abigail's voice was so kind and melodious that it comforted Ruby each time she heard it.

Ruby opened her mouth to respond, but yawned instead.

"Yes, I should like to very much. Thank you," she said, her voice sounding thick and croaky.

"Splendid! Would you like me to help you dress?"

She cleared her throat. "Oh. Yes. Thank you."

Abigail strode to the wardrobe and combed through the dresses. The one she selected was pale pink and simple yet elegant. She held it up against Ruby.

"How about this one?" smiled Abigail.

Ruby cautiously returned the smile.

"It is lovely! Thank you."

Abigail fluttered around the room to various drawers and boxes, gathering ribbons and stays, amongst other things.

As she helped Ruby dress, Abigail hummed a gentle melody. It sounded sombre, yet hopeful. Once again, Ruby struggled to take in her new reality.

"Is the room to your liking?" asked Abigail, pausing her tune.

Ruby gave a short, incredulous laugh. "It is beautiful. I cannot tell you what a change it is from—" She paused. "It is beautiful, truly. I cannot thank you enough."

Abigail smiled. "I was not enquiring to incite thankfulness. I merely wished to make sure that you have all that you need, my dear."

Ruby sighed. "I have more than I could have ever imagined," she said, softly.

THERE WAS A HOMELY ATMOSPHERE in the dining room, yet all Ruby could think was how luxurious it seemed compared to the brothel's eating hall. It was smaller, yet, owing to its pleasantness, a thousand times more grand.

Ruby and Abigail were the first to arrive. Browne attended them, and Ruby was surprised how different he looked now that he was back in his servant's outfit. He still emanated a quiet dignity, yet he had lost the appearance of a refined gentleman, despite displaying it so convincingly the day before.

"Miss Ruby." He smiled. "How are you feeling now? I trust you had a refreshing rest?"

"Yes, thank you, Mr. Browne." She paused. "I trust that you yourself are not too fatigued after our travels?"

As she took her seat, alarm filled her. How out of place

she was. It had been so long since she'd interacted with normal society. She was a fallen woman now, even though it was not by her own choosing.

She scrambled for a memory, no matter how faint, of how things used to be, long, long ago - before everything had altered so terribly.

How should she speak? Or act? She earnestly wanted to do and say the right things, but having been forced to do the wrong things for so many years, she had no idea what was expected of her now.

"Miss Ruby? Are you all right?"

Ruby stared at Browne. She realised she had not even heard his reply to her question, and for a moment she forgot what she had asked him. Swallowing hard, she nodded.

"Yes. Forgive me, I am still rather tired."

The dining room door swung gently open and Henry strolled casually into the room. Ruby was struck by how gentlemanly he looked.

It was not merely his attire, nor his pleasant manner of speaking, but something in his very air. He carried himself well, yet there was nothing false or proud about him.

There was something deeper, too, that Ruby could not quite determine. Whatever it was, it made her breath catch in her throat and the hairs on the back of her neck stand on end.

"Good evening, Aunt Abigail. Good evening, Ruby. Good evening, Browne," he smiled as he took his seat at the head of the table.

Abigail and Browne both smiled and returned his greeting.

Ruby simply nodded at him and held his gaze for a few moments. Her heart pounded faster and faster.

She had longed to wear a modest dress for such a long time, yet now that she was wearing one, she felt like an impostor. Abigail had even swept Ruby's hair back into a loose bun, tied with a ribbon that matched the dress beautifully. She could not remember the last time she had worn her hair up. Ironically, it made her feel utterly exposed.

"How are you feeling?" Henry smiled, looking at Ruby.

She curled her hands into fists, urging herself to calm down. Staring at the table, she tried to slow her breathing, but to no avail.

"I . . ." She nodded, quickly yet shakily.

"Ruby, are you all right?"

She opened her mouth to speak, but a faint croak was all that emerged. Before she realised what she was doing, she was on her feet and running toward the door.

CHAPTER 7

TOO GOOD TO BE TRUE

HER HEART POUNDED in unison with her feet as she ran down the corridor and up the stairs. Despite how new and unfamiliar the rest of the place was, she did feel a measure of comfort in her new room.

Just as she reached the door and clasped its handle, she heard footsteps tracing the path her own had taken.

Her stomach flipped at the thought of explaining herself. How unutterably rude she must have seemed. What would Henry think of her now? Perhaps she had shattered his illusion that she was in any way deserving of his kindness.

She hurried into the sanctuary of her new room. Abigail appeared in the doorway, gasping - whether from exertion or anticipation Ruby couldn't tell.

"My dear! Are you all right?" she panted.

Ruby stared at the ground, her mind racing and her stomach churning. She struggled in vain for words. Exhausted, she turned and slumped down onto the floor, losing her fight against the tears that had long been threatening to spill.

Abigail hurried to her side and placed her arm around her shoulders, drawing her close as she whispered words of reassurance.

Ruby, who had so deeply missed her own mother's embrace all these years, felt even more unravelled.

Such kindness. Such sincerity and concern they had all shown her that she felt she did not remotely deserve.

So violent were her sobs that nausea soon permeated her, but no matter how much she struggled to stop and answer Abigail, she was powerless against the overwhelming tide of emotion.

"Oh, my dear," said Abigail, in a soothing tone.

Gradually, Ruby's tears subsided. Her head throbbed and when she finally spoke, her voice was hoarse and feeble. "I am sorry."

"Oh, my dear! Whyever would you apologise? I cannot imagine what you must be feeling, but, by all means, you are free to express it. And I am here anytime you should wish for someone to speak with."

"Thank you."

"Shall I have Bessie bring some dinner up to you?"

"Forgive me, but I do not think I could eat. Not at present."

"I understand, my dear. I shall ask Bessie to send you something up in a little while, to have at hand."

"Thank you."

"Shall I leave you to rest now?"

Ruby sighed, the effects of her crying still resonating throughout her body. "I . . . I do not know . . ." Her head was so sore it might burst. She rubbed her temples distractedly. Too many thoughts were rushing through her mind. All she wanted to do was curl up and forget everything for a while.

But she couldn't forget *him*.

Fear fastened its ice-cold grip around her heart again. Millforte was a powerful man. He would find her, no matter how long it took.

But he cannot know you are here, she told herself. *Henry was careful. Browne, too. Even when he discovers I am gone, he will not have any clue as to where to find me.*

If only she could believe herself.

"My dear! You are trembling so violently - are you cold?"

Ruby shook her head, struggling to find her voice. "I . . . I am frightened," she said in a voice that was barely louder than a whisper. "I am so frightened!" She shook her head again and a fresh wave of tears took over.

"Oh, my dear. Come, now. You are safe here."

"Safe? I can never be safe. You do not know what he is like! Oh, it was folly to think that I could escape him. He knows everything! I should not have . . . Oh, he will find me - I know he will!"

She screamed the words hysterically, agitated in body as in soul.

"My dear," Abigail said, grasping Ruby's hands tightly in a bid to calm her. "Oh, my dear . . . No one there knows where you have gone. They will discover your absence, but they will not be able to trace it. You are quite safe here, my dear."

Ruby trembled as she wept. Eventually, the storm of emotion finally passed.

"He will find me," Ruby whispered, her gaze fixed on the ground, her body still quivering.

"Even if it were possible that he could, you are not alone. We will not permit any harm to come to you."

Ruby sighed, her breath ragged and irregular as it left her lungs.

Perhaps, it will all be all right.

She was not alone, after all. For the first time in years, she was with people who seemed to care enough to actually protect her.

Once Ruby's fervour had eased, Abigail squeezed her arm and repeated her offer to have some food sent up.

"Thank you," said Ruby. "I do not know how I shall ever repay you. You and Mr. Stratton, both."

"Oh, do not speak of that! Repay us, indeed!"

Abigail's expression looked pained. Ruby felt cared for yet exposed at the same time.

"I do not think that . . . I cannot quite believe . . ." Ruby trailed off, her mind struggling to find the right phrase.

"What is it, my dear?"

Ruby glanced at the floor. "It all, well, it all seems too good to be quite true." Her voice grew quieter. "I am a disgrace, and yet, you have welcomed me to your . . . your beautiful home." It took all the strength she had to say it without crying.

"Oh, Ruby."

Ruby sighed. "I do not understand it." She looked up at Abigail, who had tears in her eyes. "But I am more grateful than I can say."

Abigail embraced her, hugging her firmly. "Please do not call yourself such things, my dear. None of us have a spotless past. And Henry told me what you told him, that you were taken there against your will. Oh, my dear. You have been horribly treated. And you are not to blame for any of the cruelty that has been done to you. There is hope, my dear, though the path that lies ahead will not be an easy one to traverse. But, the Bible shows us time and again that one's past need not define one's future. God's grace is powerful to cleanse and heal."

71

With a final squeeze of Ruby's hand, Abigail left, after reaffirming her intentions to send Bessie up with a breakfast tray.

Ruby sat, stunned and still.

Her past need not define her future? That's what Abigail had said, wasn't it?

Surely that applied to everyone but herself. Yet, something within her dared to cling to the far-off hope that maybe, just maybe, it could one day apply to her, too.

Not long after Abigail's departure, a knock sounded at her door. Ruby called out an invitation to enter, and Bessie elbowed the door open, a rather large tray occupying her hands. She placed it on the table, giving Ruby a friendly smile as she had the day before, then turned and left.

Ruby tiptoed over to the tray. As she saw the plate of food and the steaming cup of tea, she realised just how hungry she really was.

Cradling the cup in her hands, she eased herself into a wingback chair situated by the fireside and closed her eyes, relishing the comforting heat of the steam and the delicate scent of the liquid effusing it.

Slightly more composed after her tea, she surveyed the offered food. Lamb chops, creamed potatoes and a delightful medley of vegetables. A veritable feast.

At the brothel, the most lavish meal she'd ever received had been bread and soup. Oftentimes, leftovers were all that were available, and they'd hardly ever been edible.

After eating until her stomach was full, she meandered back to the bed. Curling up and pulling a thick, warm blanket over her, she felt a rush of exhaustion sweep through her. As she lay still, she marvelled at how, in such a short span of time, her circumstances had altered so dramatically.

Yet, even in her slumber, she still thought of Millforte, and how angry he would be when he discovered she had gone. Perhaps he might think that an unstable client had whisked her away or brought her to harm.

But she knew him.

She should have tried to burn the cushion after all. The more she thought of it, the more anxious she felt. He was sure to tear the place apart looking for evidence. He would find the cushion under the bed. He would work it all out.

But surely he would not know where to look. Browne had not given the frontman his real name, and no one knew that he and Henry had any connection.

Perhaps, she was safe after all. She could only hope.

She stared at the ceiling, thinking of too many things at once to fully notice any of them.

Her eyelids started to feel heavy, and she relished the fact that this bed was only for her. A safe, warm place for her to sleep and rest. She almost felt like smiling at the thought, had her eyes not been closing as sleep embraced her.

She woke briefly a few times, frightening images of Millforte's wrath jolting her from her calm, steady sleep.

THE NEXT MORNING, as Ruby awoke, her gaze travelled around the room with fresh wonder. It all seemed so clean, so tranquil. The difference between this room and the one she had dwelt in for so long was almost beyond description. Never before had she woken up in such peace.

Rising slowly, she eased herself out of bed and walked to the mirror in the corner of the room. Her dress was crumpled, but not very much. It still looked far superior to anything she usually wore. Shifting her inspection to her face, her heart sank. The sleep had refreshed her somewhat, but still she looked haggard and worn, her eyes red and puffy from her earlier tears.

And thin. Too thin, after so many years of excess stress and limited nourishment.

A knock at the door startled her.

She opened the door slowly to reveal Abigail, who smiled at her kindly before asking, "Would you like to join us for breakfast, my dear?"

Ruby raised her eyebrows. She had slept all night?

"Oh, yes. Thank you."

Ruby smiled, though nervous at the thought of facing the others again. It pained her to think that her prior folly might have caused Henry hurt or offense.

As she followed Abigail downstairs, Ruby's heart quickened its pace. Soon, Henry's eyes would be upon her again. Those eyes that seemed to know what was in her soul better than she knew herself.

Upon reaching the door of the dining room, she drew an anxious breath. This time, she would not run away.

"Ah, Aunt Abigail."

Ruby could hear the smile in his voice as Henry greeted his aunt, and taking another deep breath, she followed Abigail into the room. Henry's eyes diverted their gaze to meet her own, and she felt a slight warmth in her cheeks.

"Ruby." His eyes were burning through her again, with some deep expression she could not interpret.

"Good morning, Mr. Stratton." It took all her resolve to hold his gaze. Why did she feel so conspicuous?

"I trust you are feeling better." Despite his kind tone, she imagined he must think her reprehensibly rude for her behaviour the night before.

"Yes, thank you." Should she blurt it to him now that she was sorry? Or ought she to address Henry and his aunt together?

"Well, I hope you are hungry - Bessie has prepared her finest breakfast spread for us all."

She smiled politely, her thoughts still in torment.

Henry ushered her toward a chair, and she shakily sat down. He treated her like a lady. It was wholly unnerving.

"Ruby suits beautifully the dress Lady Harford sent over, does she not?" Abigail smiled.

Henry cleared his throat slightly. "Yes. Indeed." A pale flush of pink fleetingly appeared on his cheeks.

Once the three of them had been served and Bessie had left the room again, Ruby drew a deep breath, clutching her saucer and teacup so tightly that her knuckles hurt.

"I do hope you will both accept my sincere apologies, for my terrible behaviour last night. I do so much appreciate your kindness. I did not mean to appear ungrateful . . . "

She trailed off, her voice weak, her mind racing.

"You have no need to apologise, Ruby," said Henry. His eyes, filled with deep compassion, looked intently into hers. "This will not be an easy adjustment for you. And, the past few days must have been dreadfully long, and . . . " He sighed. "I pray you do know that you can talk to us, about anything. I believe I speak for both of us in saying that we are here for you."

Abigail nodded. "Indeed, yes, my dear - as I said earlier. Whenever you may need me."

"Thank you." She paused. "I do mean it - thank you."

As she looked from one smiling face to the other, she tried determinedly to push her fears away. But no matter how happy and welcoming Henry and his aunt were, she could not shake off the tumultuous dread that Millforte would find her.

Because she knew that when he did, his retaliation would be far worse than anything Henry or his aunt could ever imagine.

CHAPTER 8
CHOICES

A FEW WEEKS LATER, one morning after breakfast, Henry, Abigail, and Ruby wrapped up warm for a stroll around the gardens. Thin blankets of snow covered parts of the ground the winter sun had not yet reached.

Ruby was in awe. It still felt so lovely, yet so strange, to go outside. She'd been like a wilted flower for so long now, cut off from the invigorating earth and air needed to flourish.

Henry slowed from the slightly brisk pace he and his aunt had shared and fell in step with Ruby. He moved his hand in a wide arc.

"I imagine all this is a refreshing change for you," he said, echoing her thoughts.

"Yes." Ruby smiled.

He smiled in return. "I truly am so glad that you are here."

She was caught off guard a little by his frankness but did not hesitate in echoing his sentiment.

"As am I." She sighed. "Thank you does not seem enough to say. I can never tell you just how grateful I am."

Henry raised his eyebrows slightly and smiled. His dark

eyes twinkled kindly. "Ruby, you do not need to say thank you *every* time we speak about your being here."

Ruby's heart and stomach twisted and turned. "Forgive me. Only . . . I feel so out of place," she blurted. "I cannot help but wonder when you will realise what a dreadful mistake you have made in bringing me here."

Henry stopped walking.

Ruby stopped a few paces ahead of him.

Her words seemed to be hanging in the air around them. She wished she could retract them. She had spoken without thinking how it might sound. A glance at Henry's expression confirmed the fear that her words had hit him like a slap across the face.

"Forgive me," she stuttered, "I—"

"Do not worry. Please," he interrupted.

His expression was painful to look at. He appeared sincerely grieved by what she had said.

She groaned inwardly, the whole incident adding to her growing anguish that her presence at the parsonage was indeed a mistake.

Henry turned to look her in the eye.

"Ruby, please do not think such things. I do not for one second regret bringing you here. There has been no error." He sighed, softness in his eyes. "I imagine it all may seem quite strange for a while, but in time I hope, nay, I *believe* that we will be able to help you secure a suitable situation. Your future is not without prospects. I believe there is a whole new chapter of life ahead. A whole new future. And we will do what we can to help you navigate it."

She looked at him, surprised yet grateful. "Thank you."

Henry gave her a mock-cautionary look as she realised she had once again voiced her gratitude despite his earlier admonition. "Ruby . . ." He paused, his look softening with sincerity. "You are not a burden here. You *are* welcome."

A strange sensation filled Ruby as she looked into his friendly eyes. He stood, looking at her, his lips slightly apart, and an expression across his face that she couldn't read.

As Henry moved to resume walking, Ruby realised she'd forgotten momentarily about everything else around her.

Walking in the direction of the canopied bench Abigail had stopped to sit on, Ruby wondered if she dared believe Henry. He seemed so earnest in what he said. There was no doubt that he meant it. Could it be that she had a future? With prospects? It was an exhilarating thought, that there was life to be lived and possibilities she had never even explored.

But as much as she wanted to embrace the relief his words stirred, she could not dissuade the lurking conviction that, one day, he would regret that he had ever met her.

"It is lovely and crisp, is it not?" Abigail smiled as Henry and Ruby stopped beside her. She rose to a stand and dusted off her skirts. The bench was sheltered by a canopy of wood and vines. Ruby studied its beauty.

"Yes, marvellous," Henry said, his eyes twinkling.

"I do believe we have been blessed with the most beautiful land in the entire country," Abigail said, looking around at the gardens and parsonage.

Ruby followed her gaze. Henry and his aunt were not wealthy, that Ruby was aware of, but the main parsonage building and a few outbuildings were nestled in lush, lively grounds that stretched out as far as Ruby could see. It was so different from the four bare walls of her room back at the brothel. It was a little unnerving to be out in such a wide-open space. She felt somewhat vulnerable, yet drank in the fresh air with a thirsty gratitude.

"I believe so, too, Aunt Abigail. Now, if you and Ruby will please excuse me, I must get back to my work."

He hesitated, then looked at Ruby.

"Ruby, would you like to accompany us to church tomorrow morning? It is not too far," he said, turning and pointing into the distance. "It is only in the little village over there. It would be lovely if you could join us, though it is entirely your choice."

Ruby felt as though she could hardly breathe. Church! After all that she had done?

Part of her wanted to accept. She'd felt a strange sense of loneliness the past few Sundays as she'd watched the others depart to attend services. But how could she face crowds of people? What if someone recognised her? She absolutely could not go.

She looked at Henry. His eyes were filled with such compassion and hopefulness. How could she disappoint him by saying no? He and Abigail had been so kind to her, so selfless.

She must go with them. Surely, it would be too vast an insult if she did not.

She opened her mouth to speak, but no sound emerged. She was torn, her mind and heart at war.

Henry held up his hand. "Do not answer now. Take some time to think about it. See how you are feeling in the morning." He smiled, sympathy and sensitivity in his eyes.

Ruby nodded.

And as she watched Henry walk back to the parsonage, she knew.

Tomorrow morning, she was going to church.

IT WAS ODD. Even though Ruby often felt so out of place at the parsonage, there was part of her that felt as though she had been there for years.

There was something about the atmosphere, something calm and inviting, as though it had been bathed in peace.

The brothel had never been comforting. Nothing about its peeling paint, stone-cold floors or scratchy, worn sheets had ever been reassuring.

And never had she enjoyed sharing a meal with others until she had arrived here. Everything was lovely, though at the same time, terrifying.

And, as much as she wished to forget them, it stirred memories of her life before the brothel, when she had been cherished as a daughter, and had never known fear or shame.

Ruby forced the painful thoughts from her mind as she meandered through the garden.

Abigail had since gone indoors, but Ruby had lingered behind, glad to be immersed in fresh air and tranquility.

Snow flitted softly down around her. As it drifted delicately through the plants and trees, it was more beautiful than anything Ruby had ever seen.

Her thoughts turned to Henry. She smiled slightly as she remembered his sincere statement that she was welcome at his home. He did not regret any of it. He did not believe he had made some dreadful mistake.

Shivering, she pulled her shawl up on her neck. With a sigh of contentment, Ruby made her way back inside the house and up to her room. Lying on her bed, she closed her eyes, breathing deeply.

Instantly, Millforte flashed into her mind. Her eyes snapped open. Her heart rate sprinted. As she tried to force her breathing into a steadier flow, her hands trembled.

I am safe here. I am safe here.

She lay still, clutching the eiderdown as she waited for the room to stop spinning.

Her grip on the blankets tightened. Had she been at the brothel, a glass or two of gin would have steadied her nerves. She rolled her head to glance at the tray on her dresser. Bessie had brought refreshments to her room. There was a beautiful crystal glass and a ceramic pitcher. Ruby's heart leaped.

She dragged herself to a sitting position, then lurched to her feet and dashed toward the pitcher. Grabbing it eagerly, she pulled it toward her and cast her gaze down into its core.

Water sloshed back and forth, lapping its sides. Her heart sank.

Reeling from the suddenness of her movements, she backed down onto the bed again, still clutching the disappointing pitcher. Her heart pounded in her ears and she blinked rapidly as her vision clouded over.

I need a drink . . . I need a drink . . .

What would Abigail say if she ventured down and requested alcohol so early in the day? And on its own, too. Each night at dinner, they all enjoyed a robust glass of wine with their meal, which had been a bigger comfort to Ruby than she had expected. Now, the realisation of her deep-seated yearning loomed before her, like a hostile impostor, cornering her and taunting her.

Spurning her desire, she stood and strode to the dresser. Shakily, she poured water into the sparkling glass, then snatched it up and drained it in one long gulp. She closed her eyes as the tasteless moisture seeped down into her body, struggling to calm her breathing and her wild, racing mind.

A fresh wave of dizziness overpowered her, and she clutched the dresser with the little strength she could summon.

It's no use.

Once the dizziness had passed, she looked up into the mirror, the cold determination in her eyes startling her slightly. She gave herself a long, deep look, then turned and headed for the door.

Let Abigail say whatever she liked.

She needed a *real* drink.

"RUBY, DEAR." Abigail smiled at her as she entered the drawing room. "How are you feeling?"

A flash of annoyance surged through Ruby at Abigail's cheerful composure.

"Fine, thank you," Ruby replied, the tone of her voice considerably cooler than it had been that morning. "I was wondering if I might have some gin?"

Abigail looked at her, unmoving. Suddenly, Ruby grew aware of her own nervous fidgeting.

"Or, perhaps, wine?"

Why does Abigail look so gentle? Shouldn't she be angry with me?

"I shall see that you have a glass presently."

A glass? I need more than a glass.

"Thank you," Ruby stuttered, taken aback by Abigail's non-judgmental acquiescence.

As she stood alone in the warm, bright room awaiting Abigail's return, she shuddered. The walls seemed to expand and close in on her at the same time. Panic welled up from her stomach and drained back down through her entire body.

She did not belong here. Henry was wrong. Abigail was wrong. They were all wrong. She was not fit to be their maid, never mind their houseguest, dining with them and being served by the same staff as they were.

But where could she go? Where *did* she belong?

Not with Millforte. He had tried for years to persuade her that she was not worthy of the life she had once known. Yet, she'd never fully bowed to Millforte the way the other girls had. She never permitted him to rearrange her broken pieces until there was no trace of herself left. Even now, her determination still bubbled beneath the surface. Fragile, but intact.

"Here you are, my dear," Abigail called out as she breezed back into the room. Ruby turned to face her and reached urgently for the glass of deep, red wine that Abigail extended to her.

"Thank you," Ruby murmured hastily, as she grabbed the glass and drained it of its contents. She closed her eyes as the soothing warmth washed through her body and the sweet vinegary taste enveloped her tongue.

After savouring the wine for a few moments, Ruby opened her eyes. Her gaze immediately routed to Abigail, standing still and silent as she observed Ruby. There was no trace of judgment on her features - only concern, which hit Ruby harder than any disapproving glare she'd expected to receive.

Her heart picked up speed as she looked at the ground. Even the floorboards shone. She shuddered to remember the floorboards back at Millforte's place - rotting around the edges and scraped so bare it was impossible to traverse them without getting splinters.

She swallowed hard, the comforting wine still fresh on her taste buds. She had been in prison, now she was in a palace. At least, that's what it felt like. And how was she repaying the people who had been kind to her? By clinging fast to her old chains - the wine, the brokenness, the anger.

The realisation throbbed like a wound.

"Excuse me . . ."

She bolted from the room - and Abigail's presence - and

with shaky legs and hammering heart she half-ran, half-dragged herself back up to her room. She had barely closed the door when her knees buckled, and she sank, crying, to the floor.

THAT EVENING, before dinner, Ruby sheepishly peered around the drawing room door, looking for Abigail, who was seated at the writing desk by the bay window.

Noticing the movement of the door from the corner of her eye, Abigail looked up. Immediately, she rose from the table and moved toward an armchair, motioning for Ruby to sit in the one opposite.

Ruby trudged over to the chair, her head low. She sat on the edge of the seat, her posture as uncomfortable as her feelings.

"How are you, my dear?" Abigail asked warmly.

Ruby's red-rimmed eyes welled up with tears again. A few spilled onto her cheeks.

"I am so sorry," Ruby said faintly, whisking tears from her cheeks. "I am so sorry about the wine."

"My dear," Abigail said, her voice soft and calm. "You are free from your old surroundings now, but you need to be freed from the chains that bind your heart. The path may not be easy, but you are not alone. I believe God has brought you here so that you will learn how you can be truly free. You are carrying a dreadfully heavy burden. But He can set you free from it. Truly."

Ruby felt so undeserving of the kindness and encouragement in Abigail's voice. She didn't know how, but she knew that Abigail's words were true. She sank against the arm of the chair and wept.

Abigail slowly got up and knelt beside Ruby's chair. She stroked Ruby's hair and hummed softly, a melody that Ruby had never heard before, but one so lovely that she hoped she would never forget it.

Ever so softly, Abigail sang in a hushed, whispered voice. "Amazing grace, how sweet the sound, that saved a wretch like me . . . I once was lost, but now I'm found, was blind, but now, I see . . ."

A wretch. That's what I am.

And she had been lost, but Henry had found her and rescued her. Is that what it meant?

One thing was clear to her now - this grace, which Abigail had mentioned a few times now, was something she desperately wanted to experience.

"DID YOU FINISH YOUR SERMON, my dear?"

"Yes, thank you, Aunt. Then I spent some time in prayer and made a list of the parishioners I must visit this coming week. I believe poor Mr. Smith has taken a turn for the worse."

"Oh, that is a shame," said Abigail.

Henry glanced at Ruby. Her eyes were rimmed with red and her demeanour indicated quiet exhaustion.

"How was your day, Ruby? Did you enjoy the garden?"

Ruby looked up at him and noticed how his eyes were twinkling with delighted contentment. How she longed for her own to do the same.

"Yes, thank you," she replied, her voice weaker than usual. "It is so beautiful."

She stared at the table. Exhaustion and shame rendered her unable to hold Henry's gaze. Upon her next glance at him she noticed how quickly his countenance had changed. Gone was the twinkling delight and, in its place, a melancholy concern. She hoped he wouldn't ask her what was the matter.

Henry sipped the last few drops of wine in his glass. Abigail's was almost empty, too, yet Ruby's was untouched. Every so often, she would extend a tremorous hand and clutch her water glass, raising it to her lips and tipping its contents into her mouth without raising her gaze from the place setting in front of her.

She could see Henry glancing at her out of the corner of her eye. The last thing she wanted was to appear rude, but she felt completely drained. She could scarcely muster the energy required to eat, never mind to make conversation and look into those knowing eyes.

As Abigail and Henry spoke, Ruby's thoughts drifted. She could not get the question of grace out of her mind. She yearned to know exactly what it was. Perhaps Henry would speak about it at church.

Oh, church! Every time she had made up her mind about whether or not she should go, she quickly decided the opposite.

"Shall we retire to the drawing room for a while?" Henry's voice pierced her thoughts.

"Yes," said Abigail.

Ruby simply nodded.

As the women followed Henry to the drawing room, Abigail gave Ruby an encouraging look. The other two entered, but Ruby lingered in the doorway.

She hesitated as she watched Henry stride to the window, peer out through the glass, then turn, walking toward one of the armchairs. He froze as he noticed her, a look of confusion clouding his face.

"You will join us awhile, Ruby?" he asked, his eyes a mix of disappointment and hope.

She clutched the doorpost. The entire room was threatening to spin.

"If you would be so kind as to excuse me," she trailed off, feeling like a disappointment. "I do not think I would be a pleasant companion this evening," she said.

Henry walked closer to her. The hope was gone from his eyes. In its place was the longing expression of missing someone's company.

"Rest." His smile seemed forced. "I pray you sleep soundly. Have you all that you need?"

"Oh, yes," she nodded. "Thank you."

She inhaled and exhaled deeply. "And . . ." Her voice was weak. She cleared her throat. "And I should very much like to go with you to church in the morning."

Her heart thudded with such force as she spoke that she thought it must have drowned out her voice.

Henry's eyebrows lifted with the hope that flooded his eyes. "Oh, Ruby, that is wonderful! Oh, I am delighted, truly."

Ruby's heart filled with warmth at seeing how happy Henry looked. She smiled softly, then clutched the doorpost as a new wave of anxiety set in.

She bade Henry goodnight, and as she turned away, she noticed a quiet joy in his deep, dark eyes.

As she ascended the stairs, she felt a medley of emotions. It was lovely to see Henry so happy, yet she was terrified to think of the practicalities that were to be navigated.

Nonetheless, it was fixed in her heart and with her words.

Tomorrow, she was going to church.

CHAPTER 9

BLAST FROM THE PAST

THE NEXT MORNING, when Ruby awoke, she looked out her window to see new snowflakes cascading delicately toward the white-carpeted ground below.

Yet, it was not the snow that sent a chill down her spine. It was knowing that just a few hours hence, she would leave the safety and privacy of the parsonage to enter a brand new social setting.

Henry had assured her of the modest size of his church, but the idea of seeing and being seen by even a handful of people was extremely unnerving.

The largest crowd she could remember encountering had been in the eating hall at the brothel. Yet the church crowd, even if it was smaller, would be very different. She would be circulating among people with whom she was no longer equal.

A knock at the door jolted her from her thoughts.

She opened the door to find Bessie, smiling as usual.

"Good morning, Miss Ruby. Mrs. Jones asked me to come and help you dress for church this morning."

"Oh." Ruby smiled, trying to conceal her nervousness. "Thank you."

As Bessie tightened Ruby's stays and helped her dress, Ruby felt faint with anticipation. She almost regretted her acceptance of Henry's invitation, until she remembered the look on his face when she had informed him of her acceptance.

Such pure happiness. She couldn't remember ever seeing such a look. Most men looked at her with impurity and impatience. But she'd never seen a hint of either from Henry. Surely he must be the noblest and kindest gentleman in the entire country.

"There you are, miss," smiled Bessie as she handed Ruby a silk bonnet that complimented her dress.

Ruby turned to look in the mirror. "Oh." She scarcely recognised herself. She looked like a lady. The pale pink silk gown was embroidered with delicate floral details and the sleeves were finished with tufts of ruffled lace. It was the finest dress she had ever seen, and couldn't believe that she was the one wearing it. Her heart raced. Though she feared she would not fit in at church, she hoped the gown would at least help her look as though she did.

She took a deep breath, fastened her bonnet with Bessie's help, then headed for the door.

THE CARRIAGE WAS ready and waiting, and Henry and Abigail stood patiently beside it. Browne was facing her direction as he spoke to the other two.

"Ah, Miss Ruby." He nodded as she walked up behind them.

Henry and Abigail turned to face her.

"Oh, my dear, you look wonderful!" cried Abigail. "I am so glad you are joining us."

When Henry said nothing, Ruby looked up at him. His eyes had a peculiar look in them, one that she had never seen before and couldn't read at all. Her stomach flipped.

Henry cleared his throat. "Shall we?"

Abigail reached for Henry's offered hand and climbed into the carriage.

This was it. Ruby's last chance to bolt back into the house. But she took a deep breath and placed her hand in Henry's, which he had kept extended.

As her gloved fingers met his, she glanced at him. He stared back at her, his face expressionless yet his eyes burning with that same peculiar, unreadable look.

She took her seat in the carriage beside Abigail and peered out, absent-mindedly, at the ground. Her heart raced. Had she offended Henry in some way? Did he dislike how she was dressed? Perhaps it was not fitting for her, considering her background. That must be it. He must think she looked like an imposter.

"You really do look splendid, my dear." Abigail startled Ruby out of her worries. "Doesn't she, Henry?"

Ruby looked down at her hands. She wanted to see Henry's reaction but was too afraid to look at him only to have her fears confirmed.

"Yes," he said, clearing his throat. "Indeed."

She glanced at him. He was gazing out of the carriage window, deep in thought, a somewhat pained expression on his face.

Abigail noticed Ruby studying Henry, then leaned toward her and whispered, "Henry does not tend to speak much on the way to church, my dear. He reflects on everything that he will be preaching about. But do not worry." She chuckled. "On the carriage ride home he will certainly make up for it!"

Ruby smiled. Maybe that's all it was. Maybe he was just thinking about his sermon. She swallowed hard and sighed.

She really hoped that was all it was.

THE JOURNEY to church was fairly short and mostly comfortable. As the horses slowed down, Ruby looked out the window and quietly gasped as she saw the building. It was slightly bigger than she had envisioned.

She was last to leave the carriage, longing desperately to stay inside its now-familiar safety. She sighed as she mustered the strength to shuffle toward the door.

Henry's hand was waiting to receive hers. He looked a million miles away.

Ruby alighted from the carriage, her eyes fixed on the ground. There was hardly any snow on the ground here, compared with the parsonage.

Henry walked briskly to the church, propped open its heavy wooden doors, then disappeared through them. He had barely spoken the whole way there, and now that he was gone from her sight, a flash of loneliness gripped Ruby, despite Abigail's presence at her side.

"Come inside," Abigail trilled, as she started walking. As they reached the doors, Ruby braced herself. She followed Abigail inside, looking only at the ground, terrified to discover how many people were there. Noticing how silent the church was, she glanced up at Abigail, then looked around. The church was empty.

"There is no one else here?"

"Oh, we are always the first to arrive so that Henry has

enough time to prepare," Abigail said.

"Oh, of course," said Ruby, her cheeks colouring.

Abigail took her seat in one of the two front pews. A red carpeted aisle ran between each side. Ruby eased down beside her.

Henry sat directly ahead of them at the pulpit, facing their pew. He was bent over, his head in his hands, his gaze fixed on the floor.

Ruby stared at him. She did not like the distance she felt between them, first in the carriage and now here. It made her feel somewhat adrift.

"Is everything all right, my dear?" asked Abigail, studying her.

"Yes, yes."

"The others should arrive quite soon. They tend to trickle in bit by bit."

Ruby looked around. The church was rich with intricate details everywhere she looked, and radiated warmth and kindness. It reminded her of Henry. She could see his character all over it.

She was about to mention this to Abigail when a man and woman walked in.

"Good morning, Mrs. Jones," they said to Abigail as they walked past, ultimately settling in the front pew on the other side of the aisle.

"Good morning Mr. Graham, good morning Mrs. Graham," replied Abigail.

Ruby sighed, somewhat relieved. They had not stopped to find out who she was, but had merely nodded respectfully to her as they passed by. She hoped others would do the same.

Before she and Abigail had a chance to say anything else to each other, a small cluster of people marched in. One young woman in particular, whose ringlets bounced with each step she took, made a direct line toward them as soon as she saw Abigail.

"Oh, good morning, Mrs. Jones," she said, smiling from ear to ear. "And who is your companion?"

Ruby froze.

"Good morning, Miss Acton," Abigail said with a smile. "This is Miss Ruby. She is a guest of mine, from out of town."

"Good morning, Miss Ruby," said Miss Acton, her voice high and soft, her eyes bright and keen. "It is a pleasure to meet you." She paused. "So, you are staying at the parsonage?"

Ruby detected a slight frown on Miss Acton's brow as she asked the question.

"Yes." she replied, unsure what else to say.

Miss Acton shifted her beady eyes to Henry, who still looked rather sombre at the pulpit.

Ruby looked at Henry, then back at Miss Acton. She looked at Henry again. He turned and glanced in their direction. Ruby turned her gaze to the young lady in front of her.

Miss Acton's eyes lit up. She dropped her head to one side and gave Henry an adoring smile.

Ruby felt a lurch in her stomach. She looked back at Henry, who just stared at the three women, a serious and almost worried look in his eyes that made Ruby's heart ache.

Miss Acton's smile faded, and her voice carried a note of embarrassment. "Well. Good morning, ladies."

With that, she strode to a pew at the other side of the church and sat down, smoothing her pale blue silk gown and fixing a forlorn yet expectant gaze on Henry.

Ruby looked at Abigail and exhaled deeply. She glanced at Henry, who was turning the pages of the large church Bible poised before him on its eagle-shaped lectern.

"Mrs. Jones, good morning."

Abigail and Ruby looked up at the distinguished gentleman and woman standing beside their pew.

"Oh, Mr. Penton, Mrs. Penton, good morning!" Abigail's smile showed deep friendship. "So lovely to see you both. I trust you are well?"

Ruby smiled politely at the middle-aged couple that Abigail conversed with, but was soon lost in her own thoughts. She felt so nervous to be out, surrounded by so many strangers. Strangers whose stations she believed to be much higher than her own.

Then there was Miss Acton, and Henry's odd behaviour. It all seemed too much to handle. She imagined running from her pew out into the open, and running and running and running . . .

"Good morning, ladies and gentlemen."

Henry's voice boomed from the pulpit, startling everyone's hushed conversations into silence. Mr. and Mrs. Penton hurriedly sat down beside Abigail. Ruby glanced at Miss Acton, whose eyes were wide with admiration and fixed unblinkingly on Henry.

"Let us all stand to sing 'When I Survey The Wondrous Cross'," said Henry, his voice commanding yet gentle.

The whole congregation stood. Abigail opened a hymnal deftly to the required page. She offered it to Ruby, who looked at her almost fearfully and shook her head. A knowing look appeared in Abigail's eyes and she subtly moved the hymnal back in front of herself. Ruby's cheeks heated as she glanced around.

She listened to the words that everyone in the church, apart from herself, were singing clearly. Her curiosity was piqued by some of the phrases.

Prince of glory? Such love and sorrow?

There was a depth to the worship that surprised and captivated her.

As the last note sounded, the congregation resumed their seats and silence. Henry placed a hand on either side of the lectern and looked intently at the open pages of the Bible.

"Colossians, chapter one." The passage he read spoke of walking worthy, being fruitful in every good work, increasing in the knowledge of God and being joyful and patient.

Ruby was fascinated.

Henry spoke on, reading aloud about the kingdom of darkness and the kingdom of God's Son.

Ruby didn't know God had a son. She'd never heard much about God, only what the vicar had said at her parents' funeral, but she had always imagined Him to be very far away. She'd never thought of Him in the way the hymn had mentioned Him, or even the way the Bible passage described Him. Joy, fruitfulness and glory were all unfamiliar to her.

Ruby was shocked to hear some of the particular verses about God's Son that Henry read out.

"In whom we have redemption through His blood, even the forgiveness of sins . . . all things were created by Him, and for Him . . . having made peace through the blood of His cross, by Him to reconcile all things unto Himself . . . And you, that were sometime alienated and enemies in your mind by wicked works, yet now hath He reconciled in the body of His flesh through death, to present you holy and unblameable and unreproveable in His sight . . ."

There was so much to take in. God's son offered forgiveness? How? And where did the blood and death fit into it all?

Had she really heard the word unblameable? God's son's blood could somehow make her . . . not guilty?

Henry cleared his throat quietly and looked up from the Bible.

"We are a blessed people. We have been given a far greater gift than any of us could ever dare hope for. That gift is redemption. Forgiveness. Atonement. That gift is the blood that Jesus - the Son of God and the Prince of glory - shed on that agonising cross. The blood that cleanses us from all sin."

All the nervousness that Ruby had felt in coming out in public and being surrounded by strangers somehow faded into the background, and a new sensation flooded through her. She struggled to understand most of what Henry was saying, but she knew, somehow, that it was of great importance. And she didn't want to miss a word.

"There are many different kinds of sin. We need only look at the Ten Commandments to find the most common ones: murder, adultery, lying, idolatry, theft."

Instantly, she remembered the lies she had told Millforte, and the coin she had asked Browne to keep safe for her, which now sat in the drawer of her dressing table. Not to mention, all the days and nights of impurity. Her shoulders slumped.

"Yet there are so many seemingly more subtle sins that worm their way into our lives day by day," Henry continued. "Greed, pride, hatred and all manner of impurity and immorality."

He paused.

"And the truth is, we all sin differently. Perhaps one of you could never imagine murdering someone, but you think nothing of telling lies. Another one of you might be honest, always telling the truth, yet be filled with such pride that you think you are better and holier than the person who *does* lie. But hear me, dear soul - whether your primary sin is lying, pride, hatred, adultery or any other kind of immoral or impure behaviour, you are guilty. We are all guilty. We have all missed the mark of God's standard, which is perfection. None of us are perfect. Not even close. We are all guilty. We are all marred and disfigured by sin."

Ruby looked at her hands. She was probably the most guilty person in the whole church.

"And this sin is the chasm which separates us from God. He is perfect, holy, righteous and true. We are not worthy to stand in His presence and cannot come near Him because of our sin. But! He is so longsuffering, so kind and so loving that He Himself paved the way we must travel if we seek to draw near to Him. He sent His Son - Jesus - to take our place. To take the punishment that you and I all deserve. Your punishment, sir. Your punishment, madam. We *all* deserve only punishment for our repeated disobedience and disgrace. But God is more kind and loving than you and I can ever understand. He came to rescue us. To snatch us out of the kingdom of darkness and to usher us into the kingdom of His Son. A kingdom of light, of hope, of peace - and of grace."

Ruby looked up. There was that word again.

Grace.

"A kingdom of forgiveness. Of restoration. Of redemption. And there is only one way that you and I may ever enter this kingdom. There is only one way that you and I may receive this forgiveness, this cleansing, this grace."

Ruby leaned forward slightly without even realising it.

"That way is Jesus Himself. Listen to what He says in John chapter fourteen: 'I am the way, the truth, and the life: no man cometh unto the Father, but by Me.' Jesus alone has the power to forgive us, to cleanse us and to make us new."

Ruby's eyebrows raised. So, God had a son who could forgive people and make them clean and new?

Surely not everyone. Surely she was too far gone, had sinned too much. These church folk had never done the kinds of things she had. Perhaps this forgiveness was achievable for them, but she was much too dirty to be made clean and new after so many years of debauchery.

Henry's bold voice startled Ruby as he echoed her thoughts. "Perhaps you feel as though you are too dirty to be cleansed by this wonderful Saviour. Perhaps you feel as though you are not worthy enough to receive His divine grace. Dear friend, you are *not* worthy enough. Not one of us is worthy enough. But He offers redemption - freely and fully - to all who call upon His name!"

Ruby was amazed. She didn't understand how this could be true, how it could be possible. Still, she told herself, she was too far gone. It couldn't apply to her. She shouldn't even dare hope.

"Or, perhaps, you feel as though you are clean enough already. Which is utterly more dangerous and damning than feeling too unworthy to receive God's grace."

Grace.

There was something about the word that captivated Ruby each time she heard it.

"Even the smallest act of disobedience toward God's holy standards is enough to banish you and I to hell forever."

Ruby gasped. She had heard the word hell. But she'd never heard of it in the way Henry had just mentioned it.

"God's Word tells us that if we have broken one of His commandments, we are guilty of breaking them all. There is no such thing as an innocent lie, or a harmless flirtation with someone who is married. Sin is sin, and God *will* punish it. But the reason we are a blessed people, dear ones, the reason we can rejoice this morning - and, indeed, always - is because there is One who was punished in our place, and He has cancelled out the list of debts that we could never be able to pay. He has purchased our redemption with the shedding of

His own precious, innocent blood. For as we read in the first few books of the Holy Scriptures, without the shedding of blood, there is no remission of sins. Sin is so serious a matter that blood is required to be spilled in order to remove it. And instead of you and I receiving the punishment we so deeply deserve, Jesus received it for us, so that whoever will come to Him in humble repentance - turning away from all their sin - He *will* cleanse and make brand new."

Ruby's mind was reeling. Oh how she wanted this to be true for her, too. But, how could it be?

"Dear ones, this morning, I beg you - if you have not repented - that is, if you have not humbly knelt before Jesus and confessed your sins, asking Him to cleanse you from them, and resolving to leave them all behind - do so now! Do so at once! He is ready and waiting to receive you. Such is His love, His mercy, His grace. I pray that you will know it today, and for all eternity."

He motioned with his hands for everyone to stand up.

"Please turn in your hymnals to page seventy-four."

Everyone stood. Abigail swiftly located the correct page as Ruby smoothed her dress nervously.

The music began to play, and Ruby's eyes widened as she recognised the tune.

"Amazing grace, how sweet the sound, that saved a wretch like me . . ."

It was surprising yet lovely to hear so many voices singing it all around her.

". . . I once was lost, but now am found, was blind, but now I see . . ."

She was enthralled to hear the other verses that Abigail had not sung. She drank in every word with deep, grateful delight.

When the song had ended, everyone sat down. Henry

prayed, then before she knew it, Ruby was looking around at the congregation, who were bustling and chattering now that the service was finished.

Abigail turned to face her as they both stood up. "Are you glad you came, my dear?"

Ruby smiled, nervous that she might soon have to converse with others in the congregation. She couldn't wait to return to the safety of the carriage and the tranquility of the parsonage. Yet, she *was* deeply glad that she had come.

"Yes, I am . . . I very much am."

"Oh, splendid."

"Mrs. Jones?"

Abigail turned around to face Miss Acton.

Ruby groaned inwardly. She had a feeling that Miss Acton was the kind of person who would gladly ask far too many questions.

"Miss Acton," Abigail said, warmly.

"Mamma asked me to invite you over for afternoon tea on Thursday, if you are free?"

"Why, yes, of course," smiled Abigail. "I would be delighted. It has been too long since I have seen your dear Mamma. Pray, is she well?"

"Oh, yes, thank you, very well." Miss Acton's cheeks pinked a little. "Mamma said also that if Mr. Stratton is not too busy, he would be most welcome to join us. I believe he and Papa always enjoy chatting . . ."

"Indeed! I cannot speak for his plans this week, but I shall certainly inform him of the kind invitation."

Relief and anticipation mingled in Miss Acton's smile. "Well, I must be going now. We are to travel to meet some friends. I cannot delay. Good day, Mrs. Jones."

Miss Acton nodded to Abigail and offered Ruby a polite smile as she left.

Ruby glanced at the pulpit. It was empty. She looked around at the people standing near the front of the church, all deep in conversation. Henry wasn't there, either.

Taking a few steps forward to continue her search, she saw a familiar form in the doorway. Henry stood with his back to them, shaking hands and greeting everyone as they exited the building.

Ruby looked intently at the people who were leaving, hoping to see Miss Acton's exchange with Henry, but it seemed she had already gone.

Turning back, she saw Abigail deep in conversation with Mr. and Mrs. Penton. She lingered where she was, aiming to avoid any awkward exchanges that might ensue if she rejoined Abigail and the various congregants who seemed eager to converse with her.

She felt quite out of her depth as she beheld all the people. Some were standing, some were still seated. Most were engaged in conversations and laughter.

As her eyes scanned the room, she felt a sinking feeling in her chest. She retraced her gaze and her eyes fixed on a gentleman standing at the back of the church. As she took in his appearance, her heart lurched.

He stared straight at her, a smirk on his thin lips and an eyebrow slightly raised.

She forgot to breathe as her mind screamed at her to run.

Run. Now!

But she couldn't. Her feet were frozen, her legs feeling ten times heavier than usual. She was rooted to the spot.

People brushed past her on their way to the door and more than once she felt as though the slightest breeze from their movements could have knocked her down.

The man started walking toward her. Ruby's blood ran cold.

Closer and closer he came. Her ears rang, her breaths fast and shallow.

He glanced at Abigail, still deep in conversation with the Pentons, as he approached Ruby. As he strode slowly past her, he whispered, almost inaudibly.

"Well now, Ruby. What is a girl like *you* doing in a place like this?"

Ruby almost collapsed. She clutched blindly at the edge of the nearest pew to steady herself, blinking rapidly to diffuse the black dots that clouded her vision.

It was no use. Her legs crumpled and a draught weaved its way around her.

"Ruby!" Abigail shrieked her name. Her vision was almost gone, her heart hammering. Desperately, she clutched to consciousness, her mind reeling, a deep desire to run still flooding every fibre, every nerve.

"Ruby? Ruby! Are you all right? What happened?"

Abigail was beside her, bending down and stroking her hair.

"I . . . I . . . H—"

All Ruby could do was pant.

Mr. and Mrs. Penton's faint voices came from behind Abigail, asking if they might be of any assistance.

The only thing Ruby could hear clearly was her heartbeat as it thundered in her ears. She just about distinguished the shapes of Abigail and a few other figures moving about.

As her senses retreated into silent darkness, a shadowy male silhouette approached her, his arms extending. The sensation of being lifted up from the cold stone floor and floating weightlessly filled her, just as she lost consciousness entirely.

CHAPTER 10

SHAKEN

Buzzing echoed through Ruby's head. Her whole body tingled and shook. Hushed voices grew louder, the blackness dispelling as the light grew stronger.

Her chest felt tight. Slowly, thoughts and words returned to her mind.

Where was she? What had happened?

She gasped in sheer panic as she opened her eyes and sensed movement all around her, even while her own body felt stuck and heavy.

"Ruby?"

Henry's voice was a calm, steady anchor.

"Ruby! Oh, we have been so worried about you! Are you all right, my dear? Whatever happened?" Abigail said, her words spilling out in a frantic flurry.

Ruby's head spun. A sudden jolt made her realise she was in the carriage.

She looked around, blinking as her vision returned to normal. Henry and Abigail were on one seat, while Ruby lay on the other, her head resting on Henry's rolled up jacket.

She looked at their faces. Abigail's was flushed with relief. Henry's was a multitude of emotions. Concern. Sadness.

Fear.

Fresh grief washed over Ruby and silent tears sprang to her eyes. She wanted to sit up, but her head was still reeling too much, and her body felt pinned down by an invisible weight.

"Ruby? What happened?" Abigail asked softly.

The man's face flashed into Ruby's mind, his leering grin and whispered words disorienting her all over again.

Her heart raced. She should never have come. Now, it would only be a matter of time until Millforte found her. What then? He would either beat her to death or force her back to the brothel. Either way, her life was over.

"Ruby? Oh, please speak to us. We cannot help you if we do not know what must be done." Abigail's brow furrowed in concern.

Ruby slowly eased herself up to a sitting position. A rush of dizziness caused her to clutch Henry's jacket with one hand and the carriage seat with the other.

Moments of silence passed, then Henry cleared his throat.

Expecting him to speak, Ruby raised her gaze to his eyes and was startled to see them downcast, unblinking as he stared at his folded hands.

Terror still gripped Ruby, like a fist deep inside her chest. She gazed out the carriage windows at the blurred landscape flitting by. Should she tell them? Should she let them know she had been recognised by one of the brothel's most frequent customers? Or should she bide her time, get back to the parsonage, then make a run for it?

Who was she kidding? She had never been on her own, had never had to fend for herself. How could she begin now, with Millforte in pursuit? Yet she could no longer stay at the parsonage. Either way, he was sure to find her.

She went back and forth between the two choices, yet all the while she felt as though she had no choice at all. Shaking from fearful exhaustion, tears escaped her stinging eyelids and she sobbed, curling her head down into her weary palms.

"Oh, Ruby." In a flash, Abigail was by her side, her arm across Ruby's shoulders.

"It cannot have been easy for you this morning, my dear. Perhaps we were all too hasty. Perhaps we ought to have given you more time to adjust before inviting you to accompany us."

Abigail's tone was one of regretful hindsight.

Ruby raised her head and shook it slowly. "No," she croaked. "No, I should not have come." Her voice cracked, and a fresh batch of sobs escaped.

"There now. It was too much too soon. We ought to have given you more time. We are sorry we rushed it on you."

"Yes," Henry agreed quietly.

Ruby shook her head again, more firmly this time. "No, no, no . . . I should not have come at all!" Her voice intensified in pitch and volume with each word.

"What do you mean?" asked Abigail, her eyes wide in confusion.

Ruby was breathing rapidly, every inch of her hunched frame trembling. She looked at Henry, her eyes wild with terror. "You should have just left me there!"

Henry looked astounded. Horror filled his eyes and confusion contorted his features.

Ruby grabbed her head with her hands and closed her eyes, as though trying to block everything out. "He saw me! And now he'll find me . . ." Her sobbing grew uncontrollable.

"He saw you?"

"Who saw you?"

Henry and Abigail spoke at almost the same time, but Ruby was so overcome that she could not answer either one of them.

Abigail pulled Ruby closer to her, tears rolling down her own cheeks.

"Ruby, please do not lose hope. Please, explain to us exactly what happened, and we will help you as best we can."

"Yes," echoed Henry. His voice trembled with agonised emotion as he spoke. "God brought you to us. You are safe now."

Ruby's body shook violently. "I can never be safe," she sobbed.

"Ruby, please! What happened? Who saw you?" Henry pleaded.

Ruby glanced at him, the fear in her eyes reflected in his own. Those eyes that seemed as though they could read her soul . . . how she wished they could read her mind so that she could avoid reliving the awful encounter.

Ruby looked at Abigail, surprised by the depth of compassion in her eyes. She breathed deeply, trying to calm her tremors.

"You were talking to a man and his wife."

"Mr. and Mrs. Penton, yes."

"And I did not wish to be questioned by anyone, so I stepped back and looked around the room." An involuntary whimper punctuated her sentence. "And I noticed . . . a man." She whimpered again, struggling to keep her sobbing at bay. "A *customer*," she whispered.

Henry's expression changed in a flash from agonised compassion to angry incredulity. "What did he say to you?"

Ruby closed her eyes, remembering the horrible moment. "He walked over to me." Another whimper escaped from her

throat. "And . . . And he said, Hello, Ruby . . . what is a girl . .
. like *you* . . . doing in a place like this!" Her voice trailed off
into a new wave of sobs.

Henry's fists were clenched as tightly as his teeth. "How
dare he!" he muttered. "Who was he?"

Ruby shook her head. "He always told me to call him Jack.
I do not know his last name."

"Always told you?" Henry paled. "You mean that you . . .
met . . . him more than once?"

Ruby nodded. "He came every week." Her face crumpled.
"And he is right. I do not belong here . . . I do not belong
anywhere!"

"Oh, Ruby, that is not true!" said Abigail, shaking her
head.

"Can you describe him?" Henry asked, his teeth still held
tightly together in an angry grimace.

Ruby shuddered as she sobbed. "He . . ."

"Oh, Henry, now is not the time. We will ascertain his
identity soon enough. Do not ask this of her now." Abigail
whispered the gentle rebuke.

Henry sighed in restless frustration. His jaw was tightly
shut, his fingers clenching and unclenching at the same speed
his eyes darted to and fro.

The carriage slowed to a halt, jolting them all into the
serene silence of the parsonage grounds. The door opened,
and Browne arranged the steps.

Abigail squeezed Ruby's arm and whispered, "Everything
will be all right, my dear. Come, let us go inside." She glanced
at Henry, then exited the carriage.

Ruby wondered how her weak legs would manage to
stand, never mind walk.

Henry's voice cut through the air.

"I will fix this. I will find out who he is, and I will ensure that, that . . ." He sighed, as if overwhelmed by his indignation. "I will fix this."

Ruby glanced up at him and felt a jagged pain pass through her heart. There was still something in his eyes she could not read, but she was familiar enough with torment to recognise its presence alongside the undecipherable emotion.

She shook her head. "Everything is beyond fixing," she whispered.

Henry shook his head, looking as though he were about to speak. But he voiced only a sigh. Then, swiftly, yet more stiffly than usual, he left the carriage.

Silent tears ran down Ruby's cheeks as she sat there, alone. A few moments later, the carriage swayed gently as Browne ascended the steps and entered.

"I came to offer my assistance, Miss Ruby. Mr. Stratton told me you had a faint. Let me help you inside, miss."

Ruby's tears flew faster as she marvelled at the kindness and gentleness Browne showed her. He was supporting most of her weight, and she felt at times that he was practically carrying her along. He was such a gentleman.

She wished all men were so noble. But they weren't, and now it would only be a matter of time until the very worst of them all would find her.

A KNOCK at her bedroom door startled Ruby, all her nerves in a heightened state of alertness.

Weakly, she rose off the chair in the corner of her bedroom and half-walked, half-stumbled toward the door. Her hand trembled as she turned the door handle.

The first thing Ruby noticed about Abigail was the softness in her eyes. Then, the small tray in her hands and the steaming cup of tea that was perfectly centred on it, framed by bread and fruit.

"I thought you might be in need of a little refreshment."

"Thank you," Ruby croaked. "Do come in."

Ruby's jaw clenched. The words flashed back memories of the many times she had opened her door in the brothel and said them to customer after customer. She stood, frozen to the spot.

Abigail frowned. "Ruby?"

Her voice jolted Ruby back to the present. She stumbled back, pulling the door open so Abigail could enter.

Abigail swept into the room. "You must be exhausted after everything this morning. I thought some sustenance might strengthen you."

Ruby sat down. After seeing the customer at the church, she had avoided the bed when she'd got back to her room. Instead, she had been curled up in the wing chair beside the fireplace, alternating between crying and feeling sick to her stomach.

"Here." Abigail placed the tray on the small round table beside the wing chair.

Ruby reached for the teacup and saucer, drawing them back toward herself with shaky hands. The aroma of the tea wafted up into her face. It smelled lovely. So unlike the cheap beer at the brothel, the stench of which had invaded her nostrils day and night.

Jack's face flashed into her mind again. The memory of his leering grin and taunting words caused her heart and breathing to speed up again. Her hands grew even more shaky, the teacup and saucer clinking rapidly together.

Abigail knelt beside the arm of Ruby's chair. She gently reached out and grasped the teacup and saucer, taking its full weight as Ruby's weak fingers slipped off it.

"Oh, my dear." Abigail sighed, setting the tea back on the table.

Ruby's whole body trembled, the man's face now fixed in her mind. The leer. The voice. Those words. He knew she didn't belong. And now Millforte would know where to find her.

She was close to overwhelm when Abigail's gentle voice filled the air.

"May I pray for you?" Abigail asked softly.

Ruby scarcely heard her above the cacophony of her racing thoughts. Vacantly, she nodded.

Abigail placed a caring hand on Ruby's arm and dipped her head.

"Dear Lord, we thank you that You know all things, and that You alone are in ultimate control of all our lives. I ask You, Lord, to please comfort Ruby."

Ruby bowed her head, her heart pounding, her breathing racing. She had never had anyone pray for her before.

She remembered praying alone a few times after she had been taken to the brothel. But as the years passed and trauma had broken her spirit, she hadn't prayed at all. Her heart had been too empty.

"Please quiet all her fears and wash away all the painful memories that she longs to forget."

Ruby took a deep breath and shakily exhaled. All she wanted to do was curl up in a ball and scream.

"Thank You, Lord, for bringing her here, to us."

Ruby looked at Abigail. She was moved by how earnest and calm she was. Had Abigail actually just thanked God that Ruby was there with them? How could the best two people in the world be glad to have a girl like her in their home? She was so dirty. So vile.

Her stomach lurched. Millforte was right. She *was*

worthless.

"Please, Lord, keep her safe from all harm, and help her not to worry, Lord. Please, grant her rest and peace."

Peace. How she longed for peace.

"Help her to heal, Lord. Cover her with Your grace."

There was that word again. Ruby shifted in her chair, curling her arms around a small cushion.

"And draw her close to You. In Jesus's name we ask, Lord. Amen."

Abigail seemed to pray quietly for a moment before lifting her head to look at Ruby.

A sudden bird call outside made Ruby jump. All her nerves were on edge. Raw sickness gnawed at her stomach. She clenched her jaw, trying in vain to suppress its trembling.

Abigail looked at her kindly. "Perhaps some fresh air would ease you. Shall we take a short stroll in the garden?"

Ruby shook her head vehemently. No way was she leaving the sheltering walls of the parsonage to stroll about in full view of anyone who might arrive. She had lived without going outside all these years. She could do it again if it meant she'd stay hidden.

Abigail rose to a stand. "I shall go for now and let you rest, my dear. Please do let us know if you need anything. I shall check on you again a little later."

Ruby nodded again. "Thank you."

As Abigail slipped out of the room, Ruby's thoughts turned to Henry and the look in his eyes on the way back from the church. It had startled her to see him look so angry.

As she puzzled over it in her mind, her eyelids grew heavy. Resting her head on the wing of the chair, she surrendered to the sleep that was slowly enveloping her body.

The customer's face flashed into her mind as she awoke with a start. Simultaneously, there was a knock on her door.

CHAPTER 11

QUESTIONS

DISORIENTED FOR A BRIEF MOMENT, thinking she was back at the brothel, she froze. Her heart thumped loudly as she scrambled to her feet.

Another knock, sharper this time.

She dragged herself to the door and opened it, expecting to see Abigail.

Bessie's pleasant smile greeted her. "Mr. Stratton wishes to speak with you in the drawing room, miss."

After tidying her appearance, Ruby approached the drawing room. Her heart squeezed as she wondered what Henry might say.

She entered the room to find it empty. Frowning, she walked further in, though she doubted he was merely out of sight. Upon closer examination, the room was indeed empty.

The door flung open. Henry strode into the room like a hunter. He looked haggard and distraught - a far cry from his typically fresh composure.

"Forgive my impertinence, Ruby, but there are some questions that I *must* ask you."

He paced back and forth, his eyes scanning the floor intently.

Ruby felt too weak to continue standing. She shuffled over to one of the armchairs by the fireside and sank down onto it.

Henry glanced over. He stopped pacing, concern etched on his furrowed brow, his eyes softening slightly.

"Ruby, are you all right?"

Ruby nodded, though she felt quite the opposite. Her heart pounded as she wondered what Henry wanted to ask her. As she observed him, worry gripped her. He seemed wholly absorbed by his thoughts.

"I do apologise for disturbing you." His face steeled again. He resumed his pacing. "I must ascertain a few facts about the . . . situation . . . that occurred earlier. I have been unable to think of very much else since we returned."

Ruby stared at him. He looked haunted. Heavy as her heart already felt, it weighed heavier to see him so affected, knowing it was all her fault.

How noble a man he was to be so concerned with a worthless wretch like her. She could not understand it. She did not deserve it.

How different he was from Millforte. A shudder passed through her as she remembered *him* - his cold, unfeeling eyes and his hulking, forceful frame.

Nausea clutched her stomach and throat. She closed her eyes, attempting to wrest the tormenting memories away.

"Ruby!"

She opened her eyes to see Henry kneeling by her side, his warm eyes wide with alarm. She batted away the thought that she could look into those eyes forever.

"Oh, Ruby, you grew so pale and closed your eyes, I thought perhaps you were feeling faint again." A long, overwhelmed sigh released itself from his lungs.

"Forgive me," she half-croaked, half-whispered. "I . . ."

She trailed off, not knowing what to say, and feeling somehow that she didn't have to say anything.

On a few occasions since arriving at the parsonage, Ruby had noticed a strange sentiment at times that seemed to pass between herself and Henry, as though they had some kind of unspoken understanding. There was an ease that she felt when Henry was near.

She had never experienced anything like it before, and she could scarcely define it.

Safety? Protection? *Home?*

These things she'd never known, never expected to experience, yet, all three she felt at Shiloh Hall.

Sudden realisation stunned her. No - not Shiloh Hall.

All three she felt with *Henry*.

He raised his gaze to meet hers. Her heart fluttered as she looked into his deep, dark eyes. They were rich with concern, filled with a protective anguish, and a flicker of something else - something she couldn't place.

"Ruby," he breathed, his voice burdened. "I am sorry to have to ask you this." He paused, as if he didn't want to know the answer to his impending question. "But can you remember anything more of his name? This man, this . . . *scoundrel!* There is no one by the name of Jack who attends the church."

Ruby frowned. She rarely knew any of their names. She knew this man's face with abhorrent clarity - the smugness, the scorn, the lust. But as for his name . . .

She lowered her gaze from Henry's piercing eyes. "He told me to call him Jack. That is all I know of his name." She paused. "It may not even be real."

Another agonising sigh from Henry caused her to glance back up at him. He looked like a man whose only exit was blocked, and who had to find another route, which didn't seem to exist.

He turned away from her, rising to a stand, recommencing his agitated pacing.

A few moments later, he stopped. Hesitating, he finally asked, "Then I must ask you to provide a description of him. I am sorry, Ruby, truly I am, but I must know who he is. I must ascertain if he is merely a passing stranger or if he is indeed one of my flock."

He was shaking his head as he spoke, his gaze downcast, his eyebrows raised in the middle.

Ruby's stomach lurched. How could she put into words how abhorrent he looked? She stared up at Henry with puzzled eyes.

Henry took a deep breath. "His hair colour. What is it?"

"Brown. Light brown - not nearly so dark as yours," Ruby said slowly.

Henry stiffened. "His eyes. What colour are they?"

Ruby swallowed hard. "Blue. Cold, pale blue."

His eyes had bored into her as he'd sized her up at the brothel. Ruby had wished herself invisible more times than she could remember, but that was a time she would gladly forget.

"Is he tall?"

Henry's face was agony, but his voice was strong and matter-of-fact. Ruby could tell it was taking all his willpower to present such a stoic composure.

She thought for a moment. "Not very tall. But he is thin. Which, perhaps, causes him to appear taller than he is."

"He is thin?" Henry repeated.

"Yes."

Ruby's heart pounded. She didn't know which outcome would be worse - if Henry knew the man or if he did not.

"Does he have any distinguishing features?" Henry asked, shaking his head slightly in mild scorn.

Ruby shifted uncomfortably in her seat. She opened her mouth to speak, but no words came out. She glanced at Henry, then her gaze fell to her lap as she stared at her hands, shame and sorrow clouding her face.

Henry spoke with shaking breath. "What is it?"

He stopped pacing and knelt beside her chair, looking down at her with imploring eyes. "Ruby, please. I know it is difficult." He grimaced. "But if you can tell me anything that will help me identify him, then . . . Please."

"He has a small scar," she said, her stomach churning and her body trembling.

"A scar?" asked Henry, his expression slightly more hopeful.

Ruby nodded. "But, I doubt it will help you identify him."

She glanced at Henry's face, then away just as quickly.

"Ruby, tell me." Henry's voice was almost a whisper.

Ruby closed her eyes as she spoke. "It is not on his face." Her heart thumped.

Gathering all her will, she opened her eyes and looked up at Henry.

His lips were slightly apart, his cheeks pale. Those eyes . . . It was unbearable to see those gentle eyes filled with such dread.

Time seemed to stand still, Henry and Ruby both suspended in agony of soul. Ruby's eyes filled. Oh, how she longed to undo the pain she was causing him. When Henry had devised her escape plan, she hadn't even considered how it all might affect him. How could she have been so selfish?

All she had thought of was her own freedom. She certainly never dreamed it would lead to such sorrow and hurt for the kind gentleman who had met her by accident in the first place.

Henry cleared his throat, the suddenness of it making Ruby jump.

A thought came to Ruby. "There may be a way," she whispered.

Henry looked up at her, his expression a mix of incredulity and apprehension.

"The scar—"

Henry winced. "Ruby, please . . ."

"—is just under here," Ruby said, tapping her collarbone.

Relief transformed Henry's face. "Oh!" He closed his eyes and breathed deeply, rubbing his forehead with his fingertips.

After a long silence, he finally spoke, disappointment clouding his voice. "I still do not think it helpful. I cannot imagine how I would ever have occasion to see underneath the man's collar."

He was right. Ruby scrambled to think of anything else that might prove helpful.

"From the details you have given, I must confess - I cannot think of anyone from the church who quite fits his description. However, I did notice a fair few strangers in attendance this morning. He must have been one of them," he said, his frown deepening to a scowl as he uttered the last sentence.

He looked up at Ruby with a hesitant expression. "The only way I believe we could ascertain his identity is if, well, if you were to attend church again next week and—"

Ruby's eyes grew wide. "No!" She cried out in alarm before she even realised she had spoken.

Henry nodded. "No. I know. It is too much to ask of you, after everything that has transpired today. Please, forgive me for mentioning it."

Henry stood up and walked over to the fireplace, resting one hand on the mantel, staring down at the dancing flames with a pensive expression that seemed almost devoid of hope.

Ruby felt a stretching sensation deep in her heart. How she longed to see his dashing smile again, to see his deep eyes twinkling with joy.

The door opened in a graceful arc, drawing them both out of their thoughts.

Alarm flashed onto Henry's face as he turned his back to the fireplace and fixed his collar.

Abigail walked into the room, stopping abruptly as she noticed Henry and Ruby at the fireplace.

"Henry?"

Ruby detected shock and surprise in Abigail's questioning tone.

Henry looked skittish. "Aunt Abigail. Do come in. I merely wanted to make sure Ruby was all right. I . . ."

As Abigail resumed walking, Ruby could see concern etched on her face. Surely she did not suspect any foul play?

But as Ruby reflected, she realised that Henry's reputation must be one of utmost purity. It would never do for him to be seen alone with a lady.

Not that Ruby was a lady. However, she was still a woman and, thus, her interactions with Henry ought never to take place behind closed doors.

Ruby felt awful. She hoped Aunt Abigail would not think ill of her, or worry that she was trying to ruin Henry, given her murky past.

"Yes . . . Are you feeling better, my dear?" Abigail said, looking at Ruby. She looked deep in thought, though it seemed as if she were trying to appear that she was not.

Ruby didn't know what to say. She nodded unconvincingly.

Henry stood awkwardly in front of the fire, his hands clenched by his sides, his gaze roaming the floor. Silence hung heavy, its weight filling the atmosphere with more and more discomfort as each second ticked by.

Abigail looked from Ruby to Henry and back again.

"I do hope I have not interrupted any sort of . . . private conversation?"

Abigail's expression was one of puzzled suspicion.

"Not at all, Aunt," Henry said, clearing his throat. "I merely wished to ascertain that Ruby had suffered no ill."

There was resignation in his voice, and a quiet frustration in his manner.

Ruby wished to defend Henry to Abigail, but she didn't know what to say, or if she ought to say anything at all.

Abigail eyed Henry, keen to detect the truth. Seemingly satisfied that there was no impropriety, she turned her gaze to Ruby.

"Shall we have a cup of tea?"

Ruby nodded slowly. "Thank you."

Abigail smiled. "I shall go and arrange some."

"I shall go, Aunt. You stay a while. I . . . I ought to be going, anyway."

"Thank you, Henry," Abigail said, her tone indicating a lingering trace of wariness.

Henry looked at Ruby, his eyes filled with uncertainty.

"Ruby," he nodded to her.

Ruby smiled weakly as she nodded. "Mr. Stratton."

Henry glanced at Abigail, then looked back at Ruby before turning away and reaching for the door.

A breeze of cool air wafted into the room as Henry left, the heavy white door sweeping shut behind him.

The two women sat in silence for a moment.

"Do not fear, my dear. Today was a shock. But it will pass.

A new day will dawn tomorrow. There are many possibilities that lie ahead for you. Much we can discuss, perhaps before long. Take heart, and do not lose hope."

The only thing Ruby had ever known of hope was that it was always just beyond her feeble grasp.

A knock at the door brought them both out of deep thought.

"Oh," said Abigail, remembering. "That must be the tea."

As Abigail opened the door and greeted the person on the other side of it, Ruby listened, almost holding her breath.

Bessie's voice trickled into the room's sombre air.

Ruby sighed. It wasn't Henry.

What was he thinking after their conversation? It made her stomach churn to think of the look in his eyes when they had discussed the man's scar. Such cruelty her presence was causing him as all the murky details of her past gradually came to light.

Ruby looked at the tea tray Abigail had returned with. Even though her stomach was still churning, she reached out and lifted a sandwich, marvelling at how fresh and soft the bread felt.

"Oh, good. Do eat something. You need to get some strength back." Abigail said, her voice mostly returned to its usual perkiness.

They ate and drank in silence for several moments.

Ruby looked up at Abigail. "Mrs. Jones, is it true that God offers grace to everyone? Mr. Stratton spoke of it this morning, but . . . but surely it cannot be for *everyone?*"

Abigail's face filled with pleasant surprise, which gave way to a deep, joyful smile.

"Oh, my dear, but He does! Why, the Bible says so."

"Yes," said Ruby. "But surely there are those who . . . who have fallen too far. Who are too vile to ever be made clean."

Compassion sparkled in Abigail's eyes. "It is as Henry said this morning. We are *all* separated from God. We are all vile, at heart."

Ruby couldn't imagine that Abigail or Henry were vile. Not like she was.

"God desires us to be reconciled to Him, but He is holy, so no sin can go near His presence. He loves us, because He created us. But He cannot tolerate sin. It is such an affront to His character that it must be punished. So, we must be washed clean of it if we ever wish to dwell in His presence."

Ruby leaned forward slightly, training her ears on Abigail's every word.

"God could have easily chosen to do nothing. To leave us all in our sins and filthiness and let us be damned. But His love for us is so vast that He desired to show us mercy. He gave us a chance to be cleansed and forgiven, through Jesus." Abigail paused. "That is what grace is. He offers us something that we do not deserve. He gives us a gift, when all we have given Him is rebellion. And He enables us to give others the same grace He has shown to us."

Ruby's mind raced. On the one hand, it sounded amazing that God would give the gift of forgiveness to people who had done Him wrong. But on the other, a question emerged that disturbed her soul. If God showed Ruby grace, would He expect her to show grace to Millforte and the men from the brothel after all that they had caused her to suffer?

Ruby looked at Abigail intently. "Is it only God who gives grace?"

"God is the only one who can forgive us. His is the only grace that can wash us clean."

Ruby shook her head. "No, no, forgive me. What I meant was, well, are we expected to give other people grace, too?"

"Oh yes, once we have been reconciled to God, He gives

us a new heart. Gradually, He helps us see things as He does. Our lives start to mirror His attitudes and actions."

Ruby's heart thudded as she tried to understand.

She looked at Abigail, whose smile she did not mirror.

"Do you mean that I would be expected to show grace to, to . . ."

Ruby couldn't speak. She could hardly take it in.

Surely not. Surely, she had misunderstood Abigail.

Abigail seemed to realise what Ruby was trying to ask.

"Oh! Oh, my dear - do not concern yourself with such things. You have been cruelly treated. Why, no one is expecting you to embrace anyone who has hurt you."

Ruby felt a rush of relief.

"It is a complex thing to try to explain," Abigail continued.

Ruby tensed. Maybe she hadn't misunderstood after all.

"All that you need to know is that God loves you. So very much. And as Henry said this morning, when we repent and trust in Jesus, He cleanses us and gives us new hearts, and He helps us to love and forgive those whom we never believed we could."

"So, God would want me to love and forgive . . . *him*?" Ruby asked, her face the picture of incredulity.

CHAPTER 12

WHISPERINGS

"THE MAN who owns the brothel? Or the man you saw today?" Abigail asked, clearly uncomfortable referencing either man.

"Both! Either!" cried Ruby.

"It is not easy to explain before one has fully surrendered to the Lord." Abigail paused. "God wants you to love Him, first and foremost. After that - indeed, as a *result* of that, He will help you to love others." Her tone softened. "Even people who have hurt you."

Ruby stared at her, blinking and open-mouthed.

"Please, do understand me - no one, that is, it does not mean that you would *engage* with them. Merely that the anger and fear that you feel now would be healed, in time. And the burden of unforgiveness would no longer weigh you down."

Ruby felt a measure of comfort from Abigail's explanation. It did not sound as impossible as it had at first.

THE NEXT MORNING, Abigail and Henry both smiled to greet her as she entered the cheerfully decorated dining room. Ruby smiled in return.

Abigail motioned to Ruby to sit beside her. "Good morning, my dear," she trilled.

Ruby had come to look forward to mealtimes at the parsonage. There was always encouraging chatter, which came mostly from Abigail, and Henry's company was exceedingly enjoyable, whether he was speaking or not.

"What are your plans for the day, Henry?" Abigail asked at a lull in the conversation.

"Dr. Shaw informed me yesterday that Mr. Griffith has taken ill, so I am to visit him and one or two others who are in need of either prayer or encouragement."

"Oh, poor Mr. Griffith," Abigail said, mournfully. "He has never been blessed with good health. I am sorry to hear that he is ill again - indeed, it does not seem so very long ago that he was recovering from another bout."

"That is true," Henry said, sympathetically. "He has rather a heavy load to carry, which is why I must endeavour to lighten it, if I am able to do so."

Ruby admired Henry's committed compassion to his congregation. Though, deep down, she never liked it when he left.

"Oh! Why, with everything that happened, I forgot to tell you," Abigail gasped, looking at Henry. "Miss Acton has invited us to have tea with herself and her parents. This Thursday, if you are . . . available?" Abigail's tone was almost playful.

Ruby remembered Miss Acton's keen interest in Henry. Her heart faltered as she wondered if he returned it.

Henry frowned as his cheeks flushed slightly. Ruby wasn't

sure if it were due to annoyance or embarrassment. "I see," he said, his voice flat.

Ruby glanced at Abigail. A smile flickered at her lips, and a few times she opened her mouth to speak, then said nothing.

"Well, I must away," said Henry, drawing himself to a stand.

"So, are you free on Thursday?" asked Abigail, a deeply curious look in her eyes.

"I cannot say for certain. I shall have to decide closer to the time." He shook his head gently as he spoke, his cheeks a flush of pale pink.

"Ah, I see. You do not wish to appear too eager, perhaps?" Abigail asked with a smile.

Henry stifled. "Aunt Abigail, I assure you—"

Abigail chuckled, interrupting him. "Oh, Henry, I am half-teasing you, my dear."

Henry's eyes darted as colour flooded his cheeks. "Only half? Honestly, Aunt, I—"

"Oh, my dear," Abigail said, chuckling. "It is entirely up to you. See how you are fixed in a day or two. Miss Acton seems a very nice girl. Perhaps once Ruby has settled in a bit more, we ought to have Miss Acton over for dinner."

Henry glanced at Ruby, then back at Abigail. "Why so?"

He didn't seem thrilled with the idea. Ruby hoped it was only because he did not have much of an interest in having dinner with Miss Acton.

"Why, Henry! You do not intend to remain a bachelor forever, do you?"

Henry's eyes widened, mirroring Ruby's at the same moment.

"Aunt Abigail!" Henry's face practically drained of colour, except for the blushes of pink on his cheeks.

Abigail's eyebrows raised and she smiled in surprise at Henry's horrified reaction.

Ruby felt uneasy. What would become of her if Henry were to marry? She could not imagine that Miss Acton would be too happy to share a house with her if she had not yet found a suitable position, knowing what she was.

Not only that, but it would change everything. Ruby would not be able to speak so freely with Henry, nor he with her. They would hardly be able to speak at all.

Ruby clutched the table in front of her. The room looked as though it were swaying.

Abigail and Henry both noticed her hunched shoulders and white knuckles.

"Ruby, are you all right?"

Henry crouched beside her, seemingly to ascertain that she was all right.

Ruby swallowed hard, her throat so dry she felt like choking. "Yes, yes, I am fine."

She looked up at Henry. Such concern and compassion flooded from those eyes. She imagined him looking at Miss Acton with the same expression. A jagged pain pricked her heart.

As her dizziness settled, she noticed Abigail quietly observing their interaction. Shifting her gaze from Henry to his aunt, Ruby noticed a strange expression on Abigail's face. Curiosity, mixed with . . . fear? It was not an expression Ruby had ever seen on Abigail's face before. Nor did she like it.

Henry straightened up. "Well, if you are sure. I had better take my leave now."

Ruby nodded slowly, her heart pleading for him to stay.

For the first time, she felt uneasy about being left alone with Abigail. Something about her expression made Ruby feel a little less welcome.

"Yes, I dare say time is ticking on swiftly. You had better hurry if you wish to return before nightfall," Abigail said as she adjusted her sleeve cuffs.

"Yes, yes." Henry said. He seemed distracted.

Ruby could hardly bear to look at his face. And she felt almost afraid to look at Abigail's.

"Farewell, Aunt. Farewell, Ruby."

A few agonising seconds later, he was gone, and with him, most of Ruby's calm.

Abigail was uncharacteristically quiet. Ruby's stomach churned. She longed to slip quietly out of her chair and leave the room without a word, yet she did not wish to appear rude.

Slowly, she stood up, pushing her chair back cautiously. Abigail was still lingering near the doorway, rearranging a few items on the bureau.

"If you will excuse me, please."

Ruby's voice trailed off as Abigail turned to look at her. It was as she suspected. There was something different in Abigail's eyes. And it was a difference that made Ruby feel as though she had been pushed farther away.

A few awkward moments passed, then Abigail opened her mouth and inhaled, about to say something. After a short pause, she exhaled.

"I am here if you need me, my dear." she said, with a polite nod.

"Thank you." Ruby said, before easing the door open and slipping through it.

Once she was back in the safety of her room, she stood by the window and gazed out at the beautiful, rugged landscape that stretched into the distance.

What was happening to her? Why did she feel so sad

when she thought of Miss Acton, and so alone when Henry wasn't around?

Racing questions pummelled her and swarmed incessantly inside her head. She thought of God. Of all that Henry had said in the church. She wished for a moment that it could all be true for her. But how?

Hot tears pricked her eye

Surely, I am the vilest of all. Why would God want me or even care for me?

JUST BEFORE DARK, Abigail was praying in the drawing room when Henry rushed in, glancing around him in an apprehensive manner.

"Henry! Whatever is the matter? How was Mr. Griffith?"

Henry sighed. "Oh, Aunt Abigail. Mr. Griffith is doing well, I am glad to say. Oh, but Aunt!"

He struggled to catch his breath. Clearly, he had rushed back into the parsonage with urgency.

"What is it, dear boy?"

"Ruby!"

"Ruby?!" Abigail interjected. She paused. "Is this about the wine?"

He frowned. "The what?" He hesitated, bewildered curiosity etched on his face. He shook his head. "I know nothing of the wine, Aunt. No - Mr. Fotherington informed me that there have been whisperings in the village since Ruby was seen at church with us. There are . . . *speculations*. As to why we have a female guest with us. All sorts of hypotheses are being bandied about! I tried to explain what you and I had settled upon, and told him that she was a guest of yours who had fallen on hard times, and that we are endeavouring to find her a suitable position."

"And how did he respond?"

Henry gritted his teeth and paced the room, agitated and angered.

"He accepted it without question, but! After leaving his house, I walked a few paces through the village, to see if all was well with Mr. Griffith. As I passed by his shop, Mr. Woods then accosted me and said that he had heard from a reputable source that a 'lady of the night' had planted herself in my keeping!"

Abigail turned pale. "Oh! They do not think—"

Henry barely noticed her interruption, such was his agitation. "And of course when I demanded to know who had told him such things, he made a vague excuse and trundled back into his shop. I sought to pursue him further on the matter, but a queue of people had gathered, and I did not wish to discuss it in front of them." He brushed his hair back, angrily. "I imagine it was *him*, the man from the church. The one who, who . . ." He sighed in irritation. "I will find him, Aunt. I will. I must."

Abigail clutched her necklace. "Oh, Henry. Oh, we should have been more careful. This could ruin your reputation, your ministry - your future prospects!"

Henry started. He fixed a bewildered gaze on his aunt.

"Aunt Abigail, you do not understand! If the *villagers* are speculating about her, why, the news could travel still further." He looked as though he had been punched in the gut. "Aunt, it could reach Millforte's own ears - and then what?!"

At the mention of Millforte's name, Henry's voice grew angry, and his expression darkened into a fierce scowl.

Abigail was speechless. She had never known Henry to be anything but a living example of love and compassion.

She forced herself to speak with a reassurance she was praying to feel. "Do not worry, my dear. No one knows who she really is, or where she has come from. I doubt that speculations from our little village would travel all the way to Millforte's ears."

Again, Henry's face flickered with anger at the mention of the man's ominous name.

"But, if by some chance it ever did," Abigail continued. "God would give us the grace we needed to endure it."

Henry's face softened a little, much to Abigail's relief.

"What about Ruby? What do we tell her?"

Abigail thought for a moment, the memory of Ruby draining the wine glass fixed in her mind. News like this would only cause needless panic.

"We need not tell her anything. I hardly think any good would come of it."

She looked at Henry, unsure whether or not to voice her deepening concerns.

"What is it, Aunt?" His agitation had somewhat dissipated, though it seemed it would take very little to ignite it again.

"Henry, you know how much I admire your kindness in bringing Ruby here. I am glad she is no longer with Millforte, truly I am." She swallowed hard, her voice betraying her. Weakness and worry spilled out where she wanted to sound firm and reasonable.

Henry tapped his foot, somewhat distracted.

"I only want you to be careful, my dear."

"Careful?"

"She is from a very different sphere. She does not think as we do. She has been treated very unkindly."

"I know that, Aunt." Henry looked bewildered and sincere. "That is why I brought her here. I want to help her. She does not deserve to be anyone's slave."

The expression that subsequently flashed onto his face indicated that he had spoken more frankly than intended.

"No one does, my dear." She paused, wondering how she could make Henry understand what she meant. "All I am saying is that you must try to understand that she may do or say things that will disappoint you. She is wounded, Henry. And although she has been removed from her damaging surroundings, the wounds will remain for some time. Perhaps, even forever."

Henry stared at Abigail, exasperation and insult emanating from his countenance.

"Must you speak with such hopelessness, Aunt? I do confess, I am surprised that your opinion of both Ruby and myself is quite so low. I am not naive, Aunt. I know she is wounded. I know that the road before her is not an easy one, but that is why she is here - that we might walk with her and give her the support that she needs. I do not expect her to be perfect, Aunt. No one is so! But she is no worse than you or I, and I do not appreciate your implication that she is!"

"Henry! I did not say that!"

"No, Aunt, but you did imply it. Do you not see? Disappoint me? She cannot disappoint me, because I know who she truly is, deep down, and that matters more than the superficial social standing that her circumstances have taken from her!" He paused, breathing out frustration. The anger in his voice dissolved into weariness. "I had *hoped* you would see her the same way."

"I do, my dear. I did not mean that we were more important or more valuable than she is. Not at all." She paused. Her voice wavered slightly, despite her attempt to stifle it from doing so. "I only wish to protect you, as you wish to protect her."

Henry frowned. "Protect me? Aunt, she means no harm! You do not need to protect me from her. She is the one who needs protection - from *them*, from . . . from *him*."

Again, his voice deepened to almost a growl as he referred to Millforte.

Abigail said nothing. She sighed, concern filling her with each passing moment. Earlier, she'd suspected some kind of attachment on Ruby's part. Now, she saw one on Henry's, too.

Deep down, she sensed it would not be long until Henry's views - and heart - were shattered. Now that the villagers were actively discussing Ruby's presence at the parsonage, a storm might break.

A storm that could destroy everything.

THE SHARP, loud call of a bird from outside summoned Ruby to her window. She lifted her gaze and looked out the window, searching the branches of the oak tree that stood not too far away. Her eyes lit upon the warbler, and she stood there watching it intently. A soft smile crept onto her face.

In a flash, the bird took flight, and was gone. Ruby gazed up into the sky, marvelling at the intricacies of nature.

She gave a happy sigh as she bounced back to her wingback chair and resumed her embroidery.

Abigail had been teaching her various accomplishments every day for a few weeks now, and Ruby was delighted to learn the new skills. Embroidery was her favourite.

She and Abigail had spoken at length about the different

options for her future. She could be a lady's companion, or maybe even a governess, if she brushed up on her reading.

For the first time she could remember, she awoke and went to sleep - and lived every moment in between - with a sense of hope. It was wonderful.

And most wonderful of all was the sense of being useful. As part of her education, Abigail assigned various tasks to Ruby after teaching her how to do them. It made her heart soar to know that Abigail - and Henry - trusted her.

Upon hearing a knock at the door, she placed her embroidery accoutrements on the side table and moved to answer it.

Henry's quizzical face peered at her. Ruby smiled inwardly, glad that he had returned to the parsonage. She felt entirely at ease with him. It was as though he saw past everything that she had been and saw her as she hoped one day to be.

At times, her insecurities triumphed, and she wanted to hide from him, to shield his pure eyes from the filth she feared still entangled her. Yet, other times - like now - she simply felt glad to see her new friend.

"Good afternoon, Ruby." There was something different in his face - some strange expression she had not seen before. Uneasy doubt surfaced in her mind, but she triumphed in suppressing it.

"Good afternoon, Mr. Stratton," she replied. How pleasant he looked, despite his frown.

He stood respectfully at the threshold. "I wondered if you might like to accompany me for a short stroll in the garden?"

"Oh, yes, thank you. That would be lovely."

She cautiously gathered up the fur-lined pelisse that was draped over her dressing chair, along with a shawl.

Henry smiled, looking like himself again, and turned to lead the way.

Neither spoke as they descended the stairs and made their way out into the crisp air. The sights and scents of the parsonage's garden took Ruby's breath away each time she encountered them. Such vivid freshness, bursting all around with imminent life.

"Are you warm enough, Ruby?" asked Henry, turning to see where she was. He had walked ahead, seemingly deep in thought.

She tucked a stray strand of hair behind her ear and pulled her shawl tighter around her shoulders. "Yes," she said, with a smile. "And you?"

He looked agitated, though whether by cold or worry she could not tell. "Yes, I am fine."

They started walking, silent once again.

A delicate scent drifted past on the cool breeze. Sometimes, being exposed in the open still unnerved her a little, but not when she was safe at Henry's side.

Ruby glanced at him. His brow was furrowed as he stared at a patch of ivy on the parsonage wall, his gaze intense yet vacant.

What was he thinking of? Miss Acton, perhaps?

Ruby looked around, imagining Miss Acton walking through the garden hand-in-hand with Henry.

It hurt.

It surprised her to realise it, but her chest tightened with grief to think of Henry and Miss Acton becoming more than they seemed to be at present.

Henry stopped walking again. "I meant to say - you truly excelled in the floral composition you arranged for the breakfast table centrepiece."

"Oh, thank you."

Henry nodded. "You have quite a skill with floristry. How is your pillowcase coming along?"

"I am almost finished embroidering one of them," Ruby said. "And then, I shall make another to match."

She smiled, looking up at him. The expression of admiration on his face rendered her speechless. His eyes were so deep she felt as though she could fall right into them.

She stared at him, every word escaping her. What *was* this?

"Well, regardless of how rapidly your skills are developing, you have my word - we will not allow you to take just *any* position. And we will certainly ensure that you do not take any until you are fully ready and able to do so."

Ruby smiled gratefully.

She trusted Henry implicitly. Never in her life had she been able to trust a man. But Henry wasn't like other men.

In truth, all the others ought to be like *him*. She had met man after man of the very worst kind. But Henry was a gentleman.

Perhaps that's why she was feeling all sorts of strange and unfamiliar things. Before Henry, she couldn't remember ever meeting such a gentleman. That must be it.

What else could it be?

CHAPTER 13

THE UNWANTED VISITOR

A FEW UNEVENTFUL WEEKS LATER, Henry left the parsonage to visit some of his congregants in town. Abigail went with him this time. Browne was still home, as was Bessie, though both were busy with their duties.

Ruby had started a new embroidery project - a surprise for Abigail, to thank her for all her kindness.

Abigail and Ruby spent a lot of time together, talking and working, and most days Abigail would read the Bible to her and pray with her.

Ruby wished she could have faith as deep as Abigail's. But she still felt too dirty for God and still struggled to understand why God would want her to love the people who had made her feel so dirty.

She heard a faint clip clop of horses' hooves. Darting to her window, she heard the sound grow louder and louder until finally the carriage burst into view.

It was Henry's carriage. She had not expected he and Abigail to return so soon. Yet, part of her was glad they had.

She stood, watching from her window as Browne attended

the carriage - settling the horses, opening the door, arranging the steps.

Abigail emerged first. As soon as her feet touched the ground she began pacing a tiny circuit. She reminded Ruby of a moth she had seen in the garden one day. Flitting and fluttering, unable to settle or be still for more than a moment.

Fear crept up Ruby's spine.

Why were they back so soon? And why was Abigail so agitated?

Henry emerged, too, and even from Ruby's distant, distorted angle, his pallor was noticeable. His fists were clenched by his side, his frame held stiff and firm.

Abigail repeatedly flitted back and forth toward him and away from him, saying something each time she moved closer to him. Henry sighed deeply enough for Ruby to see. He shook his head and turned his face away from Abigail, his narrowed eyes staring down the path toward the road they'd just travelled.

Ruby blinked, hoping she might be reading them all wrong. But she wasn't. Something must have happened.

Something bad.

A soft knock on Ruby's door startled her.

"Miss Ruby?" Bessie's gentle voice called from the hallway.

Ruby instructed herself not to worry as she opened the door.

"I am told to let you know, Miss Ruby, that Mr. Stratton and Mrs. Jones have returned and have requested your company in the drawing room. Right away."

Smoothing her dress, she joined Bessie in the hallway. With each stair she descended, Ruby tried to convince herself that all was well. Perhaps Henry and Abigail had merely quarrelled in the carriage. Perhaps the people they had been intending to visit had not been home.

Too soon, Ruby and Bessie reached the drawing room. Bessie entered first. Ruby followed, trepidation slowing her steps.

As soon as she saw Henry and Abigail, her fears were confirmed.

All was most certainly not well.

Henry stood with his arm on the mantelpiece, his jaw and fists clenched. His face wore a tight frown, deeper than any Ruby had seen on him before.

Abigail sat in one of the wingback chairs, her hands still as fluttery and fidgety as a garden moth.

Bessie took her leave, and Abigail raised worried eyes to look at Ruby.

Ruby could hardly breathe. Surely Henry and Abigail must be able to hear her heart thudding, deafening as it was. She searched for words and the strength to speak, but she had none.

Henry turned, withdrawing his arm from the mantelpiece and pulling himself up straight. He fixed his eyes on Ruby's.

"Ruby. . ."

He walked toward her, swallowing hard, a strange look of concern mixed with resolve in his dark, deep eyes.

He stood before her and sighed. Trembling consumed her, though she tried to force herself to be still.

"Ruby, Aunt Abigail and I arrived in town. I went to see another congregation member who is ill, while Aunt Abigail went to visit Mr. and Mrs. Penton."

"Henry," Abigail stood up and rushed to his side.

Henry gave her a firm, quick look, then fixed his gaze back on Ruby.

"Ruby," he half said, half breathed. "There are . . . whisperings."

Ruby felt sick. Suspecting something dreadful was one thing, but hearing it confirmed was quite another.

A tremble worked its way into Henry's voice. "The village is ablaze with gossip. There are . . . questions, and . . . speculations about . . . your presence here. We first became aware of them a number of weeks ago, but we had hoped they would all come to naught. Alas, they have persisted incessantly."

"The man," Ruby choked.

Henry's jaw grew tighter still. "I suspect so, yes. No one I have spoken with saw a man speak to you at church, so I am still unaware of the cad's identity."

"Henry," Abigail interjected mournfully.

Henry gritted his teeth. "Well, how dare he, Aunt! When I find out who he is, I—"

"That is enough, Henry - saying such things will not help anyone!"

Ruby stumbled backward, groping for something to hold onto to steady herself.

Henry reached out and caught her by the elbow, leading her gently to a backless brocade seat. She perched on it, grabbing tightly to each of its curled sides.

Henry knelt down in front of her. Abigail flitted back and forth beside them.

"I promised you that you would be safe here," he said in agony of voice and face. Ruby hated seeing and hearing such pain from a man who usually had such peace.

"I do not know . . ." He shook his head, resting his face in his palm momentarily. He sighed, a deep and shaky sigh.

Gathering his composure again, he looked at Ruby. "I

promise you this - I will do whatever I must to ensure that you are safe."

Ruby felt light-headed. Her breathing was as rapid as her heartbeat and as shallow as her hope.

"We have been discussing what ought to be done. We spoke of nothing else the entire journey home." said Abigail.

Ruby's eyes filled with hot, stingy tears.

"We think that perhaps, the best thing," Abigail continued, "Well, that it would be best for you to go and stay with my brother-in-law and his family."

Ruby's arms went weak.

"They live a five-day's journey from here. They have a fairly large property. It would be much easier to conceal you there than it is here. And they could see that you are trained as a lady's companion. It is not a situation without its benefits . . ."

The tears in Ruby's eyes spilled out, streaking down her cheeks.

Henry, who had been pacing by the window the entire time Abigail had been speaking, turned away on seeing Ruby's reaction, his head dropping low, his forehead pressing against the glass.

"I should never have come," Ruby croaked faintly.

Henry whirled around. "No! Ruby, do not say that." He knelt in front of her again in a flash. "You must not ever say that, or even think it. This is where you belong."

Tears flowed freely down Ruby's face. "No." Her whole body shook. "I do not belong anywhere!"

Henry's eyes grew moist. "Yes, you do." His voice rose with fervour. "You belong here. You belong wi—" He stopped abruptly, a strange look dawning in his eyes.

Ruby stared at him, a small flicker of hope kindled by his

passionate sincerity. Time seemed to stop. She would stay forever in this moment if she could.

"With *us* . . ." he said, his eyes blinking, his mouth slightly gaping.

"You will be safe at my brother-in-law's house," Abigail announced somewhat sharply, shattering the tender atmosphere between Henry and Ruby. "I have instructed Browne to ready the carriage and gather everything required for the journey."

Henry and Ruby turned to look at Abigail. She had stopped her flitting and was looking at them both quite firmly. Her eyes met Ruby's.

"You leave tomorrow morning. I shall send a letter with you for my brother-in-law, explaining everything."

Abigail stepped closer to them, her expression softening slightly.

"I shall ask Bessie to help you pack some dresses and things to take with you."

Ruby's heart sank. She really was leaving. Leaving Henry, leaving the safe walls of the parsonage. Would she ever be free from the threat of discovery? How long until the whisperings would catch up with her at the new house? Perhaps her entire life was to be spent on the run.

Then the worst thought of all staggered into her mind.

Would she ever see Henry again?

RUBY SAT on the chair beside the fireplace in her room. It wasn't really her room, though. Not anymore. Tomorrow she would have to leave it behind.

Bessie was busy smoothing and folding dresses into pretty cases. Ruby had tried to help her until the reality of what was happening had overtaken her. She hadn't been able to see anything through her tears.

"Have a seat, miss, I can manage," Bessie had said kindly, her usual cheery demeanour more subdued.

Ruby watched her as she worked with contented ease. She wished *she* could be a maid here. Then, she would not have to leave Henry, and the villagers would have nothing to whisper about.

Without a word to Bessie, she scrambled to her feet and flew out of the room.

Maybe she wouldn't have to leave him after all.

ABIGAIL WAS STILL in the drawing room, though Henry was nowhere to be seen.

"Ruby!" Abigail exclaimed, startled by Ruby's abrupt arrival.

"Forgive me! But, I had a thought . . ."

Ruby struggled to catch her breath after racing down the stairs.

Abigail walked over to her. "There now, my dear, calm, calm. What is it?"

Ruby hesitated. She did not want to appear ungrateful, but she knew she couldn't leave without trying everything within her reach to stay.

"Perhaps I could . . . if I . . . perhaps, if people thought that I was a maid here . . . Would that, perhaps, settle the whisperings?"

With each word that rushed out of her mouth, Ruby lost more and more confidence in what she was saying. Of course it wouldn't settle the swirling accusations and their implications. What had at first seemed like a spark of hope now seemed an ember of folly.

Abigail's expression reflected Ruby's misgivings.

"A maid?" she asked, her face incredulous. "Ruby . . . this is not a game. No one would believe it. Besides, you have all along been presented as a *guest* of mine, not a servant . . ."

Abigail sighed, seeming frustrated and a little impatient.

"I am sure it must be frightening, going to another place that is unfamiliar, but it must be so. For everyone's sake."

Ruby wondered what had caused the alteration in Abigail's approach to her. There was now distance and wariness where gentleness and softness once had been.

"Forgive me, I . . ." Ruby didn't know what to say. "You have both shown such kindness to me here. And I am so very grateful. I will miss, I will miss you all so—"

Ruby used all her determination to hold back tears.

Abigail's expression softened slightly. "And we will miss you. But it is for your own safety that you must go. It is the only wise thing to do. It is what is best, for everyone."

Everyone. That was the second time Abigail had used the word.

Realisation dawned on Ruby. She was not being sent away solely for her own safety. Clearly, Abigail felt it was what was best for herself and Henry, too.

"I am sorry if my residence here has harmed you or Mr. Stratton. I would never wish it so."

Abigail shifted about awkwardly. "You have not harmed *me*." She paused. "But, in truth, I do fear for Henry's reputation. I only hope that it survives all this."

Hearing Abigail admit what Ruby suspected felt like a kick in the stomach. Yet, even worse was the possibility that Henry's whole livelihood could be ruined by Ruby's presence.

Speechless, she turned and rushed back to her room. As

the tears rolled down her face, she resolved in her heart to do something that she knew would break it.

If leaving the parsonage would save Henry's reputation, there was no question.

Tomorrow, she must leave.

THE NEXT MORNING, everything was ready. All that remained was for Ruby to say her goodbyes to everyone at Shiloh Hall.

She glanced in her mirror. Dark circles and puffy skin around her eyes evidenced her lack of sleep, owing to the awareness that it was her last night at the parsonage.

Nausea permeated her entire being. Every limb and muscle felt heavy and stiff.

How could she say goodbye? How could she look into those eyes and bid him farewell, knowing she might never see him again?

The knock on her door was a familiar and welcome sound, despite her grief. She would miss this room, the little habits and customs of the parsonage that had quickly become so dear to her.

She opened the door slowly.

There he was.

"Good morning, Ruby." Henry's own eyes looked tired and rimmed with red. "I was hoping you might care to join me for a short stroll through the garden before . . ." His voice trailed off.

Ruby looked at him. It was clear from his stance and his tone that he was trying to appear upbeat, but she easily saw the sorrow in his eyes.

"That would be lovely, thank you." Ruby replied, forcing

every bit of energy within her into her voice.

"It is bright today." Henry said in faux cheerfulness.

"That is good." said Ruby, gathering her pelisse.

As the heavy white door closed behind them and they descended the stairs, they both sighed. Simultaneously.

Henry looked at Ruby. Ruby returned his gaze.

The depth of misery in his eyes made her want to weep.

An unspoken understanding seemed to pass between them, as it had so many times since they had met.

As they both resumed walking, silently making their way to the garden, Ruby had a sense, deep down, of how profoundly they would miss each other.

ABIGAIL WAS SEALING the letter to her brother-in-law, when Bessie entered the drawing room.

"Pardon me, Mrs. Jones, but there is a man at the door . . . asking for Miss Ruby . . ."

The colour drained instantly from Abigail's disbelieving face. She asked Bessie to repeat herself, hoping her mind had clouded Bessie's words with her own fears.

Alas, Bessie repeated the message with no alteration.

With a silent prayer, Abigail rose and followed Bessie to the door, eager to forego the traditional customs if it meant neither their plans or safety would be disrupted.

With a deep breath, she greeted the man in a cold, impassive voice. He was enormous. The first thing she noticed, other than his vast height, was the coldness in his eyes.

"Good afternoon, madam. I believe you have something of mine. I'm here to take it back."

For a moment, she thought she had misheard him. But a sickening lurch in her stomach assured her she had not.

Something. He had actually referred to a human being as a 'something'. And an 'it'. Indignation rose in her chest.

"I do not believe I have anything of yours, Mister . . .?" she replied, forcing an air of oblivion and cheerfulness despite feeling the complete opposite.

The man smiled, though it looked more like a grimace.

"No doubt you know my name, madam."

Abigail exhaled impatiently. "I am sorry, but you appear to have the wrong address. Do have a pleasant day."

She pushed the heavy wooden door, eager to shut him out in every possible way, but just before it reached its latch, the man raised a huge hand, stopping it in its tracks.

Anxiety fluttered in Abigail's throat as she pushed the door with both hands, but to no avail. She was no match for his brutish strength. He flung the door open with astonishing ease, almost knocking Abigail down in the process.

"I have no wish to be nasty, but I am not leaving without my property."

"Mr. Millforte, you are trespassing on private property. I am asking you politely to leave at once." Abigail's voice was firm and unwavering, unlike her nerves.

Then, she realised - and regretted - her mistake.

"So you *do* know who I am." He grinned. Abigail had never seen such a chilling display of what ought to have been positive emotion, yet looked more like a mocking hunger for destruction.

"As I said," he continued, "I am not leaving without my property. Would you be a dear and fetch her for me? I shall wait somewhere more comfortable, if you would be so kind as to see me in."

Abigail knew, especially now that she had accidentally

acknowledged who he was, there was no way he would leave without Ruby.

She quickly weighed her options. She had no chance to succeed in overpowering him physically - that much was out of the equation entirely. Even if Bessie fetched Browne and Henry, they would hardly succeed against him either, even if they were to resist him in unison.

It was too late. He was in, closing the door behind him. Abigail tried not to show how unnerved she really was.

It was time to employ more subtle tactics.

"Right through here, please," she said, scarcely believing her own words, as she walked toward the drawing room. She led the way, glancing behind to ensure he was following her. She could see his bulk moving close behind. Once they were in the drawing room, she motioned for him to sit.

Bessie was still there, a worried look marring her usually cheerful complexion.

"Bessie, do fetch Mr. Stratton, and ask Browne to bring Mr. Millforte some tea, please."

How she longed to be the one to find Henry and warn him, but she knew the last thing she could do was leave Millforte alone. She had no trust in him, and the worst of it was, she knew she was not being irrational.

Bessie's eyes betrayed her worry to both Abigail and Millforte, as she turned quickly and left the room.

In the garden, Henry and Ruby were strolling contentedly, their dark moods lightened by the mutual delight they found in one another's company.

"This is my favourite flower," Henry said, pointing at a viola.

"Really?" smiled Ruby. "I did not know that men had favourite flowers." Her smile lessened a little. "I am sorry. Gentlemen, I mean."

Henry ignored her faux pas and proceeded to tell her that gentlemen did indeed have favourite flowers - and colours, and that favourite delicacies were not the exclusive property of ladies.

Ruby could not help but chuckle at his mock-serious, injured tone.

She turned sharply, hearing hurried footsteps behind her, her laugh cut short in surprise.

She relaxed. It was only Bessie.

"Bessie? What is the matter?" Henry seemed to instantly detect something in Bessie's demeanour that Ruby only noticed upon closer examination.

"Oh, Mr. Stratton!" She seemed to abruptly stop herself from saying something, as though she were standing too close to the edge of an abyss and had jumped backward for fear of falling in. She sighed, evidently trying to calm and compose herself.

"Forgive my intrusion, sir. Your aunt wishes to see you, straight-away."

Henry wasted no time hanging about. "Come, Ruby," he said, starting down the path back toward the house.

"No!"

He spun on his heel and stared, stupefied, at Bessie, from whose lips the frantic cry had burst forth.

Ruby was staring at her too, imagining the very worst, yet hoping against hope that there was nothing of danger in this alarming urgency.

"Bessie? But, why should not Ruby accompany me?"

Bessie glanced at Ruby awkwardly, the fear in her eyes

confirming the fear that was growing deep in Ruby's stomach.

"Ohh . . ." Ruby stumbled, her knees weakened by fear. She sank to the ground, her heart pounding, a voice in her head screaming at her to run as fast as she could.

All she could do was hunch there, trembling. She looked imploringly at Bessie, desperate for some sign that she had misunderstood.

"Ruby!" Henry raced to assist her, and when he had ascertained that Ruby was all right, he glanced at Bessie, who was standing with her head in her hands, trembling as Ruby was.

A look of horror dawned on Henry's face. He fixed his gaze on Bessie. When he spoke, his voice was a mere shadow of its usual resonating tone.

"Is Millforte here?"

Shaken, Bessie feebly raised her head and fixed her eyes on Henry. She nodded weakly.

Henry reeled backward, as though on uneven ground. He looked at Ruby, then squeezed his eyes shut as if in a silent prayer. Upon opening them, he fixed his disbelieving gaze on Bessie.

"Bessie - take Ruby with you and head for Sir and Lady Harford's house. Now. Go through the fields, not on the roads. I want you both to hide in their attic until I come for you. Tell them it is urgent, and that I will explain all when I arrive."

Bessie nodded, wiping away her tears.

Henry reached down and pulled Ruby to a stand. She quivered under his touch.

He squeezed her shoulders gently. "I will come for you. Do not—" He choked on his words. "Do not be afraid. It will all be over soon."

Ruby looked into his anguished eyes. None of the words she wanted to say would come forward. They had all left her, and now she feared that Henry might be taken from her, too.

Bessie started to pull her away, but she turned back, grasping for Henry's arm. "Please! Be careful! He will hurt you . . ."

Tears spilled out as she whispered the last word of her warning. Bessie's strong hand clutched her, pulling her away from Henry. Her heart felt like it was tearing in half.

All Ruby could see as they ran was grass, blurred half from their speed and half from her tears. She sobbed openly as they ran through the valley, her heart filled with fear for Henry's safety, as she pictured him coming face to face with Millforte.

CHAPTER 14

A DUEL OF WILLS

As he approached the drawing room, Henry's heart seemed to thud with each step of his boots. Silence filled the halls.

A different kind of silence.

Tranquil as the house usually was, there was an unease in the air today, negativity hovering and lurking everywhere.

He steeled himself as he reached the drawing room doors, silently praying for safety and strength.

As he reached for the door handle, he thought again of Ruby, of how terrified and fragile she had looked on finding out that Millforte had arrived.

Whatever happened, he had two objectives - make Millforte leave, and keep Ruby safe.

Clutching the handle, he whispered a prayer and flung the door open. Striding in to the room, he found Abigail sitting quietly, an expression on her face he had never seen before, and hoped he would never see again.

In the chair opposite hers was a tall, sturdy man, whose

posture and attire displayed his wealth and dominance. The man turned to face Henry on hearing his approach.

"Mr. Stratton?" the rich, gravelly voice enquired knowingly as the man rose to a stand.

Face to face with Millforte, Henry struggled to think coherently. He did not appear as ogre-like as Henry had imagined. He could actually pass for a gentleman. Though, upon closer inspection, there were telltale hints of his sharpness and pride.

"Yes," Henry said, clearing his throat. He stopped himself just in time from saying the visitor's name, reeling inwardly that he might have given away so easily the secret of Ruby's presence. A quick glance at Abigail's expression caused him to wonder if she might have already done so.

"Beautiful day, is it not?" Millforte said, in a voice that sounded like a deep purr. "One always sees the very best of the weather out here in the country. I am a city man, myself, but I find it always enlivens me to reacquaint myself with the fresh air and verdant trees."

His eyes twinkled the whole time he spoke, as though he were moments away from delivering the punchline of some delicious joke.

Henry grew more appalled each passing second. All he wanted to do was flee to the Harfords' house and make sure Ruby was all right. Instead, he was face to face with her tormentor.

He prayed silently that God would somehow help him show grace and mercy to the man instead of the resentment and bitterness building inside him.

"Yes, indeed," Henry replied, the kindness in his voice somewhat more strained than usual. He forced a smile.

Millforte smiled back, his eyes still twinkling as his lips stretched wide across his face, his teeth lining into view.

A predator's smile, thought Henry. *Like a jackal just before the kill.*

"How may I help you, sir?"

It pained him to call him sir, knowing what he was. But God was his example, and God showed kindness even when it was not deserved.

Millforte fixed his gaze at Henry's eyes, the traces of his jackal-smile still lingering on his face. "I think you know . . ." he said, his tone sounding much like a growl.

Henry stifled. "Most people who visit me wish to speak on ecclesiastical matters - matters of faith."

"Do I look like a man of faith to you?" Millforte retorted.

"The gift of salvation is freely offered to all," stated Henry.

"We both know why I'm here, preacher man," snapped Millforte, impatiently. "You have something that belongs to me."

His growl had turned almost to a roar, and the twinkling in his eyes had given way to a cruel glint.

Suddenly, and with nauseating vividness, Henry comprehended just how vicious Millforte was capable of being, as he remembered details Ruby had told him before her escape.

His peaceable intentions crumbled.

"How dare you show your face here?" Henry said through gritted teeth.

He tensed, wishing he could unspeak his words. If he didn't already, now Millforte knew for certain that Ruby was there.

Millforte's scowl deepened. "Where is she?" He paced the room, alert and predatory.

"Who?" Henry croaked, lost for words.

Millforte whirled around to face him. "You know full well! Ruby, that cowering *whore!*"

He roared the last word, and Henry's outrage roared louder within his own heart. It took all his strength to stand his ground instead of launching a physical attack on the scoundrel before him.

"How dare you? You miserable blackguard! No man should ever speak of a woman that way!"

"Gentlemen, please! I must ask that you both hold your tongues before either of you say yet more that you will later regret," said Abigail, her presence almost forgotten amidst the emerging duel of wills.

"I regret nothing," growled Millforte, " . . . save that my own property has been stolen from me. And by a clergyman, too!" He laughed in contempt, his dark brow still furrowed in a scowl.

"She is not your *property!*" bellowed Henry with a short pause between each word, his cheeks red with indignance.

"You and I both know that she is. She owes her miserable life to me! And I demand to know where she is."

Henry was pale with anguish and rage. "Her life, *sir*, is most certainly not miserable. Her life is precious to God, as all lives are." Shifting his focus to his faith helped dissipate some of his anger.

"She is barely worthy of her life, as well you know. And be under no delusion about this - the longer you conceal her whereabouts from me, the more she will suffer for it." He leaned closer to Henry, his breath noisy and threatening. "Now. Where is she?"

Henry lurched forward, pushing Millforte backward. "You shall not touch her! You shall not lay one wicked finger on her ever again!"

"Henry!" shrieked Abigail.

Millforte immediately countered Henry's attack by punching him in the stomach.

Henry sank to his knees, coughing. His lungs felt empty, his throat choking on dry air.

Millforte picked him up by his coat and pulled him close, breathing threats in Henry's face.

"You may not realise who you are dealing with, my boy. But if you insist on delaying me and insulting me, you will soon find out."

He shoved Henry backward, letting go of his coat.

Henry, still coughing and straining to breathe, looked up at Millforte's threatening scowl. Fresh resolve strengthened him.

"You can—" He started coughing again, still winded. "You can do whatever you . . . whatever you like to me—" He coughed again. "You will never . . . be near her again, I assure you."

Millforte deepened his scowl, evidently riled by Henry's challenging words.

The two men looked at each other defiantly. Then, like a flash, Millforte swung his giant fist at Henry's jaw, filling the room with a loud, sickening crack.

"Henry!" Abigail shrieked again.

Agony flooded Henry's skull. He stumbled backward, disoriented momentarily by the blinding pain.

"Give her to me!" Millforte demanded.

"You shall never see her again!" Henry shouted in agony.

"Must I really beat you to a pulp over a worthless strumpet?" Millforte taunted.

Henry gritted his teeth and lunged at him again, swinging his own fist upward at Millforte's face.

Dodging the blow, Millforte grabbed Henry's arm, then jerked it downward.

"Ah!" Henry cried out, pain twisting up into his shoulder.

Millforte's growl invaded Henry's ear. "Where is she?"

Henry swung at him again, without success.

"Listen to me, boy - I *will* find her. So I suggest you save yourself a great deal of pain and give her to me *now*." Millforte practically shouted the last word.

"I care nothing for pain." Henry's voice shook with passion and determination. "You may beat me again - you may kill me if you wish! But you will never, *ever* hurt her again."

"You would really give up your noble life for her?" Millforte asked, incredulous amusement lifting his brow. "She is worthless!"

"She is precious! I would gladly give my life for hers!" Henry shouted.

Millforte smiled, then chuckled. Soon, his chuckle was a full-blown cackle.

"Oh, no . . . Really? Oh, this is too delightful for words! The holy man has fallen for the harlot!"

Henry stood motionless, staring at Millforte, endless thoughts swirling through his mind. He gaped, clamouring for words.

Abigail and Browne came rushing into the room. Neither Millforte nor Henry had noticed Abigail leave not long after Millforte had punched Henry in the face.

"You, sir, must leave at once," Browne stated calmly yet sternly.

"Henry! Are you all right?" Abigail fussed as she rushed to his side. He gave her an upward nod before turning his eyes back to Millforte.

"I will leave when my property has been restored to me," Millforte said, mockingly.

Henry's teeth gritted. A surge of protectiveness overwhelmed him, stronger than anything he had felt before.

He couldn't stop himself. "She is not your property," he muttered.

A cruel smile stretched across Millforte's scoffing face. "Oh, my dear boy . . . you believe she is yours?" he chuckled. "Or at least, you want her to be . . ."

Henry's face flushed. "She is not mine, she is God's. He created her. He—"

"Spare me your self-righteous subterfuge! You want her all for yourself. I imagine the parsonage bed gets rather lonely, and you think she is just the thing to—"

"How dare you!" Henry interrupted, his teeth grinding together, every inch of his body trembling with emotion.

Millforte's eyes glinted cruelly. "Isn't it funny, preacher boy - you long to share Ruby's bed, and I already have. Numerous times, in fact . . ."

Henry's lips contorted in a seething grimace as he launched himself at Millforte.

"Mr. Stratton, please," Browne urged, grabbing Henry's arm in an attempt to pull him back.

Browne's intervention threw Henry off course. Millforte moved back.

As Browne's grip on Henry's arm loosened, Henry launched himself forward, raising his knee with all his might where he hoped he would hurt Millforte most.

"Oof!" Millforte bent over, his lips pressed tightly shut.

Raising his head, his eyes locked on Henry's. "You've asked for it, boy. Now you will find out how powerful an enemy I can be . . ." he growled.

Millforte straightened up and barged past Henry, knocking him sideways as he headed straight for the drawing room door.

Henry immediately followed him. "Where do you think

you are going?" he asked, his teeth still clamped shut in fervour.

Without stopping or turning, Millforte barked, "To find my *property!*"

He bolted up the stairs. Henry followed. Even though Ruby was safe elsewhere, he did not want Millforte anywhere near her room. It was a safe place - the only safe place she had known for a long time. He did not want it sullied with Millforte's possessive presence as her old room had been.

"Ruby!" Millforte bellowed.

Henry shuddered. He hated hearing Ruby's name spoken by such an insolent bully.

Millforte swung the heavy wooden door of Ruby's room wide open. Glancing inside, he gave a frustrated sigh, before racing down the hallway to the next door. Room after room he found empty, and soon there were no more doors to open.

"Where is she?" he seethed, turning to face Henry.

"That is not your concern," said Henry. His voice was strong with resolve, though every fibre of his being shook with emotion.

"Do you really think you can win this?" said Millforte, his eyes narrow and full of hatred.

"Win?" Henry shook his head in confusion. "I am not playing a game. Ruby is not some trophy or trifle to claim!"

Millforte's lip curled into a sneer. "Yet, you wish you could claim her as your own . . ."

Henry gulped. "She belongs to God, as every—"

Millforte interrupted him in a loud, bellowing scream. "She belongs to *me!*"

He moved closer to Henry. "Now, for the last time, boy," he said, practically spitting at Henry. "Where . . . is . . . she?"

Henry was appalled. His disgust filled him with renewed

courage. "You are mad . . . I pity you, Mr. Millforte. I do. Your soul is frightfully dark."

Millforte frowned, taken aback.

"But you are mad if you think for one second that I would ever permit you to go anywhere near her," Henry continued, his voice clear and firm.

He leaned in to Millforte, his gaze unblinkingly fixed upon the intruder's cold, incredulous eyes. "You will *never* see her again."

With that, Henry turned and headed for the stairs. As he reached the top step, he turned back to Millforte. "Now, I shall ask you one last time. Please leave. Immediately."

"Why, you little—"

Millforte lunged at Henry, pinning him against the bannister, his back bending across the handrail.

"Ah!" Henry felt that his back was stretched to breaking point. He clawed at Millforte with his fingers, succeeding in poking one of his eyes.

"Mmh!" Millforte grunted, pulling Henry toward him and smashing his head into Henry's forehead.

A jarring pain radiated through Henry's skull. He elbowed Millforte in the stomach though it seemed to have little effect. He aimed his knee again at Millforte's crotch, but Millforte dodged him and wrapped a thick arm around Henry's neck, pulling him back against his chest.

Henry clutched Millforte's strong arm with both hands, trying desperately to ease the crushing suffocation. He thanked God that Ruby was not the one suffering Millforte's cruelty.

Millforte relaxed his arm. Henry gasped, his vision spinning. Before he could recover himself, Millforte grabbed Henry by the coat collars and drove him straight over to the top of the stairs.

"Perhaps it is you who will never see your little harlot again," Millforte said, glee and anger strangely entwined in his eyes.

Henry, gasping for breath, opened his mouth to speak just as Millforte bashed his head into Henry's forehead a second time and raised his heavy knee into Henry's stomach.

Henry buckled over, agony consuming him. Suddenly, all he felt was Millforte's large, strong hands on his side.

Without hesitation, Millforte shoved Henry with all his might.

Henry grappled in vain for the bannister.

Winded and wounded, intermittent surges of pain shot through Henry as he tumbled rapidly down the flight of stairs.

He heard Abigail shriek his name just as everything went black.

"HENRY!"

Abigail threw herself at her nephew's limp body, which lay in a heap at the bottom of the staircase. Blood trickled across his face.

Browne nudged and addressed him, but to no avail.

"What have you done?" Abigail cried, looking up the stairs to Millforte. He stood proudly on the top step, as one who had conquered a mountain. His face was twisted in a satisfied smirk, yet his eyes looked devoid of all feeling.

"Henry! Henry, can you hear me?" Abigail screeched between sobs.

Millforte slowly and steadily picked his way down the stairs, his shiny boots coming to rest beside Henry.

"You will all be sorry, I promise you that."

Abigail looked up at him through tear-filled eyes. She shook her head as tears rolled down her horrified face.

"I shall have her, one way or another," he hissed. "And when I return, you will wish you had given her to me this time."

He crumpled his chin into a determined sneer and kicked Henry forcefully and swiftly in the stomach.

"No!" Abigail screamed, her cry giving way to bitter sobs.

As Millforte swirled past them, Abigail cradled Henry's head in her arms, her anguished howls echoing down the empty hall.

CHAPTER 15

DARK VIGIL

"WOULD you care for some tea, Bessie?"

"Yes, please," said Bessie, a little sheepishly.

Lady Harford smiled. She shifted her gaze to Ruby, her smile fading a little.

"And you? Care for some tea?"

Ruby shook her head and said nothing. Decorum called for an apology and eye contact, but she had the strength of heart for neither.

Lady Harford left the room. She was a very matter-of-fact woman. Not the most likely accomplice to hide a maid and a prostitute, yet she thought so highly of Henry and Abigail, she had immediately agreed to assist the two girls, despite her apparent confusion.

Ruby stared with vacant eyes at her hands, folded in her lap. Her body still trembled, her mind racing. The sick knot she had felt in her stomach had completely engulfed her.

Bessie said something to her, but she didn't even hear what it was. All she could think of was Henry. It was agonising to imagine him in Millforte's company.

Ruby knew too well how possessive and abusive the man could be. She shuddered to think what he would say - or do - to Henry when he discovered she was nowhere to be found in the parsonage.

Please help him, she prayed silently, new tears tracing the paths of the ones that had dried onto her cheeks.

"Try not to worry, Miss Ruby," Bessie said gently. "Mr. Stratton said he would come for us soon."

Ruby glanced with weary eyes at Bessie. It was obvious from the worried crease in Bessie's brow that she was offering more hope than she felt.

Every noise outside startled Ruby. When would Henry arrive? It had been so long since he had been strolling with her in the garden. Dusk was falling now. She could feel the evening chill wafting underneath the door.

"Is he really very dreadful, miss?" Bessie asked, her voice hushed and hesitant.

The sick feeling in Ruby's stomach lurched upward as Millforte's image appeared in her mind. A heavy, cold feeling wrapped around her.

Many silent minutes passed. With fresh tears in her eyes, Ruby met Bessie's apprehensive gaze and nodded.

Bessie sighed. "I do hope—"

The door opened and Sarah, Lady Harford's maid, bustled in with the tea tray, unwittingly interrupting Bessie's lament.

But Ruby knew the rest of Bessie's sentence. And she fully agreed in her heart.

I do hope everyone at Shiloh Hall is safe.

LATER, Sarah returned with blankets and cushions, forming them into makeshift beds for Bessie and Ruby. She had cleared the tea tray away, which had consisted of Bessie's empty cup and one that Ruby had clutched for a long time. Hers had still been full, the tea that brimmed in it as cold as the night air outside.

The attic was mostly weatherproof, but patches here and there allowed a trickle of cold night air to flow in, giving rise to the occasional shiver from both its inhabitants.

Ruby sat in the corner of the attic, pulling her knees tightly to her chest. The blankets draped over her were still cold, so for a time she felt more chilled than when she and Bessie had been sitting on the wooden chairs Lady Harford had instructed to be relocated to the attic upon their arrival.

"Seems we are to be here for the night then," mused Bessie. "I suppose it is safer that way."

"I suppose it is," Ruby echoed.

The sick knot in her stomach and the numb, fluttering in her chest made her think otherwise.

Henry had promised he would come for them that evening. But, perhaps, he really did intend for them to stay there all night so Millforte would not follow him and find her. After all, that's what Millforte and his henchmen did best - preying and lurking.

But it was agony not to know.

The worry that harm might have come to Henry resonated throughout her. All kinds of violent scenarios flashed through her mind, each sending more pangs of fear and dread through her heart.

The faint whinny of a horse in the distance made her breath catch in her chest. Her eyes widened, and her already racing heartbeat charged to an even higher velocity.

Could it be?

"Did you hear that?" Ruby asked, scrambling to her feet.

The attic had no window. She longed to look out, to

search the grounds far and near for the familiar sight of Henry's carriage.

"Hear what, miss?" Bessie said, her voice soft with readiness for slumber.

Ruby listened intently, moving closer to one of the draughty spots to see if she could hear anything else.

"I thought . . ." she whispered, listening, willing the horse to make another sound.

She closed her eyes, pressing back the tears that started to fill them.

A very quiet, rhythmic thudding sound filtered in through the crack in the attic wall.

Ruby's eyes sprang open as she gasped. She pressed her ear right up to the wall, moving around until she felt a small rush of cold air.

Hooves. It *was* hooves.

And a low, dragging sound. The carriage.

It must be.

"He is here!" said Ruby, a little louder than intended.

"Mr. Stratton? Can you hear him?" Bessie rose to her feet now, too.

"I hear the carriage," Ruby gushed, her lips the closest they had been to a smile since she and Bessie had left the parsonage.

Bessie smiled at Ruby. "I knew he would be all right. If Mr. Stratton says he will do something, then you can count on it. He said he would come. And now he has."

Ruby sighed with relief.

Finally, Henry had come.

Bessie and Ruby crept quietly over to the attic door and listened.

And waited.

Ruby's heart pounded as she anxiously wondered what had transpired between Henry and Millforte that afternoon.

"I can't hear anything, miss . . ." said Bessie, her ear pressed against the door.

The silence was deafening as Ruby strained her ears, waiting desperately to hear the kind timbre of Henry's voice.

A low murmuring sound eventually reached their ears. Then, the muffled voice of Lady Harford. From her tone, it was clear she was welcoming someone. The other voice - low and deep - spoke again, followed - or rather, interrupted - by a cry of exclamation from Lady Harford.

Immediately, Ruby and Bessie straightened up to glance at each other in alarm before resuming their listening postures.

"I do not think—" Bessie hushed to listen again. "Why, it almost sounds like—"

"Browne," breathed Ruby.

The attic started to close in on her and the floor swayed.

Bessie glanced at her.

"I would not worry, miss. Perhaps Mr. Stratton thought it would be safer to send Browne to fetch us. Or perhaps something happened with one of the congregation. Mr. Griffith is quite ill, I have heard."

Ruby looked at Bessie with apprehension and uncertainty.

Soft, quiet footsteps in the distance grew louder and closer.

Bessie and Ruby had just stepped back from the door when it swung open. Sarah entered, her face as expressionless and her voice as calm as before.

"Lady Harford sent me to fetch you. Your carriage has arrived."

Bessie smiled and followed Sarah, who had turned to leave the room as soon as she had delivered her message. Ruby trudged behind Bessie, but as they reached the top of the staircase she grabbed Bessie's arm, stopping them both.

"What if it is a trap? What if . . ." Ruby's breathing was fast and heavy. "What if it is not Browne here to take us, but, but . . ."

Bessie, startled as she had been by being so suddenly apprehended by Ruby, smiled softly, pity and reassurance in her eyes and voice.

"Do not fret, miss. I have been working with Browne for years now. It is most definitely his own voice. We can hear it plain now - listen."

The two girls stood, Ruby still clutching Bessie's elbow, mostly to steady her own trembling frame. Listening a moment, they heard Browne speaking, albeit in hushed tones. He was thanking Lady Harford for her assistance. Though, at times, the words were unclear, there was no mistaking his voice.

Ruby sighed, partly relieved yet anxious to know why Henry hadn't come as he had said he would.

Bessie and Ruby hurried down the steps to catch up with Sarah, who had continued walking, unaware of their halting exchange.

Turning a corner, they emerged into the main foyer of the house, where Browne and Lady Harford stood, each silent and pale.

Ruby knew before Browne met her gaze that something was wrong. His lips were pursed tightly together, and his brow was drawn down into a worried frown.

He looked up as he heard them approach. Meeting Ruby's gaze, the sorrowful look in his eyes made the sick knot in her stomach tighten.

"What happened?" she managed to choke out, as the trembling overtook her.

Browne held his mouth even more tightly shut and cleared his throat. "We must away at once, miss. I will explain further in the carriage. We must hurry back."

THE NEXT FEW moments of saying farewell to Lady Harford and stepping out into the crisp night air all seemed to blur together in the background as frightful scenarios flashed through Ruby's mind.

Once inside the carriage, she sat motionless in agonised anticipation of learning the painful truth that was, at that moment, known only to Browne. She glanced at Bessie. There was concern in her brow, yet an element of hope underneath.

Ruby wished she were more like Bessie - always full of cheer and vivacity. But each glance at Browne's sombre face caused only dread to flood her soul.

Browne cleared his throat.

"Mrs. Jones had gone to the door in hopes of dismissing Mr. Millforte, after you were both sent here by Mr. Stratton," he said, glancing at Bessie, then Ruby. Browne spoke more slowly than usual, his tone more hushed.

"Yes, I opened the door to him and went to the drawing room to fetch Mr. Stratton, but Mrs. Jones said he was outside," said Bessie. "So, I went out to tell him and she said she would go to the door. I did not see her after that, as Mr. Stratton instructed me to take Miss Ruby here."

A sudden jolt as the carriage started to move startled Ruby. She clutched the seat, wishing she could close her ears to all the talk about Millforte. She longed only to hear that Henry was unharmed.

"Mrs. Jones tried to send him away, but he pushed his way in."

Ruby's eyes grew wide. Her heart picked up pace.

"Mr. Millforte and Mrs. Jones were in the drawing room when Mr. Stratton returned from the garden. He also tried to get the . . . *gentleman* . . . to leave, without much success."

Browne seemed to almost choke on the word gentleman, his expression clearly highlighting how unsuitable a descriptor he thought it to be.

"Mr. Millforte and Mr. Stratton exchanged some words and Mrs. Jones tried to get them both to calm down."

It hurt to imagine Millforte speaking insolently to such a noble gentleman as Henry. She hated even thinking of them being near each other.

"It was after Mr. Millforte delivered the second blow that Mrs. Jones came to fetch me."

"*Second* blow?" exclaimed Bessie.

Ruby froze. "No!" Her voice was scarcely louder than a whisper.

"I should have been there the whole time. I should not have allowed him . . ."

Browne seemed to be talking more to himself now, his eyes downcast and his head shaking slowly from side to side.

"What happened after Mrs. Jones fetched you?" asked Bessie.

Ruby couldn't get the image of Millforte's mountainous fist colliding with Henry's perfect face out of her mind. She felt sick.

"I told him to leave, but he refused. He and Mr. Stratton continued their fight. Mr. Millforte was . . . provoking Mr. Stratton, and . . . saying things that are not becoming for a gentleman."

He glanced awkwardly at Ruby.

"I tried to pull them apart, but Mr. Stratton launched back into him."

"Mr. *Stratton* did?" Bessie was incredulous.

Ruby's heart flickered. Part of her was glad it hadn't been a one-sided fight with Henry only at Millforte's mercy. Yet, part of her felt guilty. Henry was a gentleman. And a clergyman, at that. It was her fault that he had even been in a situation where his only option had been to fight.

She decided the first thing she would do when they arrived back at the parsonage was apologise to Henry. She hoped he wouldn't hate her for all that had happened.

"Yes. He was very worked up, Mr. Stratton was." Browne paused. A heavy sigh slumped his shoulders. "Then, Mr. Millforte strode out of the drawing room and up the stairs."

Ruby froze again. She shuddered to think what might have happened had she been inside the parsonage, in the room she now thought of as her own.

"Mr. Stratton raced after him, trying to keep him away from your room, miss," he said, diverting his gaze to Ruby.

A pang of gratitude flooded Ruby's heart.

Oh, Henry! How kind he is . . .

"They argued some more, then Mr. Stratton seemed to take a courageous stand against the scoundrel and he . . . he walked to the top of the stairs and instructed him to leave again . . ."

Ruby's stomach lurched. She'd never seen Browne like this.

"Mr. Millforte pushed him and smashed his head into him and almost choked him and then—"

Bessie and Ruby gasped with each new detail that Browne revealed.

"And then . . ." Browne's voice wavered. "They scuffled again, and he beat him a few more times and then he—"

Ruby held her breath.

"He pushed him down the stairs." Browne looked as though he might break down.

Bessie gasped loudly. "Oh! Oh, poor Mr. Stratton! Is he all right?"

Ruby's ears rang. She clutched the seat feebly, her grasp weak.

"I still can see him, tumbling down those steps like a . . . like some sort of doll," Browne said, more to himself than the others.

Ruby tried unsuccessfully to swallow despite the choking sensation in her throat.

"But, is he all right, Browne?" repeated Bessie.

Browne cleared his throat as his awareness of Bessie and Ruby returned.

"Dr. Shaw is with him now, and Mrs. Jones." He looked up at the girls, a heaviness in his demeanour and voice. "He is breathing, but he . . . he fell unconscious at the bottom of the stairs." He cleared his throat again. "He has not opened his eyes, or moved, since."

"Oh!" Bessie exclaimed softly.

All air sucked from Ruby's lungs as each of her muscles tightened in terrified disbelief.

"Does Dr. Shaw expect him to recover?" Bessie hesitantly asked.

Browne sighed heavily. "No one knows." He sighed again, shakily this time. "I believe, however, there is a high chance that . . . that he may not."

A knife struck Ruby right through her very core. A wailing scream burst forth from her just as Bessie began to weep.

Browne closed his eyes, his brow furrowed and his head low.

As grief and panic surged through Ruby, dots flickered in front of her eyes. She froze, forcing herself to listen for a moment to the calming sound of the horses' hooves thudding along the cloddy ground beneath her. She had often tried to focus on something when she felt overwhelmed back at the brothel - the crackling of candles, even noises that had filtered in from the street. Anything that had distracted her from the reality around her.

Bessie's tear-stained face was pale with concern and shock. "What might I do to help when we return?"

Ruby looked at Browne, silent tears trickling down her cheeks. Her head ached, and the dim interior of the carriage hemmed her in.

Browne pursed his lips and sighed. "We must go straight to Mrs. Jones and ask what she would have us do. Perhaps, if Dr. Shaw is still there, he may have some instructions."

He looked up, at Bessie first, then at Ruby. His eyes were filled with sadness.

"We must be strong for Mrs. Jones," he continued. "And for Mr. Stratton. He is a good and gentle man, who has always looked after us well. Now, it is our turn to do our very best to look after him."

Bessie nodded, her face crumpled with emotion.

Ruby sat motionless, gaping at Browne, tears still pouring down her cheeks.

A sudden jolt caused the swaying and rocking to cease.

They had arrived.

As the three of them entered the parsonage, Ruby noticed a tangible difference in the atmosphere. It was filled with a terrible silence, and heaviness weighed on the whole place.

Sombrely, she followed Browne and Bessie down the hall to the staircase. She stopped as she neared the bottom step.

This is where it had happened.

Her gaze wandered across the floor and the bottom few stairs. She noticed their hard edges, stretched unforgivingly from side to side. She was just about to resume walking when her gaze caught a small, red patch on the hallway floor.

Blood. Henry's blood.

Ruby was aghast. Her fear of Millforte momentarily gave way to rage.

How dare he?

Energised by her indignance, Ruby dashed up the stairs to catch up to Browne and Bessie. They were walking along the upstairs hallway, past her own room and past a few more doors that Ruby had never taken notice of before.

A closed door at the end of the hallway marked the end of their route. Browne knocked softly before closing his hand around the brass doorknob and slowly turning it.

Ruby tried to breathe deeply, her heart quivering.

Browne disappeared behind the half-open door, then Bessie.

Her turn.

Not knowing what to expect, Ruby slipped past the door and into the dimly lit room.

A bed jutted out from the far wall, and the first thing Ruby noticed was Abigail sitting beside it. She was curled forward, unmoving, yet obviously not asleep, as every few seconds a gasping sob escaped her chest.

As Ruby lifted her gaze, her heart sank.

There was Henry, lying motionless with his eyes closed. She might have thought he was only sleeping, except for the bandage that was wrapped around his forehead and the patches of blood that had pooled on it in numerous places.

Everything within Ruby wanted to scream.

In her heart, she flew to his side and cupped his face in her hands, begging him to open his eyes. In reality, she could hardly keep herself upright, weakness washing over her at the sight of his lifelessness.

Browne knelt beside Abigail, speaking so softly that Ruby could not hear what he was saying. Still, Abigail uncurled herself enough for Ruby to see that she half-clutched, half-stroked Henry's limp hand.

A man strode into the room. For a split second between hearing him and seeing him, Ruby feared it was Millforte, but as she glanced at him she felt a small measure of relief. It was someone else entirely.

The man walked straight over to the bed, placed his fingers on Henry's neck and slipped a pocket-watch out of his waistcoat. He held his fingers in place as he stared unblinkingly at the watch. Then, a few moments later, he tucked the etched gold timepiece back into his pocket.

"Precisely the same." He paused. "I believe I shall take my leave for now, ma'am," the man said. His voice was gruff and authoritative.

Abigail looked up at him. "Is there anything I can do?" Her voice cracked and she stared at him pleadingly.

"Only keep him warm and comfortable. I shall return at dawn to examine him again."

Abigail sighed. "Thank you, Dr. Shaw."

Ruby watched helplessly as he gathered his bag and hat and headed for the door. She wanted to stop him and insist he stay lest Henry might need him. She wanted to ask him all sorts of questions about how severe Henry's condition was and how she might help him. But she could only return his nod as he walked past and greeted her. And then he was gone, as swiftly as he had entered.

Ruby stared at Henry. She longed to see a smile break out on his face, to see his eyes open and alert. But, apart from the faintly noticeable rise and fall of his chest, he lay there, eerily still. Ruby's stomach twisted as fresh, silent tears rolled down her cheeks.

Abigail and Browne were still speaking quietly. Browne stood and walked over to Bessie. He said something to her, but his hushed tone was still inaudible.

Bessie nodded, her face lined with anxious pity. She turned and slipped quietly out the door.

Browne approached Ruby. She wiped the tears off her cheeks, though they were quickly replaced.

"Miss Ruby," Browne said, his voice barely above a whisper. "I have offered to stay with Mr. Stratton for a time to allow Mrs. Jones to rest awhile. Bessie has gone to fetch her some tea and take it to her in her room. Dr. Shaw has said he will return in the morning, so until then, perhaps, you, myself and Bessie might take turns sitting with Mr. Stratton, as Dr. Shaw has expressly stated that he is not to be left alone. Mrs. Jones has been with him since the . . . since his fall, so, I feel it is only right to relieve her and take a few turns ourselves."

Ruby nodded, the reality of the circumstances drying her throat.

"I will sit with him for now, and in a few hours perhaps you might wish to sit with him while I attend to some household duties?"

Ruby nodded repeatedly. "Yes." There was so much more she wanted to say.

Browne gave a single nod in acknowledgement of their plans. He walked gently back to Abigail and helped her to her feet. Abigail slowly turned and Browne held her arm, leading her toward the door.

Ruby barely recognised Abigail's face. Dark circles lined

the skin under her swollen, bloodshot eyes. Her hair, which was always swept up immaculately, straggled out here and there. She looked haggard and heartbroken.

As Abigail and Browne shuffled closer to the door, guilt and worry flushed over Ruby. She was responsible for this. *All* of this.

If she had never come to the parsonage, Henry would not be hovering between life and death, and Abigail would not be devastated by deep grief.

Abigail met her gaze as she shuffled past. Too many emotions flickered on the older woman's face for Ruby to read her expression.

As Abigail turned her face away from Ruby she burst into tears, burying her face in her hands. Browne placed one arm around her and held her arm with his other hand. He looked worn and worried.

Ruby wanted to reach out to comfort her and apologise.

She wanted to apologise to Henry, too.

Abigail and Browne left the room and Ruby turned to face the bed again. It was only herself and Henry in the room now. The last time it had been just the two of them had been in the garden before Millforte had arrived.

How different the atmosphere was then compared to now.

Alone with him in his pitiful state, she stopped trying to hold herself together. She stepped closer to the bed. Sobs and tears poured incessantly from her. As she reached the foot of the bed, she clutched one of the bedposts and wept.

"Oh . . ."

Upon seeing him more closely, Ruby noticed bruises that she hadn't been able to see from the other side of the room.

A sick realisation washed over her. Those bruises were from *him*.

She had been covered with them many times before, but now Henry had suffered at Millforte's brutish hands, too.

Traumatic memories flashed back into her mind. The grabbing, the hitting, the forcing. She felt as though she might vomit.

Overcome with emotion, she took a few more steps and sank to her knees at the side of the bed. She wept and sobbed until she felt empty.

Tears still streaming down her face, she looked up at Henry. Such a noble man. Such a good man.

He was laid out straight, his arms by his sides, bruises and cuts marring his hands.

Barely able to see through her tears, she instinctively yet cautiously reached out and slipped her fingers behind his. As she carefully closed her grasp around his fingers, her heart squeezed.

"Please . . . please open your eyes!"

Her words trailed off into bitter sobs, and she squeezed his fingers tighter, wrapping her other hand around them now, too.

"I am sorry . . . I am so sorry!"

She could hardly speak due to her choking sobs and wails.

A creak in a floorboard behind her made her jump. Letting go of Henry's hand, she hastened to a stand. As she turned around, she came face to face with Browne.

She fumbled to speak, fearing an accusation of impropriety for her previous actions. But his eyes glistened with compassion as he looked at her tear-stained face.

"There now, miss. It cannot have been very pleasant for you and Bessie in Sir Harford's attic. You ought to get some rest, too. I shall sit with Mr. Stratton awhile."

Ruby glanced back at Henry, unwilling to leave him. She slowly turned back to look at Browne.

"Are not you tired yourself, Mr. Browne? I do not mind staying now if you wish to rest."

Browne smiled sympathetically. "Thank you, miss, but I shall stay a while now. I told Mrs. Jones I would, and I like to keep my word." Browne sighed. "He is an excellent man." He rubbed his brow, shaking his head slightly. "I only hope . . ." His voice trailed off as he pursed his lips and gazed with melancholy at Henry's motionless body.

Ruby looked at the floor, more tears springing to her eyes.

Browne looked up at her. "I shall fetch you at the end of my shift, miss," he nodded.

Ruby felt a small flicker of relief. She still did not wish to leave, but she felt a little comfort in knowing that she would soon return and watch over Henry herself.

She voiced a gentle thank you to Browne and made her way to the doorway. Gripping the edge of the door, she looked back at Henry. Her heart burned as deeply as her eyes stung.

Noticing the open Bible on the drawers beside his bed, she remembered what Abigail had told her about prayer. Cautiously yet desperately, she spoke to God silently in her heart.

Please, God - if You can hear me . . . please, do not take Henry! Oh, please do not take him away . . . Help him . . .

As she turned and left the room she dissolved into weeping. Entering her own room, she had scarcely pushed the door shut before sinking to her knees.

"It should be me, not him! Please, do not let him die! Oh, please . . . Why him? It should be me! Please!"

Her entire body convulsed with every bitter, rapid sob. Suddenly, she remembered what Browne had said in the carriage.

'We must all be strong for Mrs. Jones and Mr. Stratton.'

Determination grew inside her. How selfish she was

being, wallowing in her grief. Browne was right. They all had a duty to do what they could for Henry and Abigail.

Especially me.

She brushed her tears furiously off her cheeks in contempt. No more crying. Henry needed her. Abigail needed her.

She must be strong.

CHAPTER 16

UNWELCOME

A KNOCK at the door pierced Ruby's fitful doze. She opened her eyes, though they felt only half-open, swollen from her weeping hours before.

Browne stood solemnly on the other side of the threshold. As he lifted his gaze to her face he started slightly.

Ruby realised how haphazard she must look. She smoothed her hair as she greeted Browne.

"I must tend to some household matters for a while now, miss, so I came to fetch you to sit with Mr. Stratton awhile, if you still wish to do so?"

"Yes, yes." Ruby nodded.

"Very well, then. I shall return to his room when I have finished. I do not expect to take very long."

Ruby nodded again, then made her way hurriedly to Henry's room.

Her breath caught in her chest at the sight of him. He had not moved at all, but more blood had oozed out across the bandages on his head.

Ruby approached him, mindful of Browne's admonition to be strong.

"Henry," she breathed. "Henry? Can you hear me?"

No movements. No flickers. He was entirely unresponsive.

Ruby nestled into the chair by his bedside, pulling it closer to the edge of his bed.

She looked at his hand, lifeless at his side. Such a gentleman's hand, she thought, bruised though it was. She slipped her thin fingers behind his and gently squeezed his hand as she had done earlier.

She looked at his face, taking in every detail. His forehead was mostly covered by the bandages and there was a deep purple bruise under one of his eyes. She noticed another bruise almost hidden amidst the dark dusting of stubbly hair on his chin.

His cheeks were pale, and dotted with tiny cuts and nicks.

Ruby timidly stretched out her other hand toward his cheek. Slowly and carefully, she placed her fingertips on it.

She pulled them back quickly, uncertainty flooding her, drawn though she was to be closer to him.

She reached out her fingers again and stroked his cheek gently.

No response.

She placed her fingers and palm on his cheek and held it there a few moments. It felt so comforting to be near him. His cheek felt so soft and warm in her hand.

She looked at his closed eyes, wishing they would open. Oh, how she yearned to look at those eyes again and see them looking at her.

She moved her hand, stroking his cheek gently.

"Oh, Henry," she sighed. "I never wanted to cause you any pain . . . I am so sorry . . . for all of it." She fought back tears, clinging to her resolve to be strong for the others. Her hand still on his cheek, she sighed, lowering her head onto his chest, a few tears streaking silently down her cheek and onto his quilt.

"Oh!"

Ruby jumped up at the sudden sound of the startled cry that rang out from the other side of the room. She turned to see a frightfully pale Abigail standing with her hands on either side of her face, her eyes wide with disapproving shock.

"What is the meaning of this?" she shrieked, walking toward Ruby.

"Mrs. Jones, please, I—"

"You wretched girl! You would take advantage of a gentleman in his weakest hour?" Abigail exclaimed incredulously.

"Take advantage?" Ruby shook her head. "No! I—"

Browne rushed in. "Mrs. Jones, what is it?"

Bessie hurried in a few seconds later. "Is everything all right, ma'am?"

Abigail glanced at them, then fixed her bewildered glare firmly on Ruby.

"This insolent girl! Why, here is poor Henry - a *clergyman* - lying at the doorway of death and what do I see when I enter his bedchamber? This dangerous girl, flouting all propriety, throwing herself on top of him!"

Ruby's cheeks flushed with embarrassment and indignance.

Browne and Bessie both uttered sounds of disbelief and incredulity.

"Please! That is not what—" Ruby protested.

"I saw you with my own eyes!" Abigail interrupted.

"I assure you, it was not as you think! I—"

Abigail waved her hand dismissively.

"Please, take her out of here - she has no right to be here at all!"

Ruby was stunned. She knew Abigail didn't merely mean Henry's room, but the parsonage in its entirety.

"Please! Listen to me!"

"Let her speak, ma'am," Browne said, his voice gentle and kind.

Abigail looked at him as though he had taken leave of his senses.

Unflinchingly, Browne spoke again. "Hear her, ma'am. Let her have her say."

Abigail's breathing was fast and firm. She shifted her gaze to Ruby and looked at her coolly.

Ruby exhaled sharply, willing herself to calm down. "I am sorry. I realise how it must have looked to you, but I promise you - it was not what you think. I was holding onto his hand - as you had been - and, and, I—"

"What made you think you were permitted to hold his hand as I had been? He is my *nephew*! My nearest family!" Abigail's voice shook, her volume increasing with each word. "You are *not* family - you are a stranger, and a dangerous one, at that! You have no right—"

Ruby struggled to shake off the blow that Abigail's words had dealt her. "Forgive me! I rested my head on his chest but for a moment. This is all my fault, I know that! And it is agony! But, I am telling the truth - I had no intention of taking advantage of him at all! I never would. He is the only person who has shown me nothing but kindness - I could never explain to you how highly I think of him!"

She panted, unsure what to say or do next. Bessie moved beside her and put a gentle arm around her shoulders.

"Do not blame yourself, miss," she whispered kindly.

Abigail looked again at Browne. He gave a sympathetic look and clasped his hands behind his back.

"Ruby . . ."

Ruby looked at Abigail, somewhat startled that she had addressed her.

"I am sorry for my . . . accusations." She released a heavy sigh. "I do believe your intentions were innocent. But you must understand, you are never to do such things again. It is most improper. Please do remember that Henry is a gentleman, and a clergyman. You must refrain from caressing him and draping yourself all over him. It is most inappropriate."

Embarrassment kept Ruby's head low. She nodded. "I truly am sorry. I assure you, it will not happen again."

Abigail sighed. "And as for all this being your fault . . . We all know who is to blame. Yes, we would not have made his acquaintance if we had never made yours, but each person is responsible for their own actions. You must not blame yourself for choices that were not yours to make."

Abigail's voice was wavering, and on more than one occasion she wiped her eyes as she spoke.

Ruby fixed her gaze on the floor. It didn't matter what Abigail said. It was her fault, and that's all there was to it.

Ruby thought back to Henry's restless anguish regarding the man who had confronted her in church, the distance and heaviness that had seemed to settle on him at various times in the carriage, and the look of horror in his eyes when Bessie had announced Millforte's arrival.

She was the one to blame for all of it.

She recalled how light and easy he had seemed the first day she had met him, despite his obvious discomfort at being in a brothel. But since she had come to the parsonage, a heavy weight had seemed to bear further and further down on him.

Surely it was her own presence, and all the filthy echoes of her past, that had infiltrated the serenity and purity of the parsonage.

She rushed past everyone, out of Henry's room and back into her own, though it was starting to feel less and less like home. After closing the heavy door, she rested against it, her head tilted back against the wood, her heart sinking deeper and deeper in her chest as it filled with even more sorrow.

It was clear now. She knew what she must do. It was the only way.

She must leave the parsonage.

It would not be without its risks. But, come what may, she must leave, in the hope that her absence would restore everyone and everything at the parsonage to their rightful state.

SOME HOURS LATER, Ruby heard hushed tones and deep voices drift past her door. Dr. Shaw had returned.

She could not decipher what he and Browne were saying. Her stomach twisted, longing to know if there was any improvement in Henry's condition.

It is none of your business now. This is not your home anymore.

She scolded herself inwardly as she pulled a warm pelisse from the wardrobe and slid her arms into it. She had been agonising back and forth in her mind, wondering whether she should leave with nothing or pocket a few necessary items from the parsonage for her journey.

Her throat felt dry and her muscles were heavy from dread. Where would she go? Who would help her? No matter what she tried, Millforte would find her.

But then, maybe that's what she deserved after all she had caused Henry to suffer.

I must go. I must.

The worst thing of all, it surprised her to realise, was not the fear that Millforte would find her. It was the agony of knowing that she would never see Henry again.

How much colder her world would be without him in it.

She pushed the thoughts from her mind. She had endured an empty life before. She would do it again.

A knock at the door broke through her melancholy. She trudged to the door, pulling it open wearily.

Bessie was on the other side, her eyes sparkling, a smile of astonishment illuminating her face.

"Oh, Miss Ruby, he is awake!"

Ruby's heart leaped. "Awake?"

"Yes, miss! Dr. Shaw has not examined him yet, but I saw his eyes open, and his hand moving - he is awake!" She was practically shrieking with glee.

"His eyes are open?" Ruby closed her own in relief.

Upon opening her eyes, she noticed Bessie observing her with a measure of suspicion.

"Are you going out somewhere?"

Ruby swallowed hard, then gaped, trying to think of what to say.

Realisation dawned on Bessie's face. "You were not leaving, were you? Why, where would you go? It is not safe for you out there. What if that man found you? And surely you would not leave Mr. Stratton while he is in need of us all? I—"

Ruby tried to find a sound to focus on, but there was none. "I must, Bessie. The very reason he is in need of us all is because of me. I cannot remain, knowing that I might bring further catastrophe on him, on everyone here."

"But, truly, it is not your fault! You heard what Mrs. Jones said. You cannot blame yourself. Besides, it is not safe! You would bring more harm to him by turning your back on him now, in his weakest hour! Browne told me how valiantly Mr. Stratton defended you, yet you would leave and allow him to awake to find you gone? You cannot be thinking straight. I know you think you are thinking of him, but you are not thinking of how it will make him feel to lose you."

Ruby was stunned. Could Bessie be right? Had she been so busy blaming herself and yearning to protect Henry that she had not even considered how betrayed he would feel or how ungrateful it would seem if she were to disappear without a word?

She realised what Bessie had said. "Lose me?"

"He cares deeply for you, Ruby, of that I am sure. He would take it very ill if he were to find out you had taken leave without a word. And he would be so worried for your safety, I expect it would even set back his own recovery."

Ruby was speechless. How would someone who had never mattered to anyone be missed so profoundly?

"Well?"

"All right. I shall stay. For now, at least."

"I am glad. I would hate to see the disappointment on his face if I had to tell him you had gone, knowing how highly he thinks of you."

Ruby stared at Bessie. "How highly he thinks? Of me?"

"Of course! I have known him a number of years now, and I have never seen him so at ease in anyone's company as he is in yours." She chuckled softly. "He never used to stroll so much in the gardens, either, 'til you came along!"

Ruby clutched the door to steady herself. To think that she had almost left the parsonage without a word . . . how insulted and hurt Henry would have been, yet all the while she would be thinking she had done him good!

Bessie slipped Ruby's pelisse off her shoulders and faithfully strode to the wardrobe, placing it back inside.

"I must see if I am needed for anything. I shall fetch you shortly, if Mr. Stratton is still awake."

"Thank you, Bessie," Ruby said, stunned at what had transpired in the preceding moments.

Closing the door after Bessie left, Ruby inhaled and exhaled deeply.

Bessie's words filtered back into her mind.

"How valiantly he defended me?" Ruby whispered. "*Lose* me?"

There was a stirring in her heart she had never known before. And with it a feeling of deep humility. How undeserving she felt of such loyalty and affection.

And how deeply she felt the very same toward him.

IT WAS THE DEEP, throbbing ache in his head that first pierced Henry's awareness. Slowly, light filtered in through his flickering eyelids, and with each passing moment, new surges of pain shot through various parts of his body.

He tried to move, but the smallest exertion surged his pain to the point of overwhelm. He groaned.

"Henry!"

A female voice called out his name, sounding very far away.

"R—" Henry tried to speak, but choked, his mouth drier than dust.

"Henry, my dear!"

The voice still sounded far away, but he realised from the words spoken that it belonged to Aunt Abigail. Not Ruby.

Pain and discomfort fogged his mind. He tried desperately to recall what had happened. He remembered Millforte. Verbal confrontations. Fistfights.

He could not recall how it had all ended.

Panic surged through him. Where was Ruby? Had Milforte taken her? No. No, he was almost sure of it.

Pain zagged through his head, rendering him unable to think.

"Henry? Can you hear me?"

He opened his eyes, closing them almost immediately due to the agony inflicted by the light, dull as it was.

Slowly, he opened them again.

"Oh, Henry, my dear!"

He heard another female voice in the distance and Abigail seemed to turn to face it, speaking softly about a doctor and rest. The other voice wasn't Ruby either.

Suddenly, two hands grasped one of his and squeezed. It hurt.

"Oh, Henry! I am so relieved that you are awake!"

His vision was blurred, but he could detect Abigail's outline as she sat by his side.

"Wh—"

He tried to speak again, still struggling to piece it all together, wanting desperately to ensure Ruby was safe.

"Do not try to speak if it hurts you too much, my dear. Rest, now. There will be plenty of time for speaking later."

Abigail placed a reassuring hand on his arm as she spoke. That hurt, too. Every inch of him felt badly bruised.

Millforte had kicked him, hadn't he? He was sure that he had. But then, he wasn't sure at all.

It was all a blur, and each time he thought he had it all figured out, he doubted it so much that none of it made sense. Scattered fragments of memory swirled around in his mind, with no way of knowing which ones were real and which were imagined.

But, still. Ruby. Finding out what had happened to her was more important than whatever had happened to him.

Suddenly, it came back to him. She was at the Harfords' house.

His heart sank. He'd told Bessie to hide herself and Ruby in the Harfords' attic. How long had they been there? How long had he been here like this?

Gritting his teeth in anticipation of the pain, he tried to move again. It was agony.

"Aunt—"

"Henry! Oh, Henry, my dear!"

"Ruby—"

"Ruby?"

"She . . . she . . . the . . . attic . . ."

Every breath and every utterance was pure agony. But he pressed on, the memory of Ruby's frightened face at the forefront of his mind.

"No, my dear, she is here. Bessie, too. Browne went to fetch them last night. That was Bessie here, just now. Have some water, my dear."

A glass bumped his lips, sloshing a few drops onto his chin.

"Oh, sorry, my dear." Abigail tried again, successfully this time. Henry silently welcomed the soothing liquid's cool relief.

"Ruby?" He called out to her.

"She is here at Shiloh Hall, my dear. Not here in the room."

"Please . . ."

He squinted, trying to focus on his aunt's blurry frame.

"I . . . must . . . see her," he breathed, wincing with pain at the last.

"You must *rest*, my dear," Abigail replied, her voice cool and calm. "Dr. Shaw is due to return at any moment. I shall sit with you until he arrives."

"Please, Aunt . . ."

"Oh, my dear, please, let us see what the doctor says. You have been through a tremendous ordeal. It is an answer to all our prayers that you are awake at all. Please, my dear, rest. He shall be here before long."

Henry sighed. He was in too much agony to argue. Plus, the pain was utterly exhausting. He closed his eyes and unintentionally drifted into sleep.

RUBY COULD HARDLY SIT STILL. Every few minutes, she kept jumping up, pacing the room, then sitting back down somewhere else.

She really couldn't wait to see Henry, to see for herself that he was definitely all right. But, at the same time, she was nervous. What if he hated her? What if she had been convinced by Bessie to stay only for Henry himself to order her to leave?

Somewhere deep within, she knew he would not. But years of being treated as worthless had led her to expect that rejection was never too far away.

A knock.

She launched herself forward, clasping the brass doorknob with both hands as she pulled the door open.

"Mrs. Jones said he has fallen asleep again and, therefore, no one is to disturb him. I am sorry . . ."

Ruby's heart sank. She had a feeling that even if Henry were still awake, Abigail would still not permit her to visit him.

CHAPTER 17

AWAKENINGS

IT WAS EERILY silent in the dining room.

Ruby had arrived a little early. She had no appetite to speak of, but she was hoping to see Abigail to ascertain some facts regarding Henry's condition and the doctor's conclusions.

Browne entered, startled to see Ruby lingering by one of the armchairs.

"Ah, I did not know you were here already, miss . . ."

"I was hoping to find out how Henry is. I thought perhaps his aunt might be here." She paused, briefly. "Do you know how he is? I understand the doctor was here earlier."

It had been a few hours since Bessie had informed Ruby of the doctor's arrival. Since then, she had not seen or heard anything or anyone. She was growing ever more anxious to discover how Henry fared now that he was awake.

"Yes, miss." Browne gave a heavy, burdened sigh. "Dr. Shaw feels that the situation is still rather grave. Mr. Stratton did open his eyes and try to speak momentarily, but even with such an encouraging development, the doctor feels that his recovery is not yet guaranteed." He swallowed determinedly. "Mr. Stratton may have a long and uncertain path before him. We must carry him along as best we can and leave the rest in God's sovereign hands."

The silence in the room seemed to grow louder. Ruby slightly choked as she swallowed, her throat constricting.

"I do not understand. Surely, if he is awake, surely, he must . . ."

Her head shook slowly from side to side as she spoke, her worried eyes darting to and fro beneath her furrowing brow.

Browne's gaze was fixed to the floor.

"I know not, miss, but it is what Dr. Shaw has warned. We can only wait. And pray."

"Warned?" Ruby shivered. "Does he think it *likely?*"

"I do not know whether he believes it likely or not, miss. Only that it is still a distinct possibility. It seems, at this stage, either outcome may transpire."

Ruby's eyes and throat were stinging. "Is there anything that can be done? Anything, to try to . . ."

She could not finish her sentence out loud. However, Browne seemed to know what she was trying to ask.

He sighed. "All we can do is what we are already doing, miss."

Ruby felt that she wasn't doing anything, except worrying and waiting.

"What can *I* do, Mr. Browne? I can clean things, I can fetch things, I can care for him . . . Only, tell me what I might do and I shall do it."

"I shall ask Mrs. Jones," Browne, a hint of compassion in his weak smile. "We must all take our lead from her until Mr. Stratton—"

Bessie bustled in, a tray in her hands. Her eyebrows raised as she looked at Browne.

"What news of Mr. Stratton? I know he awoke for a time earlier . . ."

Ruby couldn't bear to listen to the pessimistic prognosis again. She turned and headed for the dining table, and as she seated herself in her usual chair at the table, she looked at the empty seat where Henry usually sat.

She could not imagine his permanent absence from the table, the parsonage, the garden . . . from the world. And she didn't want to envisage such a bleak reality.

The dining room door opened and a pale, care-worn Abigail drifted in.

Browne and Bessie greeted her with surprised tones. Ruby remained seated and fixed her gaze on her. Abigail's accusations echoed in Ruby's mind, followed by her kind reassurances of apology. What did she think of her now?

Abigail smiled weakly at Browne and Bessie and turned to take her seat at the table. She stopped in her tracks as she noticed Ruby, then resumed her prior course of action.

"Good evening, Ruby," Abigail croaked, her voice hoarse and weak.

Ruby realised she had been holding her breath. She coughed. "Good evening, Mrs. Jones."

She almost continued with a question about Henry's state of health, but stopped herself at the last moment. Perhaps it would be wiser to permit Abigail to mention him first.

The strain in the atmosphere intensified after Browne and Bessie left the room. Abigail and Ruby ate mostly in silence, with an occasional remark or question peppered throughout, more for decorum's sake than anything. Henry's absence was painfully perceptible.

Abigail's puffy eyes gazed vacantly at her dinner plate.

"Mrs. Jones? When is Dr. Shaw due to return?" Ruby asked, her tone soft.

Browne entered the room and added some more wood to the fire, much to Ruby's relief.

"He has dedicated himself to coming every half day." Abigail said slowly. "At least for now. I am sure that he will not be able to do so for very long. I imagine there are plenty of other patients in need of his assistance."

"Do not forget, ma'am, that the Great Physician is with Mr. Stratton at all times," Browne said gently.

Ruby thought for a moment. Did he mean God?

Abigail looked at him and sighed, a hint of reassurance on her face. "Yes. That is very true. Thank you, Browne."

Some of the heaviness seemed to have lifted from Abigail's shoulders. Browne raised himself from the hearth and strode past them with a nod.

"Oh, Browne! Before you go . . ."

Browne stopped and awaited her continuation, his face lined with gentleness.

"I wanted to ask you if I might charge you with a new kind of duty tomorrow?"

"Of course, ma'am. I will gladly do all I can to help you and Mr. Stratton."

"Thank you. I intend to write a few short letters this evening. Would you be so kind as to deliver them in town tomorrow? I wish to let a few key church members know about . . ." Her voice trailed off. After a moment, she cleared her throat. "And ask for their prayers for Henry."

"Of course, ma'am. I shall leave bright and early and see to it that they are all delivered into the right hands, without delay."

Abigail sighed with relief. "Oh, thank you, Browne. I know that Dr. Shaw has had occasion to make mention to a few people, but there are others outside of his sphere . . . I wish to make it known to them, also."

Ruby's chest burned with a desire to help. She could stay silent no longer. "Is there anything at all that *I* might do to help?"

Abigail turned to look at her.

"In truth, I am not sure. I hardly know myself what more can be done."

Ruby bit her lip and looked down, though somewhat relieved that Abigail had not taken offence at her offer.

"Allow me to think on it this evening," Abigail continued. "And, perhaps, you and I might speak in the morning?"

BRIGHT STREAKS of sunlight burst in through the window, painting an illusory warmth on the drawing room walls.

Ruby drummed her fingers on the soft red velvet arm of the wingback chair she perched on as she awaited Abigail's company. She yawned, shaking her head slightly, wishing she could put the notion of sleep as far behind her now as it had been last night when she ought to have been benefiting from it.

Instead, she had spent a fitful night tossing to and fro, worrying about Henry and feeling anxious about her pending discussion with Abigail.

Now, as the time for their meeting had arrived, exhaustion enveloped her.

The hushed creak of the drawing room door caught Ruby's ear. She straightened up in her seat.

Abigail entered and sat down opposite her, frightfully pale. Ruby noticed lines and shadows that hadn't been there before.

It seemed Ruby wasn't the only one who had struggled to sleep.

As Abigail eased her stiff frame into the chair opposite Ruby, she sighed as though she'd been holding her breath.

Ruby hesitated, timidity in her voice when she finally spoke.

"How is he this morning?"

Abigail looked at Ruby blankly. She shifted in her chair as a look of reluctance washed over her tired face. "Much the same, really . . ."

Ruby yearned to see him. It was so strange being in the same building - the same corridor, even - yet, seemingly miles apart. She missed him dreadfully.

"Might I help? In *any* way?" She prayed Abigail would not refuse her.

"I own that I am exhausted from attending to him so constantly. But you must understand, I do have my reasons for being so reluctant to share the task."

Ruby's heart plummeted. Her cheeks flushed a little as she spoke.

"I know how wrong . . . how, improper it must have looked to you, but I do assure you, I—"

"Oh, my dear," Abigail said, a hint of surprise lifting her brow. "No, it has nothing to do with you."

Hope pricked Ruby's ears.

Abigail drew a shaky breath. "My husband and I were never blessed with children of our own. When Henry lost his parents, we did not hesitate to take him in and care for him as though he were our own." She blinked back tears. "When my husband died, Henry took his place as parson, as had long been intended." She sighed, a motherly tenderness filling her eyes. "I love Henry as my own son." Her voice cracked. "If he were to . . . slip away . . . whilst under someone else's care, why, I do not imagine I could ever forgive myself." A silent, delicate tear rolled slowly down her cheek. She brushed it away with a trembling finger.

Weight settled across Ruby's shoulders. Slip away?

She knew the concerns, yet had not allowed herself to imagine the prospect in such particulars. How could she bear it if Henry were to slip away whilst she sat with him?

A worse thought tore swiftly through her heart. How could she bear it if he were to slip away without her ever having seen him again?

If Henry's life hovered at the edge of a precipice, she must be right beside him, no matter the outcome. She could not bear another minute of separation. She swallowed hard, hoping that Abigail's fears would never be realised.

"I understand," she said tenderly. "I do not wish to cause any distress. I only wish to do what I am able, to help him . . . as he has helped me."

Abigail's eyes softened as she looked at Ruby. She gave a slow, short nod.

"Very well. Perhaps, then, you might sit with him until Dr. Shaw returns in an hour or so? I have no wish to sleep, but I am afraid I no longer have any choice in the matter . . . I do not think I could stay awake much longer." Abigail's yawn evidenced her sentiments.

Ruby nodded. "Of course. I do hope you are able to get some rest."

"Thank you, my dear."

They rose in unison. As Abigail left the room, she turned, clutching the door.

"Fetch me if you need me. For anything at all. And, Ruby - watch him well."

The sombre responsibility placed itself like a mantle around Ruby's shoulders.

"I shall." She nodded. "I promise."

RUBY STOOD outside Henry's room, breathing deeply yet swiftly. Mustering fresh courage, she hesitated for a moment before pushing open the heavy, wooden door.

The first thing she noticed was Browne, sitting in a wooden chair in the centre of the room.

Her eyes widened. "Oh! Mr. Browne . . ."

"Morning, Miss Ruby. I understand you have come to sit with Mr. Stratton awhile so as Mrs. Jones can get some rest."

As he spoke, Ruby's gaze drifted to the bed at the side of the room. There, nestled amongst blankets and pillows was the face she had been longing to see.

Aware that Browne had stopped talking, she shifted her focus back to him.

"Oh. Yes."

"Very kind of you, Miss Ruby. I shall tend to a few chores. If you need anything, please do fetch me." He made for the door, turning abruptly as he reached it. "And, unless there is an urgent need, I believe we should let Mrs. Jones rest as much as she is able to, miss. This has all taken a great deal out of her."

Ruby pressed her lips together and nodded. Deep within her, guilt churned again.

Browne nodded, then left, the door meeting its frame with a quiet click.

Clutching the back of the empty wooden chair, Ruby gazed at Henry. Concern drained through her as she observed the lack of colour in his ordinarily healthy cheeks.

She pushed the chair forward. A screeching scrape stopped her at once. Lifting the chair up, she carried it closer to the bed, careful not to place it just as close as she did on her previous visit. The last thing she wanted was any further suspicion or accusation.

A blade of pain jabbed her heart. How could he still look so lifeless? So dramatically opposite to the animated, twinkling-eyed, smiling gentleman she had first come to know.

Silence hung in the air like a canopy. She tucked her chin into her palms, her elbows resting on her lap. Her ears tuned in to the faint sound of his breathing.

Inching the chair a little closer, she listened more intently. In, out. In, out. Barely palpable, yet such a welcome sound.

She wondered if he could hear her. Or if he might be dreaming. What was going on behind those closed eyes?

"Henry . . ." she whispered, barely above a breath.

She was about to ask him if he could hear her, but she stopped herself just as she opened her mouth to speak.

Her hand flickered closer toward him. She pulled it back into her lap, the memory of Abigail's disapproving words ringing through her ears.

No, she would not forget herself this time, not after giving her word that she would watch him well. She must prove deserving of Abigail's trust.

Something about Henry's breathing changed slightly.

Ruby held her own breath and strained to listen. Her throat felt dry. She silently pleaded with God.

Please do not take him! Please help him. . .

Gently, wearily, Henry's eyelashes flickered.

Ruby froze. Should she call his name again? Run quickly to fetch Browne? Rooted to the spot, her eyes widened with anticipation.

"H—"

Her throat was so dry she couldn't speak. She swallowed hard.

"Henry?" she half-whispered, half-trembled.

His eyelashes fluttered again.

"Can you hear me?" she asked.

His eyes flashed open, closing almost immediately.

She gasped.

Again, he pried his eyes open, only to close them at once. The cycle repeated, each time keeping his eyes open a little longer. At last, his eyes stayed open.

Ruby's elation was quickly overshadowed with fear. What would he do when he saw her? After all that had happened, would he even want to look at her?

Surely, he would wish Abigail with him. Not an imposter.

A soft groan rose out of Henry's chest. His breathing was laboured. He was almost panting. He sucked a deep breath in, then a weak, broken version of his voice met the silent, trepidatious air.

"Ruby . . .?"

She had the sensation of being tossed at sea. Trying to say his name again, all that emerged was a half-broken cry.

Slowly, seemingly with great agony, he turned his head incrementally in her direction. His eyes continued the journey that his head could not.

He looked her in the eye.

How she had feared this moment would never again come. Yet now it had arrived, she wanted nothing but to flee from the room.

Tears rolled down her cheeks as she looked into his eyes. Those pain-filled eyes, set in that pale, bruised face.

Henry's eyes moistened. "I—"

He panted without ease, appearing too weak to talk, intermittently closing his eyes for brief snatches of time. He fought to keep his eyes open, training them each time on Ruby's face.

A frown crinkled his brow. He squeezed his eyes shut and half-gasped, half-grunted.

"Henry? Are you all right?" Ruby rushed off her chair and onto her knees at his bedside.

Henry made a noise that seemed to answer positively and nodded, more with his face than with his head. Opening his eyes again, his gaze routed to where Ruby had been. He blinked as he rolled his eyes to look at her face, closer now as she knelt beside his bed.

Neither of them said a word. Their gazes fixed directly into each other's eyes.

Time and worry stopped. The world disappeared from Ruby's mind. There was no one else, and nothing else - only she and Henry.

Warmth and a strange new feeling flooded Ruby's entire being. She had never seen so clearly, never heard so plainly. Never had she felt so *happy*.

Henry's hand moved slightly at his side, drawing Ruby's attention to it. His fingers extended and stretched ever so slowly toward her. Without a second thought, she reached out and wrapped her fingers around his.

A smile slowly broke out across his features, settling deeply in his eyes. She returned it, surprised to feel such genuine delight given how worried she had been the past few days.

"I . . . I am . . . so . . . glad you . . . are . . . are here . . ." he panted between each breath.

She looked down, blinking hard to fight the stinging tears invading her eyes.

"I am so dreadfully sorry," she whispered, shaking her head.

"Hush . . . Ruby," His voice, though likely strained from

the exhausting effort it took to speak, was gentle and soothing. "Look . . . look at me . . ."

She swallowed back her emotion. She must be strong for him, as Browne had said.

She glanced at his face a few times before allowing her gaze to settle on his eyes. Her reluctance melted, and she sighed as she looked into his deep, dark eyes, suddenly aware of their interlocking hands. Why did being close to him make her feel so weak?

"Are . . . are you well?" Henry asked, his gaze as gentle as his voice.

"Well enough," said Ruby. "More importantly, how are *you?*"

"Fine," he said, his voice a whisper.

He observed her silently for a moment.

Ruby's cheeks flushed. He'd always been accurate at reading her. She hoped he wouldn't be this time.

"You blame yourself," he said with visible effort.

Such an earnest depth in his eyes. She almost couldn't bear it.

"How can I not?" she said quietly, looking at the bandages that encircled his dark, wavy hair.

Henry's eyes moistened. He squeezed her hand tightly. "No, no . . . You . . . are not to blame . . ."

Ruby looked into his eyes again. Never before had she felt like this.

"Would you like some water?" she asked, trying to distract herself from everything around and within her.

Henry tried to shake his head, his eyes burning with pity and protest.

"Ruby," Henry said, his fingers squeezing hers weakly.

She looked at him again, searching his eyes. Surely, he must blame her even a little.

"I believe that the Lord answered everyone's prayers," Henry said, still gasping and grimacing between words. "I know that He answered my prayer that He would keep you safe. I am so glad that He did."

Ruby looked at him through misty eyes. "Glad? I would not blame you at all if you hated me for—"

Henry's eyebrows shot up as his eyes grew wide. "Hate you?" he exclaimed. "Ruby . . . I could never hate you," he said, his eyes shining with emotion.

Ruby's heart hammered. Time seemed to stop again. She pulled her hand away from his and stood, pacing nervously to the window. As she shifted her focus to the sprawling landscape outside, a new thought distracted her from Henry's magnetic ambience.

"God must hate me," she croaked, a distant look in her eyes.

"No! No, Ruby—" Henry's emphatic reply triggered a cough, which in turn made him wince with pain.

Ruby held her breath, but Henry soon recovered himself and stared earnestly up at her.

"Ruby, you must believe me. This is the most important thing that you will ever hear," Henry said, his voice still frequently breathless. "God loves you. He loves you so much that He gave Jesus to take your place. Ruby, we have *all* done wrong. The Bible says our hearts are more wicked than we can know. Everyone needs God's forgiveness. Everyone. And He offers it freely, to all who will trust in the sacrifice Jesus made on our behalf. Jesus died, taking our punishment, taking our sins away. Then He rose from death, bringing us new life. All who earnestly believe, He will cleanse and He will make new. New! All the old filth, gone. New life, new heart, new values - everything is new." He paused, looking at her attentive face. "He loves you, Ruby.

And He wants to wash away all the old pain and sin, and make you new."

Ruby looked down out the window again. She wanted to believe what Henry was saying. But he clearly didn't know just how filthy she was.

Henry seemed to hear her unspoken thoughts. "No one is beyond the reach of His grace. He loves you, Ruby." Henry's jaw clenched. "You are not to blame for all the wrong that others have done to you. Know that."

Ruby looked at him, his reassuring words a welcome reprieve from the shame that weighed her down.

"We all must answer to God for our own sins. And whatever we have done, He is willing to forgive. Ruby, He longs to give you a new heart, a new life. Do not turn away from Him. He is . . . He is all you need . . ."

The exertion of Henry's exhortations started to show. His panting intensified and he closed his eyes, his brow furrowed in seeming discomfort.

Ruby watched him, his words echoing through her mind. Quietly, he slipped back into sleep. She gazed out the window, a sense of being alone filling her mind.

An awareness gripped her. She was alone with God.

Twitching with an anxious unrest, she paced the room a few times before returning to the window. The day was bright, and a breeze gently rustled the tall, bare trees.

Understanding grew inside her, her breathing fast, her throat dry.

It was all His.

God had made it all, and it all belonged to Him. That's what Henry had told her one day in the garden. God created the world and all the trees and birds and flowers in it, too. And all the people.

Including her.

And everything that He made, well, it belonged to Him. Did she?

She realised she wanted to.

Pressing her trembling hand against the window pane, she drew a shaky breath. Time had stopped again. She felt transported from the room, from the parsonage. There was no one else and nothing else, like before, with Henry, yet stronger somehow.

There was something different about this. Something deeper.

Something even more real.

"God . . .? I do not feel worthy to even speak to You . . ." Her gaze dropped, years of accusations hurtling through her heart once again. "But I need You, God!"

She lifted her eyes and fixed her gaze on the sprawling evidence of creation that stretched magnificently to the horizon.

"I need You to cleanse me and, and to make me new. Oh, God, I am sorry." Her voice cracked and tears streamed silently down her face. "I am so sorry for all of the wrong things that I have done. Please, forgive me . . . I know I do not deserve it . . . But, please, forgive me . . ." her voice trailed off in sobs.

She remembered what Henry had told her.

As her sobbing abated, she voiced her thoughts. "I believe. I believe, Jesus, that You shed Your blood to save . . . to save a wretch like me."

She almost smiled to quote the phrase that had impacted her so deeply.

"I believe You did. And that You came back to life, to give me life. New life . . ."

As she spoke, something welled up inside her. Something she had never felt before. Squeezing her eyes shut, she silently continued her prayer, infusing it with gratitude and praise.

Upon opening her eyes, she felt as though she were seeing everything for the very first time. The room looked different. The trees outside looked different. It all seemed and looked different.

Then she realised. It was she who was different.

Everything had become new.

CHAPTER 18

A PECULIAR ARRIVAL

THE DOOR HANDLE rattled then clicked open. The door swung open in a smooth arc. Ruby was still standing by the window, delighting in the sight of all the trees and plants outside swaying in a graceful dance.

Dr. Shaw strode into the room, followed by a weary Browne.

Ruby smiled, then rushed toward them.

"Mr. Browne, he woke up! Henry woke up again!"

"When was this, miss?" the doctor asked, before Browne had a chance to say anything.

"Why, it must be only moments ago, sir - not so very long ago."

Dr. Shaw went straight over to the bed and placed two thick fingers on Henry's neck, slipping his gold pocket watch out of his waistcoat. His eyes stared at the clock's face as he silently counted the rhythm of Henry's pulse.

"Did he say anything, Miss Ruby?" Browne asked, hope filling his tired, grey eyes.

"Yes." Ruby smiled again.

It was strange. She could not remember ever feeling a smile so tangibly. Not like this. Everything seemed so . . . light. So fresh.

So new.

Delight bubbled within her. God had heard her prayer.

"We spoke. We spoke for quite a few moments. About . . . about what happened," Ruby said, her smile fading a little. "And then we spoke about God." Her smile deepened and widened.

Browne's eyebrows raised. "About God, miss?"

"Yes. Oh, Mr. Browne, it is true! It is all true, every word of it! God really does forgive - He really does!"

Browne smiled, his eyebrows still aloft. "I know, miss," he said, gratitude creeping into his voice. "He forgave me . . . many years ago now."

"And today He has forgiven me!" Ruby said, her eyes dazzling.

"Oh, Miss Ruby!" Browne's eyes looked moist. "That is wonderful, miss!"

Ruby felt as though she might burst. A glee-filled sound rose up from deep within her, punctuating the air of the quiet room as it escaped her throat.

"I am much happier with his condition today, Browne," said the doctor, without acknowledgement of Ruby and Browne's conversation. "I believe he may have settled in safer territory, though his road to recovery may still prove rather long."

"But you think he will recover, Dr. Shaw?" asked Browne, more hope dawning on his face.

Ruby looked expectantly at the doctor.

"I believe so . . . Although, I would be much happier to pronounce it for certain after seeing him in his wakeful state myself."

Ruby glanced at Henry. Even he looked different.

"I did not know what to do when he awoke . . . whether I should have fetched you or not, Mr. Browne. But then he began to speak, so I stayed and spoke with him. After a short time, he fell back to sleep. I did not wish to disturb him. And then, I was praying."

"You did the right thing to stay with him, miss," Browne said softly.

"I shall return in half a day, once again, in hopes of finding him awake once more. Good day, Browne. Miss," the doctor said, tipping his hat at Ruby.

Ruby responded with a nod and a small curtsey.

Browne followed the doctor out of the room in a less weary manner than when he had entered it. As he left, he glanced back at Ruby. The tension on his face had given way to a look of pleasant surprise.

Alone, Ruby returned to the window and gazed up at the cloud-speckled sky. It was so vast. Stretching as far as the eye could see, it seemed a visible representation of the boundless mercy that God had shown to her.

She glanced at Henry. He was breathing rhythmically, his chest slowly rising and falling. He looked so peaceful, and yet, it was obvious he was not enjoying a simple rest. Bruises marred his face and his brow was drawn down into a slight frown even as he slept.

Millforte's face flashed into Ruby's mind. It grieved her that Henry had suffered at his powerful hands.

Then, she realised.

Even thinking of Millforte was different. She still felt a measure of anxiety and repulsion, but underneath it was something that had never been there before.

Underneath it all was a deep-seated certainty that Millforte's power was nothing compared to God's.

A creak of the door jostled her thoughts back to her present surroundings.

Abigail entered the room silently, gliding across the polished floor. Her face and hair were pristine once again.

Ruby smiled as Abigail approached her, though with her lips firmly together. As glad as Ruby was to have been made new, she still had a heavy heart about Henry's condition, and she knew that Abigail did, too.

"Ruby, my dear - how is he? Has there been any change?"

Ruby smiled. Abigail sounded more like herself again.

"Did Browne not tell you? He awoke again! For a short time."

Abigail's eyes widened, eager anticipation within them. "No, I have not seen Browne for hours. He awoke? Henry awoke?"

"Yes," Ruby nodded. "We spoke briefly, and then—"

"He spoke?" Abigail half-exclaimed, half-asked, unthinkingly cutting off Ruby mid-sentence.

"Yes," Ruby said. She looked down at the floor. Her hands were clasped together in front of her, her fingers moving with nervous energy. "I told him how sorry I was, for . . ."

Abigail nodded knowingly. "What did he say?"

"He is much too kind," Ruby said tenderly. "He said he does not blame me, or hate me, and that . . . neither does God."

Abigail reached out and squeezed Ruby's hand. "Of course not, my dear. God loves you very much."

Ruby looked up at her, a smile of relief breaking across her features. "He does! I cannot explain it, and I do not deserve it, but He does!"

Abigail smiled faintly, a hint of surprise marking her brow.

"When Henry fell back to sleep, I . . . prayed."

"Oh, Ruby." Abigail's smile deepened.

"And, and I believe. And - He did it! He made me new . . ."

Abigail gaped slightly. "You mean . . . you—"

Ruby nodded gratefully. "It is all true," she said. "Every word of it. He is so wonderful to show mercy to someone like me. I know - I know I do not deserve it. But He did it!"

Abigail took a few steps forward and embraced Ruby. "Oh, Ruby, I am so glad, my dear," she said, squeezing Ruby tightly.

As Abigail drew away, Ruby realised how much she missed her mother's embrace, and felt even more grateful for Abigail's.

A thought seemed to dawn in Abigail's eyes. She glanced at Henry, motionless in his sickbed, then looked back at Ruby. She still seemed glad, yet something had stifled it. Whatever it was, it made Ruby's heart sink a little.

"Does Henry know?" Abigail asked, a heavy sigh escaping her.

"No. Not yet." A thread of worry weaved its way into Ruby's happiness. "He spoke to me of God's mercy, and then, when he fell back to sleep, I prayed." She fixed her curious eyes on Abigail's. "And I meant every word of it."

"Oh, I do not doubt that, my dear!" Abigail gave a sympathetic smile.

Ruby relaxed a little. Still, the air seemed strained, somehow.

"I cannot express to you the change that I felt - within me - as I prayed, and as I thanked Him. I . . . It is all too wonderful for me to comprehend!"

Abigail nodded slowly. "It is the most important and most wonderful thing that can happen to anyone. And with it comes more change than we are sometimes prepared for. More trials and testings. Growth and joy, yes, but many hard times, too, that chip away all the old thoughts and habits." She paused, deep in thought. "Your real life has only just begun, my dear. There will be blessings and comforts, but there will also be trials and tears."

Ruby nodded, listening attentively to Abigail's wisdom. "I do not doubt it."

Abigail smiled again, though still somewhat contrived.

Abigail's gaze shifted in Henry's direction, the smile half lingering on her lips, the worried look in her eyes deepening each passing moment.

Ruby looked at Henry, watching his slow breathing and praying for his closed eyes to open.

A faint echo of footsteps in the hallway grew louder and louder until Browne appeared in the doorway.

"Mrs. Jones, there is a man in the drawing room who wishes to speak with you."

Ruby's heart faltered. It couldn't be.

"A man, Browne?" Abigail asked, concern and confusion etched on her face.

"Yes, ma'am. He says his name is Mr. Webster, and that Sir Harford has sent him to you on Mr. Stratton's behalf."

"Oh, indeed?" Abigail breathed with evident relief. "I shall join him presently. Thank you, Browne."

Browne nodded and turned to leave as swiftly as he had arrived.

Abigail sighed. "Oh, for a moment, I thought . . ." Her voice trembled into silence.

Ruby looked at the ground.

As did I . . .

Abigail squeezed Ruby's arm. "There, now. All is well. I shall go and see Mr. Webster." She smoothed her dress and turned to look at Henry. Stepping toward the bed, she whispered a prayer that Ruby couldn't hear clearly. She stooped and stroked Henry's forehead with the back of her fingers before turning to look at Ruby.

"Might you sit with him a little longer?" Her eyebrows were elevated with a worried hope. "I cannot bear to think of him waking only to be all alone, and perhaps unable to summon anyone if he has need of anything . . ."

"Yes, of course. I will be glad to stay."

Relief swept over Abigail's face, though it didn't dispel the worry entirely. She drew herself up straight. "Thank you, my dear. I shall return as soon as Mr. Webster has taken his leave."

She gave Ruby a friendly smile as she bustled past and proceeded out the door.

Ruby smiled softly. She was so glad to have told Abigail and Browne. Now, she couldn't wait to tell Bessie and, most of all, Henry.

Without taking her gaze off him, she quietly dragged the chair closer to his bedside.

Thank You, God, for Your mercy to me. Please have mercy on Henry and help him to awaken fully soon.

As she leaned back in the chair it creaked, startling her slightly. Henry didn't flinch.

As much as it pained her to see him recumbent, she couldn't help but think that she could sit and look at him forever without growing bored. He was like a beautiful work of art that revealed something new upon each observance. She took in every detail of his eyebrows, his lashes, his closed eyelids.

Her heart was filled with a yearning to see those eyes open once again, looking into her own.

The thought of it made her heart flutter.

"MRS. JONES, allow me to introduce to you Mr. Percival Webster, a close friend and associate of Sir Harford's."

"Thank you, Browne. Good day, Mr. Webster. To what do I owe the pleasure of making your acquaintance?"

Mr. Webster gave a stiff bow. "Good day, Mrs. Jones," he said, his voice deep and clouded. "Sir Harford is a longstanding friend of my father's, and he has instructed me to lend my assistance due to the . . . predicament . . . that has befallen your nephew."

Abigail nodded and indicated with her hand for Mr. Webster to take a seat.

"Yes, poor Henry is quite ill at present."

"Have there been any hopeful improvements?"

Abigail paused. "Of late, yes. Though we are still expecting Dr. Shaw to call later and issue an update on his progress. He is hopeful that Henry will indeed recover, though it shall not be an easy road to travel."

"I do apologise, Mrs. Jones. I am dreadfully sorry that the situation is quite so grave."

"Thank you."

Bessie breezed into the room with a tea tray.

"Some tea, Mr. Webster?" asked Abigail.

"Delightful! Yes, thank you," replied Mr. Webster.

As he and Abigail drank their tea, they exchanged pleasantries and histories of their interactions with the Harford family. Upon draining his last sip from the teacup, Mr. Webster cleared his throat and looked squarely at Abigail, his steely eyes filled with serious intent.

"Mrs. Jones, I confess that Sir Harford sent me here with unequivocal intent."

"Oh, I see. Do proceed, Mr. Webster."

"Due to Mr. Stratton's indisposition, rendering him unable to carry out his ministerial duties at present, Sir

Harford - owing that he is your nephew's patron - has charged me with taking up the duty of the running of the church, until such times as Mr. Stratton is well and able to resume his duties."

Surprise lifted Abigail's brow.

"I am capable, I assure you," he continued. "My father was rector of a rather large parish in Devonshire, and I gained a great deal of experience assisting him for quite a few years as his own health declined. I assure you that I would do my utmost to ensure that proper care would be taken of everyone in the church."

He reached into his inner coat pocket and pulled out a piece of cream paper, crumpled at the edges, though immaculately smooth everywhere else. A red seal was perfectly centred on the side facing Abigail as Mr. Webster handed it to her.

"Sir Harford sends this to you with his regards."

Abigail, her eyebrows high and her mouth slightly agape, accepted the letter and quickly unfolded it, red wax breaking off into her lap as she did so.

Mr. Webster watched as her eyes scanned the page. He cleared his throat. "I do hope that none of this seems too presumptuous. But, as your nephew is under obligation to Sir Harford. . ." His words trailed off as he shrugged.

Abigail's eyes moistened slightly. "Oh, Mr. Webster, I do not know how to thank you! Your arrival, this letter - why, they are answers to my prayers. I know that Henry cares more for his flock than for his own life, and once he is awake and fully aware of the absence his condition will force him to have from the church, his pressing concern will be to ensure that everyone is looked after well. And for you to be sent by Sir Harford - a man who has been so generous and kind to Henry for so long, and whom Henry trusts implicitly - why, I know that Henry will be delighted that you have come to help us in this time of trial."

Mr. Webster smiled. "Splendid. I am only too glad to be of assistance. After all, what is our faith worth if we do not have love for one another and seek to comfort and ease one another's suffering, as the Lord has done for us?"

"Indeed, you are most right, Mr. Webster. I shall have Browne make ready a room for you. You must stay with us for as long as you wish."

"I am most obliged, ma'am." Mr. Webster smiled.

Abigail stood up, but just as she was about to take a step, Mr. Webster raised his hand to secure her attention and presence a moment longer.

"Pardon me, ma'am, but . . ." He hesitated, his serious brow wrinkling slightly. "Sir Harford made mention of another guest who is here at the parsonage. He said it was a young . . . *lady*, of . . . indecorous origin?" His concern was as obvious as his confusion at how best to put his query into words.

Abigail's brow furrowed then raised, a mix of emotions flitting across her face.

"Well, ah . . . Miss Ruby is a guest at present. She . . . She has long been held against her will in a . . . a place of . . ." She trailed off, unsure how to explain it all with decorum.

"Forgive me, it is not my wish to cause embarrassment," Mr. Webster said.

Abigail sat down again. "Please, there is no need for you to apologise. It is only right that you know the particulars since you will be staying with us. Besides, if you do not hear the truth from us, you may indeed hear all manner of rumours and whisperings in the village."

"I see . . ." Mr. Webster leaned back in his chair, one eyebrow raised in suspense.

"It was seemingly by chance that Henry encountered Ruby a few months ago, now," Abigail began. She smiled as she exhaled sharply. "Though, as you and I are well aware, what some call chance is really the Lord at work, orchestrating it all . . ."

Mr. Webster gave a brief smile in response, and nodded.

"At the heart of it . . . Her *uncle* was granted guardianship of her a number of years ago, but instead of keeping his word that he would look after her . . . her parents died, you see - consumption . . . he forced her to live and *work* in that dreadful place ever since." Abigail frowned. "She has been greatly affected by all the abuse and vice she has endured. And then, of course, there is her uncle - she fears him most of all. And for good reason."

Abigail paused, turning her head momentarily.

She turned back to look at Mr. Webster. "You see, it was this man . . . Millforte . . . who injured Henry."

"I say!" exclaimed Mr. Webster.

Abigail's gaze dropped to her lap. She squeezed her eyes shut, not wanting to remember, as she conveyed to Mr. Webster the particulars of the dreaded event.

"The scoundrel," said Mr. Webster, shaking his head. "Dear, oh, dear. I am dreadfully sorry, Mrs. Jones. I do not wish to stir up such painful memories."

Abigail gently dabbed her eyes with her handkerchief. "Well, now. There is some good news, at last." She tried to smile. "Ruby informed me, before you arrived, that she has turned to the Lord for mercy and forgiveness."

"I say!" Mr. Webster exclaimed. His brow shot upward as his eyes widened. "Unbelievable!"

"Yes, it is quite wonderful! And a very welcome occurrence . . ." Mixed emotions moved across her face as she spoke.

"Is there something wrong, Mrs. Jones?"

"No, no. Not at all. I—" She shrugged into silence.

"And what of this Mr. Mill . . . Millfont?"

"Millforte," Abigail said with almost a shudder. "Yes, Mr. Millforte. After he injured Henry, he threatened to return. He claims Ruby as his own and assured us all he would return again for her. To tell you the truth, I have been so concerned with whether or not Henry would live these past few days, I have not given enough thought to what must be done to prevent history from repeating itself."

"What a frightful thought that must be for you all. And what of this Ruby girl, if he returns?"

"He will stop at nothing to drag her back to the city again. Back to that horrible place . . . Or worse."

Mr. Webster clasped his hands in his lap and tapped his thumbs together absentmindedly. "Well then, one can only ask - is this really the safest place for her to be stationed?"

Abigail sighed. "I do confess, I do not believe it is."

"Is there nowhere else she might go?"

"In truth, the very day that Millforte arrived, Henry and I had made ready to send her to stay with my brother-in-law and his family. It is a fair journey from here, and I cannot imagine that Millforte would ever find her there."

"Well, perhaps you ought to resume your endeavour. Mr. Stratton agreed, did he not?"

"I would not say that he *agreed* . . . I believe he thought she would be safe there, but there is no doubt in my mind that he would wish her to be anywhere but here."

"What? Even with this Millforte chap casting his shadow over the whole parsonage?"

"Perhaps, even so." Abigail looked as though she intended to speak further but couldn't find the words.

"Pardon my frankness, Mrs. Jones, but it seems as though there might be more to the story . . . Pray, am I right?"

Abigail froze. She looked at him, in many ways a perfect stranger. Dare she voice the concern that had been building within her?

"I confess, I do not know. I do suspect so, but I cannot give any certainty on the matter. It is only . . . only a feeling. A suspicion, that has been growing for some time now."

"I assure you, ma'am, if you do wish to confide in me, I shall employ the utmost discretion. I have no intention of prying if the matter is one that you do not wish to discuss. But a burden shared is often easier to carry, and I am willing to aid you in carrying it if you wish it so."

Abigail sighed, much more deeply this time, drawing shaky breath as she prepared to speak. "For some time now, I have wondered if perhaps, there might be some form of attachment that has formed between Henry and Ruby. I have observed . . . glances, and attitudes. Even actions that, to me, indicate something deeper than mere Christian charity on Henry's part. And I fear that there may be something deeper than mere gratitude on Ruby's part."

"I say!" Mr. Webster sighed. "Small wonder you are concerned." He shook his head gently. "Have you addressed your suspicions with either of them?"

"Not openly." Abigail sighed. "You see, there are also times when I wonder if I might simply be reading too much into things. Yet, truly, I do not believe that I am . . ."

Mr. Webster shifted in his seat, his fist drawn up to his mouth. He appeared to Abigail to be deep in thought.

After a few moments of silence, he lowered his hand and fixed his gaze squarely on Abigail.

"It appears to me that you have two options concerning what might be done, Mrs. Jones. The first, would be to voice your concerns with Mr. Stratton, and if he confirms there to be any sort of partiality, you would then inform him of the gross inappropriateness of such an attachment, insisting that Ruby be removed to your brother-in-law's house for her own safety and for that of Mr. Stratton's reputation."

He paused.

"The other option . . . is to send Ruby to your brother-in-law's house presently, without consulting or confronting Mr. Stratton. She is still in danger of this Millforte fellow, regardless of any inappropriate attachments, so you would merely be acting in her best interests. And, indeed, in the interests of all those at the parsonage, who may once again suffer at this madman's hands."

He leaned forward, ever so slightly.

"And, of course, the distance ought to sever any improper attachment once and for all."

CHAPTER 19

ALL NEW

ABIGAIL CLUTCHED the arm of her chair, her breathing fast and shallow.

"I fear you are right, Mr. Webster. Although, I do not know which choice is best. If I were to send her away without Henry's knowledge, or indeed, consent, I do believe that as soon as he were well enough, he would rush to my brother-in-law's house to bring her back here. And if I were to wait until he were well enough to discuss it, I fear it would be too heavy a blow to him, in addition to everything that has happened."

Mr. Webster nodded slowly. "Yes . . . I say, it certainly does sound as though there is a jolly strong attachment if that is how you imagine he would react." He shook his head. "Personally, I would send the girl away as soon as possible. No discussion. Since he, as master of the house, is incapacitated, all pressing matters concerning the parsonage fall to you. And since a very real threat looms over everyone's safety - especially Ruby's - you must use any available means to secure a measure of safety for all involved. Ruby will be safe at your brother-in-law's house, and in time, perhaps, the distance will unravel whatever attachments may have already formed. Certainly, it would prevent any deeper ones from taking hold, and go a long way toward preserving Mr. Stratton's reputation while it might still be recovered."

"I do fear there has already been some damage done to his reputation. Before his infirmity he and I travelled to the village. We were dismayed to discover that all sorts of whisperings about Ruby were being passed around. Many questioned Henry's motives and . . . his purpose . . . in having her here."

"I say!" Mr. Webster interjected.

"A man at the church - we have not been able to ascertain his identity - recognised Ruby after the service, the day that she came with us to church. We later found out that he was, well . . . acquainted . . . with Ruby, through her previous station. It must have been he who started all of the rumours. Indeed, we believe that it was through him, somehow, that word of Ruby's whereabouts reached Millforte himself."

Mr. Webster's eyebrows shot up. "Oh, my dear Mrs. Jones!"

The drawing room door swung open and Bessie entered. "Pardon me, ma'am, I am dreadfully sorry to interrupt, but Dr. Shaw is here and wishes to speak with you urgently."

Abigail rose to a stand, her heart starting to race. "Henry! Is he all right?"

"Oh, yes, ma'am. Do not be concerned - only, the doctor must be going - he has an urgent matter in town. But he is insistent on seeing you before he goes."

Abigail sighed. "Very well." She turned to face Mr. Webster. "Please, do excuse me, Mr. Webster. I shall have Browne come and show you to your new room. Please, do make yourself comfortable here while you are waiting for him."

"Thank you, Mrs. Jones," smiled Mr. Webster, settling back into his chair. "Sincerely."

Abigail hurriedly followed Bessie into the hallway, expecting to see Dr. Shaw's straight, large frame standing there.

Bessie kept walking, heading for the staircase. Abigail followed.

As they reached Henry's room, Abigail froze. Was that Henry's voice she had just heard? Hastily, she followed Bessie in, and her knees almost buckled as she saw Henry's face, animated and happy, speaking to Dr. Shaw and Ruby.

Abigail's heart sank as she saw Ruby, and the look in Henry's eyes each time he glanced at her.

There was no doubt an attachment had formed. But how strong was it? And how likely that it might be broken without injury or distress?

Abigail feared she already knew the answers to both questions, and they were not the ones she wanted.

"Aunt Abigail . . ." Henry said, his voice hoarse and dry. The sweet, loving joy in his eyes as he looked straight at her sent a twist of guilt through her heart. He had no idea what she had just been thinking. Or planning.

Ruby looked up at Abigail, too. Abigail saw a freshness and purity in Ruby's eyes that it startled her to notice. As Ruby smiled at her, another blade of guilt pierced Abigail.

Looking at Henry and Ruby together, Abigail saw only good - the evidence of God's Spirit within them. Would it really be such an improper match now that Ruby had received salvation? Didn't God's forgiveness cleanse all impurity of heart and deed? Didn't His love wash clean all depths of guilt and shame?

"Henry, my dear!" Abigail rushed toward him, trying unsuccessfully to push all her thoughts far from her and enjoy this moment, this miracle of Henry's awakening.

"Are you well, Aunt?" Henry's eyes filled with concern as Abigail knelt beside him. Worry had altered her face and tumultuous emotions filled her eyes.

"Oh, I am amazed, my dear! It is wonderful to see you moving and speaking again . . ."

Tears spilled down Abigail's cheeks as she spoke. She clasped Henry's hand and began stroking his hair with her other hand. "Oh, my dear . . ."

Hard as she tried, she could no longer stifle the weeping that had been welling up inside of her. Sobs and tears poured out in equal measure, partly due to relief and concern for Henry's well-being and partly from guilt and confusion about his attachment to Ruby.

"Oh, Aunt! Do not cry . . . The Lord has been gracious. He has preserved me, and He is with us all . . ."

Abigail cried even more, her mind and heart in anguish about what ought to be done.

"There, now! Oh, Aunt . . ." Henry squeezed her hand.

As Abigail's sobs eased, she looked up at Henry. His eyes were filled with compassion.

Abigail glanced at Ruby. A flutter of trepidation filled her chest as she noticed that Ruby was holding Henry's other hand.

Lifting her eyes to meet Ruby's, Abigail was struck by how different the girl looked. There was peace in her eyes, and a purity that seemed to have completely erased the decades of darkness and emptiness that had once resided there. Gentle contentment seemed to radiate from her face.

Abigail looked down, speechless. Her conversation with Mr. Webster now seemed utterly irrelevant, though deep down she knew the threat of Millforte's return still hung over them all like a darkening raincloud.

"Mrs. Jones," said Dr. Shaw, the sudden boom of his voice scattering her thoughts.

"Oh, yes, Dr. Shaw . . ." She suddenly remembered what Bessie had said about the doctor's wish to speak with her and his pressing need to depart from the parsonage. She stood up and walked over to him. "Forgive me, I did not intend to detain you further. I understand you have important business to attend to in the village."

"Do not worry, Mrs. Jones. I understand how relieved you must be to see your nephew back from the brink. I merely wished to tell you that I have examined him, and I am quite convinced he is in no danger at present. It may not be a speedy road back to perfect health, but I am sure that with your help and support, it is a journey he will make successfully."

"Oh, thank you, Dr. Shaw! That is wonderful. Thank you."

"Well, it is as Mr. Stratton has said, ma'am. The Lord has preserved Him. And I have no doubt that He will continue to do so."

Abigail smiled and nodded in gratitude.

"And now I must away. I shall return in a day or two to assess his improvement, but I do feel it is now a case of simply moving forward, day by day. He will grow stronger over time, and it appears he has wonderful support around him here."

Dr. Shaw glanced at Ruby as he said the last few words. Abigail glanced over, too.

Ruby was helping Henry raise a glass of water to his lips. His eyes were shining with wonder and gratitude as Ruby patiently assisted him.

"Thank you, Dr. Shaw," Abigail said, barely above a whisper, as the doctor bowed and took his leave.

She stood, rooted to the spot, for a few moments, just watching. And as she watched, she was in no doubt about the depth of the attachment that had formed.

Now, she must ascertain whether it was one she should discourage or embrace.

HENRY'S HEART drummed rapidly in his chest as Ruby lifted the small glass to his parted lips. He wasn't sure why her hands were trembling. Especially when she looked so happy. He was thrilled to finally be awake and alert. Smiling, speaking . . . living.

"Thank you, Ruby," Henry rasped, his voice weak and dry from lack of use. "You look . . . different, somehow. Yet, I am not sure. There is something . . . Perhaps, it is only that I have been asleep for so long . . ."

He studied her. It seemed to unnerve her. She broke eye contact with him and her cheeks pinked ever so slightly. Yet, a moment later she raised her eyes to meet his. He smiled. What eyes she had . . . He could never tire of looking into them.

She smiled - a peaceful, contented smile. "There is something . . ." she half-whispered.

Henry fixed his gaze on her. The more he looked at her, the more he noticed changes in her appearance. Her eyes seemed . . . brighter. Livelier. Her face seemed almost smoother, the worry and fear now barely traceable.

"What is it?" he asked, eager to know the hinge upon which the dramatic transformation had taken place.

Ruby opened her mouth to speak, but no words came out.

He could see hope in her eyes, and her mouth parted in a smile. She shook her head gently. "I do not even know how to begin!"

Glee was in her voice. Henry's heart surged with delight on hearing such positive emotion from her.

"Oh, He has done it! God has forgiven me!" She half-shrieked, half-laughed. "He has made me new!"

Henry's heart fluttered. He felt light-headed.

"Oh, Ruby!"

A grin broke out across his face, as absolute happiness filled him.

"He has! Why, I can see it! You look . . . new! You do! Oh, Ruby . . ." He wanted nothing more than to embrace her, yet his injuries pinned him to the bed. Besides, there were all manner of factors rendering it improper to do so, even had he been physically able.

"Thank you," she said, her exuberant smile toning down a little. "Thank you for all that you said the last time you awoke. It was then, when you fell back to sleep, that I prayed." Her eyes filled with wonder. "And He heard me, and He forgave me." She squeezed her eyes shut and sighed quietly.

Tears of delight pricked Henry's eyes. "Oh, Ruby . . . I am so glad. Truly, this is the most wonderful news I could have ever hoped to hear!"

He noticed Abigail out of the corner of his eye. Turning his eyes to look at her, he added, "Is it not, Aunt Abigail?"

Abigail sighed, her heavy brow at odds with her words. "Yes. It is wonderful."

Ruby looked at Abigail and smiled.

"I cannot believe it . . . I am overjoyed!" Henry said with a hint of a laugh, leaning his head back into his pillow and closing his eyes. Opening them again, he looked at Ruby.

She did look new. New and clean.

For the first time since he had regained consciousness, Millforte's hulking image flashed into Henry's mind. Inwardly, he shuddered. The distance of character between that brute and Ruby seemed even more vast now. Of course, to him, it had always been. But he could not shake the thought that if Millforte were to see Ruby now, even he would not recognise her.

It was a marvel. Such an enormous change that one prayer had wrought. He looked at her. She was sitting watching him, such contented peace on her face. It made his heart melt.

"I am so grateful," Ruby said quietly. "Although, I do know that the path ahead will not be without difficulty."

Ruby glanced at Abigail as she said this, and Henry detected that the two must have already spoken on the matter.

Abigail smiled encouragingly, though an invisible weight still seemed to lay heavy upon her.

Henry looked hard at Ruby. "That is true, Ruby. Difficult times will come - we can none of us avoid them - but when they do come, you will not be facing them alone. The Lord will give you the grace, strength and courage to face even, even the most frightful trial."

Ruby looked at him, such serious conviction in her eyes that it made his heart ache. "Even *him* . . . Even Millforte. I confess, I do still fear him. But I know that God will help me. I know . . . He will."

She nodded absentmindedly, her gaze falling to the floor, as though trying to remind herself of the truth of her words.

"No matter what happens, God is with you. He is in control, He is on your side, and He will bring you through." Henry paused. "Just as He is doing now, for me."

Ruby glanced up at him. "Yes." She smiled. "He has heard our prayers and He is helping you."

Henry returned her smile. "And He will always help me. Just as He will always help you." He shifted his gaze to Abigail. "And you!" He smiled.

Abigail smiled and sighed at the same time. "So very true, my dear. We have so much for which to be thankful. And we are all safe in His capable hands."

"Shall I pray a moment?" Henry asked.

Abigail and Ruby both smiled at the same time, relief and gratitude filling their faces. "Yes," they each said.

Henry closed his eyes, offering a silent prayer of gratitude before beginning his audible prayer.

"O Lord, our God, I thank You, and give You praise, Father, for preserving my life thus far. For restoring to me my consciousness and for preserving and looking after everyone here. Thank You, Lord, more than I can say, for saving Ruby."

He couldn't stop a smile flooding his cheeks.

"For her earnest cry to You for mercy, which You have heard, Lord, and which You alone can answer. You alone can redeem us. I ask You, Lord, in the precious name of your Son, Jesus, to please continue to watch over us all with Your unfailing love and mercy. Please, keep us safe from foes that have disturbed us in the past and from the fears that linger over us as we look to the future. Lord, please have mercy on us all, and help us to always love You first and foremost in our hearts. Help us to serve You with everything that we have, and help us to love one another as You have loved us, with kindness and compassion and grace."

He heard Abigail clear her throat quietly, and a rustling of fabric.

"And help us to trust in You, to know without a doubt that

You are in control, and that You are faithful and true. In Jesus's name I ask all these things, Lord . . . Amen."

Peace was in the room and the three sat still in silent contemplation after Henry finished praying. Footsteps and muffled voices further down the hall eventually broke into the silence and Ruby turned to look at the door.

"That must be Mr. Webster," said Abigail. "I asked Browne to show him to his room."

"Whose room?" asked Henry, his brow furrowing in confusion.

"Mr. Webster." Abigail looked almost guilty. "He . . . well, perhaps, are you well enough to speak further for a short while?"

Henry groaned as he tried to shift his back and shoulders. "Yes . . ."

"Are you sure?" Abigail didn't seem convinced.

"Yes, yes . . . A short while, yes."

"Very well." Abigail glanced at Ruby. She hesitated. "Ruby, I should like to speak to Henry privately about Mr. Webster. You do not mind, I presume?"

"Oh . . . no . . . not at all," Ruby said, flustered. She rose to a stand. "I shall leave you both."

Henry opened his mouth to protest, but catching sight of Abigail's face, he detected something deeper going on.

He closed his mouth, sighing inwardly at Ruby's dismissal, and watching her as she made ready to leave. How he longed for her to stay.

"Rest well," Ruby said, some of the confidence gone from her voice.

Henry smiled at her warmly. "Ruby, truly, I am overjoyed. It is wonderful news!"

Ruby smiled back at him, then left, glancing over her shoulder at him as she did so.

Henry saw it. His heart soared.

He sank his head back into his pillow. "It is wonderful, Aunt, is it not?" he asked, a smile still lingering at his mouth.

Abigail looked at him without speaking.

Henry looked up at her. "What is the matter, Aunt?"

Abigail sighed. Still, she said nothing.

"Who is this Mr . . .?"

"Mr. Webster," Abigail answered. "He arrived here earlier, sent by Sir Harford. He brought a letter with him, from Sir Harford, to confirm his identity . . . and his ability to carry out what he has proposed."

"And what has he proposed?"

Abigail stepped over to the chair that Ruby had been sitting in and perched on the edge of the seat. "He has offered his assistance with . . . church matters, until you are well enough to resume your station."

Henry's eyebrows raised, half in surprise at the news and half in realisation that he would probably be unable to lead the church for quite some time. He didn't like the idea of a stranger stepping in, though.

"What is he like? Is he able for it? Would he have a heart for the people of the church?"

"He seems a rather serious and respectable young man."

"Young? How young?"

"I imagine he is around your age, my dear."

"Ah."

Abigail smiled slightly. "He is not so young that he would be inexperienced or uncommitted, I assure you. He helped his father - who was himself a clergyman - for a number of years. And he comes to us highly recommended by Sir Harford, who wrote so with his own hand."

"So he has experience, yes, that is good - but does he have *heart*, Aunt? Would he genuinely care for everyone?"

"I believe so, my dear. I have already seen him demonstrate great wisdom and compassion."

"How so?"

Abigail seemed to pause for a moment. Her eyes darted. "I made him aware of Ruby, and of our situation here . . ."

"Aunt! Can he be trusted?" Henry's eyes widened in concern. Fierce protectiveness flooded him.

"Henry, he was sent by Sir Harford, who himself is aware of at least part of the story. You cannot think that Sir Harford would have sent Mr. Webster if he did not believe he could be trusted with so delicate a situation!"

Henry relaxed a little. "No, I suppose not." He thought for a moment. "And he was compassionate, about Ruby?"

Abigail cleared her throat gently. "Yes . . . and glad to hear of her good news."

Henry's eyebrows raised as he smiled. "Oh!"

"He did, however, voice his concerns . . . about her safety."

Henry said nothing, apprehension gathering in his heart. He knew from Abigail's tone that she was about to say something she knew he would not want to hear.

"Millforte *has* threatened to return, after all," Abigail went on, meeting Henry's gaze only occasionally. "And now that you are incapacitated, the threat is much more grave. Browne would be *willing* to defend, but the poor man is not young. And myself, Ruby and Bessie are women - even all of us together would be no match for that . . . that brute of a man."

Henry was torn. He didn't want to hear anything about Millforte, yet he knew that a solution must be devised as quickly as possible.

He sighed. "And what of this new fellow, this Mr. Webster?"

Abigail hesitated. "I believe he would be overpowered, as you were."

Henry looked around frantically. "I must be up and about as soon as possible. We must ask Dr. Shaw on his next visit what can be done to hasten my recovery. Perhaps there—"

"Henry!" Abigail interrupted. "That is not the answer, my dear. "

Henry looked up at her, not wanting to hear the words that he knew were coming.

"There *is* a way," Abigail said slowly. "A way that Ruby can be safe, out of his reach—"

"Aunt . . ." Henry frowned.

"It is the only way, my dear! After all, it was what we were about to do, until we were interrupted by Millforte himself!"

Henry wished he could jump out of bed and do something - anything - to avoid Abigail's entreaties.

"She will be safe there," she continued. "My brother-in-law's estate is vast. There are so many—"

"How can you ask this?" Henry barked.

He didn't like interrupting her, but it drove him mad to think of sending Ruby away.

"Especially now?" Henry continued. "She is in need of our guidance and support. This is a tremendous, enormous change for her! You expect me to abandon her at the turning point of her life?"

His voice was filled with as much volume as he could muster, which wasn't awfully much.

Abigail was stunned. "Henry! This is not about you . . ."

"No, it is about you! You want her away from here! It was your idea to send her to your brother-in-law's house - not mine! I did not wish it. I only agreed because I was at a loss to know what ought to be done. But surely the fact that we were prevented is proof that it was not the right plan!"

"Do you hear yourself, Henry? What then? You would rather she stay here so you can fawn over her until we all end up battered and bruised, or even dead?"

Henry gaped. "Fawn over her? Aunt, I—" He stopped suddenly, his eyes wide as he realised what he had been about to say.

Abigail looked down. When she spoke, her tone was soft and gentle.

"I know, my dear. I know."

Abigail paused, sighing.

"You love her."

CHAPTER 20

A WEB OF DECEIT

HENRY'S EYES darted to and fro. "She has been entrusted to our care, and—"

"Then we must care for her," Abigail said, shaking her head. "By ensuring that she cannot be reached by that horrid man. By keeping her safe from what has already happened to you."

The anguish on Henry's face was almost unbearable. He was in love with Ruby, there was no question. Abigail's heart sank as she observed his agitation.

"But I would not be keeping her safe - I would be sending her away for your *brother-in-law* to keep her safe. Aunt, she needs us! She—"

"But, Henry, she cannot remain here *and* be safe! We must choose one or the other."

Henry thrust his chin up as he turned his eyes away from her, grimacing immediately afterward.

Abigail hated seeing him in so much pain - of body *and* soul. She softened her voice slightly. "My dear, you know what he is capable of doing. Surely, if we truly love her and want what is best for her, we must be willing to sacrifice our own ideas about what ought to happen. Or not happen."

Remorse pricked her conscience as she realised she had been guilty of wanting things her own way, too. She silently prayed for forgiveness and guidance.

"Aunt, I . . . I cannot do it. She needs us, at this *critical* point of her life. If ever she needed us, it is now . . ." Henry muttered, shaking his head. He sighed heavily.

Suddenly, he was completely still. After a few moments, he looked at Abigail as some form of resolve or determination seemed to return to his eyes.

"I cannot give you an answer now, Aunt. Permit me some time to consider things."

Abigail knew from his tone that he had already begun to think.

"Very well. But, do - *please* - consider it very carefully."

"I shall," he half spoke, half sighed. He closed his eyes in a frown, the look of someone in pain.

Abigail studied him for a moment. He looked so pale, so ill. So bruised.

Henry nestled his head back in his pillow, his eyes heavy with encroaching sleep.

"I shall leave now, so you can rest," Abigail said softly. She paused. "I am so glad you have come back to us, my dear. I love you . . ."

"I love you, too, Aunt," Henry breathed, just as sleep enveloped him once again.

"OH, Miss Ruby! That is wonderful news!"

Bessie's voice was practically a squeal. She could hardly stay still, her eyes wide with happy amazement.

"Oh, I truly am so glad!" She gave a happy giggle. "And Mr. Stratton waking up, too! Did you tell him?"

"Yes, he was . . . delighted!" Ruby said, struggling to take it all in.

"Ooh!" Bessie grinned. She thought for a moment, her excitement settling into awe. "What a wonderful day . . ." she said, wistfully.

Ruby cast her mind back through all its happenings. "Truly . . ."

"And, Mr. Stratton - is he improved?"

Ruby's smile faded a little. "He is still unable to move very much. And he is still frightfully pale, and bruised." She sighed and frowned simultaneously. "My heart aches to see him so."

Bessie echoed Ruby's sigh. "I know . . . We are all filled with grief at what was done to him."

Millforte's face flashed into Ruby's mind. The automatic response of every single cell in her body was still to recoil in repulsion at the very thought of him. But there was a phenomenal difference in the level of fear that she felt. It was still there, yet it did not seem to consume her as it had before.

"Are you all right, miss?" Bessie asked, jolting Ruby's awareness back to the present. She had stopped dusting to stare at Ruby, her eyebrows raised slightly. "Is there something on your mind?"

Ruby sighed and shook her head. "I cannot bear the thought that . . . that Henry - indeed, all of us - are still in danger. He is calculating, and cruel. He may wait until we have lowered our defences, but it is a certainty that he *will* return, though we know not when."

Bessie was silent, a searching concern creasing her face.

The dining room door clicked open, startling them both.

Bessie resumed her dusting and Ruby absentmindedly smoothed the skirt of her gown.

Browne entered the room with a quick bow. "Miss Ruby." He turned his attention to Bessie. "Mrs. Jones is asking for you, Bessie. She wishes to make sure that Mr. Webster has all that he needs."

Bessie briefly glanced at Ruby, her expression communicating her curiosity. Ruby stifled a smile, filled with a sudden surge of gratitude for Bessie's zesty nature and optimistic cheerfulness.

As Bessie followed Browne out of the room, leaving Ruby alone, she wondered who this Mr. Webster was, and why it seemed that he would be staying at the parsonage.

THE NEXT DAY, Ruby found only Bessie in the breakfast room, polishing the table.

"Good morning . . . am I early?" she asked, looking at the empty chairs around the empty table.

"Morning, miss." Bessie stopped her cleaning. "Well - Mrs. Jones is with Mr. Stratton, Browne is off to the village on what I gather seems to be some sort of urgent business, though I cannot imagine what it might be, and Mr. Webster, as far as I am aware, has not come down yet. I am just about to lay the place settings now."

"Who is this Mr. Webster that everyone keeps mentioning?" Ruby asked, her tone hushed, her eyes glancing toward the door.

"Well," Bessie said, her expression one of disbelief and excitement. She dropped her voice to a whisper. "Mrs. Jones told me last night that Mr. Webster will be staying with us in order to take over Mr. Stratton's duties at the church until Mr. Stratton is recovered!"

Ruby's mouth dropped open, dismay and apprehension filling her. "What? But, who is he?"

"Ah, Mrs. Jones said he is connected somehow with Sir Harford, and comes to us on his very high recommendation."

Ruby's concern partially dissipated. Sir Harford's family had been kind enough to help her and Bessie - she could not imagine he would jeopardise their safety now.

"Oh, I see."

"There is no need to worry. If Sir Harford knows and recommends him, then he will be trustworthy, I am sure." Bessie smiled, resuming her chores.

"Yes. I imagine so." Ruby sighed in relief. "What is he like? Have you met him?"

Bessie stifled a chuckle. "I have. He is . . . how shall I say it? Not quite so *animated* as Mr. Stratton."

Ruby frowned slightly. "But, Mr. Stratton is not unusually animated. No more so than anyone is, really."

Bessie grinned. "Precisely my point! Mr. Webster seems rather forty years beyond his age in terms of his temperament and mentality. I should not like to go so far as to say that he's a *bore*, however . . ." Her expression indicated her amusement at thinking that a bore was precisely what he was.

"Bessie!" Ruby chided, unable to stop a smile.

As if on cue, the dining room door opened and a man around Henry's age - though markedly taller - stood in the doorway. He glanced at Ruby and Bessie and gave a short bow. His posture was stiff and straight, and his eyes showed very little expression.

"Good morning," he said, his voice occluded, his timbre deep.

"Good morning," replied Ruby. Bessie curtseyed and nodded a greeting.

"You must be Miss Ruby?" Mr. Webster half-stated, half-asked, his eyebrows slightly elevated.

"Yes," Ruby answered, wondering how much he knew about her history and her present sphere of life.

"And you are Mr. Webster, I expect?" His sombre countenance and quizzical gaze unnerved her.

He nodded. "Indeed. I am come by way of Sir Harford to lend my assistance to Mr. Stratton while he . . . recovers."

Ruby's heart thudded. She detected a hint of blame in Mr. Webster's tone. She glanced at Bessie, whose own expression seemed to be curious regarding the same.

"So I understand. That is very kind of you," Ruby forced herself to continue. She silently asked God to help her, and for His grace to reign in the room.

Mr. Webster gave a brief nod in response. He seemed too busy studying her to form a verbal reply. His scrutinising attention made Ruby feel as though her face were too close to a fire.

"Would you like some breakfast, sir?" Bessie chimed, glancing at Ruby to reveal her intention of breaking the atmosphere of inspection.

"Yes, indeed." Mr. Webster said, turning and making his way to the table, which was now perfectly set. He stood at his chair, looking at Ruby, waiting until she would be seated before he himself could sit down.

Ruby considered fleeing from the room, but she was so hungry. She knew she would be too weak for the day's activities if she did not eat now.

Reluctantly, she approached the table, settling herself into her usual chair.

Mr. Webster sat down and lifted his napkin, shaking it open and tucking it below his broad chin.

Bessie served the breakfast, leaving the room more than a few times to fetch various plates and accoutrements.

Ruby and Mr. Webster ate in silence for what seemed an age.

"Mrs. Jones tells me that you have recently been saved. That is excellent news."

Ruby looked at him, startled by both the suddenness and kindness of his words. "Yes, I am so very grateful."

"Has Mr. Stratton been informed yet?"

"Yes," Ruby smiled as she remembered Henry's joy and surprise at the news. "Yes, he was . . . delighted."

Mr. Webster said nothing. He simply nodded, a curious look in his eyes that unsettled Ruby even more.

The rest of the breakfast passed in silence, save for an odd triviality spoken now and then. Bessie had not returned for some time, though Ruby kept hoping she would reappear at any moment.

As Ruby rose and bade the new lodger farewell, Mr. Webster raised his hand, motioning for her to wait a moment.

"Miss Ruby," he said, his voice slightly hushed. He stepped toward her and looked into her eyes with a sombre stare. "Should you ever need to speak on ecclesiastical matters, please, do not hesitate to come to me."

Ruby returned his gaze, her brow slightly deepening in discomfort at his proximity, and curious as to his intent.

"Thank you," she said quietly.

"Not at all," he replied. "I wish only to save Mr. Stratton any undue burden at present."

Ruby's heart flipped. So, this was his intent - to draw her away from Henry?

"I do not—"

"Allow me to clarify," he interrupted. "I am here to assist Mr. Stratton. Not only with church matters, for it is partially on my shoulders now to assist him in his recovery. For, indeed, the sooner he recovers, the sooner he can resume his station both in the church and in this parsonage."

He stepped closer to her again, this time so close that she could feel his breath on her face.

"I think it best that you leave him be."

Her mind reeled. Who was this man who had arrived unannounced and was now trying to keep her away from Henry? She had suspected, deep in her spirit, that his presence would be a negative one. It sickened her to realise she'd been right.

With shaking breath, she prayed silently for courage and said, "With all due respect, Mr. Webster, I—"

"Ah, but that is precisely the point," he interrupted again. "Respect. For you see, you are not his equal. And he should have your respect." He looked her up and down as though she were some peculiar - and potentially dangerous - display. "He ought not to be the target of your carnal temptations."

Ruby's blood ran cold. She almost turned to leave the room at once, but her desire for truth and justice burned stronger than her offence.

"Mr. Webster." Ruby stiffened and drew a deep, impassioned breath. "I do respect Mr. Stratton. More than I can say. You are gravely mistaken, sir, if you think that I have any ill intentions toward him."

Mr. Webster scoffed as though in disbelief.

"Mr. Stratton is the very best of men," Ruby continued. "He is unlike every other man I have ever met. And he is the *only* man I respect wholeheartedly."

She strode to the door, then turned and fixed her gaze on the audacious interloper.

"I had hoped, Mr. Webster, that you would prove worthy of Sir Harford's recommendation, and of Henry's charge. I am saddened, for all of us here, that you do not."

"How dare you . . ." Mr. Webster said slowly, his prideful tone briefly reminding Ruby of Millforte. "I am come to assist. To support. Why are you come? To bring sin and suffering to one of God's servants?"

Ruby gaped at him, disbelief dizzying her. "I am here because Mr. Stratton was so kind as to rescue me from a place of depravity and darkness."

The parallel dawned on her as she spoke.

"Just as God sent Jesus to rescue me from all my sin and striving."

Tears sprang to her eyes.

"Mr. Stratton showed me grace, and mercy - as God shows to all. And as I now choose to show to you."

The tears spilled silently down her cheeks. She exhaled sharply.

"You claim to serve God, Mr. Webster, but you are not doing as He does."

She brushed her cheeks with shaking fingers, flinging the tears away.

"Where is your grace, Mr. Webster? Where is your mercy?"

Mr. Webster's silent mouth hung open in shock, his eyes squinting in disgust at Ruby's frankness. He looked as though her words had physically slapped him across the face.

Ruby quietly opened the dining room door and slipped out into the hallway, silent but for the gentle click of the door latching shut and her shaky breathing.

She stood for a moment, evaluating all that she had said, her heart pounding. She prayed silently for wisdom and for the humbling of Mr. Webster's secret pride.

246

THE RELUCTANCE with which Abigail knocked on Ruby's door was of great magnitude. Her eyes were heavy with weariness of body and spirit, and her posture was stooped in exhausted resignation.

"Is everything all right?" asked Ruby, as she appeared in view. She was frowning slightly at Abigail, no doubt because of her fatigued appearance.

Abigail tried to formulate a response. At last, she gave a slight shake of her head and waved her hands to dismiss the question.

"I am here on Henry's orders. He wishes to speak with you."

"Of course. Is he well?"

Abigail nodded slowly. "He is a little improved since yesterday, I think. I am beginning to see evidence that he is more himself."

"Oh, that is wonderful," Ruby breathed, a smile of relief washing over her face.

"Yes," Abigail murmured. More himself indeed. He was up to something, and she knew by his manner that it had everything to do with the girl standing opposite her.

Their journey to Henry's room passed in silence. Upon entering, Ruby made a soft sound of surprise as she saw Henry in a more elevated position. He was not quite sitting up, but closer to it than he had been thus far.

"Ruby," Henry grinned, his face enveloped with a smile upon seeing her. Abigail watched as Ruby smiled in return.

"How are you feeling today?" Ruby asked him.

"Ah, I cannot complain. I am so grateful to be here and to be feeling a little stronger," he said, a wistful expression settling on his features.

"That is wonderful, indeed," Ruby smiled.

Henry motioned with a weak hand for Ruby to sit in the chair she had occupied the previous day. Once she was settled, he looked at Abigail.

"Aunt, I wonder if you might be so kind as to arrange for some tea?"

Abigail had wondered if Henry would find a subtle way of dismissing her, or if he would plainly state his wish to speak with Ruby alone.

"Of course," Abigail said quietly, as she reluctantly turned to leave.

As she walked through the doorway, she cast Henry a look of caution.

His expression in response grieved her. Fleeting as it was, he looked at her with a mix of disappointment and distance.

Her stomach wrenched as she closed the door and headed for the stairs.

With each step, she felt sorrow weigh more heavily upon her. For the first time, she felt as though the closeness she'd always had with Henry had fractured.

She was no longer the person he felt closest to in his heart.

CHAPTER 21

TROUBLED

"It really is wonderful to see you thus improved," said Ruby, shaking her head gently, a peaceful smile on her face.

Henry's heavy thoughts weighed down his attempted smile.

"Improved . . . how much I wish that I had no more improving to do!"

Ruby's brow flickered. "Are you troubled?"

Henry sighed, shaking his head. "Oh, I am fine. All is fine." He shook his head again and looked at her imploringly. "But all is not fine! Is it?"

Ruby appeared unsettled by his fervour.

"What is the matter?" she asked. "Is it Mr. Webster?"

"Mr. Webster? Oh, I had forgotten about him. Truth be told, he is the least of my worries."

Ruby glanced away, her gaze trailing the floor.

Henry's agitation gave way to concern. "Ruby? What is it?"

Ruby sighed. "I . . ."

All kinds of scenarios swept through Henry's mind. None of them pleasant.

"Ruby? You must tell me at once if there is anything improper or untrustworthy about him. He is here to replace me for however long I may be unwell. I have not even met the man! I am trusting the judgement of my aunt and of Sir Harford. According to them, he is highly recommended. But you do not agree? Please. Tell me."

Horror compelled him to ask his next question. "Ruby, was he . . . improper . . . in any way? Toward you?" Anger pulsed in his eyes.

Ruby shook her head quickly. "No," she said faintly. "He said . . ." She grew silent. She looked overwhelmed.

Henry watched her, his brow furrowing. It was agony, waiting for her to speak.

Ruby cleared her throat. When she finally spoke, her voice sounded weak.

"He is cold. And hard. I see no grace in his actions or words."

She spoke slowly, as though choosing each word with utmost carefulness. "He is very proud. And I do not feel that he deserves the praise bestowed upon him by Sir Harford."

She looked Henry in the eye, his heart surging as he remembered what he had almost said to Abigail.

He scolded himself as he pushed the thought aside. Now was not the time to think of such things. Ruby was clearly distressed.

"I fear that he may do more harm than good."

Henry gulped silently, his body filled with a sensation of standing on unstable ground.

He took a deep breath. "Why? What makes you say all this? What did he say?"

Ruby sighed again, and Henry thought he saw her chin quiver slightly.

"He . . . questioned . . . the reasons for my presence here. He thought . . . He suggested . . ." She cleared her throat. "He appears to believe that I am intending to . . . to ruin you."

She looked away from him as she said the last two words. Henry felt as though he could hardly breathe.

Aghast fury reared in him, the urge to defend her filling him with strength.

"How dare he," Henry growled, his gaze darting to and fro.

Moments later, he fixed his eyes on Ruby. "Are you all right?"

Ruby nodded silently. "In truth, I am disappointed by his character. And though I regret placing an extra burden on your shoulders, I am glad to be able to share my concerns with you."

She was looking him in the eye again, and as he looked back at her, his anger dissipated. He longed to reach out and stroke her cheek, to wrap his arms around her and shelter her from the world's cruelty.

Realising what she'd said, Henry sighed. "I do hope you know you may always speak freely with me."

She held his gaze, tenderness in her eyes that disarmed him completely. His breath sounded loud as he became increasingly aware of the silence around them.

Summoning all his willpower, he tore his gaze away. Resolution firmed on his face.

"Ruby, please can you ask Aunt Abigail to come to me at once?"

"Of course," she said.

Henry detected uncertainty in her voice. "What is the matter?"

"Nothing," said Ruby. "Only . . . I do not believe that Mr. Webster will show his true self to the others." Her features twisted with regret. "Oh, if only Bessie had still been there. No one else was there - it will be my word against his, and, well, my word is worthless!"

"Ruby!" Henry reached out his hand toward her elbow, which was too far for him to reach.

"Henry? Are you all right?" she asked, moving closer without realising it.

The corners of his eyes smiled, yet the rest of his face seemed awash with concern. He shook his head gently.

"Ruby . . ." He reached out again, grasping her elbow this time, his dark, earnest eyes looking imploringly into hers. "Your word is worth far more than you know."

Time seemed suspended.

Peace and warmth filled the space between them.

Henry's touch was firm but gentle, and Ruby felt something she couldn't remember feeling for a long time.

Safe.

Just for a moment, there was no Millforte. No Mr. Webster. No suspicions, or cruelty, or regrets of the past. Only peace. Only joy.

Only love.

Love?

Fear jolted her back. Back from Henry's touch. Back from the serenity she had been suspended in. Back to the cold reality of an impending confrontation with Aunt Abigail, with Mr. Webster, and with the designation of debauchery that clung to her like an unseen spider's web.

"Ruby?"

Henry was the picture of compassion and kindness. How

could she dare even think that what had silently passed between them could ever be anything close to love?

Mr. Webster's cold words rang in her ears.

'You are not his equal.'

A man like Henry was unattainably above her station. He could never love her. Not like that.

Sorrow pierced her heart. As grieved as she was to realise that she could never belong with Henry, she was equally surprised to realise how deeply she wished she would.

Her face burned. She turned to leave, not knowing what to say. All she wanted was to flee. Somewhere. Anywhere. Away from those eyes and the thoughts and feelings they were awakening within her.

"Ruby!" Henry called out, his tone strong and questioning.

She turned back, silently refusing to meet his gaze. "I shall fetch Mrs. Jones for you."

Her heart faltered. What a hypocrite she was! How could she maintain that Mr. Webster was accusing her of things untrue when buried deep within her heart were deep feelings of love and yearning for a future with Henry?

"Ruby, please - before you go . . ." He pushed himself up a little, his expression revealing the pain that seemed to overwhelm him as a result.

She stood, frozen, by the door.

"Forgive me. I did not mean to cause any offence, or to do anything . . . improper. Forgive me?"

His voice was tender and gentle. Ruby sighed inwardly. She loved hearing him speak as much as she loved seeing him smile.

The tremor in her voice was detectable even as she cleared her throat. "Please, do not worry."

All she wanted to do was weep.

"RUBY, I . . ."

Henry stared at the silent, pale lady at his door. As he took in the sight of her vulnerable frame, his heart ached to comfort her, to reassure her.

He could not allow Abigail to send her away. And he could not bear the thought of Mr. Webster lingering like a snake and repeating his accusations, whatever they had been.

He had to regain his strength as soon as possible.

Ruby glanced up at him. Silently, a catalogue of communication seemed to pass between them. Yet, the overarching declaration, unspoken as it was, seemed that of sorrow.

Moments later, Ruby drew her stance up straighter and smiled weakly at Henry. Just before she left, she called out, "I shall tell Mrs. Jones that you wish to speak with her."

Before Henry could utter anything in response, she was gone.

Alone in his sick room, he revisited the thoughts that gained determination in his mind each time they entered it.

He must recover. Immediately.

And he must do whatever was necessary to silence all accusations against Ruby and himself once and for all.

Frustration surged through him.

Gritting his teeth, he grabbed the blanket that covered him and threw it toward his feet. Gripping the edge of the bed, he pushed himself upright, his lower back a brace of agony.

Puffing and grunting, he forced himself to turn, his legs dropping over the side of the bed. He stopped himself from crying out in pain.

Steeling his mind, he took a deep, ragged breath, then launched himself to his feet.

Almost immediately, he thudded to his knees. His spine seemed nothing more than a column of pain, and his legs trembled with weakness. Dismay flooded him as he realised his inability to straighten his back and his legs at the same time.

Unable to suppress it any longer, he cried out - an overwhelmed, helpless note of bitter anguish.

Weak and worn, he curled his head down to the floor. Kneeling in a ball of throbbing discomfort, tears filled his eyes.

"Oh, please, God, please help me! I feel so useless, Lord! I cannot even stand . . . I cannot even stand. I feel so useless, Father . . ." He was sobbing now. "Please, God . . . I need to get well! I need to protect her!"

His exhausted panting and whispered prayers were all that punctuated the silence that surrounded him. As he earnestly sought to wait for God's response, he realised what he had prayed.

Instantly, Abigail's words came rushing back to him.

'Henry, this is not about you.'

Realisation dawned on him. All his thoughts and actions - he had been operating as though only he could protect Ruby, when in fact it was God who was truly her protector.

Henry had not been able to protect her from Millforte - God had.

And if the hulking brute kept his promise to return, even if Henry were fully mended, God would protect Ruby. Not him.

"Oh, Father . . . Please forgive me. Oh, how wrong I have been! Forgive me, Lord - I have been looking to my own strength instead of relying on Yours. I have been driven by the mistaken belief that Ruby's protection depends on me. Oh, but I am so weak, Lord. I cannot . . . Forgive me. Forgive me . . . Oh, Lord, please show me what we are to do!"

Abigail's plea to send Ruby to her brother-in-law's house returned to his mind.

He shook his head as tears rolled down his cheeks.

"No . . . Please, Lord - do not send her away! Please remove the threat of Millforte's return. Nothing is impossible for you. Please, do not send Ruby away from us. Oh, please! Permit her to remain with us, and help us to give her all the support and encouragement she needs, especially now that she has put her faith in you, Lord . . ."

Peace returned to him, melting his frustration. As he finished praying, he became aware of the draughty chill that winnowed around his knees on the cold, wooden floor.

Pleading for strength, he clambered slowly to his bedside and hauled himself up. Breathing heavily as his muscles almost gave way, he managed to recline once again under the covers. Beads of sweat lined his forehead and his limbs fell limp as he sank, panting, into an exhausted slumber.

CHAPTER 22

TRUE COLOURS

"SHE IS in the drawing room, miss."

"Thank you, Bessie."

"Are you all right?"

Ruby wanted to say yes, despite how deflated she was. Instead, she gave Bessie a quick nod and as much of a closed-lipped smile as she could muster, then headed for the drawing room.

She knocked the door lightly before opening it. Abigail sat at her writing desk.

"Yes, I know!" she said.

Ruby frowned, puzzled momentarily as to why Abigail would be speaking aloud in an otherwise empty room.

Her stomach flipped.

Abigail looked up. "Ruby."

Ruby walked in. From the corner of her eye, she saw a seated form that had been veiled by the door.

Mr. Webster said nothing. Ruby forced herself to look at him, giving a brief curtsey of acknowledgement. Still, he was silent.

She turned her attention back to Abigail. "Excuse me, Mrs. Jones, but Mr. Stratton wishes to speak with you." Ruby swallowed hard. She had almost called him Henry. That would not do, especially with Mr. Webster's eyes boring into her.

Abigail gave a slight frown. "You are certain? I spoke to him only a little while ago."

"Yes, ma'am. He said so only a few moments ago." Never had Ruby been so aware of scrutinising eyes upon her.

Abigail tucked away the papers she had been working with and smoothed her dress as she stood up.

"Please, do excuse me, Mr. Webster," she smiled at him as she walked to the door.

Ruby stepped aside to allow her to pass, intending to follow her out of the room. As Abigail sailed into the hallway, out of earshot, Mr. Webster cleared his throat.

Ruby groaned inwardly. She glanced over her shoulder at him, not caring if she appeared rude. His intense eyes were filled with knowing judgment.

"Aha," he quipped.

Ruby's heart thudded. She turned to face the door, which had swung shut in Abigail's absence. She had no intention of remaining only to receive further accusations.

"I say!" he exclaimed, jumping to his feet. He strode between her and the door.

"Excuse me, Mr. We—"

"No, excuse *me*," he spat. "How dare you attempt to leave while I was speaking to you. You ought to learn some respect, girl. Might I remind you that I am the head of the house in Mr. Stratton's absence, and as such—"

Now Ruby was the one who interrupted.

"How dare *you*! You are not the head of this house! Mrs.

Jones is, while Henry is ill." She was shaking with indignation.

"Oh . . ." He smirked. *"Henry,* is it? I say . . . You call him by his Christian name, and you spend time alone with him in his bedchamber. I do wonder what other improper intimacies you share with him." His eyes shone with a cruel glint.

Ruby was speechless, reeling at his repugnance. She hoped that Henry was at that very moment urging Abigail to dismiss the disagreeable meddler without delay.

Shaking with indignation, she marched to the door and gripped the gold handle fiercely. As she swung the door open, she glanced back at Mr. Webster's ruddy face.

"I *respect* him, Mr. Webster, which is more than I can say for you. Good day."

Not waiting for his reaction, she rushed out of the drawing room. She could feel her heart beating in her throat the whole way back upstairs. Yet, she did not regret how boldly she had spoken to him.

Back in the safe environment of her room, she flopped into the welcoming wingback chair by the fire. Grasping the blanket that was draped over it, she pulled it tightly around her shoulders.

Gently, a somewhat comforting thought drifted into her mind. Mr. Webster was the one in the wrong, in this present circumstance. Not her. And regardless of whether or not she belonged here, Mr. Webster most certainly didn't.

A desire to pray tugged at her heart.

Oh, Lord, I do not even know what to ask or say . . . only that I am sorry for all the trouble I have brought upon this household. Please, Lord, do not permit Mr. Webster to bring any further pain or difficulty to Henry, or, to anyone here. Please, Lord, help us all . . .

A sense of peace soothed her mind and the sensation of

calmness and safety that washed over her was something she could not remember ever feeling before.

Pulling the blanket closer around her, she reclined in the chair and stretched her legs out toward the fireplace. As she closed her eyes, she breathed out deeply, knowing somehow that God had everything under control.

HENRY OPENED his eyes to see Abigail standing at the foot of his bed.

"Forgive me - I was trying not to wake you. Ruby said you wished to speak with me again."

Abigail's voice was bright, yet her raised eyebrows revealed her confusion.

Henry gave such a slight nod that it seemed Abigail did not even notice it.

"I must have dozed off for a moment," he said, the exhaustion that consumed him filling his voice, too.

Abigail moved the wooden chair closer to Henry's bedside. "Is everything all right, my dear?"

Henry sighed, deeply yet silently. "Oh, Aunt. It is dreadful!"

Abigail's expression darkened. She leaned forward. "What is, my dear?"

"I knew it was not a good idea. Deep down, I knew it, right from the very start." He sighed, louder this time, his shaking breath forced out of him by the almost unbearable frustration that filled his chest.

Abigail looked at her lap. "I must confess . . . I have been thinking the same, of late. I—"

"He must go. At once!"

"Oh, Henry, I knew . . . " Abigail trailed off, blinking. Her brow furrowed as she looked squarely at Henry. *"He?"*

"Yes." Henry frowned.

Realisation of the meaning of Abigail's previous words hit him like a brick. His expression switched from confusion to outrage in a flash.

"Aunt? You cannot think that I meant— Aunt!"

He practically spat the words at her, his face twisted in disgust.

Abigail looked down. "Forgive me. I misunderstood. To whom *are* you referring?"

A scoffing sound erupted from Henry's throat as he shook his head slowly.

A few moments of painful silence later, he spoke, the offence plainly evident by the staccato in his words.

"I am referring to Mr. Webster."

Abigail's eyebrows shot up. "Mr. Webster?"

Henry looked at her, his eyes blazing. "Yes. Mr. Webster. Please would you be so kind as to inform him that his presence here is no longer required."

"But, Henry!"

"No, Aunt. He is a scoundrel. A cad. A hypocrite!"

Abigail's voice was every bit as cross as her face. "Now, Henry! You have never even met the man! You cannot level such severe accusations as—"

"I can, because they are all true. He is no longer welcome here." He snorted softly. "If he ever was . . ."

"Henry, you cannot be serious! Permit me to introduce him to you. Meet him for yourself, and you will see that he is a fine young man. He is sensible and—"

"And proud. And judgmental. And salacious!" Henry bellowed.

Abigail gaped. "Henry! Why do you say such things?"

"Were you aware, Aunt, that he accosted Ruby and

insinuated improper reasons for her presence here?" His eyes flashed with indignance.

"Now, Henry, I am sure that he only has the very best of intentions. He understands what a delicate situation it is to have Ruby here. And how dangerous it could be to your reputation. I am sure he did not mean any harm."

"He is proud, is he not? And cold?"

"No! He is reserved, and not one for idle chatter, to be sure. But he is very understanding, and I dare say, he cares a great deal that everything ought to run in its proper course. Besides, I cannot imagine that Sir Harford would entrust him with such a duty if he were not suited for the task." Abigail squinted. "Why? What did Ruby say, precisely? I am sure she must have misunderstood him, my dear."

"I am sure she did not! Aunt!" Bewilderment flooded Henry. "Have you no concerns? We know nothing of the man! We know nothing of his motivations or—"

"He comes by order of Sir Harford - your trusted friend and patron! Knowing Sir Harford as you do, you cannot suggest that he would have sent someone of such odious description to your aid! Really, Henry," Abigail said, tutting. "We know more of Mr. Webster than we do of Ruby!"

Henry felt as though he had been kicked in the stomach. Had Abigail taken leave of her senses?

SILENCE HOVERED BETWEEN THEM.

Steeling his jaw, Henry spoke with a firm, clear voice. "He must leave. At once."

He turned his gaze away from his aunt's shocked visage.

Abigail stuttered. "But, Henry, you—"

"The matter is settled," he said, without looking at her.

A few painfully silent moments later, Abigail stood. "I shall leave you for now, my dear" she said, almost in a whisper.

Henry glanced at his aunt. He seemed restless.

"I trust the next time we speak you will inform me of Mr. Webster's departure."

Abigail froze momentarily, then with a deep breath exited the room. The light was dimmer in the hallway, and she welcomed the sensation of solitude it fostered.

What ought she to do?

It seemed folly to dismiss Mr. Webster so dramatically, without a concrete reason to offer him.

And how would they explain it to Sir Harford? Henry was already jeopardising his standing with the Harfords by having Ruby here in the first place. If he were to send Mr. Webster away and permit Ruby to remain, Abigail wouldn't be surprised if Sir Harford withdrew his generosity from Henry altogether. And then where would they all be?

Yet, Henry was head of the household, and his wishes must be carried out. No matter what the consequences would be for the rest of them.

Browne emerged from nowhere, it seemed, startling Abigail into motion.

"Mrs. Jones," he nodded as he drew closer to her.

"Oh, Browne, is Mr. Webster still in the drawing room, do you know?"

"I saw Mr. Webster about ten minutes ago, ma'am - he was heading out to the village. Said something about having a few calls to do. The carriage was just setting off before I came upstairs."

Abigail didn't know if she felt relief or disappointment. At least, perhaps, it would buy her some time to decide what to say.

"Thank you, Browne."

She changed direction and headed for her own bedchamber. A rest and some prayer was what she needed now.

Her heart was heavy as she passed by Henry's door. She had a dreadful feeling that no matter what she might do, she would lose him.

Shuddering, she wondered if she already had.

RUBY WAS SURPRISED to find that she must have dozed off, as she slowly became aware of everything around her.

Mr. Webster flashed into her mind, followed by Henry, then Abigail. Her stomach clenched as she thought of the conversation that had been due to take place between Henry and Abigail.

Please, God, let them believe me. Please let them see Mr. Webster in his true light.

She noticed out her window that the daylight was beginning to wane. Soon it would be time for dinner. Dinner with Mr. Webster, who had accused her, and Abigail, who probably didn't believe that Ruby was telling the truth about him.

Oh, how she wished that Henry would be accompanying them in the dining room. It seemed like so long ago that his pleasant presence had graced the table, his smile and kind words like some kind of sweet seasoning that improved the meal.

A thud in her chest echoed the memory of their encounter earlier that day. Henry . . . grasping her elbow . . . how time had seemed to stop.

Could that be what love feels like?

Did she love Henry? She had never been in love, never suspected she ever would be . . . Is this what it was?

Her heart beat faster.

She could not be in love with him. It must be gratitude. Yes, that was it. He had rescued her from Millforte's clutches, after all. It would only be natural to hold him in high regard, as a result.

That must be all it was.

It *had* to be. Henry would never choose someone like her.

Miss Acton's hopeful face flashed into her mind, her heart sinking at the same time.

Henry did not seem to return Miss Acton's obvious affection, she reminded herself. Though, it was clear that Abigail certainly wished he would.

Ruby sighed. She could not imagine Abigail encouraging Henry to show affection to her. Not after all that had happened.

Yet, as Ruby thought of Henry - of his deep eyes, his kind voice, his strong faith - she felt as though she had discovered the most valuable treasure on earth.

A knock brought her thoughts back to her surroundings. Bessie's voice called out, muffled through the heavy door.

Oh, no . . .

It was time for dinner.

"THANK YOU, BESSIE," Abigail said as she replaced the serving spoons in the tray of steaming potatoes.

Ruby had barely been able to contain her relief on entering the dining room to find only Abigail present. Dinner was served promptly, with no Mr. Webster in sight. Yet, with each moment that passed, Ruby grew increasingly aware that the atmosphere was far from comfortable.

Bessie withdrew from the room once all the elements of the meal had been served, leaving Abigail and Ruby alone in an awkward silence.

More than once, Ruby almost spoke, but each time her voice came to the brink of making a sound, she hesitated, unsure of Abigail's mood after her conversation with Henry.

At one point they caught sight of each other, but Abigail swiftly diverted her gaze before Ruby could acknowledge it.

Time seemed to pass so slowly.

Ruby's thoughts kept drifting to Henry. She had not even told him all the details of Mr. Webster's remarks, yet he had responded as though he had been present to hear the contemptible words himself. Not for a second had he doubted her, or tried to dismiss the situation.

She glanced at Abigail. Sickening coldness settled itself in the pit of Ruby's stomach.

Despite Abigail's silence, her disconsolateness was evident. Her eyebrows were drawn down toward each other, and soft wrinkles lined her brow. When she was not chewing her dinner she chewed her lip slightly, and often seemed to gaze blankly into some far-off imagination.

The silence and thick, rich meat was soon too much for Ruby. She laid down her knife and fork, then wiped her lips with a napkin. She could not manage one more bite, or she feared it would all come back up again.

The clinking of Ruby's cutlery startled Abigail from her reverie. She looked down at her own plate. Much of the food thereon remained undisturbed. Shifting her gaze to Ruby, she lifted her own napkin and dabbed at the corners of her lips.

Ruby, aware of Abigail's eyes on her, looked up and gave her a weak smile.

"Forgive me, but I cannot eat another bite," Ruby said.

Abigail shook her head and waved her hand simultaneously. "Oh, do not— That is fine."

With a look of exhaustion about her, Abigail's head bowed, and her gaze sank to her fork, hovering in mid-air just above her potatoes.

"I find that my appetite has gone from me, too."

Ruby wanted to say something, to offer some encouragement or comfort. But each time she tried to formulate a sentence, she was left with nothing but a blank mind and a heavy heart.

Abigail delicately placed her fork and knife beside her plate. A long, weary sigh escaped her lips.

Browne entered the room, his sudden presence a welcome break in the tense, silent air.

"Mr. Webster has returned from town, ma'am, though he does not require any dinner."

"Thank you, Browne," Abigail said, her brows slightly raised though still drawn toward each other with concern. "If you could be so kind as to ask him to meet me in the drawing room shortly . . .?"

Her voice trailed off, a slight waver alongside its weakness.

"Of course, ma'am," nodded Browne. With a bow, he departed. The silence resettled around the two women, seeming heavier now, like a thick fog.

Ruby's heart fluttered and thudded at the same time. At the mention of Mr. Webster's name, her stomach lurched, her limbs trembling. She was so glad he was not joining them for dinner. Not that they were eating much of it, anyway.

How she longed that he would be gone as suddenly as he

had arrived. It would be wonderful not to have to see him again.

Yet, she regretted that Abigail had to endure the distress of giving him his marching orders. She could not imagine he would take too kindly to the abrupt change. But as she ran her memories over his insidious accusations, she could only be glad to anticipate Shiloh Hall restored to how it was without his odious presence.

Abigail rose from her seat with an air of tremulous apprehension. She glanced at Ruby, a strange mix of emotion in her weary eyes, then walked away, saying nothing.

Ruby did not know if she should speak, or acknowledge Abigail's departure in some other way. She gripped the dark wooden edge of the table, her knuckles blanching.

With a draught of air and a click of the door, Abigail was gone.

Now, Ruby hoped it would not be long until Mr. Webster was, too.

For good.

CHAPTER 23

ENTANGLED

"Ah, Mrs. Jones," Mr. Webster smiled as Abigail joined him in the drawing room.

"Good evening, Mr. Webster," Abigail said as she curtseyed absentmindedly. "Please - do sit down."

"I say - are you quite all right, Mrs. Jones?" Mr. Webster frowned, studying her as he reclaimed his seat.

Abigail exhaled shakily and sank down into the chair opposite his.

"Well, I . . . I do have some news—" She cleared her throat. "—that I must share with you."

Mr. Webster gave her a knowing look. "Ah. Allow me to deduce. It is in relation to the attachment you fear between Mr. Stratton and your . . . *lodger?*"

Abigail drew a deep breath. Should she really send him away? Had Henry fully thought it all through? He was not yet well enough yet to resume his duties in the church. Surely they were all in need of Mr. Webster's assistance, regardless of how Ruby might have interpreted his remarks?

Besides, the decision was ultimately Sir Harford's. And if Henry insisted on Mr. Webster's dismissal, Sir Harford could just as easily insist on dismissing Henry's standing in society.

She prayed silently for wisdom.

"Well, no. Not really. It *does* involve Henry." She smoothed her skirts nervously. "Oh, dear - I do urge you to understand that, for me, I do not agree with what Henry has bid me say to you."

Mr. Webster knitted his eyebrows up and down quizzically. "Very well."

Abigail looked at her hands. Surely it was folly to dismiss him. Yet, she knew she had a duty to obey Henry's instructions.

Closing her eyes momentarily, she arranged her tangled thoughts in the clearest order she could manage.

"I am afraid that Mr. Stratton has asked me to . . . to inform you that—" She cleared her throat again. "That your assistance is no longer required. Here. At present."

With a curious dread she raised her eyes to observe his reaction. Shock and confusion had rearranged his features into one of the most unpleasant physiognomies she had ever beheld.

The room was filled with a suspenseful silence, save for the monotonous ticking of the clock on the fireplace's mantel.

When Mr. Webster finally spoke, his voice was strained with offended incredulity. "May I ask, *why?*"

Abigail fumbled with her fingertips. "He . . . Well, you see, he—"

Mr. Webster raised his eyebrows, looking more than a little patronising. "He is not yet *mended*, is he?"

"No. He is improving, but, no. He is not yet well enough to resume his duties."

"Then, pray, whyever should he seek to dismiss me in his hour of need?"

Abigail's heart raced and fluttered. "He is concerned that you are not fully sympathetic toward . . . toward Ruby, and the whole situation."

Abigail blushed at the thought of telling Mr. Webster the full reason in more unambiguous terms.

"Not fully sympathetic? My dear Mrs. Jones! I am fully sympathetic to the great damage that the whole charade is doing to Mr. Stratton's reputation. Perhaps *he* is the one who ought to be more sympathetic toward his own situation!"

Abigail nodded. "That may be true. But he is concerned that you may be failing to see the *spiritual* importance of the whole situation. Rather than merely seeing things as they appear."

Mr. Webster looked as though he had been suddenly splashed in the face with ice cold water. "Mrs. Jones! I am a man of the church! Of course I see the spiritual implications, as well as the physical. But you may wish to make Mr. Stratton aware of what is being said about him in town before you permit him to send away an able man who is willing to look past it all to help!"

"He is aware there have been whisperings—"

"Whisperings! My dear Mrs. Jones, there has been a great deal more than that! I had a mind to tell you as soon as I arrived, until I noticed how pale and unwell you looked. So I waited. And now, here you are seeking to send away one who could be a witness, in Mr. Stratton's defence, to those who believe that Shiloh Hall has become a den of debauchery!"

He made a scoffing sound as he shook his head slowly, casting his gaze around the room yet not really looking at anything.

Tears sprang into Abigail's eyes as she shook her head

from side to side in distress. "Oh, Mr. Webster. Please do tell me what you heard. Tell me everything. Perhaps then Henry will—"

Her voice was abruptly cut off by the sob that arose from her throat as the tears spilled down over her cheeks.

Mr. Webster eyed her suspiciously. "There now, Mrs. Jones. Come, come. Do not vex yourself so sore."

Abigail struggled to gather her composure. "Forgive me, Mr. Webster. I do feel so very overwhelmed." A few sobs punctuated each sentence. "I feel that I must do as Henry asks, but I also feel that he is making a grave mistake in sending you away! I do not know what to think! Forgive me."

A calm satisfaction settled over Mr. Webster's features on hearing Abigail's confession.

"There now, Mrs. Jones," he repeated, his voice filled with smooth confidence. "I am sure Mr. Stratton is a reasonable man. But, I fear his attachment to this Ruby girl has clouded his judgment."

Abigail looked earnestly at him. "Yes. I must confess, I do fear the same."

Mr. Webster looked wistfully to one side. "And if he is not fully in his right mind to make such vital decisions, perhaps you ought to make whatever decisions are necessary to salvage his reputation. Or at least, what may be left of it."

Abigail's face crumpled. A pleading look filled her eyes. "Is it really so severe, Mr. Webster?"

"I'm afraid so. The town is quite alive with speculations."

"And you heard them?"

"Well, I imagine that I was only privy to a few of them." He paused, a flicker of scandal twitching his eyebrows. "Yet, owing to the comments that I did hear, I shudder to think of the ones to which I was not privy."

Abigail braced herself. "And what *did* you hear? What are they saying?"

"Well! I do not wish to be indelicate, ma'am," he said, shifting in his seat.

"Please. It is imperative that I know. Perhaps if I can pass it along to Henry, well, he may change his mind if he understood the severity of what was being said."

"Indeed," said Mr. Webster, soothingly. "Well, I heard a chap discussing the matter with another man and they appeared to be quite settled on the fact that Mr. Stratton was standing on sinking sand and that it would only be a matter of time until a more chaste man would replace him in his official capacities."

"Whoever would think such a thing! Surely, it was not anyone who actually knows him?"

"I believe the man's name was Mr. Graham. I do not recall hearing the other fellow's name at all."

"Graham?" Abigail paled. "Mr. Graham? Why, he has known Henry these ten years or more! Surely he could not think that he would turn his back on the church to revel in impurity—"

Mr. Webster tapped his fingertips together. "I'm afraid it rather seems that he does."

"And there were others, you said?"

"Others, yes. Which I dare say would not be proper to repeat in the presence of a lady."

"Oh, Mr. Webster." Abigail rose to her feet, trembling all over. "I must speak with Henry at once."

She headed for the door. As she reached it, she turned back hastily. "Oh, please, Mr. Webster - you will stay while I speak with him, will you not?"

"Of course, madam. I have no intention of leaving you in your hour of need."

273

"Thank you," she said, breathlessly. Then with great fervour of purpose, she left Mr. Webster alone in the drawing room, not seeing, in her haste, the smirk that crept over his determined face.

A FERVENT KNOCK at Henry's door startled him as he prayed.

"Come in?"

The door flew open to reveal a flustered Abigail, her eyes wide, her breathing rapid.

"Aunt? Whatever is the ma—"

"Oh, Henry! It is worse than we suspected!" She fluttered into the room, pacing to and fro in her panic.

Henry frowned. "What is worse?" His jaw clenched. "Mr. Webster?"

Abigail turned to look at him, exasperation all over her face.

"Oh, Henry! The rumours! Mr. Webster was in town earlier, so I could not speak with him until this evening to communicate your wishes to him. But when I did, he informed me that he had been intending to speak with *me*, to tell me of the things he had heard everyone saying in town! Oh, Henry, it is unimaginable!"

She swept her hand across her forehead and resumed her pacing.

"Aunt Abigail, please. Calm down."

"Oh, my dear! It is what I feared! Your reputation is in ruins!"

Henry shifted uncomfortably. He'd been feeling drained to begin with, but his aunt's excitement and commotion was more than he felt he could tolerate.

"Aunt, I am sure it will all settle down."

Abigail looked at him with incredulity. "Henry!"

She hesitated, then paced some more, then turned to him with a look of frightened disbelief on her face. "Everyone is convinced that you have absconded your duties to live in sin with Ruby!"

Henry's heart skipped a beat. Surely not.

He frowned. Then, with a gentle shake of his head, he looked away from his agitated aunt and half-sighed, half-snorted. "Yes, there have been speculations, but, Aunt, I doubt that anyone who knows me would believe such—"

"Mr. Webster heard it directly from Mr. Graham!"

Henry looked up at Abigail abruptly, his eyes wide, his mouth gaping.

A sinking feeling came over him as she continued her divulgences.

"Mr. Webster said he heard Mr. Graham speaking to another man, and they were quite convinced that it would not be long until someone more wholesome would be taking your place in the church!"

Henry's face was bewilderment itself. "Mr. Graham? No!"

"It is true, Henry!" Abigail stepped closer to him. "What are we to do?"

"I—" Henry struggled to find comprehension or words.

"I cannot believe it, especially of Mr. Graham," he eventually said. "Not after us clearly presenting Ruby as a guest of yours, Aunt, and making it known that she had nowhere else to go, and would only be staying until we find her a suitable position elsewhere."

He tried to force his invading thoughts of wanting Ruby to stay forever with them out of his mind.

"Well, here we are, Henry. Our explanation was clearly not enough."

Henry sighed. "I am bitterly disappointed by Mr. Graham. I shall have to write to him, and some of the others, and explain everything plainly." He trailed off, shaking his head in a melancholy daze.

"Letters? My dear, it will take more than that! What shall we do about Ruby? About Mr. Webster?"

Henry looked up at her, his face clouded. "We shall perhaps have to explain the situation to Ruby, at the right time. As for Mr. Webster, I see no reason why this revelation ought to change the prescribed course of action. He must leave at once, as decided."

Abigail was motionless save for the dropping of her jaw. "Henry!"

"Now, Aunt, I know that you do not agree with Mr. Webster's dismissal, but *I* do not agree with his character, such as it has been made known to me. I cannot entrust everything to him, whether he has been sent by Sir Harford or not!"

Abigail exhaled sharply. "Henry! Do you not see? There will be nothing left for you to entrust to anyone if you do not recover your reputation! Why, Sir Harford could withdraw his support and generosity! We could be outcasts in society, merely for having Ruby as a lodger here - nevermind if you send away the very man that Sir Harford has ordered to fulfil your duties until you are recovered!"

Henry said nothing, his heart and mind at war with each other. He knew Abigail was right. Despite how close he and Sir Harford had been all these years, not many patrons would likely tolerate such unconventional actions.

"Henry, you need Mr. Webster - now more than ever!"

"Aunt—"

"And we must not delay one moment longer in sending Ruby to my brother-in-law's estate. There is more than enough room for her to live comfortably without attracting all sorts of scandals and speculations!"

Henry covered his face with his hands for a moment. As he lifted them away, he fixed his eyes on Abigail and spoke with a quiet calm voice - an utter contrast to the maelstrom of emotions that raged within him.

"Ruby is to stay. Mr. Webster is to go. That is final."

"Henry, how can you be so calm? Do you not understand wha—"

Henry held his hands up in the air, seeking to calm his aunt's flurry of speech and movement.

"Aunt Abigail, I understand. The situation appears bleak, yes. But you are forgetting one very important truth. God is in control. I do not have to strive, I do not have to worry or fret. He has shown me that. I trust Him, and I trust that He will bring us all through this. No matter what the outcome with Sir Harford."

Abigail sighed deeply, awash with anxious energy. She appeared to try to speak, but without success.

Henry beckoned her to come closer to him.

She slowly walked toward him and arranged the chair beside him before perching on it, twitching her hands about, appearing too agitated to relax into the seat properly.

Henry reached out to her. She extended her trembling hands toward him. Grasping them in his own, he sighed as he looked into her eyes earnestly.

"Let us do what we should always do as a first priority when all manner of trials and tests assail us. Let us pray, Aunt."

Before she could say anything, Henry closed his eyes and lowered his head. He could still detect Abigail's nervous restlessness as he squeezed her hands.

"Oh, kind Father, forgive us, Lord, for failing to seek You

first. Forgive us for being overwhelmed and hurt and worried by this new twist of circumstances. We give it to You, Father, knowing that You alone are capable of protecting us and providing for us - in ways that we cannot even fathom. Please, give me wisdom regarding how to respond and explain the reality of the situation to others, Lord, and please help them to see the truth. Please help Aunt Abigail not to worry about any aspect of it all, but to give it all to You in faith and joy. And please protect Ruby from further distress and judgment. May those who have judged our circumstances so erroneously soon know the truth and repent for all their misconceptions and gossip. And, Lord, Your will be done with regards to Sir Harford. Please, help him to understand, and to grant me a reprieve for any actions that he disapproves of, that I have done . . . or will do." He paused momentarily. "And please, Lord, guard us from Millforte." His voice hardened as he uttered Millforte's name. "Thank You, Father, for all that You have done. For all that You do every day. In Jesus's name, I pray. Amen."

Abigail whispered a soft amen.

Henry let out a long sigh, basking for a few moments in the peaceful atmosphere that his prayer had ushered into the room, and into his heart.

He pushed himself further upright. "I shall write those letters presently. Would you please ask Browne to come up, Aunt?"

"Of course," she said quietly as she rose from the chair. She stood for a moment, unmoving, and looked at Henry. "And . . . you are quite sure that you do not wish for Mr. Webster to stay?"

Henry shook his head slightly, then looked up at her. "Aunt. I do not trust him. He must not remain here. I shall gladly accept full responsibility for it with Sir Harford, and will accept whatever consequences he sees fit to render."

Abigail looked almost mournful. "You have not even met him, Henry! How do you know you do not trust him when you have never even met the man?" she exclaimed.

Henry thought for a moment.

Yes. Perhaps, he ought to meet the fellow.

"Aunt," Henry said, a spring back in his voice. "Please send Browne up. Then, once Browne comes down to the drawing room, he shall escort Mr. Webster up to see me here. I think I *should* meet him."

His tone conveyed no intention of reconsidering his decision that Mr. Webster ought to leave.

Abigail looked at Henry suspiciously. "You wish to meet him up here?"

"Yes. I shall ask Browne to help me into the armchair over there. Once I am properly situated, I shall send Browne to fetch this Mr. Webster and shall deliver his dismissal myself."

"Oh, Henry, bu—"

Henry held up his left hand to silence Abigail. "Now, Aunt! You said I should meet him, I shall meet him. However, I know that meeting him will not change my mind. Nonetheless, it is only right that I should bear the task of dismissing him, not you." He looked at her, his eyes and voice softening as he uttered the last few words. "I fear you have taken on more than your fair share around here, of late. I may not be able to move around as freely as I would like at present, but I am still in possession of all my faculties and as such, I think it only right that I resume some of my prior responsibilities, where I am able."

Abigail looked at him compassionately. "Oh, Henry. You do not know how grateful I am that you are mending so . . ." She trailed off, tears springing to her eyes.

"Aunt," Henry said, his face shining with pity. "I am sorry that you have had to bear so much. But I am grateful for all that you have done."

"I would do far more for you, my dear."

Henry chuckled softly. "I know." He smiled at her. "I am so blessed to have such a dear, lovely aunt."

Abigail smiled lovingly. "Now, now. I shall go and fetch Browne for you."

She squeezed Henry's hand, then turned and walked to the door.

"Thank you, Aunt," Henry called after her.

She turned and smiled, then was gone.

"ARE you sure you are quite comfortable, sir?"

"Yes," Henry panted. "Thank you, Browne. I shall be fine. Perhaps, just some water."

Browne was swift in his retrieval. "Here you are, sir."

"Thank you," said Henry, sweeping the glass up to his parched lips. The soothing freshness cascaded down his throat as he gulped the glass dry.

Browne blinked at him. "Shall I fill it up again?"

"Yes, please. Thank you, Browne."

"It certainly seems to have aided you," Browne said as he handed the refilled glass to Henry.

"Quite! Now, could you fetch Mr. Webster, please, Browne?"

"Right away."

When Browne left the room, Henry prayed quickly, seeking wisdom for his impending encounter with Mr. Webster. The thought of seeing him, knowing that he had questioned Ruby's motives and integrity, riled Henry deeply.

Still, he must try to remain calm and collected. He did not want a repetition of how he had ended up acting toward Millforte.

Footsteps outside his door heightened his awareness of everything around him. He smoothed the blanket that Browne had placed over his legs and took another sip of water, gripping the cold glass with tight fingers.

Browne entered, followed by a tall, sickly-coloured stranger.

"Mr. Stratton, may I introduce Mr. Percival Webster," said Browne. Turning to Mr. Webster, he repeated his introduction with a reversal of the names.

"Pleasure to meet you at last, Mr. Stratton," Mr. Webster said with a nod. His voice had an occluded nasal quality that made the innocent sentence sound sickeningly smug.

"Good evening, Mr. Webster," said Henry, his voice clear and bold. "Please . . ."

Henry motioned to the wooden chair that Browne had placed opposite Henry's armchair. Mr. Webster seated himself with a rigid posture. He looked expectantly at Henry.

Ruby's face flashed into Henry's mind. How distressed she had looked as she told Henry of Mr. Webster's indiscretion.

Henry set his glass down on the small table beside him, then folded his hands together and looked straight back at the strange gentleman before him.

"I understand you arrived with a letter of instruction from Sir Harford," Henry began.

"That is correct," said Mr. Webster. "He and my father were very close friends."

"And you know him well, also?"

"All my life. He is a remarkable gentleman. Always eager to help those he counts as friends."

"Yes." Henry studied the interloper's face. It certainly would take very little effort to imagine the pride and cruelty he had directed at Ruby. There was something repellent about him. Even had Ruby not mentioned anything, Henry was certain that he would not have found the man easy to like.

"How are you feeling now, Mr. Stratton? From what I hear, it is quite a feat that you are up and about."

"I am feeling much better of late, thank you. Well enough that I believe I can manage now without any help from outside the household."

Henry had intended to prolong the interview, but now that he was face-to-face with Mr. Webster, he simply could not wait to be away from him.

Mr. Webster's eyebrows raised slightly, then - purposefully, or so it seemed - they resumed their natural position. "I see . . ."

"Thank you for all your help thus far, Mr. Webster, but you may take your leave in the morning."

Henry longed to urge him to leave immediately, but as it was now after dinner and dark outside, it was only right to allow Mr. Webster to stay until morning.

"I see. Well, thank you for meeting with me, Mr. Stratton." He drew himself up, quite a domineering height in contrast to the seated Henry.

"I must ask," Mr. Webster continued, "Did your aunt inform you of the unpleasantries that I overheard in town?"

"She did," replied Henry. "And I have the matter in hand. I shall deal with it presently. Please, do not concern yourself with it any further."

Mr. Webster looked decidedly unimpressed. "I see."

"Farewell, Mr. Webster. Thank you again."

Mr. Webster gave a reluctant nod and turned for the door.

Henry's heart raced as he tried to decide whether he

ought to mention Mr. Webster's ill-manner toward Ruby or not.

This was his chance. If he was going to say anything, it was now or never.

"Oh, Mr. Webster?"

CHAPTER 24

DIGGING DEEPER

MR. WEBSTER SPUN around to face Henry again. "Yes, Mr. Stratton?"

"I merely wish to indicate that I was made aware of your rather . . . judgmental encounter with Miss Ruby, and I feel it is my duty to remind you that God shows grace without partiality. And commands us to do the same."

Mr. Webster looked as though he did not know whether to laugh or fume. His voice erupted with a combination of the two. "I say! I do not know what Miss Ruby told you, but I assure you I was only speaking with your best interests in view, from my duty in endeavouring to bear your load regarding church matters."

Henry's jaw stiffened. "But Ruby is not a 'church matter'. Not in the sense of those with whom you were intending to assist me. She is a person - a fragile person - who has experienced far more trauma and horror than you or I ever shall. She needs a safe place to recover, to grow in her new-found faith, and to gather hope for the future." His tone grew impassioned. "The last thing she needs is judgment and suspicion!"

Mr. Webster scowled. "I do urge you to kindly recall, Mr. Stratton," he said, practically spitting the words at Henry, "that whatever your young lady friend may have told you, that it is her word against my own." He scoffed. "I do not think it difficult to ascertain which of the two would be reckoned a more trustworthy witness!"

Henry's fists and teeth clenched. He took a deep breath, trying his best to be calm. "Nor do I, sir." He shot Mr. Webster a challenging look.

Mr. Webster laughed a mocking laugh and shook his head slowly. "Oh, Mr. Stratton, your situation is more hopeless than I thought. You really ought to have listened to your aunt. I dare say, there may be some truth to the heart of the rumours, after all. Yet, disaster could have been averted if you had only accepted the superior wisdom of your dear, kind aunt."

Henry frowned. Mr. Webster was trying to bait him, he ought not to give him the satisfaction of a response. But he simply must know why Mr. Webster seemed to attribute such importance to Abigail's involvement with any of it.

"My aunt, Mr. Webster?" he said, trying to sound nonchalant and wise to the ruse.

"Why, yes. Her suggestion to send Ruby to her brother-in-law's estate. Had you done so, your reputation would not be in tatters and your senses would not have deserted you in inviting a prostitute to live within a parsonage!"

Henry felt almost dizzy at the thought that Abigail had discussed private matters about Ruby's situation with such a proud pretender. He battled to conceal his shock from Mr. Webster, believing that nothing would delight Mr. Webster more than to know himself to be responsible for vexing Henry further.

Henry stared straight at Mr. Webster, his face like flint. Neither man spoke for several long moments.

"Browne!" Henry called. Mr. Webster jumped at the unexpected issue and volume of Henry's voice.

As Mr. Webster opened his mouth to speak, Browne entered the room. Immediately, Henry addressed him.

"Browne, please can you ensure that Mr. Webster is taken to the coaching inn as soon as he has packed his belongings. He is leaving us tonight, with much haste."

Browne looked at Mr. Webster, who was half-gaping, half-glaring at Henry, then looked back at Henry.

"Of course, sir."

"Thank you, Browne."

"Would you like to follow me, sir?" Browne asked Mr. Webster, his voice sounding even more gentle than usual in comparison to Henry's clipped tone.

Mr. Webster gave a final smug snarl at Henry, then followed Browne out the door, never, Henry hoped, to return.

Mr. Webster's words flooded Henry's mind. If he had only listened to Abigail? In sending Ruby to Abigail's brother-in-law's estate? How much of their situation had Abigail discussed with Mr. Webster?

He felt something he had never felt before in relation to his aunt.

He felt betrayed.

Before he could ponder how to approach Abigail about it, Bessie bustled in with a tray of steaming tea.

Henry stared blankly at her for a moment, his thoughts slowly returning to what they had been before his encounter with Mr. Webster.

"Ah! Bessie . . . Could you please furnish me with some

paper and ink? I have a few letters to write and I must begin without delay."

"Of course."

He smiled his thanks to her. As soon as she returned, he would write letters to Mr. Graham and others from the church. But not before writing another letter.

Paper and ink supplied, he lifted his quill and dipped the nib into the little black pot, before scratching his lines onto the fresh, crisp paper. He half-whispered as he wrote.

"Dear Sir Harford . . ."

AT BREAKFAST THE NEXT DAY, Ruby was relieved to find Mr. Webster absent. She longed to know the outcome of Henry's conversation with Abigail.

She almost asked Bessie, since they were alone together in the dining room, but every creak and faint sound she heard startled her into holding her breath in apprehensive anticipation.

The door opened. Ruby froze. She looked up, acutely endeavouring to maintain a neutral expression.

Abigail entered the room, and Ruby almost gasped. She had never seen Abigail look so weary. Worry and exhaustion lined her face, and her posture reflected defeat and deep weariness of soul.

She took her place opposite Ruby, smiling a quiet greeting at her.

Ruby answered softly, "Good morning."

Bessie entered again with a fresh brew of tea. Ruby detected a flicker of surprise on Bessie's face as she greeted Abigail.

The meal passed in a comfortable silence, until Bessie came in to clear the dishes.

"Bessie," began Abigail, raising her hand slightly in the air to indicate her wish to delay Bessie's exit, which was usually swift when she was in cleaning mode.

"Yes, ma'am?" Bessie continued to gather dishes, then hovered in one spot, her queried gaze fixed on Abigail.

"I was under the impression that Mr. Webster would be joining us this morning for breakfast, but he has not come. Would you mind sending Browne to his room to enquire after him?"

At the mention of Mr. Webster's name, Ruby's stomach tugged. She prayed that he would not come downstairs until she was safely out of his path.

"Yes, ma'am," said Bessie, resuming her flight.

"Thank you," said Abigail, as Bessie whisked out of the room.

"It was a lovely breakfast," Ruby said, seeking to fill the silence which seemed to have amplified since Abigail's request.

Abigail, who was staring toward the window, looked at Ruby. "Yes . . . Yes, it was." Her eyes seemed dim with confusion.

A pang of sadness passed through Ruby. Abigail had been a different woman since Millforte's attack on Henry. Before, her appearance had been youthful for her years and she had graced each day with a warm and easy air. But she seemed to have aged and wearied considerably since Henry's attack.

Bessie reentered the dining room, chewing her lip slightly, her eyes flickering with confusion.

"Mrs. Jones," Bessie said, her voice different.

"Yes, Bessie?"

Bessie hovered, her hands clasped in front of her, her

fingers ceaselessly interweaving and twisting. "Mrs. Jones, I asked Browne to check on Mr. Webster, as you requested."

"Yes?"

"Well . . . Browne has told me that . . . Well, it seems that Mr. Webster is gone, ma'am."

Ruby couldn't believe her ears. Gone? Already? She held her breath, eager to hear more.

Abigail's eyes widened in surprise. "Gone? As in, gone to town again, or . . .?" Her expression indicated that she already knew the answer, but, like Ruby, struggled to comprehend the suddenness of Mr. Webster's departure.

"As in . . . gone away. Permanently, ma'am." Bessie watched Abigail with an apprehensive curiosity.

"When?" Abigail croaked, her frown deepening.

"Browne said that Mr. Webster spoke with Mr. Stratton last night and then Mr. Stratton insisted he be brought to the coaching inn down in the village right away," Bessie said, her voice failing to conceal her own surprise.

Abigail's eyebrows shot up. "But it was quite late when Mr. Stratton spoke to him. Surely—" She straightened up, then rose from the table. "Thank you, Bessie." With that, she bustled to the door and was gone.

Bessie looked at Ruby. "I cannot say that I am at all disappointed to hear of his departure," she whispered.

"Nor I . . ." breathed Ruby. It felt too good to be true.

She thought back to the sneers and slurs she had received from him. Relief tugged her heart. "Oh, Bessie! Am I wrong to find the news so wonderful?"

Bessie glanced at the door, then back to Ruby. "Between you and me, miss, I do not think so. He was a repulsive creature. To be sure, I am as glad as you that he is gone!"

Ruby closed her eyes and sighed.

Thank you, God.

HENRY KNEW who was knocking at his door before he even responded.

"Come in, Aunt," he called out.

Abigail entered, her expression askew with concern.

"Good morning," smiled Henry. He was sitting in his armchair, the breakfast tray on his lap empty save for a crumb-filled plate and empty teacup. A stack of letters were piled on the table beside him.

Abigail appeared momentarily stunned. "Henry! You look so well!"

"Thank you, Aunt. I feel a great deal better," he said.

Abigail glanced at the letters. The top one was addressed to Sir Harford.

"Henry. Bessie informed us that you sent Mr. Webster away to the coaching inn last night. Why did you not permit him to at least stay the night and set off in daylight?"

Henry's jaw tightened a little. "I had intended to do so, but after we spoke, it was clear that it was best for him to leave at once."

Abigail looked at him searchingly. "Why?"

Henry looked at her intently, then waved his hand in the air and blinked away what he had been thinking. "It does not matter now. He is gone, and the matter is done."

Abigail sighed. "I only hope that you have not made a very grave error, my dear."

Henry tried to look compassionate. "Aunt . . . Do not worry. The grave mistake would have been to permit him to stay. I do not trust him. And not solely due to Ruby's encounter with him. There was something about his very person. Something wanting."

Abigail shrugged gently. "I own that he was rather

reserved and stoic, but I do think he was amiable and would have proved to be a good help."

It was Henry's turn to sigh. "The matter is settled. And I, for one, shall be glad not to think of it again."

RUBY HAD RETREATED to her room not long after breakfast to bask in the glad news and thank God for answering her prayers.

She'd prayed for Abigail, too, that she would recover the strength and ease she seemed to have lost. And that she would not hold Mr. Webster's departure against her.

A soft sound of stones crunching under carriage wheels reached her ears. The sound grew louder and louder.

Someone was arriving at the parsonage.

Keenly trying to remain out of sight, she crept to her window and peered out.

Sure enough, there was a carriage.

She waited, her heart beating faster. She could think of only two men likely to come - Millforte, and Mr. Webster. She prayed earnestly that it was neither of them, fear gripping her throat as she whispered pleas for safety.

The carriage door opened. Skirts poked through the doorway.

Ruby relaxed. It was a woman, not either of the men whose returns she feared.

A slender woman descended the carriage steps and smoothed her lilac gown. A silky ribbon in the exact same shade of purple was woven around her bonnet. The woman looked up at the sky. Ruby saw her face and ducked out of sight, at the same time.

She knew that face. She had seen her somewhere before. A young woman, with bright eyes and—

Miss Acton!

The girl from the church. The one who seemed so besotted with Henry.

But what was she doing *here*?

A sick feeling crept into her stomach, and her heart felt heavy. Miss Acton. The one whom Abigail wanted Henry to marry.

Ruby felt as though the walls were closing in. Worry urged her to go downstairs to try to hear Miss Acton's reasons for visiting, and - more importantly - how her visit might be received by Abigail and Henry. Yet, fear compelled her to remain in her room, panic filling her more and more each second, and a crushing weight of grief welling up from deep within.

Why should she be so troubled?

The answer came to mind immediately, though she tried to hide from it.

"No," she whispered to herself. "No. I cannot."

But tears rolled down her cheeks as she admitted to herself why she felt such dismay at Miss Acton's arrival.

She did not want Miss Acton to marry Henry—

Ruby shook her head, trying to push the thoughts away.

It was no use.

She did not want Miss Acton to marry Henry, because she was really in love with him herself.

CHAPTER 25

A NEW IDEAL

"MISS ACTON! WHAT A PLEASANT SURPRISE," smiled Abigail after Browne had shown the unexpected guest into the drawing room. "Please, do have a seat."

"Thank you, Mrs. Jones," replied the gentle guest, as she perched on the chair opposite the one on which Abigail was seated. She gave a meek smile, yet Abigail could see something deeper in her eyes.

"I heard the dreadful news of Henry's attack," Miss Acton blurted. "I did not know whether I should have come sooner. I thought perhaps it might be better to wait until he was feeling better." She looked up anxiously at Abigail. "Is he feeling better?"

Abigail sighed, her mind travelling through the many events since Millforte's visit. "Yes, I am glad to say that he has begun to improve. Up until very recently, the situation was rather grave, but slowly he has returned more and more to the Henry we all know."

Miss Acton's relief was unmistakable. "Oh, I am so glad to

hear that!" She clasped her hand to her chest. "Oh, I have been so worried." She shook her head, slightly, sighing.

"Yes. We all have been. But the Lord has been with us," she said with a smile. "He has been bringing us through, day by day."

Miss Acton nodded, frowning earnestly. "Yes . . . He is so good."

"Indeed, He is."

Bessie entered with a tea tray for the two ladies. Miss Acton graciously accepted her cup and saucer. Meanwhile, Abigail studied her.

Here was a respectable young lady, from a good family, and with a comfortable dowry, from what Abigail had heard. It was beyond obvious that Miss Acton cared deeply for Henry, and her temperament and character were such as would make for an exceedingly appropriate parson's wife.

Yet, from what Abigail had seen and heard, Henry had no matrimonial interest in the poor girl. His affections instead were fixed on a troubled young lady, with no family and no dowry, whose temperament and character were only just beginning to emerge in her new-found faith.

Deep inside, as she sipped her tea and made small talk with Miss Acton, Abigail felt torn. Was she being too hard on Ruby? After all, the circumstances in which Ruby had been captive had not been her own doing.

Yet, society had certain expectations that must be met. There were rules that must be followed, conventions that one could not simply abandon — especially if one's life was set apart in the service of God.

"And then there was far too much rain, so we could not set out that day, either!" Miss Acton chirped.

Abigail smiled in response, still deep in thought.

Miss Acton would be of great assistance to Henry - a

profound help to him in his duties and would run a household well, Abigail had no doubt.

But Ruby . . . It was Abigail's main concern that Henry would be so busy trying to help Ruby that it would interfere with his duties. She feared that, ultimately, Ruby would drag him down, unable to support and encourage him to flourish in his calling.

Yet she could not deny, now that she was face to face with Miss Acton in the parsonage's drawing room, that could all the conventions and concerns be laid aside and Henry be free to choose a wife for love and not duty, that Ruby had something in her character - a depth or quality of some kind, she wasn't quite sure - that seemed to echo Henry's own heart much more closely than anything Miss Acton possessed.

How Abigail wished her own husband were still alive. She would pour out all her confusion and concerns to him, and he would know precisely what to advise her.

And then she realised. She knew exactly what he would say. Everything that Henry had already been saying.

Not even hearing Miss Acton's ramblings now, Abigail knew, with perfect clarity, that if Henry and Ruby were ever to be together, she ought to give the match her blessing - not her disapproval.

Henry was right. Ruby had been entrusted to their care, and no matter what circumstances she had been dragged from, there was no soul too far past forgiveness, no stain that God could not erase.

She swallowed hard. If the day ever came where Henry and Ruby entered into a formal attachment, it would not be easy. And it could cost Henry everything.

Still, she believed that God would give her the strength she would need to surrender to Him. He always did.

She prayed silently, asking for forgiveness for being so judgmental and suspicious of Ruby. The poor girl had suffered more than Abigail could even try to imagine. Was it not a miracle that Henry and Browne had succeeded in breaking her out of that vile prison? Was it not a miracle that Henry had succeeded in concealing her physical presence from Millforte?

How noble Henry had been. He had been willing to endure suffering and pain to protect Ruby. What had she herself done? Nothing but accuse and judge the girl.

"Mrs. Jones . . .?"

The silence into which the room fell following Miss Acton's question plunged Abigail back into the present moment.

"Oh, forgive me, Miss Acton. Forgive me. I have not been sleeping very well of late, with everything that has happened. Please . . . I am sorry. You were saying?"

Miss Acton's eyes filled with pity as she looked at her apologetic host. "Oh, Mrs. Jones, I am so sorry. It is a most dreadful sensation to reside in, not having sufficient sleep, to be sure! I know it all too well, myself."

The young lady dropped her gaze and looked to the side.

"Yes." said Abigail. "Though, I do believe I shall be able to sleep much more soundly now that Henry is on the mend."

Miss Acton's eyes darted back to meet Abigail's. "Yes," she smiled. "It is the most wonderful news."

Abigail smiled, nodding in agreement.

Miss Acton tilted her head and looked up. She reminded Abigail of a delicate bird. Melancholy flickered on her face. "Pray, when might he be returning to his Sunday duties?"

Abigail thought for a moment. "Oh, my dear, I am afraid I cannot say. I believe it may be some time before he will be fully back on his feet, able to be out and about."

Miss Acton's countenance fell. "I see." She swept a curl of hair behind her ear and shifted in her seat a little. "And . . . And, well, he does intend to return, does he not?"

Abigail frowned and raised her eyebrows in quick succession. "Why, yes, of course!"

A forceful sigh issued rapidly forth from Miss Acton as her face lit up. "Oh! I am glad!"

Abigail held her breath for a moment. "Miss Acton, may I ask why you thought that perhaps Mr. Stratton might not return?"

Miss Acton's wide eyes looked almost guilty. Abigail waited in suspended apprehension.

"I heard my father speaking with Mr. Graham." Miss Acton gave a deep sigh. She kept her gaze low as she continued. "According to Mr. Graham, there have been some rumours circulating in town."

It was Abigail's turn to sigh. "Yes. Regretfully, we have been made aware of this."

Miss Acton looked up at Abigail, obviously deep in thought. "I see. It is a frightful accusation. I know myself that not one word of it could be true." Her speech had resumed its hasty pace.

"Thank you, Miss Acton," smiled Abigail. "We knew that our true friends would not be taken in by such absurd fabrications."

Miss Acton seemed to find delight in being categorised as one of Abigail and Henry's true friends. A look of surprise crept across her features, followed by a radiant smile. "Oh, of course! I would never believe such ghastly and malicious rumours. Why, anyone who would even suggest any such thing clearly knows nothing of Mr. Stratton's impeccable character." She blushed slightly.

"You are quite right, my dear," said Abigail, gratefully.

"Pray, is Mr. Stratton likely to join us? No, I imagine not." She shook her head gently and looked away.

Abigail felt a pang of sympathy for Miss Acton. It was obvious how highly she thought of Henry, yet the poor girl had no idea that he didn't feel remotely the same.

"I am sorry, he is not yet well enough to entertain guests, at present. But I shall certainly convey your best wishes to him. I am sure your support will give him some comfort."

Miss Acton looked up, hope stirring on her face. "Do you really think so?" She blushed, her eyes looking everywhere except at Abigail.

The clock on the mantel chimed, breaking the silence that had begun to settle in the room.

Miss Acton glanced up, then rose to her feet. "I should take my leave now. I do hope I did not inconvenience you at all by calling unannounced."

Abigail stood also. "Not at all, my dear - it was lovely to see you. Do give my regards to your parents."

With a few more words of goodbyes, Miss Acton was gone. Abigail sank back down into her chair. Her thoughts returned to Henry's seemingly growing attachment to Ruby. How his countenance softened and his eyes lit up each time he looked at her or spoke to her.

Abigail was in no doubt that Miss Acton could not even come close to sparking the same reaction that one glance at Ruby, one word spoken to her or even about her, would ignite.

She headed to the stairs. Time to retreat to her room for some much-needed time in prayer. She ascended the first flight, her thoughts still weighing upon what she ought to think about Henry and—

"Ruby!" Abigail exclaimed upon seeing the very person she was thinking about sitting at the top of the second flight of stairs. "Are you all right? Whyever are you sitting there?" Fear lurched through Abigail at the thought of Ruby falling, dragging her memory back to the horrible moment she had witnessed Henry tumble down the steps like a rag doll.

"Oh, I am sorry, Mrs. Jones. I . . . I was just thinking. Forgive me."

Ruby gathered herself up and walked a few paces from the top step.

Abigail ascended and stopped beside her. "Is everything all right, my dear?"

Ruby looked forlorn. "Yes. Yes, everything is fine. Thank you."

Abigail noticed that Ruby's features had clouded, and her gaze was fixed on the small window overlooking the driveway.

"I am going to rest awhile, now," Abigail said. "But, perhaps, after dinner this evening, you and I could have some tea together?"

Ruby looked at Abigail, her eyebrows raising, then crashing down, then raising again. "Yes . . . That would be very nice. Thank you."

Abigail smiled at her and squeezed her elbow as she continued to her room. Settled inside, she sank into an armchair and slumped forward.

"Lord, please forgive me for being so unkind toward Ruby lately . . ."

RUBY WATCHED Abigail disappear into her bedroom. So many thoughts and questions swirled around her heart. She trudged back to her own room, each thought feeling like a dense fog she had to push through.

Why had Miss Acton come? Why did Abigail wish to speak with her? Did she intend to tell her of some sort of agreement between Henry and Miss Acton?

Oh, if she did, how could she bear it? How dare she even think she could have a chance with Henry!

Safe inside her room, she clutched her head in her hands, wishing she could swat the consuming thoughts away once and for all. She fell to her knees beside her bed, resting her elbows on the edge of it. She drew a deep breath, scolding herself to calm down. Visions of Henry and Miss Acton smiling and standing close to each other in wedding attire presented themselves every time she closed her eyes.

"Please, Lord, help me," she whispered. "I know I do not deserve him, Lord. I could never deserve him. But my heart! My heart feels as though it might break if I think of him marrying Miss Acton! Oh, help me, Lord!"

Her words morphed into sobs as she buried her face in the blankets, her hot tears forming damp patches on the soft fabric.

HENRY LEANED a lot of his weight on Browne's slight yet strong frame. He couldn't help but grin.

"Are you ready, sir?"

"Yes, Browne," he said, his eyes dancing like a mischievous schoolboy's. "I cannot wait to see their faces!"

"Nor I," Browne said with a tender smile.

Henry offered a silent prayer of thanks that God had brought Browne into his life. Strong yet nimble, it was only Browne's lined face and thinning grey hair that revealed his true age. And how good he had been to Henry and Abigail ever since he'd arrived at the parsonage. Deep down, Henry often thought of him more as family than a servant.

As Browne helped him out of his bedroom door, Henry tried his best to suppress an excited chuckle.

Yes . . . They *would* be surprised!

RUBY POURED some water from her jug into her basin. Little droplets of ice-cold water dotted her wrists. She lifted the flannel that was draped over the side of the bowl and submerged it in the cold, clear water. After wringing it out, she wiped the cloth across her forehead, her cheeks, her chin. With a sigh, she held the cool cloth against her closed eyes, relishing the refreshment she felt on her skin, burning from too many tears.

It was almost time for dinner, and she did not wish to arouse any questions about her state of emotions. She must press on, take her place, hide her heart, just as she had done for most of her life.

Wringing out the cloth and laying it back over the basin, she shuffled over to the mirror, dismayed at what she beheld. She barely recognised herself at first glance, in her fine pale pink gown and pretty necklace that Abigail had given to her during her first few weeks with them.

And her face . . . Dark rings ran along her lower lash line and her skin looked pale and tired. Wisps of hair staggered out in places, and her mouth was a thin, drawn line, tight with worry and sadness.

She pinched and patted her cheeks, the way she had seen Polly do once, trying to infuse some colour into them. It didn't work.

She moved closer to the mirror, inspecting her eyes for

tell-tale traces of tears. The cold water had helped somewhat. The redness was fading, though her eyes still looked a little glassy.

She sighed. "Please do not let Abigail speak of Miss Acton," she prayed as she opened her door and stepped into the hallway.

THE WHOLE WAY down the corridor to the dining room, Abigail was deep in thought about Henry, Ruby and Miss Acton. Her mind felt clearer than it had for days after praying so openly and honestly. She felt genuinely glad that she would be spending some time with Ruby after dinner, though if she spent too long thinking of Henry and Ruby forming a union, something about it still made her feel a little claustrophobic.

With a deep breath, she straightened her shoulders and walked into the dining room.

Her eyes grew wide as she noticed the man at the table.

"Henry!" she exhaled, followed by an array of gasps and noises of exclamation.

Henry's whole face twinkled with delight as he sat in his usual seat at the head of the table. The seat which had seemed so empty for so long.

"What are you— But, how! I— Oh, Henry!" she stuttered, her eyes clouding with tears.

"Did I surprise you, Aunt?" he asked, his grin full of glee.

"Oh, my dear boy, I cannot even tell you!" She clasped her hands together and raised them to her mouth. "Oh, it has been so long . . . so long since you have dined with us." She moved forward and hastily took her own seat, staring at him in wonderment all the while.

She reached over and squeezed his hand. He squeezed hers in return. Seeing him closer up, she noticed a small glisten of sweat at the top of his brow and the flicker of a grimace when he moved his back or neck.

"Are you sure you are quite well enough for a whole dinner here, my dear?"

Henry moved only his eyes to look at her. "Yes, Aunt," he said, his voice sounding tired already. "I have waited a long time for this, too. I have missed it greatly. Dining with you, and . . ."

As if on cue, the dining room door swung open and Ruby flowed in, her pale pink gown infusing her whole countenance with a bright and warm light.

Abigail glanced at Henry. There was no trace of a grimace on his face, despite how swiftly he had looked toward the door. Instead, he seemed completely captivated, his eyes glazed with amazement, and his mouth ever so slightly open. Slowly, a pure, peaceful smile spread across his face.

Abigail sighed, still wrestling in her mind about societal conventions, yet deeply moved to see Henry look so happy.

She had no shred of doubt left. Henry loved Ruby.

And judging by the wide-eyed, innocent smile of grateful surprise that Ruby met Henry with in return, the feeling was definitely mutual.

"Mr. Stratton!" Ruby exclaimed, resuming her approach now that the shock that'd stopped her in her tracks had started to dissolve.

"Ruby." Henry's voice was breathy and content. He smiled.

"I do not— How is it that you— Are you feeling better?"

she asked, gladness and bewilderment combining on her features.

Henry chuckled, his grin showing no signs of fading. "I am feeling a fair measure better, yes, thank you."

His eyes looked more like they used to, before that horrid day when Millforte had closed them by his violence. Ruby shuddered as she imagined what must have transpired between Millforte and Henry. She pulled her wrap tighter around her.

Ruby became aware of Abigail's presence and nodded a greeting to her, colouring slightly at how long it had taken her to do so. She could scarcely keep her gaze off Henry. It was so magnificent to see him at the table with them. Had she known he was to join them, she would have come down much earlier.

"What I cannot fathom, my dear, is how did you get down here? Those stairs . . ." Abigail asked, her brows knit in concern, a haunted look in her eyes.

"Browne has been helping me to move around a little more each day, in my room. I hatched this plot, and he very kindly assisted me down the stairs. Do not worry, Aunt," he smiled, glancing at Abigail, "Browne would not let me even consider attempting it alone. I am afraid my back is still much too stiff. The last thing I need is another tumble down the stairs!" His smile faded into an awkward look, then slowly returned.

Abigail swallowed hard, a sick look on her face, as if staring back into the past.

Ruby looked at her hands, folding and unfolding in her lap. She thought of the spots of blood she had seen. They alone had been more than enough to witness. Her heart filled with compassion as she glanced at Abigail. How horrific it would have been to have actually seen Henry roll down each step.

"I wonder what is for dinner! I am quite hungry after all my exertion!" Henry smiled, looking at each melancholy lady, as though willing their smiles to return.

"Yes, yes," said Abigail, emerging from her reverie. She smiled, seemingly forced at first, but a real one soon took its place. She reached out for Henry's hand and squeezed it. "It really is so wonderful to have you dine with us again, my dear."

Ruby longed to reach out and do the same, but even had decorum permitted it, the fluttering that coursed through every fibre of her being when she glanced at Henry, or when he glanced at her, would not.

He looked at her, his eyes warm and deep. She smiled, glancing away quickly as her mind filled with thoughts and realisations of her true feelings for him. It was bliss to be in his company, yet it was torture, too. How was it that she wanted to get closer to him and run further away from him at the same time?

They all shared pleasant conversation and laughter as they ate dinner, though turmoil of heart and mind surged through Ruby on more than one occasion.

"I could not eat another bite!" groaned Henry, throwing his head back and clutching his stomach in an exaggerated fashion, his plate now empty.

Abigail smiled, a greater atmosphere of peace seeming to surround her as more time passed.

Ruby smiled, chuckling inwardly at Henry's playful motion. He really was like no other man she had ever met. So gentle, so kind, so enjoyable to be around.

"Unless, of course, there is cake . . ." he grinned.

It was remarkable. He seemed so improved. So alive. So happy.

Miss Acton flashed into Ruby's mind. Had Abigail told Henry of Miss Acton's visit yet? Was that why he was so happy?

Nausea gripped her stomach.

Please ... No ...

"I am sure there will be cake, my dear. If Browne knew you were intending to dine with us, no doubt Bessie will have prepared a special dessert to celebrate," Abigail said, her eyes misty.

There was cake indeed. Moist sponge with rich glazed icing, baked to perfection. And gone almost as soon as it had arrived.

Ruby pushed the remaining crumbs around on her plate with her fork. Her conversation had grown quiet over dessert, while her thoughts had grown louder and louder. Miss Acton, Henry, smiles, weddings . . . all tumbled through her imagination like a merry-go-round. Except, there was absolutely nothing merry about it.

"Are you all right, Ruby?"

She looked up at Henry, his deep eyes pooled with sincere concern.

"Yes . . . Yes, thank you. I am quite full," she said.

"Me too." Henry returned her smile, seeming to relax a little, yet glancing at her occasionally. "That was superb. Truly delicious."

"It certainly was!" said Abigail, with a nod.

Henry wiped his brow with his handkerchief. He shifted in his chair, grimacing despite an obvious effort to appear comfortable.

Browne entered the room and looked at Henry, raising his eyebrows in a silent question. Henry looked at him, the happiness now dim on his face. He nodded.

"I do wish I could stay longer, but I shall have to retire for now," Henry said, looking from Ruby to Abigail and back again. "Please, do excuse me. And thank you for your wonderful company." His gaze lingered on Ruby as he smilingly spoke the last sentence.

Ruby felt her cheeks burn as she smiled in return. Such torture, yet such joy. It was all so unnerving.

"Oh! I almost forgot," said Abigail. "Miss Acton called today, exceedingly concerned to discover how you are faring."

Ruby froze, trying to conceal the watchful eye she had placed on Henry's expression.

A bemused and slightly exasperated expression filled his face. "Thank you, Aunt," he said with a sigh.

Abigail chuckled. "Oh, Henry, do not look so . . . The poor girl, she really is quite besotted."

Henry coloured. "Well, I wish she were not so."

Ruby glanced up at him, her heart racing. Had she understood him correctly? Had he really just indicated that he did not return Miss Acton's affections?

He looked decidedly uncomfortable, and not just from his physical ailment. His eyes were darting and on the verge of rolling, and he shook his head with another quiet sigh.

"Still," said Abigail, an awkward look dawning on her own face. "It was very good of her to call. She . . ." Abigail glanced at Ruby, then back to Henry. "She is quite understanding of the truth."

Henry looked at Abigail, confusion pulling his eyebrows into a frown. Then he glanced at Ruby and back to Abigail, raising his eyebrows slightly. "Oh, I see."

Abigail nodded.

"Ah. Yes, well, perhaps I ought to be more grateful."

Ruby's heart thudded so loudly she wondered if Browne, who was standing only a little behind her, could hear it. Of what secret truth had Henry and Abigail spoken? And why had they both looked at her?

Insecurity urged her to rush from the room. Even if Henry did not return Miss Acton's feelings, he certainly could never mirror her own. The chasm was too wide. Tears sprang to her eyes. She blinked rapidly, silently pleading with God that no one would notice.

"Good night, Aunt," said Henry. He pulled her hand up toward him and kissed it. Releasing it, he smiled. "And thank you."

He turned to Ruby. He stared at her silently, his chest rising and falling more quickly than she had noticed before. He cleared his throat slightly and extended his hand, his palm facing up.

Ruby tried not to gape at him. She slowly raised her trembling hand and gingerly rested it on his.

Her heart soared as she felt him squeeze the edges of her hand ever so gently. His hand felt warm and slightly moist. She forgot to breathe until she grew light-headed.

Henry pulled her hand slowly upward, his eyes locked on hers the whole time. Silence thundered in her ears. He looked at her hand, then what seemed a long time later, cupped his other hand over the top of hers. He squeezed his hands together, sandwiching her hand with heat and pressure. "Good night, Ruby," he said, in a strained whisper.

"Good night," Ruby breathed.

Releasing her hand, he turned to Browne, who positioned himself as Henry's support without delay. They walked in tandem toward the door, then left. Ruby's hopes that Henry would turn to look at them were not met, and suddenly the room seemed empty and cold.

Unlike her heart, and the love for Henry therein she could no longer deny.

CHAPTER 26

DAWNINGS

THE TWO LADIES settled close to the fire, cups of tea in hand, a quiet warmth in the air around them.

"Ruby," said Abigail, almost in a sigh. "There was a particular matter that I wished to discuss with you this evening. It is why I asked you for this meeting."

Ruby's stomach lurched, instantly thinking of Miss Acton. Then, recalling Henry's declaration of indifference, uncertainty settled over her.

Abigail looked at her intently. "I wanted to ask your forgiveness."

Ruby blinked, Abigail's words seeming to hang in the air momentarily before they sank in. Her eyebrows shot upward.

"M— My forgiveness?" Ruby stammered.

"Yes," continued Abigail. "Oh, my dear . . ."

Abigail gave a full-hearted sigh and shook her head gently, her eyes darting to and fro. "I have been so overwhelmed this past while. So worried about Henry, about . . . everything. I realise that I have not been behaving as I ought, and I truly am sorry." She paused. "I want to ask you if you might forgive me. If I have been unkind to you . . ." Her voice trailed off as she shook her head, gazing at the floor with a frown.

Ruby tried to smooth the tremble in her voice as she spoke. "You have not been unkind. No one here has been unkind." Mr. Webster flashed into her mind. "That is, no one *from* here."

Abigail looked at her knowingly yet curiously. "Mr. Webster?"

Ruby nodded and looked down.

Abigail hesitated. "Was he very cruel?"

Ruby kept her eyes firmly fixed on her hands. "He . . . was coarse. And cruel, yes. He showed no grace or kindness to me. But the worst part? His assumptions and accusations showed that he knew nothing of Henry's character. To suspect such . . . such a kind and gentle man as Henry to be anything like—" Ruby closed her lips firmly, shaking her head and frowning.

Abigail looked at her own lap, then back up at Ruby. She let out a long, measured breath. "You care very deeply for him, do you not?"

Ruby felt her cheeks heat up. She squeezed her hands tightly together in her lap, her fingers interlocking, her knuckles paled by the pressure.

Images of Henry filled her mind. Happy at the table that night, content on one of their walks through the garden, bruised and pale on his sickbed. The look of determination and fear in his eyes as he'd promised to retrieve her from the Harfords' house.

She sighed, her frame shuddering from its depth. "Yes. A great deal."

"And, how are you feeling about everything, now?"

Ruby looked at her, unsure how to answer. "About . . .?"

"Well, about where you are now, with God and with us. And about . . . where you were before."

"Oh!" Ruby exhaled her relief.

Abigail had not been asking her further about Henry. Good. She didn't even know how to put her feelings into words to explain them to herself, never mind to someone so close to the man in question.

"Oh, I am so grateful to be here," Ruby said with a sigh. "And most of all, to have been forgiven, by God. It all—" She raised her shoulders, shaking her head, then lowered them. "I cannot describe it. I am so very thankful. Thankful for you, and for Mr. Stratton, and for God's mercy and forgiveness. And for this place . . ." She looked around the room as though she were taking in the grandeur of a palace. "And I am so deeply thankful to not be where I used to be." Her eyes looked haunted as she raised them to Abigail. "I can never thank you enough. Never."

The last word was barely above a whisper, but Abigail seemed to hear it, looking at her with kind compassion in response.

"We are so glad that God has rescued you from that wretched place, and that He has redeemed you." A shadow darkened on Abigail's face. "And we want so much for you to be safe."

Safe. A word that Ruby had yearned for her whole life. A word that had taken her a while to realise she had become after reaching the parsonage.

A word that she longed to remain.

"I must confess, I cannot feel entirely at ease. You were not here, and Henry—" She swallowed hard. "Henry was—" She cleared her throat, her eyes cast upward as she drew a deep breath. "The fact is that Henry did not hear how cold and determined . . . I never heard such— He insisted, quite insisted, that he would return and that we would *all* suffer for it. And though I sincerely hope he shall never come back, I am quite convinced that he absolutely intends to."

Ruby pulled her shawl tighter. "If he said that he will, there is no question. Only God would be able to keep him from doing so. He always gets his way. Millforte, I mean."

Saying his name again, she felt a distance she had never felt before. For the first time in her life, he wasn't breathing down her neck, belittling her every move. Despite his threats, she could physically feel a distance from him. It felt wonderful. Though, how long might it last?

"I am quite uncertain as to what ought to be done. The only way for you to be truly safe is . . ." Abigail's voice faded into silence.

Ruby nodded, her heart sinking.

" . . . Is for me to leave here," Ruby said, completing Abigail's thought.

Her chest tightened at the thought of leaving. And when Abigail nodded reluctantly, Ruby felt as though she were falling.

Silence seemed to weigh them both down, the gentle ticking of the clock magnified in its solitude.

Just as Ruby opened her mouth to speak, tears sprang to her eyes. She swallowed and blinked them back. "You have all been so kind to me. You have helped me more than you can know. And I do not wish to bring any further suffering or torment than what I have already brought."

Ruby sighed, frustration filling her. "None of you deserve it."

A wave of grief engulfed her inwardly, yet her resolve was stronger than she expected it would be. She dropped her head slightly. "I cannot stay here if my very presence puts you all in danger." Her warbling voice cracked, and a few tears spilled out onto her cheeks. She quickly whisked them away.

"I do believe we ought to try to send you to my brother-in-law's estate. Perhaps, even for a time. Until . . . Until the threat is gone."

Ruby shook her head, her jaws clamped shut. "The threat will never be gone. I know him," she said, regret forcing her eyes shut at the truth of her words. "If it will keep you all safe for me to go to your brother-in-law's house, then I will go. But even if I do, he will come here, and he will carry out whatever he has threatened."

Abigail sighed. "I confess, that is what I fear. Even if you were with my brother-in-law, and you were safe there . . . If Millforte returns, why - Henry is only now beginning to reclaim his health. I cannot bear the thought of—" She rubbed her forehead with her fingertips.

More tears threatened to spill as Ruby sat in silent thought.

Abigail released another sigh. "If only there were a way to keep you *both* safe. If you are here, then you are both in danger. If you are gone, then Henry shall bear the weight of it. And perhaps, even the rest of us, according to his threats."

Ruby shook her head without hesitation. "I cannot bear to think that Henry will suffer more at his hands. I cannot." Emotion gripped her stomach, forcing all the air out of her lungs.

"Nor I," said Abigail.

A thought pierced Ruby's heart as she recounted Abigail's words. Her heart was heavy, her palms clammy, her mind racing.

"Perhaps . . ."

No, it was too much. Surely she could not bear that,

either. Yet, if it meant that those she cared about would be protected . . .

"What if I remain here," Ruby said. "What if I stay, and when he comes back, then he will not punish all of you as he said he would if I were to be kept from him again."

Abigail gave a confused frown. "I do not see how that would be better. He is determined to take you back. Surely, if you were here, it would make it unavoidable for him to do so."

Ruby spoke again, every inch of her screaming inside. "Yes." Her voice was a resigned whisper. "And, then, you would all be safe again."

Abigail's eyebrows furrowed, then stretched high. Her eyes grew wide in horror, her mouth gaping. "Surely, you cannot mean . . ." She stared at Ruby. "Ruby! You cannot . . . Why, you do not mean to say—"

"Believe me, I do not *ever* wish to go back there! It is a vile and wretched place. But, it is even more vile and wretched to me to think of that man hurting Henry again! How can I leave here for safety yet know that Henry is still under his threat?"

She longed to seize upon some ingenious thought, to discover a solution that would spare them all from danger. But none came.

The agony that roiled inside her shook her, her voice escalating.

"It would be better for everyone if I had never come here at all, yet, I cannot change that. But this - *this* - I can change! If he returns, I will do whatever it takes to ensure that Henry will not be harmed. If the only way to ensure that is for me to go back, to rot in that place, then I will!"

"Ruby!" Abigail flew off her seat and curled her arms around Ruby, like a mother bird covering her chicks with outstretched wings. "Ruby, you cannot believe that Henry - or

I - would ever permit that! After all that we have come through? I assure you, we will do whatever we must to ensure that you will never have to look upon that place - or that *man* - ever again."

Ruby sobbed in Abigail's arms. How she longed to believe that there was some other way. She could hardly think clearly enough to pray, yet, feebly, she asked God for His help.

Abigail stroked Ruby's hair and started to hum. Ruby's cries deepened, as she thought of all the grace she had been shown, yearning desperately that she might be shown it one more time.

HENRY SMILED as he eased his weary body back into bed. It was only after joining Abigail and Ruby for dinner that he fully comprehended how much he had missed being able to do so.

He loved his aunt deeply. Her motherly care seemed to fill the empty cracks and hollows that his own mother had left unfilled. He frowned slightly as he regretted speaking to her the way he had about Mr. Webster.

Abigail was his closest kin, and he knew that all her endeavours and encouragements contained only her hopes for what might be best for him. Perhaps he should ask Bessie to gather some of the garden's new blooms, that he might present them to Abigail. Yes. That would enrich his apology and bring her a much-needed smile.

And as for Ruby . . .

It had almost taken his breath away when she had walked in.

Something about her had always captivated him, but how altered she appeared now that she had asked for - and received - God's grace. Her once haunted eyes had been enlightened with a deep-seated peace, and the tension that used to stiffen her lips and jaw had eased into a pleasant contentment. And that dress . . .

His smile strengthened as he remembered. She had looked, well . . . beautiful.

As his thoughts lingered on her, a fluttering grew in his chest.

An unintentional sigh gathered and escaped. His mind raced with memories, with new observations.

He was growing more discontent each day to be cooped up indoors, unable to even move to another room without Browne's assistance. He wanted to walk in the garden, out to the fields, along the stone and country dirt paths. It seemed so long since he had hopped into the carriage and visited his acquaintances in the town or the city, or gone back and forth between the church and the parsonage, to pray and to preach.

He sighed, willingly this time, frustration moving him restlessly.

A flash of surprise paused his breathing. Yes. He missed all those things. But most of all, he realised - he missed Ruby. Their strolls in the garden, as they conversed easily and smiled abundantly.

He frowned slightly as it occurred to him that if he could spring out of bed right this instant, able to do anything or go anywhere, all he would want would be to venture into the garden with Ruby and walk and talk, for as long as their legs would carry them. To share their thoughts, their laughter, their - no - their lives?

He remembered Millforte's taunts, that Henry had fallen for Ruby, and the defensiveness the brute's sneering words had evoked in him.

He thought of Abigail, how she had stated with such certainty that Henry loved Ruby. Hadn't he tried, flustered, to change the subject, owing to the sparks of truth her words had echoed?

The feeling of confirmation reverberated through him like a book being snapped shut.

How was it possible that his assailant and his aunt had been more aware of his own feelings than he had?

Henry placed his palms on his forehead and swept his hands up into his hair.

It was all true. And, now, he knew it, too.

He wanted to share his life with Ruby. Which could only mean that . . .

"I love her," he breathed.

A short laugh escaped him, as much from surprise as from joy.

"I really am in love with her . . ."

CHAPTER 27

AN UNACCOMPANIED
STROLL

THERE WAS STILL a little time before dinner was due to be served.

Abigail had already arrived and taken her usual seat at the table. Ruby hadn't seen her since their conversation the previous night, when she had cried bitter tears as Abigail's arm had encircled her, both praying for a solution that would preserve them all.

A twist of guilt nudged Ruby for having skipped breakfast, and for staying in her room most of the day, to pray and think.

"There you are, my dear. How are you feeling now?"

Ruby breathed deeply as she settled into her own usual seat.

"Only a little tired," Ruby said, her mind too foggy and muddled to ascertain how she was actually feeling. "I am sorry, about last evening."

"My dear," said Abigail, love yet firmness in her voice. "You have nothing for which to apologise." She paused, looking at Ruby with earnest eyes. "And as for your *suggestion*

- I shall not hear another word about it. We are together in this, now - all of us. We must stick together, and trust that the Lord will show us a way. I am not willing to sacrifice your safety for that of the rest of us."

Ruby stared at the table until everything in her sight blurred from exhaustion.

Feebly raising herself to a stand, she looked at Abigail, hoping that what she was about to say would not change Abigail's recent assertion.

"Forgive me, but may I be excused? I think it may be best if I retire early."

Abigail's face creased with concern. "Of course, my dear. I shall ask Bessie to send you some food up. Go."

The kindness on Abigail's face made Ruby feel like crying. She turned swiftly, mumbling a tremulous thank you as she began walking toward the door.

The door handle clicked, startling Ruby to a halt. As the door swung open, she heard Browne's voice, followed by Henry's. Her heart quickened and sank at the same time.

"Good evening, Miss Ruby," smiled Browne as he entered the room.

Henry came into view next, stiffly manoeuvring himself as Browne hovered close to him.

It was so good to see him walking again, even if it was more of a shuffle at present. Yet, the burning in her cheeks and agitation in her heart made Ruby want to charge past him without a word or look.

"Ruby!" Henry smiled, a new depth in his eyes.

Ruby's whole world froze. All she could hear was the blood thundering in her ears as she tried to find her voice.

"Good evening." She looked at Henry, then Browne, then turned her head to look at Abigail again. Looking back at Henry, she noticed his look transforming to one of concern.

"Please. Excuse me. I—"

Lurching for the door, she opened it as little as was necessary to fling herself through it, her heart racing faster than her feet the whole way back to her room.

All she could see in her mind's eye was Henry. Why did he have to look so perfect? Why did she long to look at him and speak to him every waking moment?

Within the comfortingly familiar walls of her room, she sighed. She did not understand herself. She couldn't wait to leave the dining room to avoid the agony of seeing Henry, yet now that she had successfully escaped him, she wanted nothing more than to go back to the dining room to see him.

She shook her head, her mouth dry and her body restless.

If this was love, why would anyone wish to fall into it?

HENRY'S SHOULDERS slumped forward slightly as he turned to make his way to the dinner table. He had been looking forward to seeing Ruby all day, even more eager to spend time with her since his personal revelation. Now, no sooner had he arrived than she had gone.

In his heart, he longed to rush after her, to make sure she was all right. Such a twisting feeling. He had never felt anything like it before.

He looked up at Abigail after gingerly easing himself into his chair.

"Good evening, Aunt. Pray, is Ruby well?" He looked over at the door, a melancholy look on his face.

Abigail forced a smile, her eyes warm with pity. "She is . . . tired at present."

"Is anything the matter?"

Abigail hesitated. "I do not believe that she slept very well last night."

Henry studied his aunt's face. "Aunt, is there something you are not telling me? What is the matter? Please."

Abigail sighed and shook her head. "She is quite well, truly. Only, she and I were speaking last night . . ."

Henry's eyes widened with apprehension. "Yes?"

Abigail seemed to steel herself, before speaking in a clear and matter-of-fact tone. "She is still very much wounded by her past. And she fears that her presence here is a threat to the safety of us all."

Henry's eyebrows knitted in concern.

"I told her that we will find a solution, with God's help," Abigail continued. "That we will get through this together."

Henry's ears pricked with hope. "Together? You mean, all of us . . . here?"

"Yes," said Abigail, a resigned air seeming to sweep over her. "As we spoke, I realised - as did Ruby - that if she *were* to be sent away, those of us remaining here would bear the full wrath of Millforte, if he were to return."

Henry's eyes squinted at the mention of Millforte's name.

"And Ruby was adamant that she did not wish to be the cause of any further harm, to you, or to any of us." She glanced up at Henry as she addressed him.

His heart felt as though it stumbled. "She spoke of me?"

Abigail nodded. "Oh yes." An expression gathered on her face that Henry could not decipher.

Abigail looked up at him, an earnest worry lining her face. "I must ask, my dear. Have you thought of *anything* regarding what we ought to do about . . . about the threat of that man's return?"

Henry sighed. "I thought that I had." His mouth twisted in disappointment. "I wrote to a magistrate in town."

"Oh?" Abigail's voice sounded hopeful.

Henry looked at her sadly. "That is precisely why I did not mention it to you before. I did not wish to raise anyone's hopes before I knew if there would be any way the man might help us."

Abigail's face fell. "So, there is not?"

Henry's expression was one of wistful remorse. "I asked him what might be done concerning the situation. But, as Millforte is legally Ruby's guardian, he effectively told me that there is nothing that he can do. Despite all the threats and violence. Frankly, I expected as much. Though, I was still appalled." He shook his head bitterly as he spoke.

Abigail was quiet a moment. "We shall keep praying, my dear. The Lord will bring us through. He always does."

Henry rubbed his temple with his hand. "That is true. I do not have the slightest notion of how He will do it, but I do trust that He will."

THE NEXT DAY, Ruby awoke to the fading sound of the carriage wheels rolling away from the parsonage. Must be Browne again, she thought. He had been going into town a lot more, lately, on Henry's behalf.

As she rose and dressed, she regretted her hasty departure from the dining room the previous evening. How kind Abigail had been to her when she had been so upset the other night. She hated the fact that she had acted so rudely.

Venturing down to the dining room, she discovered that she had slept in. Breakfast had all been cleared away. The strong blades of sunlight cutting through the window's curtains indicated it was around mid-morning.

Oh dear.

She felt guilty about sleeping in, despite how little she had been able to sleep the past few nights.

Weaving her way to the drawing room, she knocked lightly. Too lightly, perhaps. A timid flutter rose in her throat as she tried to think of what she ought to say in apology to Abigail.

With a sigh of determination, she opened the door and entered the room.

"Ruby!"

"Oh! I beg your pardon, I knocked, but I heard no response, so I thought—"

Henry's eyes creased at the corners as he endeavoured to sit up straighter. "Forgive me, I did not hear a knock."

Ruby smiled, swallowing a gulp. Even sitting half-reclined, he looked like such a gentleman. She scolded herself inwardly for harbouring the feelings that she did. He was far beyond her hopes. She must not be so silly.

"Please - sit down." He smiled, his hand extended toward one of the armchairs.

She perched on its edge, yearning for her heart and stomach to settle. She used to feel so relaxed - so at home - in his presence. If it really was love that she felt toward him, why did it have to complicate things? Wasn't it supposed to be a good thing? Yet, what torment of soul and awkwardness of presence it had already affected in her.

"Are you feeling better?" she asked, trying to force her mind away from how handsome he looked.

"Yes, much. I still feel rather stiff and sore, but I am so grateful to be able to move around a little more without the need of constant assistance." His smile transformed into a look of sympathy. "How are you?"

Ruby stared at him a moment, surprised by the question and completely at a loss for how to answer it. "I am well, thank you." She forced a smile, yet her lips remained closed. "I am so glad that you are feeling better."

"God is faithful," Henry said with a smile.

Ruby longed to voice her agreement, but a sudden flood of emotion overwhelmed her heart upon hearing the words. She looked down and nodded.

"Ruby - my aunt and I, we will find a way to ensure your safety. Please, do not worry. This is your home, now. For . . . for as long as you wish it to be."

Ruby looked up. A melancholy look had settled on his face.

For as long as you wish it to be.

It was true, then. Not forever.

Just for now.

She tried to stammer a polite thank you, but the words caught in her throat, her heart and mind overwhelmed by the sensation that they were cascading down, down, down into some faraway abyss.

"Ruby?"

She drew a deep breath in, filling her lungs slowly. Swallowing hard, she looked up at him, a fresh flutter twisting through her as she looked into his twinkling eyes.

"Shall we go for a short stroll in the garden?" His voice was hushed, yet she could still detect the hope and excitement that infused it.

"A stroll?" she asked, her voice somewhat hoarse. She cleared her throat. "Are you sure? Are you well enough? I—"

"I am sure!" he interrupted her, a grin breaking out across his hopeful face. "A short one. I shall have to shuffle along, really, but it has been so long . . . Let us even take the air and see what can be managed!"

Her heart melted. He was so pure. Such an innocent

desire, such wholesome pleasure. A stroll in the garden. Fresh air. What could be better?

"Very well," she said, rising to a stand. "Should I fetch Mrs. Jones, or Browne?" As deeply as she wished she could be alone with Henry for an endless afternoon stroll, she knew that it would be wise to maintain decorum.

"My aunt is away. Browne, too. There were a few pressing errands to be taken care of in town, though they will endeavour to return as soon as possible."

"Oh." She remembered hearing the carriage wheels. They would likely be gone for at least a few hours. She did not know whether to be happy or nervous about the prospect of so much uninterrupted time with Henry. Either way, she knew she should ask the only logical next question.

"Should I fetch Bessie then? To accompany us?"

"I am not sure whereabouts she is. But, I think we will be fine without a chaperone. We will, in all likelihood, not be venturing out of sight. We have no chaperone here with us at present, so I own that we will not have need of one if we remove to the other side of the window."

Just the two of them, then. Ruby felt sick and elated at the same time.

"Very well. Shall I fetch you anything? A cloak? A cane?"

Henry stiffly brought himself to his feet. "No need," he grinned. "I had Browne leave them out before his departure." He pointed to a chair in the corner. As Ruby turned toward it, she noticed a thick, black cloak laid out across it and Henry's cane resting against its arm.

She swished toward them and scooped up the items with care, hurrying back to Henry to deliver them.

"Here you are . . ."

"Thank you." His eyes held hers for a moment, glistening with sincerity.

She looked away, her cheeks burning. "You are welcome."

He sighed. A blend of contentment and . . . something else. Before she could give it any more thought, he spoke.

"Shall we?"

"It is every bit as beautiful as I remember," Henry said with a sigh, standing a little down the path from the parsonage, casting a spanning gaze at the landscape that lay before them. The fingerprints of early spring had appeared, the ground a tapestry of various hues of green, save for a few white patches of lingering snow.

"Yes, it is wonderful," said Ruby.

They had not ventured very far from the house. It was obvious that each step Henry took caused him considerable pain.

Ruby drank deep the fresh air, the scent of fragrant early blooms infusing the gentle breeze. If only every place on earth were like this. She could scarcely imagine such bliss to have existed in the past. Now, here it was, surrounding every one of her senses.

"Ah, what a joy it is," Henry said, more to himself than to her.

He turned to face her, his eyes burning with delight. "Such delicate beauty, displaying God's handiwork in such an intricate way. I do not think I appreciated it fully until now . . ."

A strange look passed over him, and his gaze fixed upon her with an atmosphere that made her forget everything. Everything, except him.

A faint rattling and crunching sound in the distance grew louder and louder.

"That must be your aunt, returned," said Ruby, bending ever so slightly to inspect a new shoot that had just captured her attention.

"It cannot be. Not so soon," Henry said. "We have not been out here so long, have we?"

Ruby straightened up and turned to face him. "I do not think we have been here more than half an hour or so . . ." Her words trailed off into nothing.

She didn't like the frown that was forming on Henry's face.

Glancing over her shoulder, she breathed a sigh of relief. There was no sight of any carriage yet. Henry's frown must have been one of confusion, rather than concern.

She looked back at him, studying the way his brow ridged and his eyes changed shape when he was deep in thought.

Ruby wondered if it might be Miss Acton again. Though, she certainly would not mention her to Henry. No doubt, Abigail would encourage him to think of an acceptable woman soon enough. Until then, Ruby was glad to have full privilege of his captivating company.

A whinny pierced the silent air around them, dispersing Ruby's thoughts. Whoever it was, they were definitely approaching the parsonage.

And they had almost arrived.

CHAPTER 28

THE RETURN

BEFORE EITHER OF the two could remark on the proximity of the sound they had heard, a shiny, black carriage thundered into view.

Ruby glanced at Henry, then back to the carriage, searching for a look of relieved recognition on his features now that the approaching apparatus was in sight.

She found none.

Instinctively, she stepped closer to him, suddenly feeling vulnerable and exposed.

Henry stretched out his arm in front of her, creating a protective barrier.

The carriage halted and the footman opened the door. It was too late to run for it. Not that Henry could have, anyway.

The first thing Ruby saw was the immaculate lustre of the man's top hat as it poked outward then upward to reveal the face beneath it.

Millforte.

Ruby's ears started ringing, muffling the sharp cry that escaped from Henry. The air felt as though it had been sucked from her lungs. She wanted to run, to retreat, yet she was rooted to the path.

"Ah! I see you have recovered. And what is this?" Millforte walked toward them. "You *do* have a guest . . ." He gave a cruel smirk. "Hello, Ruby."

Ruby suppressed the urge to vomit. Her breathing was fast and shallow, which only made her head reel more.

"You are not welcome here," Henry growled. "I am ordering you to leave my property at once."

Ruby noticed Henry's hands curl into fists. She looked back at Millforte, struggling to believe that he was actually present.

"But what about *my* property?"

Ruby's stomach flipped.

Her. He meant her.

"There is no property of yours here. Now leave."

Millforte chuckled in amusement. "Oh, dear. A fool in love, eh?"

In love? Ruby balked. How did Millforte know that she loved Henry?

Wait. No . . . He had been talking to *Henry*.

So, Millforte thought Henry was helping Ruby because he loved her? Oh, if only that were true, she thought.

Millforte's smile faded into a glare, directed squarely at Henry. "I am not leaving without my property."

Ruby noticed Henry's jaw tighten. "Go. At once. As I have told you many times, now - you have no property here."

Millforte rolled his eyes and looked straight at Ruby. "Well, well. Look at you! I would hardly recognise you. You must be enjoying playing 'happy family' here in the country."

His mocking tone filled Ruby with disgust. Her whole body trembled.

Millforte stepped forward.

Instantly, Henry shuffled backward, his arm still extended in front of Ruby. She felt the warm solidity of his arm gently press across her body. She moved backward and, without thinking, reached out and grasped his cloak, clinging to the fabric that fell across his back as though it were the only thing stopping her from falling off the edge of a precipice.

Millforte laughed. "You must know by now, it is folly to resist. Is that not the truth, Ruby?" He said her name with a growl of disdain.

"You are not permitted to address her," Henry barked.

His volume and tone made Ruby jump. She had never seen him so angry. Or so protective. Her mind raced.

Please, Lord, help us . . .

Millforte levelled a cold glower at Henry. "Get out of my way, you pathetic preacher boy."

He shoved Henry's shoulder, causing Henry's arm to collide with Ruby. Henry placed himself directly between Ruby and Millforte, blocking her view of his tormenting visage.

"You - get out! Get off my property! At once!"

Henry was shouting his loudest, pointing at the carriage and the path it had travelled.

Millforte spat through gritted teeth. "I said get out of m—"

"Wait!" Ruby shrieked, moving to Henry's side in an attempt to diffuse the violence she knew was all too imminent.

Henry snapped his head around and caught her eyes. She gaped at him. His face looked pale, his eyes filled with the fear that widened her own.

Millforte grabbed her arm. "Now I shall leave."

"Wait!" Ruby exclaimed, yanking her arm away from Millforte's grip.

She was between him and Henry now. She held her hands up in front of her. "Wait, please!"

Tremors coursed through her every fibre, every nerve.

"Ruby . . ." Henry's voice pleaded behind her.

Millforte looked smugly at her, amused expectation all over his face.

"What is it, Ruby?" Again, he spat out her name like a sour taste.

"I have to tell you something," she breathed, the gentle breeze sounding louder than she did.

"Speak up, girl. And make it quick. We have a long journey ahead of us."

She looked away from the cruel glint in his eyes, praying and pleading with God to give her words and the strength to say them.

"I . . . I must tell you—"

She looked back up at his eyes, swallowing hard as she beheld the coldness in them. Coldness that was directed right at her.

Please, Lord, help me to say it.

She drew a shaking breath in, then felt resolution strengthen within her.

"I cannot go with you."

Millforte's eyebrows travelled as high up as they could go. He punctured the tense air with a short, sharp laugh. "You *cannot* go with me? You really think you have a choice? You are *mine*, and—"

"No!" She felt a boldness she had never felt, especially in Millforte's presence. "I am not. I do not belong to you - I belong to God."

Millforte looked from Ruby to Henry, his expression querying if her speech might be some kind of joke. He chuckled, then laughed in derision.

"Oh, I see! So the holy man has brainwashed you, has he?"

Millforte directed his bemused eyes at Henry. "Was that one of your tricks to win her heart?" His eyes glimmered with malice.

Ruby heard what he said but missed his meaning as she scrambled to speak.

"He has not brainwashed me," she had already begun to say. "He has shown me the truth. God is real. And He offers mercy, and forgiveness . . . and grace."

Millforte's attention reverted to Ruby, suspicion cresting his brow.

"He has forgiven me," continued Ruby. She swallowed hard and steeled herself. "He can forgive you, too, if you ask Him."

Millforte's expression altered so suddenly that he looked as though he had been slapped across the face.

"What?" he breathed, shock and disbelief almost muting his voice. His eyes narrowed, his skin and brows creasing around them in a look of utter bewilderment.

Ruby stood as still as a statue, holding her breath as she observed Millforte's response.

Please, Lord, help us. Please, let him leave.

She could hear Henry's breathing behind her, deep and rapid.

Please, Lord, do not allow Millforte to hurt Henry again. Please, help us.

"How dare you, you insolent girl!" Millforte spat. He grabbed her arm, gripping tighter this time, and turned toward the carriage, dragging her along despite her attempts to dig her feet into the gravelly path.

"Ruby!"

She felt Henry grab her other arm and pull her toward

332

him. She whipped her head around to face him. His earnest eyes made her heart thud.

Millforte turned, scowling at Henry's attempt to stop him.

"Oh, preacher boy - will you never learn?"

He yanked Ruby out of Henry's grip and shoved her out of his reach.

"I demand that you leave here at once!" Henry shouted.

"Gladly," growled Millforte, just before he kneed Henry in the stomach. Henry doubled over, winded and gasping.

Ruby watched in horror, her heart screaming Henry's name but her throat unable to make a sound.

Millforte grabbed Henry's shoulders and pulled him up. Ruby heard the sound of Millforte's fist cracking into Henry's temple just as she saw Henry slump to the ground.

"No!"

Ruby questioned if her scream had made any sound as she saw Millforte kick Henry in the stomach, oblivious to her hastening approach behind him.

"Stop!" she shrieked, grasping at Millforte's elbow.

He turned to face her, a sneer souring his face. He glanced back at Henry, who lay motionless across the path.

"Time to leave," Millforte snarled, grabbing Ruby's arm.

"No!" Ruby struggled in vain to free herself, keeping her eyes on Henry, willing him to move. She could not see his face, but it was clear that he was out cold.

As Millforte dragged her along the path toward the carriage, she wailed and screeched three words over and over again.

"No!"

"Stop!"

"Henry!"

She dug her heels into the path and furiously tried to shake her arm loose from Millforte's claw-like grip.

"Quiet!" Millforte snapped.

"Let me go! You cannot do this! Please!"

They had reached the carriage. A wave of nausea and weakness flooded through Ruby. She had to do whatever it took to stay on the outside of that door.

"No!"

"Get in," said Millforte, his tone calm and even.

Quivering all over, Ruby shook her head, tears streaking down her cheeks. "I will not! You cannot do this!"

Her heart was pulling her back to Henry. Still, she could see his unmoving form farther down the path. She attempted to rush past Millforte.

"Henry-y-y!" she sobbed.

"Get back here!" Millforte said through gritted teeth. "Do not worry - I dare say it will not take long to make you forget these notions you have about God and mercy," he said, cackling cruelly.

A searing pain shot through her head, just as everything went black.

"I CANNOT BELIEVE I was so silly - imagine forgetting the very thing that Henry insisted I not forget!"

Abigail's hands held each side of her shaking head.

"Oh, come now, Mrs. Jones, everyone is apt to forget things every once in a while. And you have had more than your fair share of . . . extra concerns of late."

Abigail looked up at Browne's sympathetic gaze. "Thank you, Browne. I am sure Henry will see it just as you do. Still, I do feel rather silly," she half-smiled.

"It will not be long now until we have retrieved it, ma'am."

Abigail nodded gladly and looked out of the carriage window. They should reach the parsonage within the next half hour or so.

The carriage lurched, and a faint neigh from one of the horses startled Abigail. Slowly, they rumbled to a stop.

"Browne? What is the matter?"

"I do not know, ma'am. Perhaps another carriage is trying to travel the other direction. That often happens on this narrow little stretch of road. Shall I go and check?"

"No, no. We shall wait a moment and see if you are right. I expect you are."

As she finished speaking, her attention was captured by a black horse outside the window, picking its way carefully past, another horse to its right and rigging that stretched back to an out of sight carriage.

"Ah. There we are. You were right, Browne."

"Nothing to worry about, ma—"

"What is it, Browne?"

Browne had stopped mid-sentence, launching himself off the carriage seat and scrambling to steady himself, bracing himself against the carriage door. His face was right up to the window, and Abigail could tell from his posture that something wasn't right.

"Browne?"

He turned back from the window slowly, bafflement contorting his features.

"It is the strangest thing, ma'am. I saw a face in the carriage - a girl. I could swear it looked— But surely not . . ." He lifted his eyes to meet Abigail's. "It looked like Miss Ruby."

Abigail's stomach lurched with the carriage as it jolted back into movement.

"Oh, Browne! You do not think—" she shook her head, the movements hasty and abrupt.

Browne's face was lined with concern, his voice hushed and grave. "I have a dreadful feeling that it *was* her, ma'am."

"Oh, Browne! But that must mean— Oh, what shall we do? Henry! And Ruby! We cannot see to both of them at once! Oh, Browne, what shall we *do*?"

Abigail's voice grew louder and more highly-pitched with each word.

"Come now, ma'am. We will be soon at the parsonage. I shall leave you there and take the carriage straight back down this road in pursuit of the carriage we saw. That is, unless we find Miss Ruby safe at the parsonage on our return."

"Thank you, Browne." Abigail dabbed at her eyes with her handkerchief. "Oh, I do hope Henry is not— I hope he has had no further injury!"

"I know, ma'am," said Browne in a soothing tone, though his wrinkled brow expressed the depth of his own concern.

"Let us pray, ma'am. Let us pray all the way back home."

HENRY FELT a cool breeze ruffle his hair and brush across his face. He opened his eyes, blinking at the sunlight, and at the pain he felt on moving his face. He blinked in confusion as he realised he was lying on the garden path.

It all rushed back to him.

Scrambling to his feet, he called out her name. "Ruby!"

He limped and dragged himself down the path toward the road, a bitter taste rising from his gut, his muscles weak and thrumming.

"Ruby!"

He sank to his knees, tears rolling down his face. She was gone. He had failed her.

He remembered now - Millforte had knocked him out. Again.

His heart gripped with fear as he pictured Millforte being rough with Ruby, forcing her into his carriage. What was happening to her now? How long would it be until . . .

Henry cried out with all that was in him, as despair and devastation flooded through his being. "No!"

A faint rumble in the distance made him freeze. He held his breath.

Hooves.

Very faint, but he could hear horses.

And wheels.

He clambered to his feet, straining his eyes and ears to ensure he wasn't imagining it.

It grew louder. Slowly, yet surely.

It was definitely a carriage. And it was headed for the parsonage.

"Ruby . . ." he whispered.

Could it be Millforte's carriage? Could he be returning her? Though Henry knew deep down that it would not be Millforte, he knew that with God, nothing was impossible, no matter how unlikely it may seem.

After what felt like an age, the carriage rolled into view. It wasn't Millforte's, but Henry's own. His shoulders sank.

Lord, please keep her safe! Please, show us what to do!

No sooner had the carriage stopped moving than Browne shot out of it. Spotting Henry, he kept his gaze fixed on him the whole time he helped Abigail alight.

"Mr. Stratton!" Browne started running toward Henry.

"Browne!" Henry exclaimed, his voice cracking.

"Henry!" Abigail cried as she bustled over to him. "Are you all right, my dear? Is—"

"She is gone! He has taken her! I could not stop him!" Henry fought back the wails that threatened to engulf him. "He knocked me out, and he took her!"

"I shall do as I said, ma'am," said Browne, turning to leave. He stopped, turned back to Henry and grabbed his arm. "Are you well, sir? Do you need my assistance?"

"I am all right, Browne - but Ruby! He has her! He will hurt her—" Panic shook Henry's head as he spoke.

"I must away. Pray. Both of you."

Browne turned and darted back to the carriage with the nimbleness of a man half his age.

"Wait! I am coming with you!"

"Oh, Henry - perhaps you should rest. You are only recovering from the first time, and now—" Abigail's face crumpled.

"I cannot remain here and do nothing, Aunt. I must help her."

Henry's eyes burned with an earnest resolve.

Abigail nodded. She waved the carriage off, silent tears and prayers pouring from her heart.

CHAPTER 29

BELONGINGS

"I MADE such haste to leave, sir, because Mrs. Jones and I saw the carriage go past on our way back to the parsonage. I could not be certain, but I did think it looked like Miss Ruby."

"You saw her?" Henry's eyes widened. "How did she look?"

Anguish tore at Henry's heart as he envisaged Ruby alone in the carriage with Millforte. He was beyond frustrated with himself for not protecting her.

"She, why she looked as though she were sleeping, sir. I was—"

"Sleeping? Oh, Browne! He must have knocked *her* out, too!" A fresh wave of horror chilled Henry's spine. "Oh, Ruby."

"Do not fret, sir. The Lord is in control. He has kept her safe thus far - He will not abandon her now."

Shame coloured Henry's cheeks as Browne's words stopped him in his tracks. Should he not be the one speaking thus? He was the clergyman, after all. Shouldn't his faith dispel the fear that clutched at him, choking him every time he pictured Ruby with her repulsive captor?

"I am glad for your company, Browne. And for your encouragement."

Browne looked surprised momentarily, then gave a gentle smile. "And I, yours, Mr. Stratton. God will help us, sir. We will find her."

Henry tilted his head back against the carriage wall. If only they could have gone faster. But he was not yet mended enough to travel on horseback. Besides, the horses had already been hitched up to the carriage.

He exhaled bitterly. If only, if only, if only. That phrase had seemed to dominate his thoughts of late. If only Miss Acton would transfer her affections to some other young man. If only Millforte would leave them all alone. If only he could fully express his affection for Ruby. If only he had been able to protect her today and not be so easily knocked out again.

Was this how it was always to be?

He frowned, his mind flitting with hopes and dreams, worries and fears.

A streak of clarity pierced his thoughts.

How long would he continue to wish his life away, rather than live it?

What if he were to stop yearning for the 'if only' scenarios - the thoughts that fuelled his discontent - and start fully trusting that God was in control of everything - all that was happening now, and everything that would happen in the future?

If he wanted Miss Acton to relinquish her romantic affections toward him, he should let her know that his heart belongs to another.

If he wanted Millforte to stop being a threat, he should

stop allowing himself to feel threatened by the man and instead entrust it all to God.

If he wanted to express his true feelings for Ruby, well then - he should express them. After all, she belonged to God now. What did it matter about her social standing when her spiritual standing was ultimately what truly mattered?

His heart fluttered at the thought of telling Ruby that he loved her.

If only he had protected her today. He had tried. But he couldn't. Was that what God was trying to teach him?

He suddenly recalled the time, not so long past, when he had knelt in prayer in his room, surrendering everything to God and relinquishing his faulty belief that it all depended on himself.

He knew it didn't, though time seemed to have faded his realisation. But now, it returned.

He knew that he was merely human, and certainly not equal to the task.

Praise God, Henry thought. *It all depends on Him. As it should.*

He sighed, lowering his head as he raised a silent prayer.

Forgive me, Lord. I have neglected to acknowledge Your rightful place as One who has all authority and power - the One upon whom everything depends. Oh, Lord, please, forgive my folly, my short-sightedness. I do not know what to do when we arrive, Lord, but please - help us again to rescue Ruby from that man's evil clutches. Please, keep her safe. Do not permit any harm to come near her. Oh, Lord, show us what to do. I trust You, God. You alone can rescue her. You alone can protect us all from danger and harm. Please, Lord - help us.

Henry breathed out a long, deep sigh. A comforted feeling settled in his stomach, replacing the turmoil that had been tossing in it moments before.

He squeezed his eyes shut.

Thank you, Lord.

WHEN RUBY OPENED HER EYES, she reeled as she took in the dark, velvety interiors of the carriage.

Millforte's carriage.

Acid rose in her throat as she turned her head and saw him.

"Well, hello again," he said with a smirk. The coldness in his eyes was unbearable to behold. She turned her head back to the window without hesitation.

"Oh, are you not my friend anymore?" His taunting tone made Ruby feel sick.

Please, Lord, help me.

"A friend does not treat others thus," she said coolly.

Millforte chuckled. "Oh, now! I see you have found your tongue."

Ruby stared at the carriage floor, fighting her hardest to shake off the despair enrobing her.

"Look at me, girl, when I am talking to you."

Ruby hesitated, then turned to face the man she had hoped never to see again.

Like a lightning strike, he grabbed her face in his strong fingers and squeezed her cheeks hard.

As a cry of pain tried to escape her, he pulled her face close to his.

"How dare you be so insolent! Need I remind you that I hold your miserable life in my hands? If you wish to keep your tongue, I advise you to hold it silent."

Tears of horror pricked Ruby's eyes. She knew him well enough to know that this was not an empty threat. And that he would enjoy dangling the suspense of violence overhead for as long as he could.

He let her go with a shove. Instinctively she rubbed her

face, disgusted and devastated by his menacing presence and violent touch.

She fought back tears as she thought of Henry. Had he woken up yet? Was he all right?

Would he come and rescue her again?

As the carriage pulled her farther and farther from the parsonage, she battled to keep her grasp on hope. It *had* all seemed too good to be true, after all.

Maybe Henry wouldn't come. And, perhaps, God didn't want her anymore, either.

Clearly, it had all just been a lovely yet impossible dream.

"I have a surprise for you when we get back home," Millforte said, an ironic emphasis on the last word.

Ruby's stomach flipped. No surprise he could offer would be one that anyone would wish to receive. Besides, the brothel was not her home.

Please, Lord, do not let that place be my home ever again.

She closed her eyes and feigned sleep, shuffling as close as she could to the carriage wall, trying desperately to get as far away as possible from the man whom it seemed she could never escape.

"HOW FAR BEHIND them do you think we are, Browne? Should we not have caught up to them by now?"

It seemed like years to Henry since he and Browne had set off from the parsonage.

"Well, now." Browne looked deep in thought. "I think we may yet be a fair distance away from them, Mr. Stratton. We may not entirely catch up with them until we reach the city."

Henry exhaled heavily. Poor Ruby. To endure being in such close proximity to that monster for hours on end, as she was

343

ushered toward the wretched place that had stolen so many years of her life.

It was agony. He felt a restless clawing in his stomach, in every fibre throughout him. It took concentrated effort to remain still and seated rather than writhe in his seat.

"Do not worry, sir. We will catch up to them soon enough."

Henry sighed, nodding in response to Browne's calm reassurance.

"Sir?" Browne continued. Henry looked up at him. "I was wondering if you have anything in mind? Any plan of action, so to speak, of what we might do when we have reached them at last?"

Henry sighed as he leaned his head back against the top of the carriage seat. His blank gaze darted to and fro as scenario after scenario played through his mind.

He looked back to Browne, who was sitting in expectant silence, his gentle eyes fixed on Henry. With another sigh, Henry squeezed his lips together and shook his head slowly.

"I am afraid I have none, Browne. But I will do whatever it takes," he said in a low voice, his eyes steeling with resolve.

"And I will help you in whatever way I can," nodded Browne. He gave a gentle smile. "I am truly quite fond of Miss Ruby," he said, a melancholy expression softening his face.

Henry looked up at him. "You are?"

"Yes, sir. It is remarkable how much she has changed already since her encounter with the Lord. Even before it, she was a gentle soul. But now . . ." His eyes creased as his smile deepened. "Why, I believe her to be one of the kindest and loveliest young ladies I have ever met. She has such a depth of feeling and understanding. She is quite unmatched."

Henry smiled in response, his heart swelling in his chest as he reflected on all of Browne's observations.

"Yes," he half-laughed, half-sighed. "She is wonderful."

Henry looked again at Browne. He hesitated. "I think very highly of her. Very highly indeed."

A knowing smile crept over Browne's features as he gave a soft chuckle. "I know."

Henry's heart felt like it stopped, then restarted at double speed. "You, you know?"

Browne gave him a fatherly smile of encouragement. "I know that you and she think very highly of each other. And I can think of no two people that it would make me happier to see settled and wed than you and Miss Ruby."

Henry's jaw dropped. Browne really did know. And what's more, he actually approved.

It was too much for Henry to take in. He exhaled a shaky breath.

He had borne his heart and met with approval. He had not expected such an outcome. Nor had he expected to feel such a depth of joy at the affirmation that Browne's encouragement had given him.

Henry sighed and rested his head again, closing his eyes and reflecting on what Browne had said.

I know that you and she think very highly of each other.

His eyes snapped open and he looked at Browne, pushing himself up straighter in his seat. "Browne, did you say that you believe Ruby and I think highly of each *other*? Do you mean that you think she might think of me as highly as I think of her?"

"Without question, Mr. Stratton! I may be an old man, but I am not without my wits yet," Browne said with a chuckle. "I have seen how affectionately you look at her, and though she has never said so to me, I believe she returns your affections entirely."

Henry felt as though he could burst.

Could it be true? Did Ruby really feel the same way about him?

He looked at Browne, his mouth poised to speak but his mind tumbling with so many thoughts that he could not issue any of them.

Browne smiled, amusement flickering in his eyes. "Does this come as news to you, sir?"

Henry felt as though the carriage were spinning.

"Yes!" he managed to voice, his throat dry. "It certainly does."

He searched back through all his encounters with Ruby. There was no doubt that they seemed to share a special connection. But in all his remembrances, he could find no evidence of any romantic attachment on her part.

Henry looked up at Browne, a crushing feeling slowly deflating the hope he had felt.

"Are you quite sure, Browne? I cannot think of anything that has transpired between us that would affirm your belief."

"Well, as I said, Mr. Stratton, she has never expressed anything of it to me directly, but I dare say that not all of the expressions I have noticed could have been imagined or mistaken. I think it highly likely that she *does* return your affections. However . . ."

"Yes?" Henry asked eagerly, as soon as he became aware of Browne's pause.

"Well, we must remember - she has not been treated kindly by men. And so, I imagine it would be quite a challenge for her to trust a man with her heart. Even one so trustworthy as you, sir."

"Of course," Henry nodded.

He knew it, though it sickened him to think of it. Ruby had undoubtedly experienced the very worst examples of how cruelly a man could mistreat a woman. Abuse and fear, objectification and lust. No one had cared for or cherished her. Only used and discarded her.

No one had taken the time to notice her heart.

Except Henry. He had looked past her circumstances and seen into her soul. And in doing so, he had discovered a precious heart, a gentle spirit and an answer to his deepest prayers.

As the carriage rumbled onwards, contentment and peace overwhelmed Henry. Soon, they would arrive. And when they did, he would somehow rescue her again.

Ruby.

The woman with whom he hoped to spend the rest of his life.

RUBY'S STOMACH lurched with the carriage as it came to an abrupt stop.

She glanced at Millforte as he rose off his seat and reached for the carriage door. He craned his head outside and shouted something to the footman that she couldn't quite make out.

Air wafted into the carriage, but the smell that circulated was anything but refreshing.

Smoke and filth. They must be at the brothel.

Her heart fluttered and pounded at the same time, a strange sensation of weakness yet alertness coursing through her in discomfiting waves. Part of her felt frozen to the seat, yet part of her practically twitched with a readiness to run without stopping until she was far, far away from her cruel captor.

Millforte descended the steps the footman had manoeuvred.

Ruby wondered what lay beyond the carriage door for her now. Beatings. Customers. Those were guaranteed. But what of hope? Or peace?

Would she ever know safety again?

A dark thought troubled her. Had she ever really known safety, even at the parsonage?

After all, since the day she had arrived, everyone in the household had lived under Millforte's threatening shadow. After he had failed to reclaim Ruby, each day had been filled with grief, sorrow, terror and pain, both at Henry's injuries and at Millforte's responsibility for them.

Perhaps they really were better off without her.

Maybe now that she was back where she belonged, they could go back to their safe and pleasant lives.

Yet, a simultaneous notion struggled within her that this wasn't where she belonged at all.

In truth, if she reached past all her fear and sorrow, she felt that where she belonged wasn't even a place, but a person.

Henry.

CHAPTER 30

AN ARRESTING VISIT

"WE'VE REACHED THE CITY NOW," Browne announced, bringing an abrupt halt to Henry's whirling thoughts.

"Oh." Trembling tried to consume Henry. He had no idea what lay before them, what he and Browne might encounter.

He looked at the age-worn man across from him. How noble he was. How deeply Henry appreciated Browne's presence and loyalty.

"Let us depend on the Lord, sir. He is our strength. He will help us."

Henry clung to Browne's words like a thirsty man clutching a glass of water. He closed his eyes in silent prayer, consciously determining to trust God, no matter what. To depend on His grace and strength, instead of trying to orchestrate or accomplish everything himself.

Help us, Lord. Keep Ruby safe. Please, help us free her.

Henry opened his eyes and fixed them on Browne, then gave him a ready nod.

His gentle companion mirrored his gesture, just as the carriage bumped, then slowed, then stopped.

Out in the street, the stench of tobacco and rotten food accosted Henry's senses with such force that his stomach churned.

As he and Browne began their purposeful march toward the vile building where he'd first encountered Ruby, a voice calling his name from behind him stopped him in his tracks.

"Not much different than when you left it, I imagine?" sneered Millforte, loosening his grip on Ruby's arm and pushing her into her old, hateful chamber.

"The room may not have changed, but I have," Ruby said, her voice almost without a waver.

"I am sure it will not be long until you change back," Millforte said coldly, spitting the last two words slowly.

"I never shall."

Ruby held his gaze, even though it repulsed her to look at him.

She didn't fear him as she once had, she realised. She was different now. She would not relinquish her faith for Millforte, his customers, or anyone. Let them do what they may to her. This was no longer her home, and she could no longer pretend that it was.

Millforte lashed out whip-fast, his fist punching pain and blurred vision into her left eye socket. "Ungrateful girl," he growled. He grabbed her shoulders and shook her violently. "How dare you try to defy me."

Ruby grabbed her head where Millforte had hit it. She squeezed both eyes shut, tears welling up in them. "I cannot deny who I am. I am forgiven. I am *clean*," she said, her voice trailing off into a whisper.

She was so grateful toward God for all that He had done,

yet now that she was back in this place, with the man who had done nothing but treat her cruelly, and a fresh infliction of the pain he loved to cause, she could scarcely cling to her hope.

"Forgiven? Clean?" Confusion contorted Millforte's features. He made a sound a little like a laugh, yet his face indicated that he was more bewildered than bemused.

"Yes. We are all far from God because of our sin. Everything we do that breaks any of His laws, well, there is a debt to pay. And because we sin every day - all the time, really - we owe a debt that we would never be *able* to pay. But *He* paid it for us, to bring us back to Him. That is why Jesus died - to pay the debt for the sins that we have done, so that God can declare us free, not guilty - forgiven!"

Hearing the words as she said them, she almost forgot where she was. Such joyous hope and truth - she really was forgiven. For all of it.

Hope stirred within her. No matter what lay ahead, her past had been washed clean.

Millforte's brow hardened in a suspicious scowl. "Why," he scoffed, "Why would anyone die for someone who has done nothing but rebel against them? Why would anyone allow themselves to be punished in someone else's place? Especially someone who deserved it!" He exhaled sharply in derision.

Ruby drew a courageous breath. "Love."

Millforte looked at her incredulously. "Love?"

"Yes. Love. We deserve his punishment, without question. But He loves us so much that He was willing to be punished in our stead. So that we could be reconciled to Him." Tears pricked her eyes. "And I have been."

Her voice wavered now, yet she had never felt such strength.

"I asked Him to forgive me and make me new, and He has. I have no control over your actions, but I promise you - I will never willingly betray my God. He gave everything for me. I will give everything for Him - my life included, if I must."

Millforte stared at her aghast, his features twisted in disbelief.

"So you may strike me again, if you wish. But, you cannot change me. I belong to God now, and I will never be yours again. No matter what you may do to me."

"He will do nothing more to you, Ruby."

The familiar voice came from the doorway.

It couldn't be.

Ruby spun around.

"Henry!" Ruby's voice was weak. He was actually there.

Henry walked into the room, straight toward her, followed by Browne.

Then, a man in a brown suit strolled in behind them. Ruby frowned. Surely she couldn't have a customer already.

Henry marched up to face Millforte, his arm extending protectively outward to shield Ruby as he stationed himself between them.

Millforte looked at him, a distracted expression on his frowning face. As he glanced at Browne and the man in the brown suit, he seemed to refocus on his current surroundings.

"What is the meaning of this?" he growled. Still, he was calmer than usual.

Henry motioned with his other arm toward Browne. "We have come to take Ruby back home with us."

Home. With them. Ruby's heart felt as though it could burst. That was where she belonged. Not here.

Millforte made a cynical sound. "Oh? Really?"

"Yes. And there is positively nothing that you can do to stop us this time."

This time? Ruby wondered. They had both stated determined defiance to Millforte's face multiple times now, and been defeated. What made this time different?

"Mr . . . Whatever your name is, as I have said before—"

"Stratton. Mr. Stratton. And yes, you have stated many vile things to Ruby and to myself," said Henry, leaning closer to the towering man. "But I am telling you, Mr. Millforte - you shall never see either one of us again after this day. We are leaving. And this time, there is nothing you can do to stop us."

There were those words again. This time.

Ruby studied Henry, though she could only see the back of him. There was a calm confidence in his voice, a decisiveness that she didn't think she had heard before.

Hope stirred in her heart. Maybe, somehow, this time *would* be different.

Before Millforte could respond, Henry motioned toward the man in the brown suit.

"This is Mr. Gibbons. He is an acquaintance of mine, whom we happened to meet with upon our arrival. By chance, some might say, but I believe it to be by God's design."

"Of course you would," muttered Millforte. He nodded abruptly at the stranger, then spoke with a mocking disdain. "Mr. Gibbons. Are you a clergyman, too? Come to snatch one of my other girls away from my wicked influence?" He sneered, his eyes narrow and glinting.

"Mr. Millforte." The stranger returned the nod. "So you are, in fact, the owner of this establishment?"

Mr. Gibbons spoke with a thin, nasal voice. His beady eyes were fixed steadily on Millforte.

"What business is it of yours?" Millforte asked, suspicion creasing his brow.

"Mr. Millforte, I am a magistrate and it has come to my attention that a substantial amount of counterfeit banknotes were forged earlier this month. Originally, my colleagues and I suspected an establishment on the other side of the city. Our investigations there met with no success. However, of late, I received an anonymous letter from someone who named you as a potential suspect. After conducting some undercover investigations of your premises, I happened upon the counterfeit currency. It is more than enough proof that you are, indeed, the person responsible. I am here to announce that you are under arrest and I compel you to accompany me at once to be held in custody, awaiting your trial at the Old Bailey without delay."

Henry had moved backward midway through Mr. Gibbons's speech, stopping by Ruby's side, leaving her with a clear view of Millforte.

She had never seen him so pale. The colour seemed to drain from his face before her eyes as Mr. Gibbons so eloquently revealed the reason for his presence.

Ruby looked up at Henry, struggling to believe what was happening. Henry glanced at her, hope in his eyes.

His expression changed rapidly upon seeing her face. "Ruby! Are you all right?"

Henry's hand gently cupped her chin and tilted her face upward. He frowned as he studied her right eye. Ruby noticed his jaw tighten as he glanced from her eye to Millforte.

"I am fine," she stuttered. She could hardly think, never mind speak.

Millforte stood pale and frozen.

Mr. Gibbons moved toward him, reaching out to grab his

wrist. Millforte instinctively pulled his arm away, his eyes narrow.

"Mr. Millforte, you are legally bound to accompany me," Mr. Gibbons said, his expression and manner unchanged by Millforte's resistance.

"Allow me to help you, sir," said Browne, moving toward Millforte, though his words had been directed to Mr. Gibbons.

Ruby watched and waited. She knew Millforte. He would not give up without a fight. And, though there were two of them, she doubted that Browne and Mr. Gibbons would be able to match Millforte's brutish strength.

Then, Mr. Gibbons spoke again.

"I must inform you, that if you resist arrest, I shall be obliged to call upon the three Principal Officers of Bow Street who accompanied me and who are waiting in the hallway, ready to deal with any incivility, in order that no one else here might meet with any harm. Is that understood?"

Ruby's heart skipped. Three officers were waiting outside? How could this be?

She glanced at Henry, silently searching for a sign that Mr. Gibbons' words had been true.

Henry looked at her, his face radiating grateful satisfaction.

Time seemed to slow down. Ruby could only blink.

God has surely answered our prayers.

Browne and Mr. Gibbons flew to either side of Millforte, each grasping one of his arms. As they started toward the door, Millforte glanced at Ruby.

She steeled herself for whatever threats he would level against her, whatever he might say that would become the latest phrases to haunt her.

His eyes were cold and narrowed, yet he appeared deep in

thought. She stared at him as he passed by her, expecting any moment that he would shake the men off and resume his poisonous tirade of malicious threats.

He was silent.

Once he had passed her, he looked away. His heavy frame slumped slightly at the shoulders.

And then, he was gone from the room.

Ruby stared at the doorway, listening for some impending commotion, some cry of anger.

There was nothing. No sight, nor sound.

Just silence.

Henry broke it with a sigh of relief. He turned to Ruby and seized her hands in his, grinning from ear to ear.

She looked up at him, still stunned, not really seeing him in her perplexity.

"Ruby?" Henry frowned. "Are you all right? Are you not happy? Why, you are free from him!"

Free from him? Free from Millforte?

Silence screamed all around her, her heart thudding and rushing in her ears.

Free from him.

"Ruby?"

Free from him.

"Well, sir, that is that! Did I not tell you that God would bring us through?"

Browne's voice cut through Ruby's maelstrom of thoughts. She turned to look at him, his lined face bathed in jubilant contentment.

Browne looked at Ruby and smiled, sympathy in his eyes and expression. "How are you feeling, Miss Ruby?"

She heard him, and saw him, but she could not speak. Her blank gaze passed from him, to Henry, to the empty doorway.

"I think it has all been quite a shock," she heard Henry

say. "Perhaps we ought to take her outside for some fresh air."

"Capital idea." The triumph in Browne's voice was unmistakable. "It has been a very unusual day for all of us. How are you feeling yourself, sir - your back?"

"Oh, a little stiff, but no matter. I am overjoyed and more thankful than I can say!"

"I think we all are, sir." Browne paused. "We should see that Miss Ruby takes some air."

Henry and Browne gently escorted Ruby from the room where she had spent so much of her life in misery and pain. She was in such a daze that she followed without a glance.

Still, as they shuffled along the corridors and down the stairs, she expected Millforte's voice or presence to stop them in their tracks. Finally, they filed through the main door.

Outside, the light was so bright that it hurt her eyes. She squeezed them shut, disoriented and dizzy.

As her vision adjusted, she looked at the outside of the building she had been kept inside for so long. It was a dingy, dirty looking place. Dark windows were set underneath a faded blue sign. She didn't take in what the words said. But she knew they wouldn't have given any indication as to why people actually frequented the place.

"Ruby?"

She looked up at Henry, her eyes glad to turn their gaze away from the gloomy building.

"Do you require some more air, or shall we set off for home?"

Home.

Such a beautiful word. She felt as though she were hearing it for the first time.

This wasn't home. The parsonage was. Henry had said so.

Miss Acton flashed into Ruby's mind.

Ruby's chest tightened as she thought of Henry marrying. Even if it wasn't Miss Acton, someone would one day take their place as his wife. Maybe until then, she could call the parsonage home.

She gave Henry a weak smile. Why did she feel so deeply connected to him?

"Home," she exhaled.

She felt a twist in her heart as she said it, thinking not of the parsonage, but of Henry.

"I SEE THE CARRIAGE, MA'AM!" Bessie's voice was breathless with urgency.

Abigail started. "Oh!" She hurried to her feet. "Light the fire, please, Bessie!"

Had they found Ruby? Had Henry been attacked again? So many questions swirled in Abigail's mind as she raced down the corridor toward the front door, then out onto the gravel path. A chill wound its way around her.

The carriage rocked its way up the driveway. Abigail squinted, trying to ascertain if there were two shadowy figures inside, or three.

Dusk had settled around the parsonage and despite her best attempts, she could hardly see any movement through the carriage's small, dark window.

She paced nervously, her insides feeling weak at the thought that further harm might have befallen Henry.

The carriage rumbled to a halt, agonising seconds ticking by until the door opened.

Rushing forward, Abigail's heart was racing.

"Henry?"

Shuffling out of the carriage, Henry's feet gingerly landed

on the gravel path. He looked up at Abigail, a satisfied grin on his face.

"Oh, Aunt - you will never imagine!"

"Oh, Henry!" Abigail exclaimed, throwing herself toward him and embracing him with all her strength. She released him from her clutches and looked searchingly at him, tears misting her eyes. "You found her?"

Henry nodded. He was still grinning, then began shaking his head slowly. "Oh, Aunt. We have so much to thank God for this evening. So much!"

"Is she unharmed?"

His smile faded. "He hit her twice. Her eye is bruised." His jaw was tight now, yet a peaceful certainty remained in his eyes. "But he will never hurt her again."

"Indeed, I do hope not," Abigail said, her voice heavy with longing.

Henry's smile returned. "We may be absolutely certain. He is currently awaiting trial for forgery. And the magistrate has unequivocal evidence that he is guilty."

"Magistrate? Oh, Henry! Forgery?" Abigail's eyes moved as rapidly as her thoughts as she processed Henry's triumphant statements.

"I will explain it all inside. It has been an exhausting day. Especially for Ruby."

Glancing back at the carriage, Abigail saw Browne disembark, then extend his arm back inside the dark interior of the berlin.

"She barely spoke a word the whole journey home," Henry said. "I do not think she can quite believe that the threat is gone." A short, hope-filled sound escaped him. "I do not think I can, myself!" He swallowed hard. "Though, I have not lived practically my whole life under his shadow."

Abigail looked up at her nephew, his ardent eyes fixed on

the girl stepping out of the carriage. Such compassion and care radiated from his face.

Such love.

Abigail smiled softly as she turned her attention to Ruby. She stifled a gasp as she saw the bruising around Ruby's eye. Hastening forward, she pulled Ruby into a warm embrace.

"Oh, my dear," she breathed, clutching Ruby's shivering frame.

As they moved apart, Ruby wiped at her cheeks. She looked up at Abigail with a grateful smile.

"You must be freezing, my dear," Abigail said, realising that Ruby had no coat or covering about her. "Come, let us all go inside to eat and get warmed. Bessie will have finished lighting the fire for you, by now." She blinked away the tears that brimmed in her own eyes.

"Thank you," Ruby said, her voice faint with fatigue.

The party of four made their way up the gravel path toward the welcoming glow of the parsonage. As they entered, Abigail silently thanked God for the safe return of all the people she loved most in the world.

CHAPTER 31

A WELCOME RESOLVE

RUBY COULDN'T STOP SHIVERING, despite the fact that Henry had seated her in the closest possible proximity to the fire.

Henry's words from earlier that afternoon still echoed through her head.

Free from him.

"Oh, this fire is a welcome blessing," breathed Henry as he lingered in front of it, warming his hands.

Ruby looked up at him. She felt a pang of guilt. She hoped she hadn't been rude in the carriage. The whole journey, it had seemed as though all her words had been trapped in her mind, unable to find their way to her tongue no matter how much she had willed them to do so.

Henry's face glowed, and not just from the firelight. The deep joy he had expressed verbally at various moments on the journey home was entirely visible on every feature of his smiling face.

It made him all the more lovely to behold.

Ruby looked away, turning her gaze to the mesmerising dance of the fire's nimble flames as they flickered and rolled in a merry jig.

Why couldn't she speak? There was so much she longed to say. Apologies, thankings, rejoicings. Yet, none of them would come forth.

"Shall we take our seats?" Henry smiled down at her.

Ruby looked around, surprised to see Bessie bringing the dinner accoutrements in. She hadn't even heard the announcement that dinner was ready. She sighed, longing to break free of her consuming, deafening thoughts.

She looked up at Henry and smiled, a slight nod all that she could manage in response.

He extended his hand to help her up.

As she placed her fingers in his thermic grip, warmth radiated through her whole body.

They moved toward the table as one. As he delivered her to her seat, he squeezed her hand gently. Gratitude and reassurance flooded her.

She relished being close to Henry, yet a sense of feeling exposed unsettled her. She glanced at him. His dark eyes were so kind and gentle. She looked away again, her stomach flipping.

He seated himself in his usual place, his stiffness evident in his staccato movements. He looked at Ruby and Abigail, back and forth, like someone who had just discovered something marvellous.

"Shall we give thanks?" He sighed, a long, grateful sigh. "We have so much to be thankful for." He looked at Ruby. She thought she detected a slight change in his expression. "So much," he said, softly.

"Yes," breathed Abigail.

Ruby wanted to agree, but still her voice would not cooperate. She nodded, a brief smile moving her lips, then bowed her head low.

"Oh, Lord, we cannot even begin to thank You enough for all that You have done for us and delivered us from this day. Thank You, Lord, for Ruby's safe return to us. Thank You that justice has finally caught up to those who flouted the law. Thank You for this food, this warm fire, this warm company of people to share it all with." He sighed, relief and exhaustion mingled together in it. "Thank You, Lord. Thank You. I can think of no other words, yet these do not seem enough. May Your name be praised, Lord. You have done marvellous things. And we are glad. Thank You, Lord. Amen."

"Amen," agreed Abigail.

Ruby cleared her throat. "Amen." Her voice was little more than a breath, but Henry smiled at her as he heard it.

"Let us eat," Henry said with a smile as he picked up his knife and fork.

Glancing at Abigail, he frowned. "Is something the matter, Aunt?"

Abigail glanced at Ruby, then back to Henry. "No, no. Only . . . forgive me - I am beyond curious as to how everything transpired today, but, no. Let us not think of it now. Let us focus on happier thoughts."

Henry nodded, a solemn look clouding his face. "Yes, we may speak of it later," he said, his tone hushed. He raised his voice back to its normal level. "Let us all enjoy this evening. Safe, and together."

Sadness settled on Ruby, though she knew she ought to be overjoyed instead.

Safe. Together. But for how long?

What if Millforte was set free? Would he return again? Was it all *really* over? Could it ever be?

And if it was, what of the other dreaded event? How long would it be until Henry took a wife?

Questions assaulted her from every direction. How could she settle into a happy life at the parsonage knowing that someday - whether by being sent away as a companion or governess, or whether by the demands of whomever Henry would marry - it would all be ripped away from her?

A lump formed in her throat as a brick weighed on her chest. This home she now had, this place she felt so attached to, it was all just an illusion, really. Fleeting. Unfixed. She was just as homeless as she had ever been.

Only now she had been given a glimpse of how lovely life could be.

In that moment, it seemed worse to her to gain a temporary glance at loveliness than to have longed for it most of her life.

Trembling, she silently ate the lovely meal that Bessie had prepared, though a sick knot filled her stomach, leaving room for little else.

"Ruby?" Henry said, his voice filled with a questioning hope.

She widened her eyes to disperse the tears that threatened to fill them, then looked at him. Another pang of emotion shot through her. She raised her eyebrows to indicate he had her attention, trying to look calm and content despite the storm of emotions surging within her.

"I was wondering if you would care to have a picnic with me, tomorrow, in the garden?"

Millforte's towering bulk casting its shadow in the parsonage's beautiful garden flashed into Ruby's mind. She shuddered.

Looking at Henry, she nodded, then spoke with more strength in her voice than she'd had since the journey home.

"Yes."

Millforte had dominated her life for so long. Too long. No more. She would not allow his prior presence to ruin the beauty and tranquility of the parsonage or its garden.

"That would be lovely," she said.

Yet again, her stomach twisted with conflicting emotions. She would gladly spend every day of her life having a picnic with Henry, yet her feelings toward him filled her with an agony of soul that made her want to run as far away from him as she possibly could.

He smiled, satisfaction and anticipation mingled on his face. "Wonderful."

The smile lingered as he continued to eat, his eyes filled with a deep happiness.

Abigail glanced from Henry to Ruby and back again. As she lowered her head to resume eating, Ruby thought she noticed the hint of a smile on Abigail's face, too.

HENRY STARED at the dining room door, replaying in his mind the words and smiles he and Ruby had just exchanged as they'd bid each other good night.

He exhaled deeply, his thoughts skipping ahead to the picnic that was arranged for the following day. Would he tell her then?

He hoped he would. He must.

Yes. Especially after all that had happened, he must delay no longer.

Fear pierced him. But what if she did not return his affections?

Oh, Browne was convinced that she did. But did she? Really? He had no proof.

How insensitive and cruel it would be if he were to declare his love for her just as she was settling back into feeling safe at the parsonage. Perhaps he ought to wait. But could he?

He sighed, his heart and mind a jumble of conflicting notions.

"Henry?"

He turned back to face his aunt, her face kind and calm in the flickering candlelight. He raised his eyebrows slightly in response.

"Do you have time - or indeed, energy - to tell me about today before you retire?"

Henry's heart sank. Part of him never wanted to think of Millforte again. Never wanted to relive the events of that day. Yet, he wanted to share with Abigail the amazing way God had interceded for them when everything had seemed so uncertain.

"Of course," he said, moving toward the armchairs by the fire. Settling himself in one, he stiffened with the pain he felt in his back. He drew a deep breath and released it slowly.

"Oh, my dear, if you need to rest now, you could tell me in the morning." Abigail's face was etched with concern.

"No, no, I am all right." He would tell her now, and that way, he hoped, he would never have to mention Millforte again. Enough days had been marred with the mention of that sinister name. From this point on, surely no other day need be.

Abigail nestled herself in the chair opposite him, a ready expectation animating her face.

Henry sighed, then gave a short laugh. "I do not even know where to begin!"

Abigail smiled in sympathy. "It has been a long day for

you, I am sure. It has been long enough for me here, wondering and waiting. But for you and Browne to be in the thick of it . . ." She shook her head gently, a haunting look flitting over her features.

"To tell you the truth, when Browne and I arrived in the city, we were without a settled plan of how we ought to proceed. The whole journey, we thought and prayed and spoke, yet we truly had no notion of what we would do once we arrived."

Abigail listened intently, her eyes wide and fixed on her nephew.

"We alighted from the carriage," he continued. "And we stood a moment, gathering our thoughts. We had not been there longer than half a minute, and I heard a voice behind me call out my name."

Abigail's eyebrows shot up in a graceful arc, her eyes a little wider still.

"I turned to see who it was, and it was Mr. Gibbons."

"Mr. Gibbons?" Abigail asked, frowning in attempted, yet unsuccessful, recollection.

"Yes, Mr. Gibbons. He is a magistrate. I wrote to him around the time that Mr. Webster left us, informing him of the destructive visit that Millforte had paid us, but he replied with the sorry news that there was nothing that he could do about the whole affair. *Apparently*, people are rarely held to account for such things. Especially people with Millforte's dominance. The few that *are* tried in court are often released with little or no punishment."

He shook his head, a bitter noise escaping his throat.

"Oh, how terrible," Abigail said, sorrow clouding her eyes.

"He happened to mention in his letter about a forgery he was currently investigating on the other side of the city." Henry gave a sharp, almost bitter laugh. "In my frustration that forgery seemed to be of more concern to the lawmen than . . . than what had been done to Ruby, I wrote in my reply that Mr. Gibbons ought to investigate Millforte's establishment, since he was clearly a man of unscrupulous actions."

Abigail nodded gently, her interest unwavering.

Henry sighed. "I confess, I thought nothing more of it, owing to his dismal descriptions of how *justice* seemed to weigh heavier on people who forged banknotes, rather than on people who . . ." He cleared his throat and paused a moment. "Another dead end, it seemed at the time."

Abigail nodded expectantly. "But it was not?"

"Well, when Mr. Gibbons approached me today, he conveyed his surprise to see me there. I indicated the same toward him, and then he told us - Mr. Stratton, he said, I cannot thank you enough for the information you gave in your letter, for we investigated the man in question, and found some of the counterfeit banknotes on his premises."

Abigail's mouth dropped open. She gasped quietly.

"I could not believe it. And then he told us that he had come, at that very moment, to apprehend Mr. Millforte."

"Oh!"

"And what is more, he had with him three Principal Officers of Bow Street, to ensure that Millforte would not try to resist or escape him."

"Three officers?" Abigail echoed, seeming engulfed by incredulity.

"Yes! So I did not hesitate. I made my way up the stairs, as quickly as I could despite my stiffness, and into the room that Ruby—" His face flooded with joy as he remembered. "Oh, Aunt, she was standing there - so courageously - declaring her complete reliance on God and devotion to Him. She was standing up to that—" His jaw clenched. "That bully, and announcing her refusal to comply with whatever he would try to compel her to do."

Henry leaned forward, his joyous eyes fixed hard on Abigail's. "She actually told him that she would happily give her life in order to remain faithful to God."

Abigail's expression filled with a softness and warmth that mirrored Henry's own. He laughed, a short laugh of pure wonder. The smile lingered as he shifted his gaze toward the warm glow of the fire.

"I was amazed. I must have prayed in thankfulness for most of the journey home! Such timing! Everything lined up so, so perfectly. I truly believe that God answered our prayers, and that it was really He who made everything transpire as it did. All we had to do was walk in and take her with us - Mr. Gibbons and the officers took Millforte, and Browne and I escorted Ruby out of that horrid place once and for all!"

Abigail shook her head, a smile of stunned amazement fixed on her face. "Oh, thank the Lord! You are right - He answered our prayers!"

Henry's heart stirred to think of Ruby and how brave she had looked standing up to Millforte. He silently thanked God for what he thought must have been the millionth time that day.

A flutter seized his heart as the memory of his conversation with Browne came back to him. Ought he discuss it with Aunt Abigail?

Perhaps he should ask for her thoughts on whether or not it might be too soon to tell Ruby how he really felt. Or, perhaps, he should wait to see how things developed at the picnic tomorrow. Yes. Surely it would be better to try to read the situation once he was spending quality time with Ruby, without the stifling dread of Millforte's threats hanging over them anymore.

"And so, what are your plans?" Abigail asked, almost shyly.

Henry looked at her, his face blank yet his mind racing. She couldn't mean what he had just been thinking about. Could she?

"My plans?" he asked, his heart racing in unison with his mind.

Abigail smiled gently, her head and eyes low. She looked up at him, a knowing look and gentleness on her warm face.

"With Ruby."

Henry's throat felt dry. He gave a quick cough, partly to clear it and partly to give himself more time to decide how to respond.

"Well . . . I . . . We must all continue to support her as she, as she continues to grow and heal."

He hardly sounded convincing, even to himself. He lowered his brow and rubbed his forehead.

"You have my blessing, my dear."

Henry yanked his head upward, out of his hand. He stared at his aunt, unblinking and hardly breathing.

Abigail smiled and repeated her words, her tone hushed and gentle. "You have my blessing."

Henry was astounded. First Browne, now Aunt Abigail.

The smile that seeped onto Henry's face was soon replaced with a look of crushing concern.

"Do you think— Do you think that she might . . . That is, I know how I feel about *her*," he said, a faint blush forming on his cheeks. "But I do not know how *she* feels about *me*."

Abigail smiled again, the knowing look still dancing on her face. "I believe she returns your affections, my dear. It has been quite apparent to me, for many weeks now, that she cares very deeply for you. And I do believe that, whether she realises it or not, she loves you."

Henry forgot to breathe.

Could it be true? Could Browne and Abigail both be right?

A fragile but welcome resolve filled him. Did Ruby love him, too?

Tomorrow, he would find out.

CHAPTER 32

PERFECT PLANS

THE SKY HAD BEEN grey all morning. Darkening clouds and shifting sunlight encroached on the parsonage, just as nerves and uncertainty mingled with Henry's thoughts.

Ruby had not joined them for breakfast. Bessie had announced to Henry and Abigail as she brought their food to the table that she had spoken briefly to Ruby, who was feeling extremely fatigued due to the previous day's exertions, and who asked her to please make her apologies for not joining the others.

After wondering all through breakfast if Ruby might not join him for the prearranged picnic either, Henry had asked Bessie if she might check on Ruby to ascertain her wishes.

The glad response came to him a little while later, as he sat in the drawing room.

"Pardon me, Mr. Stratton, but I thought you might like to know that Ruby says she does intend to join you for the picnic at the arranged time."

Henry tried to conceal the depth of his joy and relief. "Thank you, Bessie."

Bessie curtseyed. "I shall go now and prepare the items that you have requested. Is there anything else?"

Henry smiled at her cheerfulness. "No, nothing, Bessie. Thank you. Thank you very much. I do so appreciate all that you are doing."

"Not at all, Mr. Stratton," she smiled as she exited, the faint sound of her happy humming fading with her footsteps down the hall.

Henry sighed happily, despite the unsynchronised tremblings of his heart and stomach.

The picnic was still on.

And thus, so was his proposal.

RUBY LOOKED up at the gloomy clouds overhead as she stepped out of the parsonage. Henry followed her, his presence casting a warmth that was lacking from the weather.

"I do hope the rain holds off." He smiled at her as they walked down the gravel path toward the garden.

"Yes," she replied, distracted somewhat by unwelcome memories of the day before. It was this very path they had been on, just as they were now, when the ominous sounds of Millforte's approaching carriage had interrupted their peaceful stroll.

"How are you feeling now?" Henry asked, studying her with a kind expression.

"I am well, thank you. And you?"

He sighed, and she thought she heard a faint laugh. "Truly, I feel better than I have for a long, long time."

She glanced up at him, though kept walking. His deep, dark eyes were full to the brim with sincerity and wonder. It made her want to weep. She turned her gaze back to the path as she felt the familiar twist in her stomach. If this was love, why was it so torturous?

"I am glad," she managed to say, aware that perhaps she ought to have responded a little sooner. She glanced at him again and offered a quiet smile. "Truly."

Henry grinned in return, then briskly shuffled ahead a few paces. He turned to face her, standing in the middle of the path. His eyes twinkled. "Shall we?"

He raised his arm and extended his hand, gesturing toward an alcove sheltered by freshly budding honeysuckle.

Ruby looked over to the spot he motioned toward and gasped.

Two wooden chairs were perfectly placed beneath a small table furnished with plates, napkins and utensils. A large wicker basket overflowed with bread, cakes and other victuals.

She exhaled sharply, stunned, and looked back at Henry.

He was observing her as though with pride, yet not of the picnic, nor of himself. It almost seemed that he looked as though he were proud of *her*.

She felt her brows furrow slightly, trying to understand his expression.

At once, he looked down, a nervous uncertainty taking the place of the mysterious look. He cleared his throat and hesitated a moment, before looking at her with an almost curious gaze as he raised his elbow. Ruby looked at his arm, then realised he intended for her to take it.

Her heart picked up speed as she wove her arm around his and settled her hand on his coat's forearm. She could barely look at him, afraid her feelings would be immediately exposed if her eyes met with his.

Silently, they made their way to the beautiful nook that had been prepared with such care and consideration, Ruby's mind indelibly aware of the solidity of Henry's arm beneath her fingertips.

Henry delivered her into one of the chairs and gently withdrew his arm. Ruby felt a sadness at the parting of their touch.

She watched him shyly as he eased himself onto the other seat. He still seemed a bit more stiff than usual, but every day he was getting back to the way he used to be. Before—

No. She forced Millforte from her mind.

Here she was, in a beautiful garden, for a delightful picnic, with a wonderful gentleman. Millforte had poisoned her life long enough. His claim upon her was at an end. She would not allow him to ruin this precious afternoon.

"Tea?" Henry smiled, his visage as captivating to Ruby as the fresh and delicate scents all around them.

"Yes, please." She smiled, her inner anguish melting into joy as she allowed herself to relax and drink in the beauty all around her. A box hedge encircled them from behind, and above them the fragrant honeysuckle wove around a graceful arch, obscuring the original structure beneath it.

Henry poured them each a cup of tea. Ruby hadn't even noticed the cups or the teapot until now. As her gaze wandered across the table's contents, she was amazed anew.

She shook her head gently, marvelling at the effort Henry had expended. He had done all this, for her?

"A sandwich first, or some cake?" he asked, his eyes twinkling.

Ruby laughed before she realised she had. "I think . . . cake?" She smiled at him, the freest smile she had ever expressed.

Henry chuckled as he prepared two plates of cake. It was sweet, like his eyes. And every bit as appealing.

Ruby dismissed her appreciative thoughts and turned to

look around at the flowers and boughs all around them. To most people, she imagined, it was just a garden. But to her, it was like another world.

A perfect world. No pain, no fear, no rubble. Just freedom. Wide open freedom. And fresh, clean air to breathe.

She drew in a deep, deep breath, dizzying slightly due to the extra air. Her breathing had become shallow over the years. Withered, and stifled, as she had been. But now, she felt as though she could uncurl, stretch tall and just . . . breathe.

"Ruby."

Henry's voice turned her back from her reverie. His breathing was as shallow as hers usually was, his knuckles almost white as he gripped his teacup in one hand.

Worry flitted through her mind. An automatic thought of Millforte's approaching presence caused her to glance about her, seeking to allay her fears, desperate for reassurance that they were safe.

"Oh, forgive me. I did not mean to startle you," Henry said, a look of alarm on his face that no doubt was a mirror of her own.

She relaxed slightly, her nerves still somewhat on edge.

Ruby observed him. He seemed strained somehow. It was odd. Partly, he seemed at ease, yet another part seemed almost timorous.

"I . . . I only wished to tell you that . . . I am so very grateful . . . that the Lord had us meet," Henry said, an expression in his eyes that she couldn't quite decipher.

She drank in his words as though they were delicately flavoured tea and smiled.

"As am I," she said softly.

Her thoughts still pestered her. Thoughts of Millforte, of Miss Acton, of Henry's eventual wedding, but she diligently batted them from her mind each time they dared to enter. Just for this one afternoon, she wished to think of nothing else.

It seemed as though Henry was going to say something else, but he smiled after a moment and they resumed eating. All that punctured the silence was the clink of tableware and an occasional fleeting whisper of wind.

"More tea?" Henry offered, looking at her with that strange expression again.

"Yes, please," she said softly.

"Ruby? You look sad," Henry said, interrupting her thoughts. His expression was all concern and compassion. It made her heart ache to look at him and pretend that all was well.

"Oh, no, I am fine," she said, forcing a smile.

She felt guilty. Had she lied to him?

"Please, share your burden with me. You may speak freely with me. I cannot think of anything that you may not say to me. What is it that troubles you?"

How good he was. How kind. It made it all so much worse.

Tears stung her eyes. Her heart felt heavy with all she wished to share with him. Her very life, too. Yet that could never be.

She searched for words, but none came. His earnest eyes burned into her. She wanted to run away again. Overwhelmed, she stood up, shaking her head and waving her hands.

"I am sorry, I—"

Henry sprang to his feet, a short wince following straight after. He moved toward her and clasped her shaking hands in his.

His hands were warm and strong. Ruby felt as though hers

melted right into them, holding her steady lest the slightest gust of wind swept her away.

"Ruby, I must tell you something . . ."

She thought she noticed him shudder slightly. Overcoming all the inner turmoil that was screaming at her, she looked up into his eyes, her heart and breath both rapid.

As their eyes met, everything around her faded away.

She exhaled, her breath slow and shaky.

A cold, wet drop landed on her hand. And another. Then, others with them.

They looked up in unison at the darkening clouds, which could no longer contain the moisture they were storing.

As the rain fell on them and around them, they remained, unmoving. Ruby was fixed to the ground. Locking eyes with Henry once again, she felt as weak as air.

"Ruby," he said again. "I have questioned over and over again whether I ought to speak now or if it is too soon, but I cannot . . . I cannot bear it any longer."

Her heart sank, expecting bad news. Was she still being sent away?

"You are unlike anyone I have ever met," he continued. Sincerity and earnestness consumed his expression. "And from the moment I met you - from the moment we got you out of that terrible place, I knew. I knew that this was where you really belonged." He motioned with his eyes, looking around them.

Ruby's mind reeled. He was saying that she belonged here? At the parsonage? Surely, she had misunderstood.

"Here." He looked at her, his expression changing into the most vulnerable look anyone had ever given her. She forgot to breathe.

"With me." His eyes widened slightly, his eyebrows gently lifting.

Ruby's mouth dropped open.

She stared at him, unblinking.

Did he really say—? No. He cannot mean—?

"Ruby, I—"

The rain gained intensity.

"—I love you."

Relief and terror seemed mingled on his face. Still holding her hands, he gave them a gentle squeeze.

Time stopped. Just like before, in his room, when he had held her elbow, and she had realised the depths of her feelings for him.

She gasped silently. Could it be? Had he felt the same even then?

She tried to speak but choked, her throat drier than dust. Swallowing hard, she looked at him. Was she dreaming?

"I . . ." she practically whispered.

A question shot into her heart. A heavy question, filled with a weight that dragged her hopes downward. She looked into his waiting, searching eyes.

"Why?" she asked.

His gaze softened, love shining in his eyes.

A series of similar expressions came flooding back to her. Love. Could that have been what it was - that look in his eyes she had so often been unable to decipher?

"Because you are precious, and kind, and lovely. You have an honest heart, and a genuine soul - a deep and darling soul," he smiled affectionately. "And I truly believe that God made you to be the other half of me. There is no one else in this world with whom I could ever wish to be paired with, and never parted from."

Delight and disbelief broke out across her face.

A dawning of hope filled his expression.

She smiled at him, completely amazed. "Nor I," she whispered, her chest so full she thought it might burst.

Henry's face was the picture of surprise and elation.

The rain was falling, fast and fierce, as he pulled her to him in a firm embrace. Her heart sent a thrill of incredulous joy through her every vein, a tingling through her every nerve.

Gently his lips brushed hers. She pulled her head back, glancing up, into his eyes. He looked at her, his eyes soft with love, pure and sweet. Her gaze relaxed into a smile and as another rush swept through her, their lips met again.

Surely, this was the meaning of happiness, Ruby thought, delighting in the warmth that radiated from Henry's face amidst the icy rain.

"Here," he said as he straightened up, guiding her along as he half-walked, half-ran toward the archway not too far from them. It was a meagre shelter, yet better than nothing now that the rain plummeted to the earth in sheets.

They both laughed, looking at one another in stunned delight.

"Oh, Ruby, since the moment I met you, there was something about you . . . I feel as though our hearts have been woven together - a threefold cord, as we read about in Ecclesiastes, with God in the centre."

She gave a short laugh, tears filling her eyes. She looked up at him, savouring every feature. "As do I."

He looked happier than she had ever seen anyone ever look.

Lifting her hands in his, he fixed a steady gaze on her.

"Ruby, will you marry me?"

She could scarcely believe what she was hearing. Surely it was not possible to know joy as deep as this.

She was shaking now, not only from the cold downpour,

but from excitement and anticipation. Never had she dreamed that she would marry, for she had never thought that anyone would want her. Least of all a clergyman.

And never, had she dared to dream that if she *did* marry, it would be for love. But here he was - the very best of men - standing before her, declaring his devotion and asking for her hand.

Though the icy rain was still falling, so heavily that the archway appeared to be curtained all around with waterfalls, she was oblivious to it. All that mattered to her now was finding her voice, that she might give Henry the answer he was visibly hoping for.

She beamed. "Yes." Her voice was tremulous. "Yes, I shall marry you, and love you - with all of my heart."

Henry's expression was one she would never forget.

They embraced in joyful exuberance. Henry lowered his head at an angle, meeting her lips tenderly with his own.

Once the rain had slackened off a little, they decided to venture back to the house, still holding hands and grinning dreamily.

The warmth inside the parsonage felt as though it was burning Ruby's freezing face. She and Henry could scarcely look away from each other, grinning and gazing at one another in unuttered delight.

Shifting uneasily in his soaking clothes, Henry spoke, an unwillingness in his voice. "We ought to change . . ."

Ruby didn't want to part from him, either. "Yes, we really should . . ."

He smiled, exhaling in almost a snort. He looked up at the staircase then back at her. "Come. Let us change. It will not take long, I suppose." Yet his unwillingness to leave her was evident by his unmoving stance.

She looked at him. He was completely drenched. Drops of

rain streaked from his hair, rolling down his grinning cheeks. He was magnificent. And now, someday soon, she would be his wife.

Henry let out a frustrated sigh. "As much as it pains me to be parted from you even for a short while, I must insist that we go now and change. I do not want my precious Ruby to catch cold. That would not do," he said, his eyes twinkling.

Ruby smiled, starting to shiver. Her happiness had prevented her from noticing just how wet and cold she really was, but now she could feel it with full force.

They held hands as they ascended the wide, wooden staircase. At the top, Henry kissed her hand before they moved apart to go to their separate rooms.

"Ruby," he said, smiling. "Meet me in the drawing room when you are ready? We have much to discuss."

A thrill shot through her. "I will."

He smiled and turned to go.

"And, Henry?"

He turned back, his eyebrows raised, his face full of joy as he looked expectantly to hear what she would say.

"I love you. So very much."

"THE REASON I asked you all to join me here, is so that I might thank you all sincerely for all of your prayers, support and kindness these past few months during my recovery. God has truly blessed me with knowing each of you."

Henry looked around the room of kind faces. His heart was bursting with excitement as a grin broke out across his face. "And He has blessed me in a very special way this afternoon, also."

He turned to look at Ruby, her eyes shining with the joy in his own. He motioned for her to come and stand beside him.

A shy smile crept onto her face. She took her place at his side, making his heart swell even more as he addressed the now-smiling faces.

"Ruby and I are engaged to be married," he beamed, unable to hold the glad news back any longer.

Bessie half-shrieked, half-gasped. Browne's face transformed into the widest, most delighted smile Henry thought he had ever seen him give. Abigail looked at her nephew and Ruby with a face full of tender love and contentedness.

"Congratulations!" Browne was in front of them now, warmly grasping Henry's hand and shaking it. Turning his attention to Ruby, he nodded his congratulatory delight to her, looking as though he wanted to embrace her.

Bessie approached them as Browne moved to the side, her eyes wild with surprise and happiness. "Oh, this is such wonderful news! I am so happy for you both!" she trilled.

Bessie had scarcely moved out of the way before Abigail approached the new couple and threw her arms around them both.

As Henry embraced his aunt tightly, he silently thanked God that she was now in approval of his union with Ruby.

Stepping back, Abigail looked from Henry to Ruby as she said, "I am so glad to hear this wonderful news! I pray that God will bless you both so richly, my dears."

Henry smiled as he saw Ruby's expression of purity and gratitude as she looked up at Abigail. He felt so blessed that the two women he loved most in the world had such deep and amiable regard for each other.

He looked again at his captivating bride-to-be. He drank in

every feature, every twirl of hair, every delicate blink of her eyelashes. How blessed he was.

He became aware of Abigail's eyes fixed upon him, just as Ruby looked up at him. He flashed a joyful grin at Ruby as he turned to his aunt.

She looked at him expectantly, seemingly awaiting his response. He hadn't even noticed her speaking.

"Did you say something, Aunt?"

Abigail chuckled in amusement and shook her head slightly. "I was merely enquiring when the happy day might be?"

"Oh!" He sighed, gladness and wonder beaming from him. "Well, Ruby and I spoke a little about it this afternoon, and we see no reason to delay. As soon as we are able to make all the necessary arrangements, then we shall be man and wife." He could hardly keep his eyes off Ruby as he spoke.

"Oh, my dears! We have much to prepare!"

Henry smiled at her. "It need not be a complicated affair, Aunt. Ruby and I are both happy to proceed without fuss and flounce."

"Indeed, but it is such a special day, that you will only experience once."

"Mr. Stratton, sir?"

Henry looked toward the door. Browne was re-entering the drawing room. Henry realised he had been so busy talking to Abigail that he hadn't even noticed Browne leave the room.

"Yes, Browne?" Henry smiled.

"You have a visitor."

There was nothing in Browne's expression to indicate that the visitor might be an unwelcome one, yet Henry's stomach gripped upon hearing the pronouncement. He glanced at Ruby. She didn't seem to have heard, deep in conversation with Abigail as she was.

Henry walked toward Browne, his smile fading and his brow furrowing.

"Is everything all right, Browne?" he asked, as he reached the door.

Browne's eyebrows shot up in realisation. "Oh, my apologies, Mr. Stratton - yes! There is no need for alarm. It is Sir Harford."

"Oh! Sir Harford? Well, please - see him in."

"Ah, well, he said he was hoping to speak to you privately first."

"He was? Very well. Where is he?"

Browne led the way down the hallway to the main hall, where a damp Sir Harford was pacing a small, square track, his expression shadowed with concern and hesitance.

"Sir Harford!" Henry smiled, extending his hand as he drew near the man.

"Ah, Mr. Stratton," Sir Harford said, worry in his voice as he absentmindedly shook Henry's hand.

"Is something the matter?"

"Oh, I do not even know where to begin. I came in person, as I felt that a letter would be too impersonal, and not nearly solemn enough for what I must convey to you."

"My dear man, whatever is so serious as that?"

"I am sorry, Mr. Stratton. You must believe me. If I had known, I would have never—" He was shaking his head, regret weighing his expression down.

"Come, come. You are one of my oldest and dearest friends - I cannot imagine anything for which you might need to apologise. Tell me, what is it that troubles you so?"

"I thought I knew him," Sir Harford said, a wounded look of betrayal twisting his features into a frown.

"Knew whom?"

"Mr. Webster."

Henry groaned inwardly upon remembering the odious interloper. "Mr. Webster? Why, what has he done?"

"Had I known what he was really like, I would never have written a letter of recommendation for him. He took liberties and played upon my deep regard for his father. Had I known that he was nothing like his father, I would have had nothing to do with him."

Henry had never seen Sir Harford so upset.

"But what has he done? I confess, I did not warm to him while he was here. He was unkind toward Ruby, and eventually toward me. He seems a very proud man, and to tell you the truth, when I sent him away, I rejoiced to see the back of him!"

"Oh, Mr. Stratton, I am dreadfully sorry. I cannot believe that I was so poor a judge of character."

Henry waved his hand in dismissal. "There now, he seemed a very persuasive man. My aunt was quite taken in by him. But he is long gone from here. Do not worry yourself - there is no harm done."

"But Mr. Stratton, there *is*. That is why I have come."

Henry frowned in confusion. "What?"

"I have been speaking with some of the church folk and have gained a clear picture of the man's true character. He told you that he heard various gossip and accusations, from Mr. Graham and others, did he not?"

"Yes . . ."

"Well, I was speaking with Mr. Graham only yesterday, and he told me that it was Mr. Webster himself who had called on churchgoer after churchgoer, and elaborated on the smaller rumours that some other fellow had started, and it was he - Mr. Webster - who accused you of dreadfully wicked, reprehensible actions that I cannot even repeat!"

Henry's brow darkened. "What?" he asked, almost under his breath.

"His whole intention was not to help you at all, but to sabotage you in order that he might replace you! Oh, Mr. Stratton, I feel like such a fool, and I bitterly regret any part I had in the whole ordeal. I would never have recommended him if I had known—"

"Sir Harford, I know you. To tell the truth, there was something about his association with you that I questioned. He seemed so eager to insist on such a familiar regard between you. Something about it did not seem entirely genuine." Henry shook his head slowly. "The cad! What of him now?"

"Well, according to Mr. Graham, he has fled town, owing to the fact that his ruse was unsuccessful. No one knows whence. The whole town is quite dismayed by his audacity."

Henry sighed. "It is certainly for the best that he is gone from us."

Sir Harford looked at Henry in astonishment. "Why, Mr. Stratton - you have borne all of this quite remarkably! I was praying that you would not be devastated. You have been through so many ordeals of late. It pained me to be the bearer of yet another."

Henry couldn't help smiling. "In truth, Sir Harford, I doubt that any news could dull my spirit today. I have quite a wonderful reason to rejoice."

"Oh?"

"Ruby and I are engaged to be married," Henry said, beaming.

For a moment, Henry wondered if Sir Harford had heard him. The older man's face was motionless. Then, all at once, about five different expressions each took their turn on his countenance.

"Oh, Mr. Stratton . . . That is wonderful . . ."

Henry looked at him, puzzled. "You do not seem entirely convinced, Sir Harford."

"Oh, no, of course - it is wonderful news. I am so pleased for you both."

Again, Henry doubted him. "However?"

Sir Harford looked conflicted. "Only, I do wonder how it might be received by the others, in light of Mr. Webster's allegations." He paused, deliberating. "My only concern is that it may, unintentionally, cause questions or doubts in some of the minds of the church folk, upon hearing that there *is* something more to the lady's presence here than mere charity."

Henry felt somewhat crushed by Sir Harford's words, though he knew the gentleman spoke only from loving friendship and genuine concern.

A niggling worry started to grow in Henry's own mind. Could his and Ruby's engagement really give credence to Mr. Webster's slanderings?

"Mr. Stratton, forgive me if I have offended you, I—"

Henry held his hand up. "I am not offended, Sir Harford. I was merely thinking of how I might set the record straight with all at the church."

He paused, thinking through his slim array of options.

Sir Harford watched him intently, then jumped at Henry's sudden animation.

"There is only one thing to be done. If you would be so kind as to lend your assistance . . .?"

"Absolutely, Mr. Stratton. Whatever it is you need, consider it done."

"Thank you, Sir Harford," Henry nodded. "Now then, here is what we must do."

CHAPTER 33

AN IMPORTANT MEETING

RUBY'S STOMACH fluttered and jumped with every bounce of the carriage. It was the first time that she, Henry, Abigail and Browne had all travelled to church together. Yet, it wasn't a Sunday.

Henry had called a church meeting to explain everything in hopes of settling the rumours. Ruby's heart quickened as she imagined the looks on peoples' faces when Henry would inform them that their beloved parson was about to marry a prostitute.

She glanced at Henry. His jaw was clenching, then unclenching, again and again as he stared out the opposite window of the carriage. Ruby longed to reach for his hand and squeeze it in encouragement, but she still felt shy at the thought of doing so. Especially considering all that awaited them at church.

She thought back to Henry's announcement at dinner the evening that Sir Harford had visited. A meeting at church - a public declaration of the truth about everything that had happened since Ruby had come into their lives.

Mr. Webster had spread vicious rumours in town, unbeknownst to them all. Henry felt a meeting was the best option they had, to bring everything out into the open in order to reassure the churchgoers that there had been no sins committed and no secrets kept or hidden. They had been completely unaware of Mr. Webster's deceit and treachery.

Ruby glanced at Abigail. She looked more sombre than Ruby had ever seen her. The poor woman had been devastated upon hearing the truth about Mr. Webster. Ruby was convinced she had heard bitter weeping coming from Abigail's room the past few nights. The puffy redness around Abigail's eyes offered evidence in agreement.

Since the revelation of Mr. Webster's malevolence, Abigail had repeatedly blamed herself, once the initial shock had worn off, for entrusting too much information to Mr. Webster's confidence. Henry had tried in vain to soothe her these past few days.

Browne appeared immoveable. His lined face was the picture of contentment. Ruby wondered at him. To look at him, one would never know the nerve-wracking trial that would soon be upon them. She wondered if his tranquility emanated from a root of deep faith. She prayed that God would make her own faith deeper still.

The carriage slowed. Glancing at Henry, Ruby started to feel light-headed as she saw him shift in his seat and gather his belongings.

It was time.

THE FACES in front of Henry depicted a range of emotions. Some smiled kindly, others looked worried, some were expressionless. But all were familiar, and in his heart, he was deeply glad to see them all again.

"Thank you so much for coming," he bellowed, addressing them not from the pulpit, but from a few paces before the front row, which was empty save for Abigail and Ruby. Browne stood at the back, and Henry gladly glanced occasionally to him for reassurance as he addressed the crowd.

"I thought it imperative to ask you all to gather here today, in the hope that I might allay any concerns you may have and might impart to you my genuine affections and intentions for your spiritual wellbeing."

He paused before continuing. "Sir Harford came to visit me a few days ago." Henry stretched out his arm in Sir Harford's direction and gave him a smile indicative of gratitude for the older gentleman's supportive presence.

"He informed me that a man you know of - Mr. Webster - had been intentionally spreading confusion and rumours amongst you all, accusing myself and my household of impropriety, impurity and other indelicacies. I was dismayed to hear this, as was my aunt. We trusted Mr. Webster to carry out my duties while I was incapacitated, and instead, he betrayed us."

Henry paused, a deep sigh issuing forth from him.

"I do not know the specific details of what he told you, but I can assure you that anything he may have insinuated that is sinful or scandalous, is simply untrue. And so, I feel that it is my duty to communicate to you all the true and actual sequence of events of these months past."

He paused again, looking around the room earnestly. A few faces he had expected to see were absent. He wondered if they had not been notified, or if they had gone so far as to dissent due to Mr. Webster's meddling.

"Some months ago, a misunderstanding brought me to a certain location in town. A less-than-noble establishment, to say the least. I had believed that I would be meeting with a doctor, when instead I found myself in a brothel."

A few gasps broke out in various parts of the room.

"Needless to say, I was astonished. And I was even more astonished when the woman whose room I had entered in such naive circumstances seemed shy, deep of thought and as unwilling to be there as I was. I spoke with her briefly and learned that she had been taken there a number of years before, against her will . . ."

As Henry continued to recount all the recent events of Ruby's transcendence from city prostitute to born-again young lady, the church folk listened with rapt attention.

Occasionally, eyebrows raised or furrowed, mouths gaped or tightened, heads nodded or shook. Overall, it seemed the truth was bringing clarity and compassion to the roomful of people who listened intently to it.

" . . . And I am very glad to say that he is now no longer a threat, due to his arrest for forgery of a large sum of counterfeit banknotes. Browne and I brought Ruby back to the parsonage, to provide her with a safe place to recover from all the traumatic events she has had to endure."

He drew a deep breath, knowing that what he was about to say next had the potential to undo all the sympathy and understanding that his chronological discourse had fostered.

"And, I wish you all to know, that in very recent weeks, I gained awareness of how deeply I admire and cherish Ruby's kind personage and gentle spirit. I realised something. I realised that I am in love with her, and a few days ago, I asked for her hand in marriage."

A surprised murmur flooded the room, whether of approval or dismay Henry could not tell.

"I am completely aware that it is improper for two persons who are attached but not yet married to live in the same dwelling, especially in light of all the rumours that have been circulating. And that is why I intend to marry Ruby immediately."

He glanced at Ruby, whose gaze met him with a delighted smile.

Fixing his eyes on her as a louder murmur swept through the crowd, he walked over to her and extended his hand. His smile deepened, his gaze transfixed by the purity of her countenance.

"Right now, in fact," he said.

RUBY'S SMILE transformed into a look of joyful disbelief.

Abigail stared up at Henry, her expression alternating rapidly with unspoken questions.

Browne smiled knowingly and walked forward. When he had reached Henry's side, he turned to face the back of the room and motioned with his hand for someone to come forward.

Abigail and Ruby turned in unison to see a gentle, thin man make his way to the front of the church.

Henry grinned at Ruby before raising his voice to address the room of now-astonished people.

"Everyone, this is Mr. Bertram, the clergyman from our neighbouring parish. He has kindly agreed to take charge of the ceremony, since I cannot be the officiator and the groom at the same time."

A gentle chuckle trickled through the room.

"I invite you all to witness this marvellous occasion. I have seen with my own eyes how God has transformed Ruby with His love and grace, and I know that, in time, as you get to know her more and more, you will join me in giving thanks to the Lord for her remarkable redemption."

Mr. and Mrs. Penton strode to the front of the church and warmly embraced Henry. Turning their attention to Ruby, they clasped her hands, welcoming and congratulating her. She rose to a stand, too, unsure what else to do and still reeling with joyful astonishment at Henry's words.

One by one, the others approached them, until Henry and Ruby could hardly see one another without stretching up onto their tiptoes.

Once everyone was seated, Ruby looked at Henry, completely at a loss to know what was to be done next.

He ushered her and Abigail back to their seats and knelt in front of them.

"But, my dear! How can all this be? Why, there have been no banns read! You cannot—"

"We have no need of banns, Aunt. I enlisted Sir Harford's assistance to ensure that everything was taken care of, to the finest detail. Do you remember when I made a trip to town the day after Sir Harford's visit? I did not tell you at the time, but my main purpose in going was actually to purchase a common licence. And to ask Mr. Bertram if he would be so kind as to officiate the ceremony. He has brought with him a clerk to record everything in the register, and - you did not know this, either - but Sir Harford brought Bessie here before we left the parsonage and she has been hard at work preparing a few decorations and delicious treats for our celebration afterward!"

"Oh, my dear!" Abigail looked as though she might burst.

Ruby looked at both of them in amazement. She had no idea what was legally required for a wedding, but it seemed that Henry and Abigail certainly did, and that Henry had taken care of all the practicalities.

All that remained was . . .

"Ruby, will you marry me? Here and now?" Henry grinned, his eyes ablaze with hope and love.

She could hardly breathe as she tried to take it all in. This morning she had been fretting about the meeting and what might happen. Now here she was, at her own wedding.

"Yes," she breathed, wonder overwhelming her heart and mind.

As everyone took their appropriate place, Henry whispered a few directions in her ear, for which she was exceedingly grateful.

She turned to look at Browne, who raised his elbow toward her. As she placed her hand on his arm, they began walking to the back of the church.

"Congratulations, Miss Ruby. I am overjoyed for the both of you," he said, his gentle voice a calming anchor in Ruby's sea of amazement.

"Thank you, Browne," she smiled. "I cannot believe it all."

"A blessing from God, miss—"

Ruby nodded, then stopped walking in surprise as Browne continued his statement.

"—that is what you are to all of us."

He looked at her, surprised by her sudden halt. She quickly resumed her pace, blinking as she replayed his words in her mind.

She? A blessing? To them? But, they were all such blessings to her!

Excited joy bubbled up from deep within her as she stood beside Browne at the back of the church, awaiting the signal that would beckon her forward to marry the man she'd never dreamed could actually exist until a few months ago.

He was saying something to a young lady who was seated at the pianoforte, then he was back beside Abigail, whispering something to her. He looked so alive, so happy.

The girl at the pianoforte pressed down on its keys, enjoyment of the music etched on her face.

Browne started forward, startling Ruby into step with him. And then she recognised it. The tune that was floating through the air from the pianoforte.

"Amazing grace, how sweet the sound . . ." Browne sang softly as they walked slowly down the aisle.

Tears sprang to Ruby's eyes. Henry stood at the front of the church, his gaze fixed on her, his broad smile radiating exuberant delight.

As she beamed at him in return, she silently thanked God for the man she was about to marry, and for the amazing grace that God had shown to her.

And for the first time in her life, she felt something she had never truly felt before.

She felt . . .

Free.

WHAT DID YOU THINK?

I really hope you enjoyed reading this book
as much as I enjoyed writing it for you.

If you did, please consider leaving a rating or review on
Amazon, BookBub or Goodreads.

A review doesn't have to be a long, in-depth critique — just a
line or two about what you liked about the book would make
my day and help other readers find my stories.

Reviews really are so helpful and encouraging for authors,
and your feedback on *Ruby's Redemption* (no matter how
short!) would be so very much appreciated.

Thank you.

READING GROUP
RESOURCES

Want to read *Ruby's Redemption* with your book group?

Get free downloadable questions and goodies at
edwinakiernan.com/reading

ACKNOWLEDGMENTS

This novel would not be what it is without the spectacular help I received from the following brilliant people:

Jenny Proctor at Midnight Owl Editors -

Thank you for your editing. Your comments and suggestions not only improved my writing, but also made me chuckle! I am so grateful for your honesty, generosity and encouragement.

Hannah Linder at Hannah Linder Designs -

Thank you for the gorgeous cover. You did a stellar job, and your friendliness, professionalism and patience are very much appreciated. Can't wait to see the next book's cover!

Rachel Knowles at Regency History -

Thank you for kindly allowing me to mine the depths of your historical knowledge, and for your prompt and in-depth historical detail edit. It's my aim to one day know as many facts about history as you do!

And a huge special thank you to:

My husband, Paul, and son, Luke -

Thank you for helping me to have some extra time to write and publish, and for bearing with me through it all.

Proverbs 15:15 says "a cheerful heart has a continual feast", and that is exactly how I feel about living with both of you!

You are my two biggest blessings on earth and I love you both so very much more than I can express.

ABOUT THE AUTHOR

Edwina Kiernan is the Christian author of the award-winning novel *Ruby's Redemption*.

An enthusiast of classic novels and history, Edwina combines her faith, imagination and research in hope-infused tales set in times past.

A lifelong word admirer, with Welsh and Irish heritage, she started writing stories early in childhood.

She is a committed follower of Jesus (the Living Word), and endeavours to use her pen to point others to Him.

When she's not writing, Edwina loves spending time with her dashing husband and lively little son, reading and studying the Bible, getting lost in a captivating novel and drinking more types of tea than most people realize even exist.

Join her mailing list for free gifts, updates, regular giveaways and lots of classic and historical fiction goodness.

Subscribe at: **EdwinaKiernan.com**

- amazon.com/author/edwinakiernan
- bookbub.com/profile/edwina-kiernan
- goodreads.com/edwinakiernan
- twitter.com/EdwinaKiernanHQ

PEARL'S PROMISE

2022 READERS' FAVOURITE AWARD WINNER
IN CHRISTIAN HISTORICAL ROMANCE

Book 2 in the Gems of Grace series

A duty-bound heir. A dejected spinster.
A love that could ruin both their families' demands for their futures...

Pearl Acton's worst fear is coming true: she'll be trapped in a loveless marriage—just like her parents—as her family seeks to quickly marry her off to a wealthy stranger. Until an encounter with a gentle heir sparks a fragile hope that somehow Pearl might aid her family *and* marry for love.

Nicholas Dalton has always been a disappointment to his father, with his poetic soul and disorganised nature. In London for the season, Nicholas finds an instant connection with Pearl, but it would seem her future is promised to another. Isn't it?

Pressures soon mount, compelling Pearl and Nicholas to uphold their family duties. Is it too late to escape their crushing obligations and forge a new path - together?

Available in Paperback, eBook and Kindle Unlimited at

edwinakiernan.com/pearl

BERYL'S BLESSING

Book 3 in the Gems of Grace series

She's used to being alone.

He can't get away from his guilty conscience.

Will an arranged marriage help them heal, or force them to confront long-hidden truths and new depths of despair?

Five years ago, Beryl Haywood was crippled in an accident that claimed two lives. Since then, reading and painting have been the only companions to/in her long, lonely days.

Frederick Sinclair is struggling to adapt to normality after returning from the French battlefields. A hefty weight of guilt and regret weighs on him, taunting him that he'll never be free from it.

As the newlyweds begin to wonder if love might lie ahead, a startling discovery shakes them each to the core, threatening to snatch away the future they'd begun to hope they might share...

Available in Paperback, eBook and Kindle Unlimited

at

edwinakiernan.com/beryl

ALSO AVAILABLE

RUBY'S REDEMPTION AUDIOBOOK

Narrated by **Sophie Linfield**

Listen now:

edwinakiernan.com/rubyaudio

(Visit the link above to listen for FREE with a 30-day Audible trial!)

GEMS OF GRACE BOXSET (EBOOK ONLY)

All three *Gems of Grace* novels in one handy package!

Includes:

- *Ruby's Redemption*

- *Pearl's Promise*

- *Beryl's Blessing*

Read now:

edwinakiernan.com/gems

Penniless and alone... A stranger takes her in.

But will her presence ruin his chance to restore all he's lost?

heartsofthehall.com/restoringmisshastings

THE LETTER

Book 1 in the Victorian Virtues series

She wants a new life.

He's in danger of losing his.

Will love solve everything — or immerse them in even worse peril?

Restless and ready for a change, Grace Stratton gladly accepts the opportunity to leave her remote parsonage home to serve as a wealthy spinster's companion in the idyllic country town of Lindenfell. Its warm atmosphere and friendly inhabitants sooth Grace's lonely heart. But when a mysterious stranger arrives, she soon discovers things aren't always what they seem.

Convinced chloroform will revolutionise the medical world, Dr. David Carbury frequently administers it to his London patients — until one of them dies. Facing a grave trial to prove his innocence and defend a drug most people view as poisonous, he makes hasty plans to buy time to bolster his case. But he wasn't expecting to face an even deadlier challenge.

As attraction sparks not long after they meet, Grace soon suspects he's hiding something, and David knows he can't run from the truth forever.

But neither of them could imagine the sinister threat lurking just around the corner...

Available in Paperback, eBook and Kindle Unlimited

at

edwinakiernan.com/letter

AUTHOR'S NOTE:

The Letter features Henry & Ruby's daughter, Grace.

Revisit Shiloh Hall (and discover Lindenfell) with more faith, romance and danger.

Read now!

COMING SOON

In the bleakest of circumstances...

...can joy still be found?

COVER NOT FINAL

Pre-order the second book in

The *Victorian Virtues* series...

THE LAMP

edwinakiernan.com/preorder

WANT TO BE FIRST TO GET MY NEXT BOOK?

My author newsletter
gives you all the latest
updates - plus freebies,
book recommendations,
exciting treats *and more...*

Subscribe now:

EdwinaKiernan.com